The Abbess Rebellion

Oren Ashkenazi

Published by Mythcreants, 2024.

Copyright

Table of Contents

This book is dedicated to all the fantasy authors who came before me, and to the ultimate American fantasy: what if we made the rich pay their taxes?

Chapter 1

Twenty-three years ago

Sophie struggled alongside the other rebels, rushing to build a barricade that might delay her grandmother's army. Inch by inch, they shoved a rubble-laden wagon across the bridge's smooth paving stones until it finally ground into place. Lengthwise, the wagon blocked about half the bridge's width: not enough.

Sophie eyed the far end of the bridge, where stately buildings of marble and brick stood in orderly rows lining wide streets. They held no sign of imperial legionnaires yet, but that wouldn't last long. Soon the empero's forces would be upon them, overwhelming the rebels on the bridge and invading the narrow, broken streets on their side of the river. The close packed tenements of wood and straw would burn so easily.

Exhausted, some rebels sank down to the bridge's paving stones and leaned against the raised edges. The summer-solstice sun beat down on them, sapping at strength already depleted by days of hard fighting. They wore a motley collection of boiled leather and old chain mail as armor, nearly all of it stained and abraded from constant use.

Beside Sophie, Faidra wiped sweat off her brow, her pale skin long tanned from years of marching with the legions.

"Let's get the other wagon up here," Faidra said. "Ironheart isn't resting, neither can we."

Ironheart. Sophie grimaced. In her childhood, she'd been proud of this epithet for her grandmother. She hadn't realized what it truly meant—that Empero Irena cut down the poor and hungry for the smallest acts of defiance. The rebels had waited until she was away to begin the uprising and seized the capital, Heratia, with little bloodshed. Then Irena had force-marched her army back to the city faster than anyone had believed possible. The rebels had fallen back again and again. Now they were surrounded, barely holding on to the poorest districts as their supplies dwindled.

Faidra reached out a hand. Sophie clasped it, her own dark-brown skin standing out against her dear friend's ruddy tan. But while Sophie stood, many of the others stayed where they were, gazing blankly over the river's dark water. They were losing hope.

"Let Ironheart try to get past us," Sophie said, loud enough for the other rebels to hear. "Then she'll find out what the citizens of Heratia are made of!"

Cheers answered her as the rebels rose to toil again. But as Sophie returned to her task, the hard knot in her chest only grew. The hope she offered was a lie. The rebels had no way of turning the tide now, only delaying the inevitable. And as they delayed, losing one life after another, Irena Ironheart gathered her forces, tightening the noose around them.

The rebels had risked everything in this uprising. After her father, Sophie was second in line for the throne. More cautious voices had suggested they wait until Sophie was empero, but Irena's land reforms had forced the rebels' hand. The new law would coerce poor citizens to sell their farms to vast estate holders. Families would end up paying to work the fields they had owned for generations. What middle class remained would become poor. The poor would starve.

Irena had even overridden the elected People's Chamber to make it possible. All to enrich aristocratic senators, scions of families with more gold than they could ever spend.

Frantic signal horns interrupted Sophie's thoughts. The rebels had no more time; the imperial legionnaires were here. Heavily armored, the legionnaires marched toward them through the central district's wide streets. Steel helmets protected their heads, and each soldier carried a stabbing spear in one hand and a broad shield in the other.

The rebels scrambled to form their battle line, those few with complete armor or a shield taking the front ranks alongside the half-formed barricade.

The legionnaires charged the bridge. Over their heads, the Laskaris banner fluttered as though its diving falcon swooped down to catch rebel prey.

Sophie took up her shield and raised her sword high. She wouldn't let the uprising die here, not yet. "We push them back," she shouted above the din, "for the uprising, for Heratia, for all Meyathans!"

Faidra and the other rebels roared their response, raising the uprising's black sunburst banner high. On Sophie's signal, they charged from behind their partially completed barricade, meeting the imperial attack with momentum on their side.

A spear jabbed for Sophie's face, and she batted it away with her shield, plunging her sword into her enemy's lightly protected armpit. The imperial soldier choked on blood, their dying eyes wide with fear and pain. Sophie shoved the soldier aside. This wasn't the first enemy she'd killed to protect the uprising; it wouldn't be the last.

Beside Sophie, Faidra flexed her powerful shoulders and rammed forward into a small gap between two legionnaires. The enemy shield wall buckled, and Faidra pushed through with a shout of triumph. Sophie followed her friend, widening the breach.

An imperial officer stepped forward to block them. Shining steel scales protected her from head to toe, and even the gaps at the neck and joints were covered by tightly woven chain. Only her visor slit showed eyes and skin nearly as dark as Sophie's own.

The officer's gaze fixed on Sophie, a look of recognition. "The rebel heir," the officer muttered, and her mace swung in a deadly arc. Sophie took the blow on her shield, iron-banded wood cracking under the impact that reverberated up Sophie's arm.

Sophie dropped the broken shield and gripped her sword with both hands. Her instructors would have told her to fall back, but there was no time for that kind of caution. The officer recovered and lashed out with her mace again. Sophie stepped into the swing, blunting its impact, and checked the officer with her shoulder.

The officer stumbled back a step and Sophie was on her, sword striking a heavy blow, then another. The officer's armor held, but the impacts jarred her arm, sending her mace clattering to the cobbles. As the officer reached for the shortsword at her belt, Sophie thrust forward and up, the swordpoint shearing through chain and leather to cut open the officer's throat.

As the officer's lifeblood spilled onto the bridge's paving stones and into the Marshrun's dark water, the imperial vanguard sounded a retreat. Sophie let out a shout of triumph, but it died on her lips as she beheld the carnage around her.

A few dozen legionnaires lay dead on the bridge's paving stones, their shining armor torn open by spearpoint and encrusted with red. But scores of rebels sprawled over and around the imperials, coating the bridge in their bodies and blood. Their armor was thinner and made of poorer metal; each fallen enemy cost several of their lives. Basil, who had stood shoulder to shoulder with Sophie as they pushed the wagon into the barricade, slumped with a blade still in his chest. Helena, who had handed out their lunch rations that afternoon, was cut open from shoulder to waist. They had taken up arms only to defend their rights, and now they were gone forever.

Sophie's throat tightened. Was it right for her to sacrifice their lives when the war could not be won? The rebels had pushed back the legionnaires this time, but with their numbers so diminished, they would only be overrun by the next attack.

Sophie cast her gaze around; where was Faidra? Her friend wasn't with the rebels who limped back behind the barricade, nor with the ones gleaning weapons and armor from the dead. *Please, no.* Sophie couldn't do this without her.

Then, with a huff, Faidra pushed a fallen soldier off her and clambered upright, wiping blood from her face.

Sophie let out a ragged breath. "Faidra, thank Sol."

"Sol's not ready for me yet." Faidra grinned.

Sophie tried to grin back, but her smile faltered. "We lost too many. You know we won't hold this position for much longer."

"And where do you suggest we fall back to?"

Sophie had nothing to say. If they couldn't defend the narrow bridge, they couldn't defend anywhere else.

Faidra clapped Sophie on the shoulder. "Come on, *Rebel Heir.* We're not dead yet." She turned to the other rebels and shouted, "Back to the barricade! We need to finish it before they return."

Sophie joined her friend in the grim work of hauling their dead and wounded back across the river. The physicians' tents were already overflowing, and there was nothing to do with the bodies but stack them along the street. Messengers came to them with accounts of other imperial attempts to cross the river, with local commanders pleading for reinforcements from the Solstice Council.

As two of the council's six members, Faidra and Sophie knew all too well that they had no reinforcements to send. Every report they received added more imperial units to the map. There was even a line of trebuchets being rolled into place across the river. Sophie's grandmother held most of Heratia in an iron grip, and each probing attack weakened the rebels' hold over the city's western districts. Food was in short supply, and they had burned through nearly all the weapons provided by Tribune Styliani Delis and her sympathizers in the People's Chamber.

Faidra took a final look at their crumbling situation on the map and flicked some dried blood out of her hair. "It's just as well," she said. "The Mother knows I never planned to run from this. If

Ironheart wants our ground, she'll have to spend legionnaire lives clearing us out street by street." She grinned at Sophie and turned away from the map. "Come on, we've got a last stand to organize."

Sophie followed her friend out of the command tent, but she couldn't match Faidra's bravado. Fighting to the end would indeed cost the empire dearly, but it would cost the rebels far more. They might sacrifice the lives of everyone who trusted them yet gain nothing for their cause.

A runner approached, and Sophie braced for another desperate plea that she could do nothing to answer. Instead, the young rebel boy drew himself up and held out a sealed letter. "Councillor Sophie," he said, "a message for you—from the enemy."

Sophie took the letter and beheld the Laskaris's purple falcon seal, a symbol of imperial power. Her brows raised. What could her family possibly have to say to her? She glanced at Faidra, who gave a bored shrug. Sophie broke the seal and scanned the flowing script within.

Dearest Sophie,

I write because too much blood has already been spilled, and I pray to the Mother and Her blessed daughters that it has been enough. I know you care for Meyatha's citizens as an imperial scion should. Please help me ensure that no more die today in a pointless quarrel. Parley with us on Luna's Hill, and perhaps we can staunch this wound in our nation. As heir apparent, I guarantee your safety and freedom while you are our guest.

—Your loving father, Mihail Laskaris.

Sophie handed the scroll to Faidra. She wasn't naive enough to believe her father's kind words anymore. They were the same kind words Mihail used whenever Irena put some new hardship on Meyatha's citizens and he did nothing about it. He used his compassion to pacify, not to seek justice. Mihail was the heir; he had real influence. If only he weren't so concerned with family unity at any cost.

She quelled the well-worn resentment. If her family wanted to negotiate, then Irena must have realized how much a prolonged battle would cost the empire. Western Heratia wasn't wealthy, but it hosted most of the capital's smithies and workshops. While the rebels didn't have the time or supplies to make use of them, Irena would need weapons and armor to keep her soldiers equipped. Even if she didn't care about lives, she would care about the ironworks.

"I should meet with them," Sophie said. "If Irena agrees to rescind the land-reform order, this could still be a victory for us." Her fallen comrades wouldn't have given their lives in vain.

Faidra handed the scroll back with a raised eyebrow. "You won't get anything out of Ironheart. She'll have us all hanging from the walls before she gives an inch."

Sophie sighed and crumpled the scroll in her hands. "You're right, just wishful thinking."

A grin spread over Faidra's face. "I didn't say you shouldn't accept. Buy us a few hours to reinforce the bridges and it'll make a real difference."

Sophie laughed and clasped her friend's hand. "I'll see what I can do."

She decided not to bring an escort with her so as not to test whether her father's guarantee of safe passage extended to anyone else. As the letter promised, imperial soldiers made way for her when she crossed the bridge, a dozen or so even falling in behind her as a distant escort.

Luna's Hill was the highest point in Heratia's central district, kept clear of any buildings or development aside from the second blessed daughter's shrine. It was a logical place for Irena to make her command post, with the way it overlooked both the harbor and western Heratia. Sophie's breath grew labored as she climbed, and the city shrank behind her. The bridge her comrades had died defending only a few hours before looked small, fragile.

At the hilltop, the Laskaris imperial guard marched in formation to meet her, their plated armor gleaming in the setting solstice sun. These were the best soldiers in all of Meyatha, and before the uprising, they would have protected Sophie with their lives. Now they watched her closely, ready to cut her down at the slightest wrong move. She shivered under their dispassionate stares.

With practiced precision, the guards parted ranks to make way for the imperial family. Irena Ironheart led the way, the dark skin of her face lined with age, her helm and shining armor bearing the scratches and pits of recent use. No blood though. Sophie's grandmother would never be so careless as to return from battle without cleaning her armor.

Just behind Irena stood Mihail, his armor limited to only a light breastplate that showed no signs of use, the curly black hair he had passed on to Sophie unencumbered by a helmet.

"Sophie," Mihail said with a smile. He reached out to offer an embrace. "Thank the Mother and Her blessed daughters that you're—"

Irena blocked him with an outstretched hand. "This is not a social event, Mihail," she said. Her dark eyes bored through Sophie. "Your attempt to hold the Dawn Gate was feeble, Granddaughter. Did I not teach you better?"

Sophie's eyes fell. She was a child again, learning the craft of war from her uncompromising grandmother. The work was hard, the approval rare. Sophie shook her head. This was not a classroom, and she had chosen justice over approval.

"Your Majesty," Sophie said. "I am here to negotiate a peace."

A shout preempted whatever Irena might have said in response. "Sophie, Sophie!"

That was Taisa's voice. Sophie's shoulders relaxed, and her lips twitched toward a smile before she stopped herself. This wouldn't go well, not under their grandmother's cold gaze.

Taisa had pushed her way past the back rank of imperial guards, but the second rank formed a wall to block her progress. Two years younger than Sophie, Taisa's features were slighter and more delicate, her face more elegant, though they shared the same dark skin and curly black hair.

"Let me through!" Taisa said. "I have to see my sister!"

Taisa wore plated armor of the same make as Irena's but without the marks of use. That didn't surprise Sophie. Irena would never risk one of her granddaughters in battle while the other had risen in rebellion.

The imperial guards held Taisa back until Irena motioned them away.

Taisa marched forward and stopped abruptly, staring at Sophie eye to eye. "Tell me it's not true. Tell me you aren't leading this attack on our country, our *family*." Her eyes glistened as her voice caught. "Please, if they lied to you, if they took you hostage... we can fix this."

Sophie's chest tightened at the distress on Taisa's face, but lying would only insult them both. "I chose this," Sophie said softly. "You and Father wouldn't have been hurt, but I had to stop Irena."

Sophie reached out a hand, but Taisa slapped it away, the metal of their gauntlets ringing through the air.

"Why?" Taisa asked. "The throne would have been yours someday, but instead our soldiers die and our capital burns." Her voice rose. "Why?"

Sophie held up her hands. "We couldn't wait. The new land reform will starve our people." She'd imagined convincing Taisa after the uprising had won, when there would have been time to show her sister the true cost of their grandmother's iron heart.

"If you cared for our people," Taisa said, "You should have *talked* to Grandmother about the land reform!"

"I did," Sophie said. "Father and I both tried to change her mind. But you know how Grandmother is." She didn't say that the long arguments against her grandmother's unchanging expression had left Sophie wanting to scream, and her father's eventual capitulation had steeled her to the need for a rebellion.

Taisa spat at Sophie's feet. "You've betrayed everything we stand for."

"Taisa, please," Sophie said. "If there had been another way—"

"I looked up to you!" Taisa shouted. "I wanted to *be* you. But I never knew you, did I?"

"You did, I—"

"Enough." Irena's voice cut through the argument. "Taisa, come away from her."

Taisa's face went rigid. "Yes, Grandmother." She took a step back, then another, her gate stiff and her face unyielding. The cold expression, so similar to Irena Ironheart's, cut Sophie like a blade that her armor couldn't stop.

Mihail spoke up, his expression pained. "Perhaps we should focus on our purpose." He coughed into a silk handkerchief, a symptom of the illness he'd struggled with for as long as Sophie had been alive. "There is still time to prevent more bloodshed."

"Thank you, Father," Sophie said. She straightened as she turned to face Irena's implacable stare. Sophie had to draw the negotiations out to buy time, and that meant feigning more confidence than she had. "If you rescind the land-reform law, we will return control of western Heratia and recognize your authority as empero."

For the first time since Sophie's arrival, Irena's expression changed, lips pulling back to reveal her teeth. Then she laughed, an uncharacteristically gentle sound that Sophie had rarely heard in all her twenty years. It set her teeth on edge.

"Little Sophie," Irena said. "That is not the hand you're holding." She took a step forward, her armor plates rasping softly. "All of your traitors will immediately surrender. You, Granddaughter, will be exiled somewhere you can't cause trouble. The other rebel leaders will be executed. In return, I'll spare your rank and file instead of slaughtering them all for taking up arms against my family."

Sophie had expected such an offer, but it still rankled. "I'd never accept exile while my fellows are killed."

"Oh yes," Irena added, "and the People's Chamber will be disbanded for its role in this treason."

Sophie reeled. Dissolve the People's Chamber? No empero would do such a thing. "You can't," she gasped. "The People's Chamber was founded by Heratia herself! It's one of Methaya's three pillars."

"A rotted pillar is of no use. Best to knock it down before the rot spreads."

Sophie clenched her fists, struggling to get her outrage under control. Irena was trying to rattle her—and succeeding. She took a breath. "Without the People's Chamber, the citizens will have no voice. No outlet for their discontent. You'd only face more uprisings."

"Wishful thinking does you no favors, little Sophie. The People's Chamber *creates* such uprisings. It promises too much to the citizens, and then, once the chamber is overridden, the citizens become discontented. Just as they are now. Once the chamber is gone, the people will have no choice but to put their faith in their empero, as they should."

Sophie stifled her retort. Irena had clearly thought this through and made her decision; arguing the point would accomplish nothing. But Sophie couldn't go to her death knowing that she'd destroyed what little power the people had. She had to stop this. "Make a public vow to leave the People's Chamber in place, and we will surrender."

Irena smiled ever so slightly. "No."

Sophie's eyes widened. "No? You can have everything else you ask for. Execute me, if you wish."

"No. Fight and die, or surrender and live. It makes no difference to me." Irena glanced at Mihail. "I'm only here because my son begged for mercy on your behalf."

"To the grave with your parley, then!" Sophie said. "If you don't meet our demands, we'll destroy Heratia's ironworks before you can take them back, and your legionnaires can face their next battle without weapons."

"Is that so?" Irena lifted an eyebrow. "Come, I have something to show you."

The Laskaris guard parted for Irena as she made her way to an overlook, motioning for Sophie to follow her. Irena stopped at the edge of the ridge to stare down to where straight streets met the Marshrun where it sparkled in the early evening light. Near the riverbank, the imperial trebuchets rested in a line. They were aimed toward the western districts, but at that range, a heavy load wouldn't make it across, and a light load would do little damage.

"What is this?" Sophie asked. "You can't stop us setting alight the ironworks with a few trebuchets."

"Stop you? On the contrary." Irena turned to a legionnaire. "Commander, you may light and loose."

The commander lifted a horn and blew a brief signal. Below, the soldiers attending the trebuchets brought torches and set the loads alight. Sophie held her breath as the trebuchets sent a volley of burning pitch across the river. The aim of trebuchets was poor; some of the pitch hit the streets or was snuffed out by the wet riverbank. But one firing missile struck a wall and another a roof.

The rebels scurried to form a bucket line, dousing one of the fires. For the other building—a cooper's, perhaps—it was too late. The roof was bowing as it shriveled in the blaze, and once it collapsed, the rest of the building would go up. The occupants ran and yelled; some struggled to carry belongings while others only fled for their lives.

Sophie tore her gaze from the chaos and rounded on Irena. "You'll burn down all of western Heratia before you defeat us this way!"

Irena fixed Sophie with a stony glare. "What care I for ramshackle huts that house traitorous vermin? Only the ironworks cannot be rebuilt before I have need of them, and, as you said, your rabble will burn those anyhow."

"Those are your people! Few of them have done anything to aid us."

"You forget what's important. Your betrayal will leave my legionnaires short on weapons, so I must preserve their numbers. Why would I expend my force rooting out your rebels when I can burn them out instead?" The evening sun threw a red-and-orange glow across Irena's armor as she took a step toward Sophie. "I'll set alight any corner of this city you scurry into."

Sophie shrank back at the hard contempt in Irena's voice. That's what Irena had sounded like before she'd razed the city of Athianople to the ground. She really would torch her own capital rather than give the rebels the smallest concession.

Sophie turned to Mihail, who stood a respectful distance away, watching the exchange. He was the only person who might help her.

"Father, please. Tell her this is folly. Tell her we need peace."

Mihail fidgeted. "We *can* have peace, Sophie," he said. "But treason has its consequences."

Sophie sought Taisa's eyes, but Taisa only glared back.

"You have your answer," Irena said. "Will you accept my mercy or force my hand?"

The fate of her comrades, of all of western Heratia, weighed down on Sophie's shoulders. Whatever she had thought Irena's terms would be, this was worse. If they gave in, they would see their lands taken away, and then the next year the hereditary aristocrats of the Senate would be hungry for more still. If they fought, it would be the same, except they wouldn't even live to see it, and everyone in the rebel-controlled districts would suffer with them.

"Let them live," Sophie said, the last flickers of anger gone, leaving only numb despair.

"What?" Irena asked. "Who?"

"The other Solstice leaders," Sophie said. "I don't care what happens to me, but spare their lives along with our rank and file, and I'll agree to your terms." If the other leaders lived, perhaps they could plant tiny seeds of change that would someday bloom anew.

Irena made a dismissive gesture. "And leave the snake's head intact? I think not."

"Your Majesty," Mihail said, putting a hand on the empero's armored shoulder. "Perhaps we can do this small thing. If we spare them, we can watch them and those who associate with them. A snake we know rather than a danger in the dark."

Irena looked at her son for a moment, then shrugged. "Very well," she said. "If they swear never to speak or act against the empire again, they may live also."

Sophie's whole body felt leaden, a greater exhaustion than all the day's fighting could account for. "Thank you, Father," she said, with a slight nod to Mihail. The words were ash in her mouth, but at least Faidra, the other Solstice leaders, and those who fought for them would live. She grasped that one mercy like a lifeline.

She gave a mechanical bow to the empero, her voice flat as she promised to deliver the terms to her side. Mihail tried to console her, but Sophie couldn't bear to be in her family's presence any longer. She turned her back on him and retraced her steps toward the rebel barricades. None of the imperial soldiers interfered.

At the bridge, Sophie faced her comrades as they stared at her over the barricades, their expressions a mix of fear and determination. Faidra leaned down and offered a hand to help Sophie clamber over the piled rubble and debris.

On the other side, Faidra gave a grim smile. "We've reinforced and are as ready as we'll ever be. When do they attack?"

"They won't," Sophie said. The words were heavy stones in her throat. "It's over, the uprising's over."

Faidra's eyes narrowed. "What in Sol's sight are you talking about? What were their terms?"

Sophie took a deep breath and told her: that the land reform would stay, that the People's Chamber would be dissolved, and of the empero's mercy. The explanation made Sophie feel sick all over again. It was the end of everything they'd worked for, that they'd fought and died for.

"Mother and Her blessed daughters," Faidra said, her face a mask of fury. "You've sold any hope Heratia's downtrodden might have had."

"I bought our lives," Sophie said. "I bought *your* life."

Faidra slammed her fist onto the barricade. "I would rather bleed my life away on this bridge. The future will need martyrs to inspire it."

"History is full of martyrs," Sophie put a careful hand on her friend's shoulder. "We built this uprising with the living, and we can again, or whoever comes after us."

Faidra knocked the hand aside. "I don't care what you promised Ironheart. I'll fight until they kill me."

"No, you won't." Sophie set her jaw. "The council will decide this." Comrades in the uprising preferred to settle their differences through long debate, but when a quick decision was needed, the Solstice Council provided the final say.

"Then Alexandra and Styliani will back me." Faidra crossed her arms. "And your surrender is *still* dead."

"Alexandra I'll grant you, but Styliani?" Sophie shook her head. "She may have put her life into the People's Chamber, but she won't sacrifice half the citizens of Heratia for it. Makis and Petros will follow her lead."

Faidra's nostrils flared as she glared at Sophie. Then, in a voice that was deathly quiet, she said, "You've destroyed our cause more thoroughly than Irena Ironheart ever could."

Faidra stormed off past the bridge, leaving Sophie with the desperate stares of their comrades. She opened her mouth to announce the surrender, but then only bowed her head.

Chapter 2

Present day

With the closest imperial garrison several days away, Sophie had to keep the peace with only the resources of her abbey and a few kind words. It might not be enough for the two families arguing in her rough-walled chapel. After living on a knife's edge for years, the upcoming tax season made them desperate to claim what scraps were left, lest they starve or rot in an imperial prison. Desperate enough to hurt each other.

"Welcome in peace," Theano Patra said to both families' representatives. A few years older than Sophie, Theano was the abbey's most senior acolyte. "With the Mother's wisdom, we will find a solution to your dispute."

"I don't see why we should have to bargain," the Tocci elder said. He was a lean man, his face tanned to a light bronze from long days in the sun. "We already paid for those calves by building that windmill for last year's harvest. Now they want out of the deal."

"We've no choice," the Panos elder said, her face leathery and her back bent, nearly a mirror of her Tocci counterpart. "We don't have the calves to give you, not anymore. We'll gladly pay the debt when we can, but you can't expect us to starve ourselves over it."

"You'll starve *us* if you don't pay," the Tocci elder said. His mouth set in a thin line. "Maybe we'll just take that mill back. Get something for the lumber, at any rate."

Sophie cleared her throat, and the argument died. She raised a dark-brown hand toward the high ceiling, which bore a painting of the night sky roughly shaped into a woman's silhouette. "We must not threaten our neighbors in the Void Mother's house," she said, keeping her voice soft so they had to lean in. "Whatever our earthly troubles, remember Her tenets." This was Sophie's traditional opening gambit, appealing to the faith nearly all Meyathan citizens shared.

"Forgive me, abbess," the Tocci leader mumbled.

Sophie waved the apology away. "You are forgiven." It was her own family who bore the blame, in any case. In twenty-three years, Irena's reforms had accomplished their precise intent: subsuming Meyatha's best land into aristocratic estates. Most families now toiled on those very estates, while a few, like the Panos and Tocci, had retreated to the rough hill country around Sophie's abbey and claimed what little land was left.

Sophie addressed both leaders. "Tempers are high," she said. "But the Mother and Her blessed daughters know you mean no harm to each other."

Theano spoke up. "Indeed. Your families are blood of the same earth." She turned to the Tocci leader. "Wasn't it just last year that your daughter found that Panos boy swept downriver? Saved him from drowning, didn't she?"

Sophie pressed the attack, addressing the Panos leader in turn. "And your whole family pitched in to move the Tocci's valuables into the abbey the last time raiders came south. These aren't the kinds of ties to be quickly forgotten."

The heads of both families looked away and muttered sheepish agreements, which signaled to Sophie that the immediate danger was past. They didn't truly want to hurt each other over livestock; they simply knew no other option. How many other families spilled each other's blood, far from where Sophie might help them? She'd had the chance to save them all from this, years ago. She'd failed.

Now that she and Theano had reminded the farmers who they were, it was time to discuss the details and negotiate a settlement. Taking careful notes, Sophie extracted the whole story. The Tocci had built a windmill for the Panos' farm last year so the latter wouldn't have to haul their grain all the way to the abbey's watermill for grinding. In payment, the Panos had promised four calves come spring. But a pest had struck their herd that winter, and they had only two calves, both of which they desperately needed.

Both families wanted to make good—that was the way of close-knit communities in the empire's remote provinces—but neither could afford to. The Panos had nothing to equal the worth of four calves, and the Tocci could not afford to cancel the debt if they wished to keep their farm when the tax collector came.

"That is a tangle, even in Sol's sight," Theano said when the entire story was out. She turned to the Panos leader. "Perhaps a few of your youth could clear an extra field for the Tocci to plant come spring. We could apply to the tax collector for a deferral until then. It would be tight, but the extra crop could be enough to stave off the worst."

"Aye," the Panos woman said. "My grandchildren are ready to do their share."

The Tocci leader shook his head. "We've asked for three deferrals already. The collector will never give us a fourth."

Sophie kept a flare of old anger off her face. It wasn't enough for the empire to push citizens off their family holdings; the tax bureaucracy then still assessed them as being on prime farmland.

An idea flickered in her thoughts. She cleared her throat. "The pest only struck the Panos herd *after* the tax collector had departed last year, yes?"

When both leaders agreed, she continued. "Then we will tell the tax collector that the calves were given to the Tocci, who then sent them to be sold at market in Heliopolis, making their taxation a matter for that city's officials. We should be able to draw up a convincing contract to that effect."

Theano's brow arched ever so slightly, while the two family leaders stared at her, eyes wide.

"Abbess," the Panos leader said at last. "What of next year, when the capital's clerks see no sale on their ledger?"

Sophie nodded. If there was one thing Meyatha excelled at, it was keeping records. "We will tell our collector that the calves never arrived, likely seized by raiders. By then, the Tocci's field will have a harvest to pay the empero's tab." It would still cut deep, but not fatally, if the Mother was just.

The chapel was silent for a few moments before Theano spoke. "I shall write to a friend at the Heliopolis temple. She can give us details of the market there, so we will have enough for a convincing story if the tax collector grows suspicious."

A smile tugged at Sophie's lips. It was just like Theano to think of a contingency like that. In more than two decades of exile, she had often found her fellow acolytes to be resourceful accomplices when their neighbors were in peril.

"Abbess," the Panos woman said, a slight tremble in her voice, "If we are caught..."

The Tocci leader stayed silent, but his clenched fists gave away a similar fear.

"There is risk," Sophie said. "But I ask you both to take it with us, to show the Mother's loyalty to your neighbor and fellow citizen." She had never been especially religious as a youth, but after twenty-three years at the abbey, she found the Void Mother's tenets gave her a clarity of purpose and rallied her fellow Meyathans in ways not even the finest political rhetoric could.

Exchanging a glance, the two family heads nodded their agreement, and Sophie permitted herself a smile. Her family had abandoned the people to fend for themselves, but at least she could still make a small difference.

"I will draw up the sale contract to show the tax collector," Sophie said. Local families often got such contracts through the abbey, so it shouldn't arouse suspicion. "Do you have time for a blessing?"

They agreed to stay for the blessing, of course. Sophie took Theano's hand, and they each clasped hands with one of the family leaders. All four of them knelt and gazed up at the night-painted ceiling. Sophie spoke, the familiar words springing easily to mind after decades of practice.

"Sacred Mother and Her blessed daughters, see that we adhere to your tenets. May that we have the wisdom to be loyal to those closest, show kindness to whomever we meet, and, highest of all, pursue your justice with our every step."

The four of them hummed the blessing's affirmation, then rose together. Sophie hid a wince behind the sleeve of her wool tunic. No matter how many prayers and blessings she led, her knees never learned to be happy with it. She admired Theano with a hint of envy, a woman fifteen years Sophie's senior who rose from each ritual as if she had wings to lift her.

They led the Tocci and Panos heads from the meditation-chamber-turned-meeting room to the abbey gates and let them go only after promises to see them and their families at the solstice feast. Sophie took a deep breath of cool autumn air, relieved to be finished with the last petitioners of the day in time to catch up on the records before the sun disappeared entirely.

"I swear there are more every season who need our counsel," Theano said once their guests had disappeared round a bend in the gravel road.

Sophie grimaced. "My father, hard at work doing nothing to change my grandmother's laws." Her past had been a secret in the first days of exile, but after so many years in a small abbey, nearly all of the acolytes knew or at least suspected.

Theano nodded. "With each new empero, there is a chance for change. Perhaps Heir Taisa will do better."

"I can only pray," Sophie said. All she knew of Taisa came from the occasional imperial herald announcing the heir's latest campaign in the south. She hadn't seen any of her family in person since the day of her exile.

Sophie shook her head. Futile to dwell on bonds long broken. Peaceful Rest Abbey was her home now, and a fine home it was, with half a dozen buildings composed of warm red-brick and roofed in dark clay tiles, built into the foothills of the snowcapped Serate Mountains. From those peaks ran an endless torrent of water over the mountain's gray stone, powering the abbey's mill and giving the province of Gray Falls its name.

Sophie glanced toward the main building, steeling herself for the hours of scribing ahead. Dozens of acolytes, young and old, crossed the grounds before her: some carried water for the kitchens or bore sheaves of wheat from the fields while others tied cloths round their faces to keep the bees off as they tended the abbey's hives. Like Sophie, the acolytes all wore wool tunics over loose trousers. The garments were dyed in shades of green, blue, and yellow, but most of the colors were long faded. Sophie tried to find the silver for her acolytes to have pleasing clothes, but it wasn't often possible when the priority was keeping bellies full and bodies warm. Sophie's only affectation as abbess was a shawl of darkest black, the Mother's sacred color.

"Sophie!" A high, familiar voice cut the air along with the pounding of booted feet. "Sister Sophie!"

Sophie turned back to the gate, exchanging a raised eyebrow with Theano. A young woman of eighteen years pelted round the road's bend, a long staff in one hand, her heavy boots crunching the gravel. She skidded to a stop, breathing hard, sweat rolling down over light-brown skin and dampening her short black hair.

"Fryni, dearest one," Sophie said, enveloping the sweaty younger woman in a hug. Fryni Kota, second-in-command of the abbey's militia, had been out on patrol for two weeks, climbing into the Serate Mountains to keep in contact with remote mountain villages.

"What's happened, Fryni?" Theano asked. "Why did you run so? Where's Captain Iris and the rest of your patrol?"

Fryni leaned into Sophie's embrace, taking in deep, gulping breaths. "They'll be along," she said between lungfuls. "We were at Sol's Ridge when we saw the strangest thing, so Iris sent me ahead to warn the abbey."

"Warn us?" Sophie asked, relaxing her arms so Fryni would have more room to breathe. "Of what?" In the eighteen years since Fryni had been left at the abbey as a babe, Sophie had learned to trust the young woman's instincts.

"Imperial soldiers," Fryni said, taking a step back and standing on her own. "Six of them, by my count, with the purple standard and everything. Four on horseback, two on a big carriage, coming this way."

The breath froze in Sophie's throat. Imperial soldiers here? No, why would they be? She'd been so careful, never once violated the terms of her exile in twenty-three years.

Theano turned to Fryni. "Soldiers, are you sure?" she asked. "Not raiders pretending?"

"I couldn't very well go up and ask them," Fryni said. "But if they're pretending, they pretended themselves into the shiniest armor and the biggest horses I've ever seen. If raiders could afford that kind of gear, they wouldn't be raiding, now would they?"

Sophie took a breath to gather her resolve. It didn't matter why they were here; she'd always known they might come for her one day. She was officially stripped of inheritance rights, but she was still a Laskaris. It was only a matter of time before someone in Heratia decided she was a liability.

"Sophie," Fryni said, some of the excitement gone from her voice. "Is something wrong?"

"No, I'm sorry," Sophie said. She had to put the other acolytes off before they realized the soldiers were here to kill her. They might try to stop it, especially Fryni, who had more courage than was good for her. There would only be more blood spilled. Sophie cleared her throat. "It's probably the tax collector, come early and with extra protection on account of the raids. Fryni, see that their horses are watered."

She turned to Theano. "Sister Theano, establish them in the dining hall with food and drink, then wait for me. We must begin our deception on the Panos and Tocci's behalf earlier than expected."

Theano accepted the lie without objection, but Fryni caught Sophie's gaze for a long moment before finally following suit. Sophie plastered a smile on her face. She needed to appear as if nothing was wrong, as if this was simply a normal visit from a tax collector who would take more than they could afford. Sophie took measured, regular steps back to the main building. She had to ensure the abbey would carry on after she returned to the Void Mother's embrace.

***

Sophie's office was a converted acolyte's cell, into which the sisters had carefully fit a small writing desk and shelves for the abbey's vital records. It possessed one luxurious feature that Sophie would sorely miss, a window of clear glass that looked out onto the falls and gave her good light for most of the day. For the last five years of exile, she'd used this office to make small differences where she could, but that was all over now.

First, Sophie found her ring of keys and slipped them into a tunic pocket. Then she wrote a short note to Theano, explaining the abbey's filing system and offering suggestions for who should take over as recordkeeper. Naturally Theano would be abbess when Sophie was gone, though she didn't write that. The acolytes would choose their new leader by vote, but Sophie couldn't imagine them choosing anyone else.

Finally, Sophie addressed a separate note to Fryni alone. Her quill hovered above the coarse paper. There was too much to say. The entire abbey raised the children left with them, but Sophie had spent more time with Fryni than anyone else, watched her grow into a brave young woman who never slowed down for anyone.

She was running out of time. Sophie put quill tip to paper.

Dearest one,

I am gone, and not even the Mother can change that. You will find no justice for me through violence, and I pray you will think of loyalty to your fellow acolytes first. They will need your strength now more than ever. You are a fire I am proud to have helped light.

A tear fell from Sophie's eye, and she only just jerked the paper aside in time to keep it from splashing. She set the note out so the ink would dry. She had no time to write more; the soldiers would be within the abbey by now. She took a final moment to let the sun bathe her face through the perfectly clear window, then turned and padded out of the room.

Sophie reached the dining hall's double doors without encountering another soul. Her luck ended there, as a dozen acolytes of all ages gathered round the threshold, whispering to each other and glancing inside.

Sophie sighed. She couldn't blame them. The closest many of them had ever come to seeing imperial soldiers was encountering the rough mercenaries the Gray Falls tax collector used as guards.

She cleared her throat. "Have we all not duties to be about?" she asked.

Several acolytes jumped at her words; others flushed and looked away. All of them muttered apologies and scattered, leaving only Theano behind them. The older woman opened her mouth to speak, but Sophie held up a hand.

"Later, Sister, please," she said. "I must get to work."

With a solemn look, Theano nodded and stepped aside. Inside the dining hall waited six imperial soldiers. They were arrayed in their shining-scaled mail, spears leaned against tables and helmets doffed as they drank the watered wine and ate the dark bread a team of acolytes put before them. The soldiers' shields were strapped to their backs, each bearing the purple falcon of Meyatha's empero. Below the falcon, each shield also displayed the green crest of a crouching panther.

Sophie frowned. Imperial soldiers rarely displayed any device but the empero's. These soldiers could only be from a senator's house guard, a senator high enough in imperial esteem for their soldiers to wear the purple. The crouching panther tickled her memory. It belonged to House Kalgari, if she recalled correctly, one of the oldest and most influential families to be granted a Senate seat and longtime ally of House Laskaris.

When she was last in the capital, the House Kalgari senator had been aged; a new member of the family had likely inherited his seat since. Even so, they would be loyal to the empero. Had her father sent these soldiers himself? More likely someone in his court, possibly even her sister. No doubt Taisa still hated Sophie, as she had the last time they'd laid eyes on one another.

Only one of the visitors did not wear armor: a gray-haired woman with skin nearly as dark as Sophie's, a shade common among the capital's elite families. She stood in robes of vibrant red, with intricate patterns sewn in gold and silver. Sophie's wool tunic scratched at her as her eyes took in the other woman's clothes, likely the height of fashion in the capital. It had been so long since she'd worn something like that.

Neither the senator nor her soldiers looked up when Sophie stepped into the dining room. Without a sound, Sophie motioned the serving acolytes out, ignoring their curious looks. When they were out of the room, Sophie closed the heavy wooden doors and locked them tight with one of the keys from her ring. Now no one would interfere.

The senator looked up as the doors thudded closed, and her eyes fixed on Sophie as her mouth became a frown. "Acolyte," she said. "We're here for Sophie Laskaris, where is she? There's little time."

Sophie swallowed. She'd done her best in exile to live by the tenet of justice and perhaps left Gray Falls a little better than she'd found it. That was enough.

She stepped forward. "Pardon, Senator. I am Abbess Sophie. We should be about your business quickly so you can leave this abbey in peace."

The senator tilted her head, looking Sophie up and down. "My word, it *is* you. I didn't recognize you in those clothes." She cleared her throat, and her soldiers stood, each staring at Sophie. Sophie braced herself, unsure who would deliver the blow.

The senator spoke again, her tone formal. "I am Demetra Kalgari, speaker of the Meyathan Senate. It is my solemn duty to inform you that your father, His Imperial Majesty Mihail Laskaris is dead, as is his heir—your sister—and her family. You must return with me to the capital and take your place on the throne, Your Majesty."

Chapter 3

Sophie's mouth worked, but no sound emerged. They were all dead? How was that possible? Even in a poor and lightly traveled province like Gray Falls, they had known when Sophie's grandmother passed. While it was no secret that her father, Mihail, had been ill, her sister, Taisa, had been a vigorous heir apparent, or so the few visitors from the capital had claimed. And Taisa's children too? They could not yet have been out of their teenage years.

Her knees buckled, and she sat down hard on the smooth wood of a dining-hall bench. She had broken with her family twenty-three years ago, had disavowed their tyranny, but she hadn't wanted them dead. Not even when her grandmother was ready to burn half of Heratia to crush the Solstice Uprising. Sophie had never known her niece and nephew, never seen the ruler Taisa would become, and now she never would.

"Luna and her starry children," Sophie whispered. "Guide them swiftly to the Void Mother's embrace." It wasn't her place to pray for a family that had cast her out, exiled her on pain of death, but she spoke the words anyway. Taisa's children, at least, had been innocent of any imperial crimes.

Sophie met Demetra's waiting eyes. The older woman's face sparked a memory now: an ambitious courtier in Empero Irena's retinue. Sophie took a deep breath, forcing down the lump in her throat. "I believe we should speak privately."

Demetra nodded. "Indeed we must."

Sophie gestured for the senator to follow her and tried to steady her legs as she strode to the dining-hall doors, unlocking them with the turn of a key. Past the threshold, Sophie faced a wall of what must have been every acolyte at Gray Falls, all of them packed into the corridor staring at her. Fryni and Theano stood at the crowd's front, the younger woman gripping her staff in both hands while the older looked on with a pensive frown. All of them gazed at Sophie expectantly.

Sophie raised her hands. "I apologize for acting so secretive, but I promise to explain everything once our guest and I have had a chance to talk."

Some of the gathered acolytes let out long-held breaths, but Fryni did not relax. She glared at Demetra. "We won't let them hurt you," Fryni said. "None of us will."

Her words steeled the other acolytes, and they stared daggers at the senator's guards, who exchanged bemused glances with each other.

Sophie hid a grateful smile at the acolytes' concern. "I swear, they mean me no harm," she said. She glanced at Demetra's impassive face. No immediate harm anyway. She put a hand on Fryni's shoulder and squeezed. "Will you let me pass?"

Fryni's stance relaxed, and her expression turned to a sheepish grin. "Sorry, Sister Sophie, got carried away." She stepped back as other acolytes drifted away toward their ever-present duties, the crowd dispersing, though a few hung back to gawk at Demetra's fine silk robes.

"This way," Sophie said. She led Demetra through the abbey's red-brick corridors and up a narrow staircase to Sophie's small office. Once there, Sophie busied herself lighting a small fire to heat water for tea and dug around the cupboard for the last of her honey-cake stash. If she had to hear how every member of her family had died, she could at least do it with a few warm comforts.

Demetra looked on, tapping her fingers and fidgeting, until she finally cleared her throat with a pointed cough. Sophie sighed and poured the water for tea into chipped clay cups. She couldn't put the conversation off forever. She placed one cup and the plate of cakes before Demetra and sat down across from her at the desk. "Please, tell me what happened."

Demetra's expression soured further as she sipped the bitter tea, but after a moment the practiced calm returned. "Empero Mihail's consumption had grown worse for some time, and his death did not come as a great shock, Mother embrace him." Something caught in the senator's voice. Expected or not, Demetra at least had grieved the empero's passing. Sophie pretended not to notice.

Her father's illness had been an ever-present aspect of Sophie's childhood. The consumption had carried off her mother, Athina, before Sophie's tenth year, and it had been hailed as a miracle that neither of the imperial daughters had taken sick with the disease themselves.

"So my father passed," Sophie said. "My sister?"

"As Mihail faded," Demetra continued, "Taisa took her husband and children north for a tour of the border fortresses. She had spent most of her military career in the south, and she believed it important to be on good terms with the northern commanders before her ascension."

Sophie nodded. That was a logical move for a new empero: build connections with the empire's military elite to ensure her control. It was exactly the kind of political pragmatism she and Taisa had learned as children. Sophie dabbed moisture from her eyes with a sleeve. Taisa would never have visited a province like Gray Falls; it had no power to offer her.

Demetra took a long sip of tea, barely grimacing at the taste. "Her route was meant to be secret, but somehow the Skaldre knew. Her retinue was ambushed near Ilitia. By the time the garrison arrived, there were no survivors." The speaker's eyes focused on Sophie. "I left the capital to find you as soon as word reached me. If we hurry, we can return and have you enthroned before anyone knows Taisa is dead."

Sophie stifled a raw laugh. Her, empero? It was as absurd now as when Demetra had first announced it in the dining hall.

"How old were they?" she asked. "My sister's children."

The senator frowned. "Dafni had just turned sixteen. Iason was nine."

Sixteen and nine. Sophie drained the last of her tea. Children crushed in the wheels of imperial power. They were hardly the first, but they had been her blood, even if she hadn't known them, even if they had been taught to hate her.

Demetra stood and paced the narrow office. "But that isn't the worst of it. The Skaldre are massing their army on the border. An invasion is imminent, and after the defeats we've suffered in the last five years... it is critical that the empire have a leader."

Sophie shook her head. The Skaldre she was familiar with, at least. Though the name implied a single people, it was only a Meyathan term for the broad coalition of northern kingdoms that had banded together to oppose the empire. Raids and counterraids went back generations, and provinces like Gray Falls were a favorite target. Raiders would often bypass the well-garrisoned northern provinces entirely to reach unprotected Gray Falls. And this senator imagined Sophie would be the empire's protector from a vengeful Skaldre army?

"No," Sophie said. "I'm sorry you wasted your time, but you cannot think to make me empero."

Demeta stopped her pacing. "Were you not paying attention? You have no choice. The Skaldre sword is at our neck; Meyatha needs you. Did the failure of your uprising teach you nothing?"

Bile rose in Sophie's throat. Twenty-three years in exile had given her plenty of time to think on what she had done, and she had never been more certain. The absolute rule of one over many was incompatible with justice, the Void Mother's most critical tenet. She could not be the heir to a despotic family then, and she could not be their standard-bearer now. "Find someone else."

"There isn't anyone else."

"There is always someone else," Sophie said. "Surely some power-hungry senator wishes the purple for themself?"

The speaker's robes rustled as she leaned against the cold stone wall. "Yes. Savvas Carenthus, a hero from the Skaldre's last invasion. His family owns half the vineyards in southern Meyatha. Without a Laskaris to oppose him, the Falcon Throne will be his within a month."

"Let him have it then. With war on the horizon, a military empero is what Meyatha needs."

"You don't understand," Demetra said. "Only a Laskaris can hold the empire together. If he takes the throne, we will be awash in rebellions."

"And Savvas will crush them," Sophie said. "It will be brutal, but no worse than you can expect from crowning a former rebel as empero."

Demetra took a deep breath, folds of her scarlet robe held tight in her hands. "He wants to end the rights of citizenship."

Silence hung heavy in the small room. Sophie's thoughts reeled. End the rights of citizenship? Impossible. Citizenship *was* Meyatha, had been since the empire's earliest days. Every citizen had the same rights to life, travel, and property. It was how the empire absorbed conquered peoples, making them Meyathan over the generations. Even Sophie's Solstice Rebels had seen the rights of citizenship as a stepping stone to something greater. Without those protections, Meyathans would be completely beholden to their patrons. Not citizens but serfs.

"He can't," Sophie managed at last. "The people would revolt."

"They might have once," Demetra said. "But things have changed since you left the capital. Our citizens depend on their senatorial patrons the same way foreign peasants depend on their lords. That's been the trend for a long time, but it got much worse when Empero Irena had to dissolve the People's Chamber."

Sophie's nails dug into her palms. Demetra spoke as if Irena's actions had been an unfortunate necessity rather than vengeance against her own citizens. Sophie's grandmother had seen the opportunity to remove Meyatha's highest elected body and seized it.

"You are speaker of the Senate," Sophie said through clenched teeth. "Where were you as Meyatha crumbled so?"

To Sophie's surprise, Demetra looked away, her eyes downcast. "I was occupied," the speaker said. "Holding the empire together has not been easy. Mihail was... He tried to please everyone and ended up pleasing none."

"My father was never cut out to be empero, you mean," Sophie said. "And he let the senatorial houses push him anywhere they desired until there was nothing left to give up."

The shame vanished from Demetra's face, and her voice turned sharp. "Your father is the only reason you're still alive, why anyone from your damned uprising escaped the Mother's embrace. Show some loyalty."

The words stung, though Sophie made her face a mask to hide it. Her father had been a kind man, soft and gentle with his children, whereas Sophie's grandmother was hard and demanding. And Mihail had been the one to offer a peaceful end to the uprising, sparing Sophie's comrades from the sword, albeit at a heavy price.

Her father's face, what Sophie recalled of it, appeared in her mind. His curly black hair was so much like hers, and his kind smile was always a comfort to Taisa and herself. She had given up that comfort to rebel and never once regretted it, not when others had given up so much more, but now he was gone, and she would never see his smile again.

But his smile did not change the suffering his carelessness had caused. Her father had never meant any harm to his people, and yet under his rule he allowed the senatorial families to bleed their client citizens dry.

Demetra cleared her throat. "Arguing over who is responsible for our problems does not change what they are. The empire needs you, Sophie Laskaris. Its people need you. Will you help them?"

Sophie closed her eyes. The empire. Its people. *Her* people. She had turned against her own family for her people, and she lost both her family and her ability to fight for justice. Now she had another opportunity, one that would not come again. How could she call herself loyal to Meyatha if she turned it down? Her family bore the responsibility for Meyatha's decline; perhaps by wielding their standard, she might redeem their legacy in the Mother's eyes.

"Yes," Sophie said. "I will return with you and take up the Falcon Throne if it can be done." She met the speaker's gaze. "But you must see how difficult this will be. The army will not choose me over their beloved war hero, and the Senate will want nothing to do with a former rebel."

Demetra nodded. "Nevertheless, we must succeed. The empire depends on it."

A chuckle rose in Sophie's throat. The empire depending on *her*. "You may regret it even if we do win, Speaker. I may become empero only to abolish the monarchy and declare a republic."

"I will put out that fire when it ignites," Demetra said. She rose, grimacing as she nearly bumped her head on the low ceiling. "But if we succeed, you will discover what your father did: noble ideals are never so easy as we imagine them."

***

With little ceremony, Sophie said her goodbyes and gave over her office to Theano until there was time for a formal vote.

"As if they would choose anyone else," Sophie said, with the keys outstretched. "And with luck, you won't have to forge the sale of any cows." She lowered her voice with a grin, as if she was sharing a scandalous secret. "It seems I have some sway with the imperial tax collector."

Both women laughed, but then Theano's tone turned serious. "Go in the Mother's grace," she said. She held Sophie in a tight embrace. "And do not lose yourself."

Sophie was glad the other acolytes were too busy for long farewells. She wasn't certain she'd have been able to leave otherwise, and time was of the essence. It would be best if they reached the capital before others learned of Taisa's death.

She emerged from the abbey into the afternoon light with a heavy pack and staff in hand, only to come up short as Sister Iris Kappa, leader of the Gray Falls militia, blocked her path. The captain was broadly built, with the curly brown hair and ruddy skin common in the empire's southern provinces. A dozen of the abbey's younger acolytes stood behind Iris, Fryni among them. Each carried a heavy pack, and they wore tough boots fit for miles of walking.

"Abbess," Iris said, her voice crisp like she was addressing a superior officer, "I've been informed that you shall journey to the capital."

"Yes, Captain," Sophie said. With any other acolyte she was always informal, sister rather than abbess, but Iris had been a legionnaire for years before the abbey, and she was still more comfortable with a clear chain of command.

Iris nodded. "Then I shall lead this patrol to accompany you."

A lump formed in Sophie's throat as she looked at the determined faces of the young women. She had worked beside them in the fields, ground wheat in the mill with them, huddled together for warmth when the snow was deep and the fire low. In all the empire and beyond to the four seas there was no one she would rather have at her side. But she could not drag them into the danger she faced.

"No," Sophie said. "You cannot come with me." She addressed all thirteen of them. "If I fail, it will mean death for me, I cannot risk you as well. The Mother would never forgive me."

Iris pursed her lips. "Sister Fryni," she said after a moment. "Explain our situation to the abbess."

Fryni grinned. "We're only acting as the Void Mother would have us, Sister Sophie." She stood to her full height, the top of her head just above Sophie's chin. "The Mother asks for loyalty. It would be disloyal of us to let you walk into danger alone. The Mother asks for kindness. Helping you prevent civil war is certainly a kindness to all Meyatha. The Mother asks for justice. You should have been empero years ago, we will right that wrong."

"By the Mother and Her blessed daughters," the other acolytes said in unison as Fryni finished her sermon.

Sophie held up her hands. "Mercy, I admit defeat!" She had no conviction left to argue with them, and she found herself choking up. "I would be honored to have you with me." Gray Falls had been her home for more than half her life; now she could take a small piece of it with her. They all gathered together for a brief moment, clasping hands and embracing, before the acolytes fell into a marching formation behind Sophie.

They met Demetra and her house guards at the abbey gates. Four of the soldiers were mounted; the fifth held the carriage's reins while the sixth opened the ornately carved door and offered Demetra a hand up. Demetra waved the armored woman's hand away and looked from Sophie to the other acolytes, her eyes questioning.

"My escort," Sophie said. "They won't slow us down." Her acolytes had no mounts, but they walked and climbed to remote Gray Falls homesteads so often that she'd wager on them over the imperial horses in a distance race.

"Very well," Demetra said, shifting her gaze to Sophie's fresh traveling tunic, a serviceable garment of faded blue. "I thought you were going to change into something more appropriate. You can't go before the Senate dressed as a barb— dressed like that."

Heat blossomed in Sophie's cheeks. Was she some vain aristocrat to be insecure that she did not have the finest material or the latest cut? "This is what we wear out here, Speaker," she said with a steadying breath. She clutched her black shawl tight around her, the only part of her wardrobe with any luxury. "We are first concerned with survival. Sometimes looking our best must take second place."

"Very well, we'll get you suitable clothes in the capital." The older woman shook her head. "Something that doesn't look like it's been washed and repaired ten years running." She climbed into the carriage and gestured to Sophie. "Come up then, we're losing light."

Sophie took a step back. Ride in the carriage while her acolytes walked? She couldn't. Fryni giggled into her sleeve, and some of the heat returned to Sophie's cheeks. "I cannot," she said. "Not while—"

Demetra slashed the air with her hand, cutting Sophie off. "No. You are to be empero, you cannot be seen walking to the capital like a commoner." She stepped down and leaned in close to Sophie. "It may upset your radical beliefs, but consider how important appearances are to the people whose favor you must win. Are you committed to this or not?"

With a defeated sigh, Sophie acquiesced and climbed into the carriage. The cushioned seats were a deep red, and as she sat down, the soft velvet molded to her spine, easing aches so constant Sophie had nearly forgotten about them. A quiet groan of relief escaped her lips. Even the vibration of carriage wheels churning up gravel could not diminish the feeling that Sophie was sinking into a cloud.

"It does wonders for the back on a long journey, doesn't it?" Demetra said, leaning back into her own cushions with a smirk. "Naturally, you'll have a carriage like this every day of the week once we reach the capital."

Sophie winced but did not reply. Out the small window, her acolytes walked without complaint. Was a little comfort all it took for Sophie to hold herself above them?

The miles passed in silence. The capital, Heratia, lay to the west, but to reach it, they first had to take a winding path out of Gray Fall's mountainous terrain to the imperial highway. After that, Heratia was only a few days away. That was why Gray Falls had been chosen for Sophie's exile: the province's poverty made it impossible to engage in politics, yet she was close enough to be easily sent to the Mother's embrace.

Behind them, the snowy caps of the Serate Mountains rose up to scrape the sky. Ahead, Gray Falls' alternating pattern of marshy forests and narrow fields spread out, the Meyathan citizens there working themselves to the bone to bring in what meager harvest the poor soil gave them.

The ache of old, scarred-over guilt flared up in Sophie's mind. The uprising had been her chance to make a better Meyatha. Did she have another chance now? Or would she only bargain this one away as well?

As the sun fell toward the horizon, the gravel path met the paving stones of the old province road, a relic of times when the Meyathan Empire built great works in even its poorest provinces. Sophie's father had often spoken of building such works again, but ten years on the throne had produced little effect that Sophie could see.

Demetra dozed, but Sophie stayed alert. The speaker had claimed secrecy, but they couldn't know for certain what dangers awaited them. Was she merely racing to the capital on a doomed errand? How many people had died the last time she tried to help? She shook her head. She could not afford to think that way. She walked the Mother's path; it was her only option.

To distract herself, she voiced the question growing in the back of her mind. "You have told me how Savvas can destroy the rights of citizenship, but not why."

Demetra blinked her fatigue away. "If you must know, he believes—or at least claims to believe—that citizenship has weakened the empire against Skaldre attacks. He compares us to those southern realms where feudal lords have total control over their people. Not only have they no difficulty with the Skaldre, but they have even seized some of *our* territory in recent years. Many in the Senate are sympathetic to his arguments."

Sophie shook her head. Realms south of Meyatha suffered no Skaldre attacks because the empire held all major crossings of the Serate Mountains and the imperial navy blocked raiding longships from reaching southern waters. Still, she could see how the argument would persuade senatorial families who stood to profit if their free citizens became serfs.

"So Savvas has support in the Senate," Sophie said. She hesitated for a moment. "What did my family think of his proposal?"

"Mihail always rebuffed him," Demetra said. "Even as the empero's illness grew worse." She sighed. "But after our most recent losses to the Skaldre, Mihail did not have the clout to keep others from rallying around Savvas's banner. As for Taisa... she kept her own counsel. I do not know if she would have given in to Savvas or not."

An unexpected hint of pride sparked in Sophie's memory of her father. Whatever his faults, he had at least known to defend Meyatha's founding principles. "And when we arrive in the capital," she said, arching an eyebrow, "do you expect it will be a simple matter of imprisoning Savvas and decreeing his views never be spoken again?"

"No," Demetra said, her voice tired. "The army, the courts, all of the empire's institutions have become dependent on personal contributions from the richest senatorial families. Many commanders and judges are more loyal to their patrons than they are to the state or the empero."

Sophie relaxed back into the enveloping cushions. She could not remember her grandmother having any difficulty getting what she wanted. Irena Ironheart spoke, and legions marched. Perhaps imperial fortunes had declined since her reign, or perhaps her rule was not as absolute as it appeared to her granddaughters.

Demetra went on, "Even so, with the right maneuvering, we should be able to secure key allies and ensure stability for Meyatha. It is very important that you do as I say if we are to succeed."

Sophie said nothing. It was unlikely that her own idea of success would mesh with Demetra's quest for stability, but if she was to make things better, or at least stop them from getting worse, she would need Demetra's help.

A rapping on the carriage windowsill interrupted them. Sophie leaned toward the square opening and was greeted by Iris's stern expression.

"Abbess," the captain said. "Sister Fryni saw someone watching us from the north, just beyond the tree line."

Sophie leaned further out to see Fryni running up to the carriage with mud on her boots, staff slung under one arm.

"I saw at least one," Fryni said. "Big fellow too. Might have had a friend with him, or might just have been shadows playing tricks. They both scampered when I went to check. I didn't find any clear prints though, just a bit of mussed underbrush."

Demetra opened her own window and looked to one of her mounted soldiers. "Did you see the same?"

"I saw no one," the soldier said. He cast a look at Iris and Fryni. "But the forests are wild here. I cannot be certain."

Fryni and Sophie exchanged looks of their own. It could simply be a local farmer supplementing their family's diet with poaching, frightened by their approach. Or it might be someone following them. Perhaps Demetra hadn't left the capital as unnoticed as she believed. If Savvas and his allies learned why she had left, they could mobilize the empire's elite against her before she even arrived.

"If we're being shadowed," Sophie said, "we best quicken our pace."

Demetra agreed, and the carriage's wheels rattled and squeaked as they picked up speed over the stone road. Sophie tried to ignore the pang in her chest as Fryni and the other acolytes broke into a jog, still bearing their heavy packs. If someone were stalking them, less time on the road was more important than her acolytes' discomfort, but she wished she could share it with them.

Chapter 4

They made camp at an old hill fort; once a legion outpost to protect travelers, it had then been abandoned as the empire's military priorities shifted to guarding the frontiers. They set out again at dawn, but if anyone shadowed them, neither guard nor acolyte sighted anything. They kept their course toward the main highway, the mountainous highlands slowly giving way to Gray Falls' scant portion of flat farmland. As they came closer to the provincial border, the small patches of near-barren farmland gave way to larger agricultural estates.

These estates were owned by senatorial landlords, nearly all of whom made their homes in cities like Koriopolis, Melestar, or the great capital Heratia. And while the piles of harvested wheat grew with each passing mile, those who worked the fields remained thin and ragged.

Sophie closed her eyes and hummed the first notes of a sacred hymn. "Sacred Mother," she intoned. "As you sent forth your daughter Sol to light the world, allow me to do some good with the chance I have been granted."

Demetra nodded along with the prayer but did not echo the words.

A guard rapped on the carriage door, interrupting Sophie's thoughts. "Another party, Speaker Kalgari," he said and indicated with an outstretched arm. "They're approaching from the northern side of the highway."

Demetra and Sophie craned their necks out the carriage windows. Beyond the imperial highway's great stone thoroughfare, a column of wagons rolled south toward them, perhaps a dozen in all. The wagons were pulled by heavy draft horses, with perhaps thirty people either seated on the driver's benches or riding alongside. Each wagon was stuffed with heavy bundles—a merchant caravan coming south to trade. Gray Falls wasn't a common route for such travelers, but with goods from faraway Kalyune flowing into northern Skaldre ports, even backwater provinces were bound to see some traffic.

Demetra clicked her tongue. "Can we beat them to the intersection?"

The guard captain shook his head. "I do not think so, they are too close."

Sophie tilted her head, confused. "Why is it so important to reach the intersection first?"

"Because once they are on our road," Demetra said, "we would need to put ourselves in among them if we wished to pass. They would have us surrounded."

Sophie frowned. "Do you think they mean us harm?"

"They are Free Province mercenaries coming south with wagonloads of goods from our enemies," Demetra said. "Of course they mean us harm, even if they have no immediate plans to attack. If they knew who you were, they would take you for a hostage with no hesitation."

Sophie sighed. The Free Provinces were what the empire euphemistically called its former southern territories that had broken away centuries ago. The "provinces" were really a collection of fractious city-states and aristocratic fiefdoms, constantly warring with each other or raiding imperial territory.

Sophie had no love for the Free Provinces, but she didn't share Demetra's intense animosity. The taxes from Free Province trade ships and caravans stopping in Heratia had funded a third of the imperial army when Sophie studied such things in her youth.

"They are strangers," Sophie said. "And the Mother asks that we treat strangers with the same kindness we show our friends."

Demetra snorted. "Perhaps the Free Provinces could have listened more closely to that tenet over the last decade, if they weren't too busy plundering our southern lands."

A clopping of hooves on stone cut off Sophie's retort. A detachment of riders had broken off from the slower wagons and cantered across the highway toward the Meyathan party. Sophie surveyed the strangers as they drew closer. The riders wore serviceable clothes of wool and cotton, but Sophie's gaze passed over a fine silk scarf around one rider's hair, a flash of crucible steel as another checked their sword, and the red glint of rubies not quite hidden beneath the leader's tunic. These were very successful merchants, it seemed.

The merchant riders reined up as Demetra's guards came together to block their path, Iris and the other acolytes watching from further back.

The lead rider raised her hands. She was a handsome, round-faced woman with lightly tanned skin and flowing black hair. She might have been Sophie's age, but neither her face nor her hands showed the wear of hard labor. "Peace, friends," she said. "And well met. I am Constantia de Beltane, proudly of Gallia."

Gallia... From her long-ago geography lessons, Sophie remembered it as an up-and-coming power among the Free Province city-states. If they were sending caravans this far north, their fortunes were indeed on the rise.

Demetra opened the carriage door and placed her foot on the step. "Peace, then, but we've no wish to tarry. See that your wagons keep moving and we can both be on our way."

The Gallian woman laughed. "Apologies, I didn't mean to intrude, honored Senator. I simply thought it would be safer if we traveled together, robbers being what they are on these old roads." She swept her hand round Demetra's guards. "We would be honored by the protection of such fine imperial soldiers."

Iris and Fryni gave the armed Gallians appraising glances while Sophie winced at the sweet condescension in Constantia's voice.

Demetra's teeth ground together. "These roads are perfectly safe from robbers. Be on your way."

"As you say," the Gallian said. But instead of turning her horse, she looked past Demetra into the carriage, gaze sweeping over Sophie's faded wool tunic, so out of place among the luxurious cushions and next to Demetra's fine robes. "A further moment, though," she said, a smile baring her teeth. "That isn't senatorial fashion to my eyes. What brings you to this road, friend?"

Sophie and Demetra both spoke at once.

"I am a priestess on pilgrimage—"

"She is my cousin from—"

Constantia laughed again as both Meyathan women went silent, Sophie's face turning hot. "Well then, cousin on a pilgrimage, may the Mother give you a blessed journey." With that, she wheeled her horse around, leading her party of riders back to the main caravan.

Demetra let out an angry breath. "Keep us half a league behind them," she said in her guard captain's direction. She slammed the carriage door shut and pointed a finger at Sophie. "You must follow my lead from this point on. If someone like her found out who you were, we would be finished!"

Sophie grimaced. "Speaker, she would never have believed we were cousins." She held the rough wool of her sleeve next to Demetra's silk robes. "Our clothes mark us as coming from different worlds."

Demetra's lips pressed into a thin line, swallowing whatever retort she had planned. "That's true," she said after a few moments. "We must coordinate our stories better should this happen in future." She rubbed her temples. "But I implore you, whatever kindness the Mother demands of you, do not trust that Gallian. Your father trusted envoys from that city once, and it cost Meyatha half its merchant fleet. The stakes are much higher now."

Sophie let the argument drop. There was no convincing Demetra. The Gallians were enemies in her mind, and nothing Sophie said would change that. And yet there was some merit in her suspicion. Certainly Sophie would be hesitant to trust a Meyathan senator with the kind of wealth that Constantia de Beltane's hidden rubies hinted at. One did not become that rich on strong devotion to the Mother's tenets.

***

They traveled behind the Gallian caravan for the rest of the day, Demetra's guards keeping a constant lookout. Just before sundown, the farms and fields gave way to the mill town of Tallirod. Possessing the only watermill in Gray Falls outside the abbey, Tallirod was well-off by the standards of its neighbors. Some of the roofs were of clay shingles rather than straw thatch, and the fragrance of frying olive oil wafted out from a few of the open windows.

That smell glided into Sophie's nose and made her mouth water. At the abbey, they fried with butter and animal fat, when they fried at all. Since there was always the question of making sure everyone had enough to eat, it was more common for the acolytes to boil their food. Sophie had never quite lost her taste for the olive oil and southern spices that had been ever present in her youth. She frowned. She would need better self-control in the capital, where oil and spices were the least of the temptations her imperial rank would offer, while much of the citizenry could barely avoid starvation.

Demetra directed her soldiers and the carriage toward Tallirod's only inn, a two-story building of sturdy timbers built upon a tall hill. Some townsfolk looked up in awe at the imperial soldiers in their shining armor, while others only hurried to get out of the way. The wagon jolted as one wheel struck a cracked paving stone, and Demetra cursed the provincial roads. Sophie shook her head. Despite Tallirod's relative wealth, the deteriorating roads were just another sign of how much she would have to do when she became empero. If she became empero.

The carriage came to a halt at the inn's stable, and Demetra groaned. The Gallian caravan's wagons were already parked in the stable yard, their horses safely ensconced in the warm stalls.

"If only we'd beaten them to that intersection and been here first," Demetra said. She swore under her breath. "I will see about lodging. Speak to no one while I am gone if it is not absolutely necessary."

She motioned for two of her guards to flank her and marched up the hillside to the inn proper. Sophie watched her go with an exasperated half smile. The people who lived here were still Gray Falls folk, many of whom had traveled all the way to the abbey for aid when it was most needed. They were hardly the sort to turn on her.

Sophie got up slowly and took careful steps out of the carriage onto the soft grass. She arched her back in a long stretch, bones popping in an unsettling chorus. The carriage cushions were comfortable indeed, but sitting on them all day had left her stiff. She looked to her acolytes and immediately regretted complaining, even to herself.

Iris, Fryni, and the others were all red-faced from a long day of marching on foot, sweat soaking through the rags tied round their foreheads. They set their heavy packs down and leaned against the stable wall, taking long breaths of cool evening air and draining the last of their water.

Several more heavy waterskins hung off the back of the carriage. Sophie took down as many as she could carry and passed them out among her thirsty acolytes. They took the water with hurried thanks and drank it down as fast as Sophie could offer it.

"Mother admonish me," Sophie said as Fryni drained one of the skins. "I shall ensure we make more stops tomorrow, or set a slower pace. You're all parched!"

Fryni waved the words away with one hand and dried her mouth with the other. "That little stroll? It was nothing! We could march twice as fast."

An exaggerated groan rose up from the other acolytes, and Iris crossed her arms. "I see Sister Fryni has volunteered to scout ahead tomorrow."

This brought a round of good-natured chuckles from the other acolytes, while Fryni made a flourishing salute to her captain.

Sophie leaned against the stable wall and put her arm around Fryni. "Thank you for coming with me. But remember that a wise commander always gives their soldiers rest when they can." She let the younger woman lean against her without explaining that one did not need to be abbess to see how tired the acolytes were.

"What's important," one of the other acolytes said after a final pull of water, "is we kept up with those house guards and their monster horses." She turned to the others. "Have any of you seen beasts that size before?"

The others shook their heads.

Sophie had, when Irena Ironheart's elite cavalry rode through Heratia's shattered gates, and again when she was first delivered into exile.

"I half expected that someone would stop us before we left Gray Falls," Sophie said. "That this would all turn out to be a test and I'd be executed for breaking my exile. But it seems we are going to the capital after all."

"We're with you," Fryni said.

"By the Mother and Her blessed daughters," Iris and the other acolytes chorused.

Fryni poked Sophie in the ribs. "It's for the best anyway. You always said that climbing mountains was a young woman's game. Now you can rest your bones on a padded throne."

Sophie laughed and patted Fryni's head. "And while I'm resting, you'll have time to memorize the maps of every mountain in Meyatha. Then you'll be ready to climb them."

Fryni laughed in return, and the other acolytes joined in. Sophie kept a jovial expression even as her mind's eye went to the imperial throne room in Heratia. The Falcon Throne had not looked padded the last time she laid eyes on it. Her eyelids grew heavy in the warm sunset light. Where was Demetra? They would all fall asleep on their feet if she didn't return soon.

"Abbess Sophie!" a masculine voice called. Not Demetra then, but familiar. Sophie turned to see a gray-haired man with light skin and a soldier's build striding toward her. He wore robes of a style similar to Demetra's, though the red dye looked pale in comparison. "They told me you were visiting, and I wanted to welcome you—"

Two of Demetra's guards stepped between the man and Sophie, hands resting on the hilts of their shortswords. He came up short, his mouth snapping shut. The man's voice and face clicked together in Sophie's memory. *Mayor Niko.* He had asked for the abbey's help two years previous when a sickness struck Tallirod and had promised any assistance he could give as payment.

"It's alright," Sophie said to the soldiers. "Please, let him through."

They looked at her for a moment before stepping aside.

Mayor Niko straightened his robe and gave a deep bow to Sophie. "You honor my town, Abbess. How can we be of assistance to you?"

"The Mother and Her blessed daughters smile on Tallirod," Sophie said. "But I'm afraid my business is my own." There was no reason to drag anyone else into her quest, and it wouldn't hurt for fewer people to know why she journeyed to the capital.

Before Sophie could say anything else, Demetra stormed out of the inn and down its steps, her two guards trailing behind.

"The nerve of that Gallian," she nearly shouted. She waved a hand back toward the inn. "She's taken every room they have, but, oh, she'd be pleased to let us pay *her* for use of the stables." She went silent as she took in Mayor Niko.

The mayor cleared his throat. "Of course, your business is your own, Abbess Sophie. But if you lack lodgings, I insist you stay in my home tonight." He looked around the gathered soldiers and acolytes. "It may be a bit snug in the guest rooms, but we should have space for all of you."

"A moment," Demetra said. She put a hand on Sophie's shoulder and led her around to the other side of the carriage. Sophie went without resistance. The speaker would need to be calmed down, and that would be easier with fewer ears.

"Who, exactly, is that?" Demetra asked, her voice a brittle calm.

"The mayor of this town," Sophie said. "I have told him nothing dangerous, and he has graciously offered to solve our problem this evening."

Demetra shook her head. "No, out of the question. This inn at least is on a hill, defensible. I saw the mayor's house when we came into town. It's on flat ground, easily assaulted. And he would be one more person who could betray you for coin."

"Betray me to whom?" Sophie asked, spreading her hands.

"To that Gallian woman, if she's figured out who you are," Demetra said, one hand drumming on the carriage's smooth wooden side. "To any spies who might have followed me from the capital. To whoever was shadowing us yesterday, if anyone was."

Sophie put her hands on the older woman's shoulders with a light touch. "Speaker Kalgari, we have nowhere else to stay. Mayor

Niko is a friend, he will not turn on us." And letting him discharge his debt to Sophie would let her leave Gray Falls with one fewer loose end.

"We can keep going down the highway until we find a place to camp," Demetra said, her words coming out faster. "Or we could commandeer some of the more defendable houses, that way only we could go in or out."

"No," Sophie said. This was too much. "My acolytes are tired, and even if the Mother did not expect it of me, I would show them the kindness of a good night's sleep now, not force them to march further in the dark." She turned. "I shall accept the mayor's offer. You are free to join us, if you like."

Without another word, Sophie returned and thanked Mayor Niko for his gracious offer. He beamed at her acceptance and offered Sophie his arm. Fryni, Iris, and the other acolytes picked up their packs and followed. After a few moments, Demetra and her soldiers followed as well.

The mayor's home was a villa built in the classic Meyathan style of four wings set in a square around a central courtyard. The front steps were of smooth white marble, and the same river that powered the mill fed a stone fountain of the Mother sending Her daughters Sol and Luna on their separate paths. It was a house few in the empire could afford; even Demetra gave it the slightest nod of approval. But in Sophie's youth, she had read of times when such homes had been available to successful artisans and scholars. Those times had long given way though to an era when wealth flowed into vast senatorial estates and stayed there.

It was past the dinner hour, but Mayor Niko roused his servants long enough to provide a meal of cold bread, cheese, and a few wedges of sweet fruit. It was welcome after a day of hard travel, and they all ate the plain fare without complaint. Niko insisted he would take no payment, but Sophie's eye caught the empty wall space where tapestries had hung when she last visited. The finely carved decorations of two years previous had been replaced by rough-hewn. It seemed that in Gray Falls, even a mayor was not immune to the declining times.

As the mayor had predicted, the guest rooms were a snug fit, with many mats laid out on the floor to make extra sleeping space. Sophie and her acolytes were given the larger set of connected rooms while Demetra took the smaller set, announcing that her guards would keep watch on the guest wing's entrance.

The bed had enough room for three, so Sophie cut up straws to draw for a place on the mattress. The acolytes briefly tried to assign Sophie one of the spaces by default, but she gave a firm no. She drew with the rest of them and had no complaints when the lucky three straws all went to others. The arrangements were close quarters, but it was nothing they hadn't done on cold nights in the abbey.

Before lying down to sleep, Sophie led her acolytes in an evening prayer, much abbreviated in acknowledgment of their fatigue. "Sol embodies the tenet of kindness," Sophie said. "Lighting the way for all beings, without thought to how deserving they may be. Let us all endeavor to walk in her light."

"By the Mother and Her blessed daughters," the acolytes agreed. They lost no further time in stretching out on either mattress or floor mat, their heavy traveling clothes now piled up as blankets. Sophie laid her own head down on the bundle of reeds that served as a pillow and let her eyes close.

Chapter 5

Sophie's eyes opened. She was back on the bridge to western Heratia, half its span blocked by a rubble-laden wagon. Had she ever left? Somehow, she always seemed to come back to this place.

Her sword shook in her hand as the screams and clamor of battle drew closer. The empero's forces were over the eastern walls; this was Sophie's last chance to stop them before the entire city collapsed and the Solstice Uprising died. Round the corner came the thunder of hooves on stone: the imperial cavalry, rebel blood running off their shining armor.

Empero Irena rode in front, the Laskaris falcon emblazoned across the steel of her armor. She charged with deadly grace despite being well past sixty, and as she closed in, her lance aimed straight for Sophie's heart. Sophie raised her shield. The blow connected and sent her sprawling off the barricade. Her vision swam from the impact, and a shadow fell across her. Sophie looked up. The empero stood over her, sword raised. Sophie struggled to lift her own sword, but her arm was caught beneath Irena's boot.

"Traitor," her grandmother said. "I would destroy the empire before I handed it over to you."

Sophie's fellow rebels screamed and died around her. Smoke from the burning buildings poured into her lungs. Irena raised her sword for a killing strike.

Sophie opened her eyes to find cold sweat running down her forehead, her arm pinned beneath the acolyte sleeping next to her. Silver light drifted in the window from a waxing moon. A dream—it was only a dream. She took slow, deliberate breaths. She had never met her grandmother in battle during the real Solstice Uprising; she wouldn't have survived if she had. The image was only her nervous mind playing tricks.

Then why was smoke still tickling her nose? Why did she still imagine she could hear screaming and the clash of steel blades? Sophie blinked herself fully awake. It wasn't imagination; someone was fighting out in the guest wing's corridor.

"Up," Sophie said, in a voice pitched to carry. "Up, my sisters."

Iris was already on her feet while the other acolytes stirred and muttered. Fryni sat up, eyes blinking and head tilted sideways.

The main door swung open and Demetra rushed in, a bloodstained shortsword in one hand. She slammed the door behind her, brought the bar down, and pressed her back against it. "We are under attack," she said. Her breath came in short pants. "Get dressed, we must leave at once."

Iris and Fryni pulled the other acolytes to their feet in moments, all of them throwing on their tunics and trousers like they hadn't spent all of the previous day marching. Doors to the adjoining rooms opened and the remaining acolytes rushed in, staves in hand and heavy packs already on their shoulders.

Shouts sounded through the main doors in a Skaldre tongue, then the sound of steel against steel and the wet scream of a person's death. Sophie's feet hit the floor as she shrugged into her own tunic. If the attackers were Skaldre, then it was likely they had been sent to prune even the disgraced branch of the Laskaris family.

"How many are there?" Sophie asked. "How well armed?"

Demetra's expression was a mask of calm. "I saw at least a dozen with axes and shields, but I heard more on the way. Lightly armored, thank the Mother for that, but there are too many to fight."

The speaker's report confirmed Sophie's suspicion: Skaldre hunters, traveling light in service of speed. The enemy would not have attacked unless they were confident of victory. If Demetra's six soldiers weren't dead already, they soon would be.

"Staying here was my error," Sophie said. "I will see us delivered from harm."

The door shuddered under a heavy impacted from the other side. Sophie suppressed a grimace. Her promise would not be easy to keep.

"You can feel guilty later," Demetra said. "Now we must be away." She pointed at the shuttered window. "That is our only way out."

Fryni pressed a hand to the heavy shutters. "It's big enough, and the drop is short."

Iris shook her head. "There is no cover on the other side. Any archers outside could pick us off at their leisure."

Sophie had to agree with Iris. "If it were my plan, I'd be prepared for the quarry to flee that way and have archers ready to cut them down. Our only way out is to use the door and fight through."

Demetra stifled a desperate laugh. "Fight? Have you lost your sense? My guards are paying for our escape with their lives, but you propose we fight the Skaldre with no soldiers and just your staves as weapons? The window is our only chance."

"To arms and armor," Sophie said. "May the Mother see that any blood we spill is necessary."

At this signal, the acolytes drew open their heavy packs and drew out shirts of chain mail that glittered in the silver moonlight. Next emerged long spearheads, small round shields, and thick leather helmets.

The door shuddered again, long cracks breaking open along the wood's grain.

Demetra gawked as the thirteen acolytes donned their chain mail and bolted the spearheads to their staves.

Sophie couldn't resist a grim smile. "There is no imperial garrison in Gray Falls, Speaker, but we have raiders and bandits like any other province." She raised her hands so that Fryni could slip chain mail over her head as Iris organized the other acolytes into a wedge formation that was narrow enough to fit through the guest room's threshold. "When I came to the abbey those decades ago, I taught the acolytes to protect their flock with steel as well as faith."

A third blow struck the door, bending two of the iron hinges. More Skaldre shouts came from the other side. The door wouldn't last much longer.

Sophie strapped a round shield to one arm and raised her spear with the other. She had shed blood several times since coming to the abbey, but it was always to drive off marauders who sought profit rather than death. She gritted her teeth. This would be a battle for survival, the likes of which she hadn't fought since the uprising, and it brought old pains bubbling to the surface.

Iris gave orders in a low voice that wouldn't carry to the enemy. "Unbar the door; it will unbalance them when they break through. When they do, charge with all your strength. Protect Abbess Sophie and the speaker, and make for the woods."

Two acolytes tore the splintering bar from its brackets. The rest raised their round shields and leveled their spears, forming a line of glinting steel teeth.

The door burst open and half a dozen men and women stumbled through with a rough-cut statue they'd turned into a ram. They wore light, padded armor, with all but two sporting the blond hair and pale skin so common among the Skaldre.

Sophie had no time for further observation. In a single voice, she and her acolytes shouted, "To Void we return!" as they charged.

The enemy hesitated, some backing away while others let go of their improvised ram and reached for weapons.

The acolytes' spear line smashed into them, steel points biting through leather and cloth to the flesh beneath. As Sophie's spear sunk home, the impact jarred her arm. She clenched her teeth and pushed the dying Skaldre off her weapon with a shove of her foot.

"On and through!" Sophie shouted. The surviving attackers slumped aside, broken by the acolytes' ferocity. Outside the guest rooms, the villa was burning. Several of the corridor's lamps were fallen on their sides, spilling flames and oil onto the wooden floor.

Four of Demetra's house guards lay dead against the walls alongside two of the mayor's servants, their blood leaking to mix with the burning oil. Seven of the attackers had joined them in death.

Ahead lay the guest wing's outer doors and the sweet scent of night air. Demetra's guard captain and his last remaining soldier fought side by side to keep a second group of Skaldre from closing the doors. The two house guards stood outnumbered three to one, their armor rent and bloody, but they rallied as Sophie and her acolytes charged toward them.

One tall Skaldre barked a command to her companions, and the six of them made a short withdrawal, joining another half dozen of their kin at the guest wing's threshold. Together they blocked the only line of escape, shields locked and axes raised. These were the kind of soldiers who anchored the line in battle: broad shouldered and stoutly built, with armor of steel mail. More Skaldre shouted from elsewhere in the villa, rushing back to join their comrades. The Meyathans couldn't stay here; they could only go forward.

Sophie sprinted toward the door and its waiting guardians, her acolytes following in a wave. Fryni and Iris flanked Sophie on either side while the others formed a knot around the unarmored Demetra. Two acolytes were struck; they slid back to the rear of the formation so their comrades could take up the slack. The two surviving house guards joined the attack, seemingly unfazed by the chain-mail-clad acolytes that had come to their aid.

Sophie angled for the leftmost Skaldre, forcing him to break the shield wall to face her. The big man roared a sour-smelling challenge and thumped his axe against his shield. Sophie thrust low, aiming for lightly armored shins, but the man slid his shield into the spear's path and brought his axe down in a scything arc. Sophie raised her own shield. The axe head bit almost clear through it, and a shock of pain reverberated up Sophie's arm. The force of the blow nearly knocked her off her feet. Sophie grunted and gave a step of ground. She wasn't twenty anymore; she couldn't trade blows with a soldier in his prime. She retreated further, letting her shield arm hang limp and lowering the point of her spear. If he thought she was weak, maybe—

The Skaldre charged, swinging his axe at Sophie's hanging shield arm. Fryni darted in from the left, spear aimed to catch him in his side. The big soldier spun like lightning to deflect the attack and knocked Fryni back with a blow from his shield, leaving her stunned and exposed.

In a surge of fear, Sophie pushed forward to help, but Iris was faster. As the Skaldre warrior lunged after Fryni, Iris stepped to his other side, sinking her spear deep into a seam of his armor. The Skaldre groaned and toppled sideways, blood sheeting down from the wound as his head struck the villa's wall.

Sophie let out a relieved breath and glanced to her right; the rest of her acolytes and Demetra's house guards had broken through the remaining Skaldre, sending them into a retreat for the time being. More acolytes were wounded, leaning on those who were not.

Iris motioned the other acolytes forward, spear raised and expression set in a rare smile of triumph.

With a quiet hiss, a feathered shaft pierced the chain mail just below Iris's throat, splitting the metal rings and burrowing itself up to its fletching. Her face went slack as she sank down, folding in around the arrow.

Nausea and shock rolled over Sophie. She knelt by the stricken captain. Iris's chest was still; the breath she'd used to shout encouragement during long marches had left her forever. There was nothing to be done.

The other acolytes rushed to surround their fallen comrade. Sophie looked back. More armored figures poured into the guest quarter's main hall behind them, several putting arrows to string. Fryni put her shield arm around Iris's shoulders, straining to lift her body.

"No," Sophie said, ignoring the cold pit in her gut and pulling Fryni up. "We've no time. Out, now!"

Grief twisted Fryni's face, but she obeyed. Sophie led her acolytes, Demetra, and the surviving house guards out into the night as Skaldre arrows buzzed through the dark around them. The wounded leaned on the healthy, and the image of Iris's abandoned body tore at Sophie with every step. The first person to die under her command in twenty-three years, but there was no time to mourn now—only to run. In seconds they were past the villa's open grounds and into the full dark of night, with only the moon's light to guide them. Where it would guide them, Sophie wasn't sure.

Chapter 6

Sophie led the party to a small copse of trees on the riverbank beside the mill. The trees would give some cover from sight, and the rushing river would obscure any sound they made, or so Sophie hoped. If any Skaldre still pursued them, they were lost to her senses.

They lay the wounded down to rest in the softest undergrowth and did their best to examine the injuries by moonlight. After Fryni scouted behind them and confirmed that they had left their pursuers behind, Sophie allowed them to light a few candles from their packs. In the wavering light, she beheld the damage. Calliope had bled badly before Fryni wrapped a bandage around her ribs; she would need a warm place to rest and recover her strength. Anna's arm was broken, the bone snapped clean in two. Sophie would need better light than this to set it properly. Several of the others were in no shape for long marching.

"What happened back there, Captain?" Demetra asked, addressing the senior of her surviving house guards.

The old soldier wiped blood and grime from his sword. "They had the villa surrounded before we realized there was an attack. And they knew their work. The Mother abandon me if they were anything but Thane Eidsson's elite scouts."

Sophie recognized the name: Starkad Eidsson, thane of the largest realm in the Skaldre lands, frequent nemesis of Meyatha in the last decade. He had almost certainly been behind Taisa's death, and now his killers had come for Sophie as well.

Demetra absorbed the news with a stony expression. "And the mayor? Was he in league with them?"

The captain shook his head. "I do not know. I saw his servants struck down where they stood, but the mayor's quarters were on the other side of the villa. He might have let the Skaldre in, or he might have been slain in his bed."

Sophie looked up from examining Anna's arm. "We cannot know," she said. Then she sighed. She had been safe in the abbey for too long, with only occasional raids to deal with. Her new enemies played for far greater stakes. "But whether Niko betrayed us or not, it was a mistake for me to accept his hospitality."

Panicked shouts echoed through the trees. Sophie's gaze snapped back toward Tallirod. Smoke and an orange glow rose over the town, waking the citizens to the reality of flames engulfing the mayor's villa. Sophie wished them the Mother's blessing in putting out the blaze before it spread. They had a good chance, with the open green around the villa, but nothing was certain with fire.

"We can't stay here," Demetra said, cutting in on Sophie's thoughts. "We have to move before the Skaldre find us."

"Yes," Sophie said with a nod. "But one moment, please." She had a sacred duty to perform, even if it seemed a small thing in the face of death.

She gathered the healthy acolytes together around the wounded. "Our brave sister Iris is fallen," she intoned. Her voice caught, and she swallowed. "She came to us from the legions because she would not follow orders to evict citizens from their land and homes. She lived a sacred life and passed in the service of loyalty. Luna and your starry children, carry our sister to the Void Mother's warm embrace."

"By the Mother and Her blessed daughters," the gathered acolytes said together.

Sophie breathed in. "Who will sing her rites?" By custom, a dying Meyathan chose their closest loved one to perform this final blessing over them, but when someone passed suddenly, the choice fell to their kin.

One of the acolytes lifted her eyes to meet Sophie's. Alkestis Saitta was her name. She was taller and a few years older than her fellows, her skin paler than most, and she had sandy-blonde hair that hinted at Skaldre ancestry, though her family had lived in the empire for generations. "Iris was my dearest friend," she said. Her eyes were red. "I would take this charge, unless there are objections."

The other acolytes bowed their heads in assent. Alkestis's voice shook, but she pitched it low so as not to carry beyond the clearing. "The sun will light your way, dear friend, you have no need to fear this end."

Iris had been despondent when she first arrived at the abbey. The legion had been her entire life.

Alkestis steadied her voice. "The moon will guide you at night, dear one, if ever you should miss the sun."

When Sophie had trained them in spear, the other acolytes had left a suit of practice armor out for Iris each day until, finally, she ventured out of her room to join them.

"For you will sail on the starry sea, they know the course that's set for thee."

When Sophie's militia needed a captain, Iris was the obvious choice. By then, the taciturn ex-soldier would stay in the dining hall for late-evening chats with the other acolytes, usually just to listen.

"And then you'll rest in the Void, dear friend. Eternal rest in the Void." Alkestis's voice broke on the final syllable, and several of her fellow acolytes embraced her as she wept.

Sophie let out her breath. There should have been more. They should have covered Iris's body in a shroud of deepest black and sang songs of her life and sacred hymns of her passing until the sun rose. By sacred duty they should also sing for Demetra's fallen guards and the slain servants. But they had no bodies, no shroud, and no time.

Demetra paced up and down as Sophie turned away from the makeshift ceremony. The speaker's graying hair was unkempt for the first time since she had arrived at the abbey, and her robe was badly arranged. "Our supplies were stored in the mayor's stables along with the horses," Demetra said. "The Skaldre will have them by now."

"Most likely," Sophie said. Her acolytes carried a little food in their packs, but most of it had been with Demetra's carriage. She was even more concerned for how they would travel undetected. The Skaldre were accomplished scouts, more than capable of hunting Sophie's party whether they traveled by road or cross-country. She glanced at Demetra. "Regardless, there are too many of them for us to fight, nor can we take shelter with the townsfolk. Even if they are trustworthy, I will not draw this danger to the doors of more innocents."

The candlelight illuminated Demetra's grim expression. "I should have brought more soldiers," the speaker muttered. "Even if it meant a greater chance of discovery. Our only choice now is to make for the garrison at Kambre. It is the closest bastion of imperial power."

Sophie shook her head. "Kambre is two days away, too long on the road with so many of Thane Eidsson's soldiers stalking us."

Fryni stood up from bandaging one of her wounded comrades. "We should return to the abbey." She bared her teeth. "It's closer, we can rouse the rest of the militia to hunt these murderers down and bring justice to them."

"Have you lost your wits?" Demetra said to the young acolyte. "We must get Sophie to the capital, not leave her holed up at the nether end of the empire!"

Fryni took a long step forward so she was inches from Demetra's face. "Do you care about Sophie's life at all? Justice for our fallen sister, for your own soldiers?"

Sophie slid her shoulder between the two, forcing them each to take a step back. "Peace," she said. She looked at Fryni. "We cannot return to the abbey either. We would have to leave the wounded, and at such a price, Iris would find justice hollow."

Fryni's shoulders slumped, and her eyes fell. "Forgive me, Sister Sophie. I didn't think of that." She gripped her spear harder. "I just want them to pay for her life."

Sophie put her arms around the younger woman and held her close. "You are now captain of the Gray Falls militia. Learn this lesson and remember it: preserving your own force is your first responsibility. Iris traded her life so the rest of us could live, the speaker's house guards too. We must honor that."

Fryni gave a shuddering sob in Sophie's arms. Her voice was thick. "I understand, Sister Sophie."

An echoing sob built in Sophie's chest, but she held it in check. Now more than ever, her acolytes needed to see her in control.

Demetra coughed. "Yes, well, we must decide where to go soon. They will find us here if we give them the time." She nodded to Fryni and the other armed acolytes. "You surprised them before, when they expected peaceful sisters. But they will be ready this time, and they do not seem in the mood to take prisoners."

Sophie released Fryni and turned to the speaker. Demetra was right, but they could go neither forward nor back in their present state.

"There is one group of armed warriors closer than either Kambre or the abbey," Sophie said. "If we can reach the inn, the Gallians may grant us protection in their caravan."

"I would almost rather face the Skaldre," Demetra said. "*If* Constantia agrees to help us, it will not be due to the Mother's kindness." She brought out an embroidered purse, unfastening it to reveal a few scores of silver coins. "This is all I had the time to retrieve," she said. "Not much to a wealthy Gallian merchant."

"It will have to do," Sophie said. "I do not see that we have other options."

Demetra tucked her coin purse away. "Agreed, but you must let me speak for us. As a senator far from home, I have the resources to interest the Gallians, but I am not so valuable that they will be tempted by the reward Thane Eidsson might give them for me."

Sophie nodded. "Fryni, get the wounded moving. We must reach the inn with everyone still breathing."

***

They crept at an agonizingly slow pace around Tallirod's outskirts. Nearly half their number couldn't walk unaided, and the predawn darkness slowed them even further. Sophie couldn't risk any lights giving away their location, and so those in front had to feel for obstacles with their spears.

Tallirod's narrow river lay between them and the inn. The nearest bridge was in the center of town; they couldn't reach it without being illuminated by the townsfolk's lanterns and the still-burning villa, and any Skaldre in the shadows would be sure to see them. They would have to ford the river instead.

Sophie and Fryni went in first. The hungry cold of the mountain springs shocked the breath from Sophie's lungs. She gave silent thanks that it was autumn rather than spring, when the river would be swollen and even colder from snowmelt. They pushed on through the thankfully shallow water, probing the riverbed with their spears for any submerged stones or crevasses. Halfway across, Fryni gave a warning hiss.

Further downstream, closer to town, three figures knelt at the riverbank. Sophie hunched her shoulders. She couldn't see much of the strangers in the dark, but judging by their height and their lack of any light source, they could be no one but Skaldre on the hunt. She lowered herself in the water, letting the chilled current rush up to her throat. Fryni mirrored the move beside her. If the Skaldre looked in her direction in the dark, they would see only the outline of river rocks just breaking the surface—or so Sophie hoped.

The Skaldre took their time searching the riverbank, likely looking for tracks or other signs of their prey's passing. Sophie kept perfectly still, praying that her acolytes on the far bank had realized what was happening and would do nothing to give themselves away.

Feeling drained out of Sophie's legs, and a shiver ran up her core. She couldn't keep still much longer, and any movement would give her away. Finally the Skaldre stood and crept further toward town, their steps impossible to hear over the water rushing just below Sophie's ears. Even when they were out of sight, Sophie kept her steps measured so splashes would not draw the Skaldre back. Finally, she and Fryni stood shivering on the opposite bank, water running off them in rivulets.

The rest of their party waded through the dark water without interruption, helping the wounded across until they all rested on the far bank. Sophie gave them a few minutes to catch their breath, doing her best to wring water out of the tunic and trousers beneath her armor, before setting out again.

***

At the inn, lanterns blazed in every window, and the Gallians kept a relaxed sentry, occasionally glancing out into the dark as they played at dice or cards. They stood and put hands on their weapons as Sophie's bedraggled party approached.

Demetra stepped forward. "I would speak with your lady, Constantia de Beltane. I have a proposition for her."

After a whispered exchange, the Gallians escorted Demetra, Sophie, and their party into the blessedly warm common room where Constantia waited for them beside a crackling hearth. She had exchanged her plain traveling clothes for a gown of dark-red silk, with no attempt to hide the ruby cluster on a silver chain around her neck. Long lashes framed deep-blue eyes.

"By the Mother and Her blessed daughters," she said with raised eyebrows. "Whatever has happened?"

Demetra faced the Gallian woman. "No doubt you've seen the smoke; brigands tried to rob me as I was escorting these holy sisters to the capital." She indicated Sophie and the Gray Falls acolytes, then drew a dozen silver coins from her purse. "If you will grant us protection, I can offer you what silver I have with me now, plus four times that from House Kalgari's coffers in Heratia."

Sophie kept a blank expression, but several of her acolytes' eyes widened. The speaker was discussing more money than any of them had ever seen in one place.

"Most generous, I'm sure," Constantia said with a wave of her hand. "But it will not do, not for what you ask."

The fire cast Demetra's scowl into sharp relief: the expression of a woman unused to being spoken to with such dismissal, least of all by a foreigner. "The price is negotiable," the speaker said between clenched teeth. "Name the number of coins you require for our safe passage."

"It isn't a matter of price," Constantia said. "You can claim brigands if you like, but I know Meyathan politics when I see them." She lounged back in her cushioned chair, plucking a peach from a nearby bowl. "Whether your enemy is another senator or Thane Eidsson of the Skaldre, it will take more than what you can muster to get me involved in such costly business."

"More than the speaker of Meyatha's Senate can offer?" Demetra asked.

Constantia shrugged. "You may be the speaker, but your family's finances have been stretched thin in recent years. I suppose that will happen when one spends all their time propping up an empire that has seen better days."

Demetra's hands balled into fists at her side, and Sophie slid a steadying arm around the speaker's shoulders. An outburst wouldn't help their situation, no matter how righteous Demetra's anger.

"If you will grant us a moment," Sophie said to their Gallian host. "We must confer."

Constantia did not object, so Sophie guided Demetra to the furthest corner she could find, hoping they could speak without being overheard.

"I do not think silver will be enough," Sophie whispered, keeping her voice as low as possible.

"No." Demetra took a breath. "I see nothing else we can offer her. Even if you revealed your identity, the imperial finances are not in the best condition either. We may have to risk the roads on our own."

The speaker's words hung between them. If they traveled without the Gallians' protection, they would have to abandon the wounded or else be set upon again by Thane Eidsson's hunters. *No.* Sophie would go to the Void first.

"Tell me," Sophie said. "Are the Falcon Piers still reserved for only Meyathan ships?" Those piers had been the finest docks in the capital during Sophie's youth, a real jewel for any merchants allowed to use them.

Demetra's whisper turned indignant. "Of course they are. The Laskaris family keeps them for only our own people. No foreigner will ever..." Her eyes widened in realization. "No, you cannot! It is too great a price to pay, to this Gallian or to anyone. It would enrage the Senate, and you need them to confirm you as empero."

"The Senate's anger is moot if we die here," Sophie said. "Alive, perhaps we can mitigate it."

"Even should your plan work, how can you begin your reign as empero by giving away imperial holdings?"

"Do you see another path where I live long enough to become empero at all?"

The silence stretched for several moments. Finally Demetra shook her head. "I do not."

Sophie nodded. "Then I will try to save our lives."

She strode back to the Gallian woman. There was no more time for deception. "My name is Sophie Laskaris, empero of all Meyatha." Technically she would not be empero until the Senate voted to confirm her, but, with luck, that fine point of Meyathan law would slip past the Gallians. "I have been attacked, and I require your assistance. Protection for the rest of our journey, dry clothes, and care for our wounded."

Constantia showed no sign of surprise. She took a deep bow, the silk of her gown whispering as she moved. When she straightened, her mouth was set in a wide smile that showed all her white teeth.

"Your Majesty," she said. "It is an honor. For my humble part, I am Duchess Constantia de Beltane, on my way to your glorious capital to trade northern goods and oversee the family business." With a graceful hand, she indicated a bench beside the hearth. "Will you sit?"

Sophie nodded and lowered herself down with precise care. The battle's rush was gone, leaving her exhausted and barely able to keep herself from shaking, but she could not afford to lose control in front of this predator.

"Now," Constantia said. "Let us speak of what you can offer me. I am happy to provide all the empero asks, but it will not be cheap."

Demetra stood over Sophie's shoulder, her face masked in a friendly smile. "Does Gallian philosophy not teach the value of having the Eternal Empire in your debt?"

"Our philosophy teaches us to get the most we can in any circumstances," Constantia said. "And your circumstances are that you came to me bloody and begging."

"Then consider this offer," Sophie said, rapping her knuckles on the table to draw back Constantia's attention. She could attempt to haggle further, start with a low offer and work up to a compromise, but Constantia was right: the Gallians held all the cards. Sophie needed them to understand she was serious. "If you help us, your family's ships may dock at the Falcon Piers."

The Gallian woman whistled a low note. "Your Majesty truly is prepared to bargain, then. How many ships, and for how long?"

Sophie glanced back at her acolytes. Some of their wounds needed more attention, and they would be worse off the longer this continued. "I will allot one quarter of the berths to your use for five years."

Constantia tapped a finger on her chin. "Hmm. I would normally demand half the berths for twenty years, but you seem to be in a hurry." She followed Sophie's glance to the wounded acolytes. "Shall we skip to compromising on a third for ten years?"

"Yes, please," Sophie said, ignoring Demetra's rigid stance beside her. "If you'll see to my people's injuries, then it is done."

"One more thing," Constantia said with a raised hand. "Your offer is generous, but how can I trust it? We might arrive in the capital only for you to pretend we've never met."

Sophie nodded. A reasonable concern. "Write a formal contract. I will put my signature upon it. If I break my word, you will have proof. It will be inconvenient for a new empero to be seen as a liar."

"An empero's word should be enough," Demetra muttered, but she raised no further objection.

Constantia clapped her hands. "Excellent. I will have it drawn up." She motioned to one of the other Gallians. "Make space for them to rest and have their wounds cared for." She turned to one of her subordinates. "Unload all but the lightest cargo so that we might set a faster pace. We shall sign on more swords at the next town."

The other Gallian frowned. "A high cost in losses and expenditures, Your Grace."

"A cost worth paying," Constantia said. She grinned at Sophie. "Until we reach Heratia, the empero's safety is my sacred responsibility."

Sophie dipped her head. "Thank you, Duchess de Beltane." She only hoped that this Gallian magnate had the steel to protect them from Thane Eidsson's knives and that making this deal did not spell the end of her reign before it began.

Chapter 7

At dawn, the wounded acolytes were loaded into the wagons in place of the Gallians' abandoned cargo. Those still healthy perched on drivers' benches and running boards, weapons ready.

With Sophie's signed contract in hand, Constantia set a brisk pace, changing horses at every imperial waystation with a generous display of silver. Fryni and a troop of Constantia's guards looked for signs of pursuit, but they reported only a few scattered sightings that soon ceased altogether. If the Skaldre still followed, they kept their distance.

Soon they reached the border of Syracos Province, where the road widened and the estates along it grew more prosperous. Though its mountainous soil wasn't much more fertile than Gray Falls, Syracos had the wealth of gold and silver mines to depend on. Important civic buildings displayed marble facades, and imperial patrols were a common sight on the roads.

Syracos's grain silos were full, and in one town alone the butchers hawked more meat than the abbey had seen in all of the previous year. A temple they passed had most of one wall covered in a mosaic of Sol's first steps across the world. They encountered more traffic as well, from farmers carting their harvest to gentry in lavish carriages like the one Demetra had left in Tallirod.

Yet even in Syracos there were cracks in the road that Sophie did not remember from her trip into exile. Bridges showed signs of makeshift repairs, and mortar crumbled off city walls even as the senatorial villas grew ever more prosperous. Workers returning from the mines looked in little better shape than Gray Falls' tenants, haggard and thin. This was the imperial heartland; how had circumstances slipped so far?

Finally, as the sun set on their fourth day of travel, the Serate Mountains to their left gave way to foot hills, revealing the shores of a vast blue expanse: Godstep Lake, one of the only ways to cross the mountain range that bisected the continent, a gateway between north and south. The water swept out in a great mirror of the sky for as far as anyone could see, broken only by the swarm of boats and ships that sailed upon it.

The next morning, the party boarded a single-masted ferry heading to the capital. Sophie crowded with the acolytes on the ship's raised forward deck. The rail was worn smooth by the passage of many hands, and they pressed close to it to avoid being under foot as sailors loaded crates and livestock from the pier. An officer whistled and lines were cast off, some of crew unfurling the sail while others took up oars. A strong north wind gusted across the lake, pushing the ferry south toward waiting Heratia.

As the rising sun burned off the early-morning fog, the first tower came into view, an obelisk of black stone and brick. More towers emerged over the horizon, flowing down into walls that themselves rose well above the water. Several acolytes gasped. They had never seen a city before this journey, let alone the mighty seawalls of Heratia, capital of the Meyathan Empire, the city at the center of the world.

That title was only a modest exaggeration. Heratia controlled access to Godstep Lake and from it controlled an empire. The two great southern rivers, the Marshrun and the Silvervein, ran through the city. They powered Heratia's mills and provided drinking water for the populace, but, more importantly, iron grates could be lowered across them at any time, cutting vital trade arteries between north and south.

The city's eastern land walls were just visible as the ferry joined a teeming flotilla waiting for a berth in the harbor. These were even taller than the seawalls, their towers rising up to rival the mountains. A river of people surged in and out of Heratia through the eastern Dawn Gate, where twenty-three years ago, Empero Irena's army had breached the Solstice Rebels' defenses. The empero had launched a diversionary attack from the lake, luring the defenders away until her real force struck. If Sophie had seen through the trick, maybe... She shook her head. She was here now, with greater enemies to face than family ghosts.

The ship passed underneath a great arch in the seawalls into the harbor itself, and the acolytes' eyes went even wider. Hundreds—thousands—of ships were tied up at the sprawling docks, a torrent of dock workers loading and unloading them. The most prominent docks were the Falcon Piers, standing in the deepest part of the harbor, with berths for even the largest vessels and mechanical cranes to move cargo faster than any team of workers.

Constantia stood beside Sophie, her long black hair blown back by wind off the lake. Her eyes followed Sophie's to the promised docks, and her expression became a satisfied smile. The wind turned chill, and Sophie shivered. What else would she have to sell for a throne she had never wanted?

***

Their ship put in at a berth close to where the Silvervein flowed out of the harbor, running through Heratia's rich eastern side that held senatorial mansions, the great Senica Cathedral, and, of course, the imperial palace. Before the dock's eastern Coin Gate stood a black marble statue of Empero Hera the Great, founder of the Laskaris dynasty, with sword raised high and armor shining in the sun. At her back were the Coin Gate's high stone battlements and thick walls that separated the harbor from the rest of the city.

Constantia nodded to the statue. "Welcome home, Your Majesty. Your ancestor certainly knew how to found a city."

Sophie hid a wince. Few outside the Imperial University knew Hera the Great as anything but Heratia's founder, but the title was an exaggeration at best. Though Hera had rebuilt many parts of the city, it was already here when she chose it for her new capital. Still, if Sophie were to take the Falcon Throne, the Laskaris legacy would be critical. She couldn't afford to damage it. "Indeed she did," Sophie said. "We are pleased to behold it again."

Demetra took a step toward the rail as sailors and dock workers lowered a boarding ramp into place. "We should be on our way," she said. She gave a stiff bow to Constantia. "Thank you for your assistance."

"So soon?" Constantia said. "I would be happy to escort you at least as far as my home in the Senatorial District."

A flush crept up Demetra's neck at the Gallian's words, and Sophie took an easy guess as to why. Foreigners buying homes in the Senatorial District, a part of the city traditionally reserved only for Meyatha's most elite citizens, was just the sort of thing to rankle Demetra Kalgari, speaker of the Senate. But to Sophie, where the ultrarich bought their houses seemed of little import compared to how much less walking her recovering acolytes would have to do if Constantia's carts took them part of the distance to the palace.

"Your offer is most generous," Sophie said. "We happily accept." She took Demetra aside as Constantia went to organize her people. "The longer we are with her, the longer we seem to be Gallian traders, beneath the notice of anyone. That is worth tolerating her barbs, yes?"

Demetra bowed her head. "As you say. Better to keep an eye on the viper for as long as we can."

Most of Constantia's caravan split off, the wagons headed either for warehouses or the city's many markets, but two were held back. Fryni stopped staring at the endless expanse of people to organize the wounded acolytes into the carts before leading the others in a loose escort formation. Together with a dozen of Constantia's guards, they disembarked the vessel and entered the swirling crowd of the docks.

Merchants and their customers from all across the empire and beyond crowded around. Sophie heard a dozen dialects of Meyathan in a few minutes, plus snatches of southern tongues and even a few words in Skaldre. Some of the traders were clearly from beyond the continent itself, representing the many nations of Ethicar and Kalyune.

Despite the chaotic crowd, Fryni and the other acolytes kept their formation ordered, staves held at a relaxed guard. Sophie stood a little taller for watching them. Before today most of them would have considered a hundred people a great crowd. Now they walked through the largest city on the continent, and still their responsibilities kept them focused. She could die proud even if they were her only legacy.

Something caught at her vision: clusters of armored Meyathans scattered along the crowd's edges. It was normal for the city watch to maintain a presence across Heratia, but not in these numbers. Nor was it the watch's practice to patrol in full armor in times of peace. At least it had not been twenty-three years before. She turned her eyes to the closest knot of soldiers. Their crests were the imperial purple falcon, not the watch's bronze shield. These were units of the capital garrison.

Sophie leaned in toward Demetra and gestured toward a passing knot of soldiers. "When did my father task the garrison with patrolling Heratia's streets?"

"He didn't," Demetra answered, casting her own glance at the armored soldiers. "This must have happened since I left. Perhaps there was unrest, and the Senate called them out to keep order."

That was an unhappy thought. Sophie had seen the garrison tasked to *keep order* before, and it rarely ended without hundreds of injured Meyathan citizens. Often it was much worse. She breathed out. Yet another thing for her to put right.

"We should avoid them," Demetra was saying, inclining her head toward the nearest patrol of soldiers. "Most of the garrison are loyal to the Laskaris line, but it only takes one of them to report to Savvas or his allies. I don't want them to know you're here until we walk you in for the confirmation vote."

They passed by Hera the Great's black marble statue and under the Coin Gate, following the main road along the Silvervein's banks. Here the streets bustled with craftsfolk, artisans tinkering away in their workshops or putting out their goods to sell beneath the mighty columns and swooping buttresses of Heratia's civic center.

For a moment it seemed that Sophie had never left. Everything was the same, from the great dome of Senica Cathedral to the gray-robed scholars hurrying around the Imperial University and its Eternal Library. In her adolescence, Sophie had often snuck out from the palace to attend classes in disguise, a carefree time before she learned how much suffering her family's rule inflicted.

Sophie's reminiscence came to a halt as the great number of panhandlers caught her eye. Several sat at every street corner, with most of the better-off citizens trying to ignore them. Some of the ancient masonry showed undeniable wear; even the great land walls were missing parts of their facade. At some intersections, Sophie smelled the stench of raw sewage, a sure sign that the pipes below their feet were damaged.

An ache grew in Sophie's chest. This was Heratia's wealthy eastern side. What must the west be like, with its smoky forges and close-packed housing? How could her father have let things get so out of hand? Her gaze fell to the street. How could she be here, taking up a mantle that had failed the people so badly?

Fryni's hand found hers and squeezed. "It isn't all grandeur and great buildings, is it?" she said. "People suffer here just like they do in Gray Falls."

"Yes," Sophie said. "It's so much worse than before I left."

"We'll make it right," Fryni said. "The Mother's justice."

Sophie smiled. "Thank you, Captain. We will." She had to believe it. If she didn't, who would?

Ahead, the road fell into shadow beside one of Heratia's great stadiums. Sophie had spent more time in such places than she cared to remember, watching from the royal box as chariot racers churned up both dust and the crowd's emotions. Sophie much preferred oratory and debate at the university, but Taisa loved the races, and it was important for the imperial family to be seen enjoying Meyatha's most popular sport.

The stadium's main doors were shut, not unusual for early in the morning, but they were reinforced with heavy iron chains. Sophie blinked; that she had never seen. The smaller doors were boarded up entirely, and one of the charioteer statues that flanked the entrance was missing an arm, showing only jagged stone at the shoulder. A closer look showed scorch marks on the stadium walls and dark-brown stains on its outer courtyard stones.

Further along the street were more signs of past violence: places where cobblestones had been pried up, carts splintered, and street lanterns cast down. Heratians hurried past damaged areas, giving many a sidelong glance but never slowing down.

Constantia tsked when her eyes fell upon a broken signpost. "A difficult time for the city at the center of the world." She winked at Sophie. "I suppose your job will be interesting at least."

Demetra made a disgusted sound in her throat. Sophie ignored the Gallian duchess and kept her eyes focused ahead. Heratia was no stranger to riots; sometimes the wrong winner at a chariot race was enough to set them off. Perhaps that was all this was.

Ahead, a crowd gathered in the street, packed close enough that Constantia's wagons had to stop as the drivers searched for a path through. The crowd stood before the smashed-in doors of what Sophie guessed had once been a shop for expensive cloth judging by the mural of luxurious silk bolts above its front. She craned her neck to look. Residents had studiously ignored other signs of violence; what made this one different?

Past the crowd, the shop's interior was a wreck, its wealth of fabric either gone or torn to shreds. A few clerks scribbled notes down into books, likely assessing the damage, while armored soldiers of the city watch stood sentinel. On the shop's wall, thick letters of black paint spelled out "Those who starve us will face justice," followed by a black sunburst.

Sophie froze. It was the same symbol chosen for the Solstice Uprising twenty-three years ago. Part of the surrender terms were that the black sunburst would never be displayed in Heratia again on pain of death. Yet all these years later, someone did it anyway. Did they truly hope for another uprising? So much bloodshed, so many friends lost, for nothing.

Sophie shook herself free of the painful memories; she couldn't afford to stop and stare. Instead she turned to Demetra with a raised eyebrow, schooling her face to serenity. "You did not tell me there were rebels in the city."

Demetra shook her head and glanced at Constantia riding ahead of them. "Later."

Sophie let the speaker keep her silence. It wouldn't help her position with the Gallians to discuss rebellion in their midst. But if someone was bold enough to use the black sunburst, what else were they doing? Did the rebels cause the riot at the stadium and elsewhere? Possibly, but when Sophie had been part of it, the Solstice Movement had been more targeted in their destruction. Perhaps as Heratia crumbled, the movement had grown desperate.

They parted company with Constantia at the duchess's home, a great mansion of white marble indistinguishable from the other homes of the Senatorial District. Constantia offered the loan of her carts, and Sophie accepted without hesitation. More experienced with horses than her acolytes, Sophie took the lead cart's reins herself, with Demetra sitting beside her on the driver's bench.

To Sophie's surprise, signs of damage appeared even among the homes of Heratia's most elite. It was better disguised and repaired, but she still noted windows with cloth hung over them to hide broken glass and cleaners hard at work scrubbing scorch marks off walls. *That* was certainly unusual. As far as Sophie could remember, none of Heratia's riots had ever reached the Senatorial District. The district's residents had house guards to make sure of it.

Despite the signs of violence and the near-empty streets, Demetra's mood improved as they continued on, winding through the opulent homes of Meyatha's rich and powerful toward the imperial palace. "Enough of traveling and battles and grasping foreigners all," she said. "Soon we'll have you properly ensconced where you belong, with all the honors due an empero."

"But before that," Sophie said. "You will tell me about whoever painted the black sunburst over that shop."

Demetra's lip curled. "They are nothing. Vandals who destroy shops because they think it will make the sky rain bread." She stared hard at Sophie. "Empero Irena made sure Heratia would never rise up again. The people who looted that shop have no power, and even a hint of sympathy for them will turn the entire Senate against you."

Sophie raised her hands to avoid further argument. She would not turn Demetra into a radical with one conversation. "I've already agreed to follow your path, Speaker. I am merely curious about the capital's state." If Sophie were to look into these new rebels, she would need to do it on her own.

Demetra nodded, seemingly mollified. "Good, then we can focus on returning you home." She glanced up, and her eyes widened. "Stop the cart, now."

Sophie tightened the reins, bringing the well-trained cart horse to a halt. She raised a hand to signal the acolytes to stop the second cart behind them as well, then followed Demetra's gaze.

Ahead, half a dozen Heratians in the fine silks of Meyathan senators strode together, surrounded by thrice as many retainers. The whole group wore green cloth bands tied around one arm. They moved close together, their eyes wary, like they expected trouble. They were the first people Sophie had seen walking the Senatorial District's streets. She had attributed it to the early hour, but another possibility made the hair on the back of her neck prickle.

Several of the group glanced toward Sophie, Demetra, and the two carts of acolytes, then turned their eyes back forward and hurried on their way. They soon disappeared around the corner of a manor house's outer wall.

"Something is wrong," Demetra said, her eyes trained on where the group had disappeared.

Further down the street, Sophie glimpsed several more knots of well-dressed Heratians moving in the same direction as the first, also wearing the green armbands. "Green is your house color, is it not?" she asked. "They would seem to be your allies. I wonder that they do not recognize you."

Demetra held up a sleeve of her travel-stained clothes. "They are not used to seeing me in such a state. What concerns me is they display my colors when the Senate is not in session." She stood and dropped down from the driver's bench. "I must learn what is going on. You should find somewhere out of sight to wait for me. If there is trouble, the way to the palace may not be safe."

Fryni jogged up from the second cart, staff in hand. "Do we know why so many aristocrats are headed in the same direction, and with the same color sense?"

Sophie covered a chuckle at the younger acolyte's irreverent tone. "No, but the speaker means to find out, and the two of us will accompany her. Alkestis?" Sophie motioned the acolyte forward. Alkestis had been a city acolyte before she was sent to Gray Falls as a punishment for stating her opinion too loudly, and her sense of direction had never failed when she was out on patrol. "There should be a small temple just south of here, do you know the district well enough to find it?"

The sandy-haired acolyte studied the southern road. "Yes, Sister Sophie" she said after a moment. "I delivered scrolls there once, I can find it again."

Sophie nodded. "Take the wagons and wait for us there."

As Sophie climbed down to join her, Demetra sighed. "You should go with them to the temple. There's no need to risk us both."

"I trust Alkestis to look after the others, and I do not intend to lose track of my speaker before I have even set eyes on the throne."

Demetra let out a tired laugh and motioned to her two guards. "Then let us see what is causing such a stir among my supporters."

They followed the stream of people toward one of the Senatorial District's great public parks, wide-open meeting spaces that Sophie had occasionally visited in her youth as part of one imperial function or another.

Raised voices greeted them as they neared the park, where a large crowd gathered around a raised podium. Too many gathered for an exact count, but Sophie estimated in the hundreds. Many wore the fine silks of aristocracy, while others had the less ornate but still serviceable garb of merchants and artisans. All of them wore bands of green cloth tied round their arms or foreheads.

A tall, slender woman with pale skin and light-brown hair stepped up to the podium, a green ribbon looped around one wrist. She raised her hands to quiet the crowd, all of whom fell silent and stared with rapt attention.

Demeta let out a relieved breath. "Ah, that is Senator Ariadne Ducas. Her vote is always dependable; she can no doubt tell us what has happened." They reached the crowds' outer edges, where a few of the district's residents gave them puzzled looks.

On the podium, Ariadne began her speech. "Meyathans, citizens all," she cried, her voice ringing out over the crowded park. "We have been terrorized, forced to endure the indignity of a mob rampaging through our streets, all on the behest of one man. One traitor who could barely wait for Empero Mihail's funeral to begin his grasping quest for power."

The crowd booed, already primed for the target of their ire.

The senator waited for their jeers to die down, then continued. "Already Savvas denigrates Heir Taisa's memory. He stirs up the mob when we should be mourning her loss!"

Demetra swore. "Taisa's death is already common knowledge? Little wonder there has been so much unrest. I must learn what Savvas has done." The speaker took a step forward, then glanced at Sophie. "It would be best if you remain here. If Savvas has spies in this crowd, they will be close to Ariadne." She turned to her two surviving house guards. "Stay with the empero. I shall return soon."

The guard captain opened his mouth to reply, but Demetra was already shoving her way through the crowd.

Ariadne's speech was in full swing now. "Savvas Carenthus will destroy everything that makes Meyatha strong, he will gut the Eternal Empire for his own vainglory, he..." She paused, glancing down at where Demetra had just reached the podium's base. "Speaker?" Ariadne asked. "What is—"

Angry shouts and thundering feet cut her off as more people poured into the park. These newcomers wore bands of red, many bearing clubs or chunks of masonry. Those in the front ranks pointed their weapons at the podium and charged, racing toward the green-clad crowd with the ferocity of imperial shock troops.

Demetra vanished behind the recoiling crowd. Around Sophie, green supporters recovered from their shock and turned to meet the attack, bracing shoulder to shoulder and producing makeshift weapons of their own. The two sides collided, blows and curses flying.

Sophie brought up her staff. "Fryni, to my left." She gestured to Demetra's guards. "You two, my right. We must help the speaker." It was easy to guess who these new arrivals supported with their bands of red.

She held her staff before her and pressed two shouting men aside to clear a path. She'd barely gone two steps when the green supporters gave way around her, and a wave of red supporters crashed upon them.

A club flashed at Sophie's head, which she just barely deflected with a flick of her staff. She struck out with her fist, catching her burly attacker in the gut with an impact that bruised her knuckles but sent the red supporter gasping to the trampled grass. Beside Sophie, Fryni lashed out with her staff in vicious jabs, keeping several attackers at bay. On Sophie's other side, Demetra's guards used their armored gauntlets, slow to draw their swords against fellow Meyathans.

Sophie tensed for another push forward, but Fryni put a restraining hand on her arm. "They're surrounding us!" the young acolyte said. "We need to get back."

It was true: red supporters now surrounded them on three sides, dragging their green opponents off their feet. The path of retreat narrowed by the moment. Sophie nodded and turned to Demetra's guards. "She's right, we'll be overwhelmed if we stay here. Follow me."

To Sophie's surprise, the guards obeyed, the four of them backing out of the closing trap. They broke free of the melee at the park's edge even as more supporters of both sides arrived to swell the churning brawl. Where was Demetra? Sophie turned her gaze left and right.

Enough red and green bands had fallen now that it was difficult to tell the two sides apart, much less find someone in the crowd.

"It's time to go," Fryni said. "The reds are better prepared for a fight, and if any of them recognize you…"

Sophie hesitated. "Demetra may need our help. We must find her."

"We can't, not in this." Fryni gripped Sophie's hand, voice turning rough. "I can't let anything happen to you. Not after Iris went to the Mother for us."

Sophie let out a long breath. Fryni was right again. Demetra might not even be in the park anymore. If her allies had recognized her, they would have taken her to safety. More red supporters arrived every moment. She needed to find Alkestis and the other acolytes to keep them safe in this hostile city.

She squeezed Fryni's hand and addressed Demetra's guards, both of whom stared into the roiling crowd. "Find the speaker. We will meet you at the palace."

The guard captain made a quick bow. "Thank you, Majesty." He and his comrade set off around the crowd's periphery, looking for an opening to push through.

Sophie turned her eyes south, away from the park. "Your counsel was wise," she said to Fryni. "Let us return to our sisters."

Together they hurried to put distance between themselves and the ongoing brawl, ducking down a side street with high mansion walls on either side. Soon the sounds of fighting faded, and Sophie had time to get her bearings. The temple was right where she remembered it, a domed building of black stone squeezed into a patch of land between two senatorial manors.

The two wagons barely fit into the temple's small courtyard, where Alkestis and the other healthy Gray Falls acolytes stood watch, staves in hand. They were watched in turn by a wary collection of city acolytes and clergy from the temple's main entrance.

Alkestis's shoulders relaxed as they approached. "There you two are," she said. She glanced at the temple doors behind her. "I don't think the locals enjoy having us here, and..." She trailed off. "Where's the speaker?"

"We're on our own," Fryni said. She motioned to the other Gray Falls acolytes. "Everyone, up on the wagons, it's time to move." The sisters scrambled to follow their captain's command, and Sophie was close behind them, climbing back up to the first wagon's driver's bench.

Sophie snapped the reins, urging the horse out of the courtyard and leaving the nervous temple clergy behind. Demetra could be anywhere in the Senatorial District by now; Sophie's only option was to make for the palace and hope for the best. She set a quick pace, putting as much distance behind them while keeping the carts as smooth as possible. The wounded were still recovering; rattles and jolts would do them no good.

Sophie guided them through the district's backstreets. She had to keep her acolytes out of sight until they reached the palace where the Laskaris guards could offer them protection. As the sun crept toward noon, they reached the empty causeway that ringed the palace so that, should every other defense fail, an enemy could not use nearby houses to reach the imperial walls.

Finally they rounded the last bend and beheld the Laskaris palace. Even within the Senatorial District it was a grand structure, with turrets stretching higher than any other building in the city and great stone arches that had stood for centuries. An outer wall separated the palace complex from the rest of the city, fronted by stout iron gates.

Those gates were smashed open, one hanging on by a single great hinge, the other flat on the ground of the courtyard. Sophie blinked. Past the gates, glass lay in glittering shards below the empty windowsills of the once-great palace. Soot stains around the sills showed where some rooms had burned, even atop the mighty turrets.

Sophie's eyes were drawn to the great falcon mosaic above the entrance. Most of its purple-and-white tiles were pried from the wall and shattered across the courtyard. The falcon's head tile was still in place, though cracks ran across its surface. The painted eye glared out at Sophie, daring her to enter the family home.

Chapter 8

Sophie felt a great weight pressing down on her from two directions. This palace symbolized everything the Solstice Uprising had fought against. They had always planned to pull it down once victory was theirs. But the palace had also been her home for twenty years. Someone else had shattered the windows and scorched the walls. She hadn't even been there to bear witness.

"Sister Sophie," Fryni said. "We have to keep moving."

The other acolytes eyed the surrounding streets, staves held in tight grips.

"Keep moving?" Sophie asked. She slid down from the driver's bench, landing hard on the stone street. She couldn't leave; this was her home. She had to learn what had happened, see how bad the damage was. Didn't she owe that to the rest of her family, the ones who could no longer see it for themselves?

Fryni took her hand. "Demetra said you would be safe here, but she must not have known about this." She gestured at the ruined palace. "We'll find somewhere secure, then work on contacting the speaker."

"Halt," a voice boomed out from within the palace walls' ruined gates. "By order of the watch!" Boots crunched on broken glass. Fryni pushed Sophie back a step, the other acolytes dropping down from the two carts, their weapons held in deceptively loose grips. A troop of soldiers emerged from the ruined gate's shadow, the city watch's bronze shield crest emblazoned on their armored shoulders. Below the shield, each soldier bore a second crest: a rearing stallion. Sophie remembered that crest, the symbol of House Carenthus. These soldiers served Savvas Carenthus, the general with his eyes on Meyatha's throne.

Demetra had warned Sophie about senators buying influence with the military, but for the Heratia city watch itself to wear the crest of a patron? It was an affront that set her teeth on edge. How could anyone expect justice when the law proudly advertised those who had purchased it?

The guard captain, a tall woman in her twenties, stepped forward. "Approaching the palace is forbidden, by order of the Senate." She paused, taking in the acolytes' dusty and mud-stained clothes. "What is your business in the Senatorial District?"

Sophie suppressed a grimace. Here it was, the watch more concerned with keeping commoners out of the city's rich neighborhoods than justice. "Mother keep you and your troop," she said to the guard captain. "I am the abbess of Gray Falls, I sought only to show my acolytes the splendor of Heratia on our pilgrimage." Often an appeal to faith succeeded where an appeal to decency did not.

The guard captain's stance relaxed a touch. "Ah, I see. Forgive me, I did not realize you were sacred sisters. Mother keep you." She glanced at her soldiers, and they let their hands fall away from their weapons. "All the same, Abbess," the captain went on, "this part of the city is not safe." She looked at the wounded acolytes resting on the borrowed carts. "I recommend you head to Senica, they can offer you shelter."

"Yes, Captain, we surely will do so." Sophie bobbed her head in thanks. "But if you would indulge a sister's curiosity, what has happened here? How did such destruction reach the heart of our Eternal Empire?"

"You haven't heard?" the captain asked. "No, I suppose you wouldn't have if you were on the road. Empero Mihail passed some days ago, which was bad enough. Then news reached us that Heir Taisa and her family were dead as well, Mother embrace them, murdered by Skaldre in the north." The woman shrugged. "There was panic. People believed the Skaldre would invade that very hour. It took days for the General Carenthus and Senate to restore order, and by then, the mob had already done this." She swept a hand behind her to encompass the ruined palace.

A second soldier chuckled. "It was a mess for certain, looting from the empero's own home. Savvas will have a bear of a time fixing the place up before he moves in."

Several others echoed his laugh until the captain silenced them with a curt look.

Sophie kept her expression blank. It seemed Savvas Carenthus was already speaking as the voice of law and order, and these watch soldiers wore his standard. She had her explanation; it was time to go. "The Mother thanks you, Captain. We shall retire to Senica and let you resume your duties."

"Wait," another of the watch soldiers said—the oldest, judging by the flecks of gray in his beard. His gaze focused on Sophie. "I know you."

She'd stayed too long. Sophie took a step back. "I am sorry, but I don't believe we've met."

"Yeah, how could we have?" Fryni said, her eyes widening and her voice taking on an awestruck tone. "We've never stepped foot in this magnificent city before, I think we'd remember if we had." Behind her back, Fryni motioned other acolytes to close ranks in front of Sophie.

"Mother abandon me if I don't know her face," the older guard said, staring openly at Sophie now.

The guard captain made a frustrated sound. "How can you?" she asked. "These sisters have never been to Heratia before."

"She's no sister," the older guard said. "I remember her, from the Solstice, the uprising. She led the rebels when they captured most of the city and put the watch under siege in its barracks." He pointed with a calloused finger. "That's Sophie Laskaris."

Fryni swore and raised her staff even as the other soldiers exchanged puzzled looks.

"The heir's big sister?" one of them said. "But she's banished to far Kalyune, can't return on pain of death."

"No, you've got it wrong," said another. "She *is* dead. Ol' Ironheart cut her to pieces when the Solstice Treason was put down."

"It *is* her," the oldest guard said, his voice rising. "I remember, she set the city ablaze!"

Sophie winced. There had been some chaos in the uprising, but the Solstice Rebels had done everything they could to preserve Heratia. The real destruction had started when Empero Irena breached the walls, but Sophie doubted this watchman was in the mood to debate.

"I'm sorry, Sister," the guard captain said, speaking over her patrol's clamor. "I'll have to bring you in for now, at least until we straighten everything out." The other watch soldiers stepped up beside her, hands resting on weapons.

"You'll do no such thing!" Demetra's voice rang out, echoing off the palace walls. Acolyte and watch soldier alike turned to stare as the speaker led a column of green-wearing Heratians up to the ruined palace gate, Senator Ariadne Ducas at her side.

Demetra came to a stop inches from the guard captain's face, her crowd of supporters easily surpassing a hundred. "I leave the capital for a few days to find the city watch committing treason? Is that the Mother's reward for all my labors?"

"Treason?" the guard captain gasped, her expression waring between confusion and panic. "Honored speaker, I would never—"

"You know who this woman is," Demetra said, jabbing a finger toward Sophie. "With Mihail and Taisa dead, she is empero of all Meyatha, and you would *arrest* her?"

The guard captain shrank away from the speaker's lashing voice. "Well, no, I didn't understand."

"Bow to her," Demetra said, in a voice that could strip bark off an oak. "Bow and Empero Sophie Laskaris may forgive your transgressions against her sacred bloodline."

To Sophie's amazement, the watch troop obeyed, turning and bowing down to her, eliciting a few cheers from the ground of green-supporting Heratians at Demetra's back.

The speaker nodded. "Good. Now go. Go and tell Savvas that an imperial heart still beats in Meyatha."

The watch soldiers straightened and beat a hasty retreat, eyes darting between Sophie, Demetra, and the green-banded crowd at their back. Fryni whistled. "Now, that was some *speaking*."

"Yes," Sophie said. "Thank you, Speaker." She raised her voice so the green-banded crowd could hear as well. "And thanks to all of you. I would not want to begin my reign by fighting with the watch."

Demetra's shoulders slumped as she took in the ruined palace. "It was a small thing. Probably not enough." She gestured to Ariadne beside her. "Tell the empero what you told me."

The pale-skinned senator looked Sophie up and down, one eyebrow raised. "Your Majesty..." She paused. "Word of Heir Taisa's death, Mother embrace her, reached us just after Speaker Kalgari left to find you. Without the speaker here to counter him, Savvas seized the opportunity." She indicated toward the palace. "This is his doing. As fear swept the city, his agents whipped up a mob to storm the palace. It frightened many senators into supporting him as the only one who could restore order, and it ruined the most public symbol of an empero who had rebuffed him for years."

Sophie had to acknowledge the plan's cunning. With so much genuine chaos in the city, no one would be able to prove Savvas was behind the palace's desecration, and it served his goals well. He might even be able to blame it on whoever had put up the black sunburst at the clothier's shop. Neither did Sophie miss the hesitancy when Ariadne first addressed her. This senator at least had doubts about a long-banished heir taking the throne.

Demetra addressed the crowd of her supporters, her mask of confidence back in place. "We have won our first battle against the usurper. Now each of you must tell others what you have seen. The city must know that a Laskaris empero is still with it. As goes Heratia, so goes the empire."

The crowd cheered, and several well-dressed supporters came up to speak with Demetra. As the rest of the crowd dispersed, they spoke to her of oration strategies for the Senate's next meeting and whether to change their colors from green to purple now that they had an imperial heir among them. While that was no doubt important, Sophie needed to get her still-recovering acolytes inside and see how badly the palace had been ravaged.

The speaker's voice faded as Sophie passed beneath the broken gates and approached the main entrance. Inside, the grand hall was in even worse shape than the palace's exterior. The gold-and-silver trim that had once circled the high walls like ivy was all torn away, tapestries were shredded to rags, and statues of imperial heroes were smashed to pieces across the floor.

Sophie took a deep breath of the palace air, still coarse with the remnants of smoke. "Fryni, dearest one," she said. "Find somewhere the wounded may rest. I need to walk this place for a time, see how bad the damage is."

Fryni nodded, pushing aside a shard of white marble with her staff. "I'll get them settled, Sister Sophie." She gazed around the cavernous hall. "Shout if you get lost, this place looks worse than the Serates at night for finding your way."

Sophie smiled at Fryni's playful tone. She'd taken these young acolytes away from everything they knew, and Fryni was still the same as always.

She left the others behind in the grand hall, picking a corridor at random and following it until it opened into one of the many palace gardens. Half the abbey could have fit here, and many a past empero had awed guests with the garden's splendor. Now the long rows of bright southern flowers lay burned and trampled. Many of the trees had been chopped down, with drag marks on the ground where they had been hauled away for what, firewood? Had the looters been that desperate?

Sophie's boot squelched in the ground, churned to mud by hundreds of frantic footprints. She and Taisa had played here when they were young, running about the hedgerows and pretending that they were Hera the Great fighting off the barbarians. As the eldest, Sophie always won these mock battles, until Taisa's lip quivered and Sophie let the younger girl have a few victories of her own.

Taisa's last battle had been all too real. Sophie chose to believe her sister had died well, with sword in hand, facing her enemy.

Past the garden, Sophie's feet brought her to the palace library, home to the finest collection outside the Imperial University. The library had long been a special place to Sophie. Her father would read to her from any book she liked, changing his voice to embody different characters. When it came to battles, he smashed iron pokers together to make the ringing of sword on shining mail. He would have been a grand court storyteller, Mihail Laskaris, but birth destined him to be empero.

The library shelves held mostly ash and char now. The few books that had not burned were torn to shreds, their little fragments fluttering whenever a breeze drifted in through the broken window. Sophie could not begrudge anyone for taking gold and silver to sell or for breaking the symbols of a family that had held them down for so long, but the books? Many of the volumes in this library had been irreplaceable, accounts of Meyatha's history that were gone forever.

Sophie hoped some of them had been taken before the library was burned. At least that way their knowledge wasn't completely lost.

The ash and soot beneath Sophie's feet gave way to crunching glass: the shattered wall mirrors of an imperial training hall. Training mannequins lay in splinters; wooden practice weapons and padded armor were strewn over the reflective shards. Among the martial tools lay a few broken quills, cracked inkwells, and torn parchment. Sophie's mouth quirked up into an amused smile as she imagined looters breaking open the cabinets and wondering why in the Mother's name there were school supplies packed in with tools of martial training.

They wouldn't know that Empero Irena once preferred that her grandchildren use the training hall for academic and martial learning both. More efficient, she had always said. Sophie and Taisa never dared argue with their grandmother. They learned whatever material she put before them and practiced with the wooden weapons until their clothes soaked through with sweat.

Had Taisa continued this tradition with her own children? Had Dafni and Iason learned geography and strategy in this room? Sophie had never met them. They would not have wanted her grief, not after what she'd done, but tears pricked at her eyes all the same.

Sophie had walked nearly the length of the empty palace, several city blocks at least, and there it was: the imperial chapel. It was a small room, warm and dark, nothing like the soaring dome of Senica Cathedral. The imperial family always took service alone.

Sophie stepped inside. The only light came from glass windows stained dark purple, not nearly enough to see by. The windows were intact. That was a first for any room Sophie had passed. Even a panicked mob had their limits, it seemed. She felt along the wall until she found an alcove that held a box of candles, sulfur-treated tinder, and a flint striker. With practiced motions she lit several wicks, stuck them in a candelabra, and held it before her to light the way.

The candle flames shed a rippling pattern of light across the chapel walls, illuminating the sacred murals so they seemed to move with each of Sophie's steps. Tiled representations of the Void Mother, Her daughters, and Her granddaughters danced beside Sophie. It was a reminder; she was never alone so long as she upheld the Mother's tenets. Sophie let out a long breath. The abbey had a similar chapel, but its walls possessed only crude carvings and rough drawings made by the acolytes themselves, not the masterwork of this chapel, done by the finest artisans imperial gold could hire.

Sophie found the rear door and pushed it open, blinking in the sunlight of a walled courtyard. In the wide-open space, dozens of purple glass statues faced her, each standing on a disk of black onyx. Common Meyathans marked their graves with a circle of dark stone to invoke the Mother; the poorest citizens made do with tar-painted wood. No such simplicity for the imperial family.

Atop their discs of finest onyx, they placed life-sized likenesses, captured in a special kind of glass. The glass was clear at first, but after months and years in the sun, something within it transmuted to purple so that the dead would be forever possessed of the imperial color. The statues posed heroically with weapons held high or peered out with expressions of contemplative wisdom. There was one for every Laskaris who had died since Hera the Great built this palace.

Like the chapel, the imperial burial grounds had been spared the looters' wrath, likely because there were no entrances other than the way Sophie had come and the mob had chosen not to tempt divine wrath by damaging one of the Mother's temples. Sophie set the candelabra down and approached the nearest rank of statues.

There on the end were three figures she would never forget. Her grandmother Irena shone in deepest purple. Her glare was almost as intense as Sophie remembered it being in life, her hands balanced on a sword hilt as if in judgment. Sophie's mother, Athina, had a heavy tinge of the imperial hue. Her statue had been there the longest of the three, but crenulations on the walls kept it in partial shadow. Athina was sculpted in scholar's robes with a scroll in hand, which Sophie thought her mother would have liked. Her father's statue was as clear as water. Mihail was posed with sword arm raised, his torso clad in plated mail. Sophie had to stifle a laugh. They'd have done better to give him a wine glass and a book of poetry.

Enough room remained in this row to place four additional graves, something Sophie would need to attend to for Taisa and her family. The cost of four glass statues ran in her mind, and she winced. A score of people could eat for a year on that money. "Only stone markers from now on, I think," she said to the statues before her. "I cannot prioritize the pride of the dead over the hunger of the living."

A chill breeze blew through the cemetery, rustling leaves around the statue's feet. Sophie chuckled. "Indeed, where are my manners?" She fished in her pocket and came up with four black pebbles picked from the Godstep's northern shore while the caravan was loading. She placed one pebble on the base of each statue and a fourth on the empty grass for Taisa. It was the Meyathan custom when visiting the fallen, each stone a tiny piece of the Void.

"There," Sophie said. "I hope we can be civil now. None of us wanted this to happen, but—" She paused and gave a short bow to her mother's statue. "Apologies, Mother. You were gone before you could give an opinion, and I'm assuming..."

She stopped. Took a breath. They were dead. If she couldn't face them now, then when? "None of us wanted this, but Meyatha is mine now." If she could take it. If Savvas or one of his allies didn't stick a knife between her ribs.

"I won't be the empero you'd have wanted, but I will do everything I can to see the empire flourish." She bowed her head to her glass family. "I will find justice for our dead, I will correct the mistakes of our past. I will make the Laskaris name something to be proud of."

Sophie lifted her head. Sunlight glinted off her grandmother's statue, giving Irena the same expression she'd once used when Sophie was struggling through a sparring match. A challenge to do better. Sophie turned away. There was nothing left to say on that account.

She took up the candelabra and returned the way she had come. She passed through the chapel, but shortly after she found herself turned around in a hall she didn't recognize. The palace was a maze, and she hadn't set foot here in over two decades.

Before her stood a small door that was still intact, though the lock had been smashed. She ducked down to fit under the lintel and found herself in the corner of a cavernous chamber. High above, light filtered in through shattered panes of stained glass in the ceiling. The remnants of heroically posed statues of black marble, once tucked into alcoves around the wall, were scattered across the floor.

A thick white carpet, soiled and torn now, led from the room's main double doors to a raised dais with a black seat surrounded by a semicircle of smashed chairs. Sophie's breath caught. This was the audience chamber, where Empero Irena and Empero Mihail after her had met with Heratia's wealthiest petitioners. Those petitioners who could not afford the bribes and entrance fees would be lucky if they spoke with a lower official. More often they were turned away entirely. That would change. If Sophie had no choice but to seek an unjust power, she could at least equalize access to it.

She had entered through one of the many hidden servants' doors. Now that she was here, at least it was a simple route back to the entrance hall. But to get there she'd have to pass the raised dais. She was nearly through when her eyes caught upon the black chair that rested upon the dais. It was tall backed and made of polished onyx, the black broken only by a diving bird of prey inlaid in amethyst. The Falcon Throne.

There were other chairs, but this was the throne that her father, Mihail, and grandmother Irena before him had reigned from. One of the armrests was broken off, leaving a jagged edge, but the rest was intact. She could sit there; she would have to eventually. That was her role now. Empero Sophie.

Sophie turned and strode out of the audience chamber.

Chapter 9

By the time Sophie returned to the entrance hall, Fryni and the other healthy acolytes had cleared most of the debris into one corner. Those who were still recovering sat leaning against their heavy packs, polishing spearheads and chain mail with oiled rags.

Demetra paced before the open doors to the courtyard, conferring with a servant who bore the Kalgari crest. "Tell the others we will not be switching from green to purple," Demetra was saying. "That color is for the imperial family and their sworn soldiers. It would look presumptuous."

She turned to greet Sophie, her voice tired and thin. "There you are, is the damage as bad as it looks from outside?"

"Perhaps worse," Sophie said. "Other than the chapel and cemetery, I doubt any part of the palace is untouched." She had only explored a fraction of the palace complex, but what she had seen left little room for optimism.

A defeated sigh escaped Demetra's lips. "This is the result of my clever play at stealth and secrecy. Your family's treasures scattered to a frothing mob, or, worse, swelling Savvas's vault. He must have had agents in the north I didn't know about; that's the only way news could have reached the capital so quickly. I was so careful to keep that information secret, and for nothing. He's been laughing at me this whole time."

"Palaces can be rebuilt," Sophie said. She had very different priorities in mind for the empire's finances, but the speaker looked in need of some encouragement. "Lost treasures can be replaced."

"It's worse than that," Demetra said. "Ariadne tells me that a near majority of senators already wear Savvas's red band, and more go over to him each week. He might openly declare his claim on the throne and be confirmed any day. He'll cast you out, if not worse. Meyatha will cease to be."

Sophie blinked. Savvas had his rise to power well in hand; he was ready to fill the vacuum if she only stepped out of the way. It would be so easy to let him have it all and go back to the abbey like she'd never left. But she couldn't. If Savvas couldn't hold the empire together, it would mean civil war. And even if he could, he would destroy the rights of citizenship, effectively turning all Meyathans but the senatorial class into slaves.

If Demetra despaired, Sophie's gambit for the throne was doomed. She squeezed Demetra's shoulder and put on the voice she used with acolytes who had newly arrived to the abbey, distraught that their lives were over. "This is a setback, but it is not the end. You are the speaker of the Senate; you have held the empire together for fifteen years. You are not finished yet."

Demetra shook her head and pulled away from Sophie, hands running over her soiled robes in a futile attempt to straighten them. "Yes," she said. "Yes. There's too much at stake. I'll call my allies together, convince them to at least meet you before they consider Savvas for the throne. For your father the vote was a formality, but under the circumstances we'll need overwhelming support if we want to avoid a civil war." She straightened her shoulders. "In the meantime, we'll gather what documents we can from the palace and retreat to my home."

"Well said, Speaker." Sophie nodded. "Except that my acolytes and I will be staying here."

"What?" Demetra said, raising an eyebrow at Sophie. "Are you serious? You are the empero of Meyatha; you do not have to live in a ruin."

"This ruin is my home," Sophie said. "If it is reduced, so my family is reduced. Staying here will be my message to Heratia and Meyatha that House Laskaris shares at least some measure of their hardship."

After a few moments of silence, Demetra shrugged. "As you say. Will you at least let me send servants to help make this place livable and guards for security? I'm told that the Laskaris staff and house guards scattered when the mob came. As far as they knew, the family line was over, and Mother only knows how many of them we can convince to return."

"Extra hands would be welcome," Sophie agreed. The imperial palace was far too large for herself and thirteen acolytes to clean on their own. Twelve acolytes. With Iris dead in a village most Heratians had never heard of, there were twelve left. Sophie's hands shook for a moment before she stilled them. Demetra's guards would make it easier to protect the rest. And yet Sophie couldn't simply relax in the speaker's protection.

"How confident can you be in the loyalty of your guards and servants?" Sophie asked. "Someone informed Savvas of Taisa's death, possibly someone in your employ."

Demetra nodded with a grimace. "I have considered that since speaking with Ariadne. The truth is I cannot be completely certain. Any investigation will take time, and, at present, all I can offer you are the retainers who have served me longest and most faithfully."

"You are most generous," Sophie said. It was the best they could do for now.

The speaker shrugged. "I am loyal, both because the Mother asks it, and because the empire demands it."

"One thing more," Sophie said. "Your friend Ariadne does not seem thrilled with me as the greens' choice for empero. Do you anticipate a problem there?"

Demetra shook her head. "Ariadne is a staunch traditionalist, and a Laskaris on the throne is our most sacred tradition. She would fight any revolution with her bare hands, but we can count on her here."

"Very well," Sophie said. She had little choice but to trust Demetra's instincts and hope that Ariadne and the other greens' devotion to tradition would keep them opposed to Savvas and his radical plan to abolish the rights of citizenship.

Demetra took her leave shortly after. Sophie hoped the senator would take a few moments to rest and refresh herself before leaping into work. Demetra hadn't complained about their rough travel since the ambush in Tallirod, but it was clearly weighing on her.

But no matter how much energy Demetra put into her political maneuvering, Sophie doubted it would be enough. Savvas had too much of a head start. Sophie would need more allies if there were to be any chance of success. If any in Heratia had drawn the black sunburst in earnest rather than to stir up Savvas's mob against the palace, they were her best chance. Her old comrades from the Solstice might even be involved, and they would help if she asked.

She had to be discreet. Demetra had made it quite clear what she thought of the uprising, but, more than that, Demetra's entire strategy depended on the legitimacy of Meyathan traditions. She would never allow Sophie to consort with those who tried to disrupt or even overthrow the established order.

Sophie gathered her remaining acolytes together. "Our first task is to clear out a place to sleep," she said. "After that we must salvage any surviving imperial records. They will be invaluable if Demetra's gambit succeeds." She and Fryni organized the others, with those who were still recovering taking on the lightest work.

As the acolytes broke up to begin their task, Sophie pulled Alkestis aside. "A moment, Sister," she said. "I have a favor to ask you, if you are willing."

"Of course, Sister Sophie," Alkestis said. "I'll help if I can."

"You've seen the Imperial University?" Sophie asked. When Alkestis nodded, she continued, "I need you to take a letter there."

She dug through her pack for paper and ink. She laid a sheet out on a flat piece of broken masonry and scratched out a few short lines:

Makis,

I have returned to the city, and I need your help. If any of our dear friends are about, please bring them to see me at the palace. Hurry, there is little time.

Yours,

Sophie.

She blew on the ink to dry it. Makis had been one of her fellows on the Solstice Council, the only one whose identity had been kept secret from imperial authorities, so far as Sophie knew. Twenty-three years ago, as a radical student, he was the uprising's historian, uncovering centuries-old records of a time when Meyatha flourished without an empero to run it.

There had been six of them in total on the Solstice Council, and together they led the capital into rebellion. Those were heady times. The six of them had rarely been far from each other's sides, debating some new plan or dreaming what Meyatha would be like without an empero controlling it.

Sophie knew even less about the others' fates than she did of Makis, but her father's agreement to end the uprising had guaranteed their lives. Sophie sealed the letter and held it out to Alkestis. "Find Scholar Makis Logos and give this to him. Give it to him and no one else, and do not let the speaker or any of her people see you."

Alkestis took the letter. "I will keep to Luna's own shadows, but I cannot promise total stealth. The speaker has many eyes, and I doubt she would respond well to such subterfuge."

"Nevertheless," Sophie said, "this is something we must risk, if you are willing. We will need other allies if we are to triumph."

Alkestis nodded and took the letter. A few moments later she was gone, striding out into the Meyathan capital, looking for all the world like a Heratian citizen on her evening errands. Sophie whispered a prayer to Luna. Makis's involvement with the rebels had stayed hidden all these years, and now she was jeopardizing that by contacting him, much less asking him to speak with the others. Eyes were on her now. If Savvas or anyone else discovered Sophie had contacted a former rebel, there would be no mercy. Even Demetra might decide Sophie was more trouble than she was worth, leaving Sophie and her acolytes stranded far from home with nothing but enemies on every side.

***

The sun vanished below the horizon shortly after Alkestis left, but Sophie and the other acolytes kept up their task of cleaning up the palace. They found a stash of candles to light their way, determined to keep working until they had somewhere comfortable to rest.

Sophie and two healthy acolytes laid down padded mattresses for the wounded to rest on. They had the last one in place when Fryni bounded up, candle in hand and a grin on her face. "Sister Sophie, we've found some of those documents you wanted. This way!"

Sophie sprinted after the young captain, the two of them racing through the palace corridors as they had raced along mountain trails at Gray Falls. Fryni was damned fast, but Sophie had the longer stride, and in moments they were side by side.

They rushed deeper into the palace, where even the ruins of pomp and splendor vanished, replaced with plain white walls only occasionally marred with scorch marks. The two of them both laughed as they leapt over a fallen set of shelves like they were rockfalls in a narrow pass.

Then Fryni put on a burst of speed, just beating Sophie through a narrow doorway before skidding to a stop. Sophie nearly collided with the younger woman, and the run left her breathing hard, sides aching.

"What's the matter?" Fryni asked, wiping sweat from her brow. "A little stroll like that have you tired out?" She held a prideful grin for a moment until she broke down gasping for air too.

Sophie chuckled and hugged Fryni to her. "You're fast, dearest one. Just don't run so fast that you lose the air to keep going." She released the young captain. "Now, let's see those documents."

They were deep in the palace now, past the ruined audience chamber and inside a room full of cracked and broken desks. Soiled paper and spilled ink covered the floor. In the candlelight, some of the paper was still legible: figures and sums in imperial currency. This was the palace accounting room, which meant there would be a vault for storing valuables.

Two more acolytes held candelabras at the room's far end, illuminating a smashed-in set of iron-reinforced doors. Inside the vault, a third acolyte used her candle to reveal long rows of shelving. Some of the shelves were empty or held the splintered remains of lockboxes where the palace's modest stores of coin had been kept. With imperial wealth spread throughout Heratia and the empire, there was little need to keep hoards of currency in the palace. The looters must have been disappointed.

What remained was box upon box of heavily annotated figures. If there was one thing the Meyathans, and the Laskaris family in particular, excelled at, it was keeping records.

"Yes," Sophie said. "This is what we need. Help me get some of it into the light." With these, she could finally pinpoint the state of the imperial finances.

The four acolytes carried boxes to the lone surviving desk while Sophie lit extra candles. The records would still be here in the morning, but she wanted to look at them without Demetra over her shoulder just in case the situation wasn't what the speaker had described.

Sophie selected the records for Heratia first. The rest of the empire could wait; right now the capital mattered most. She spread the records out over the wide desk, careful to balance the candle so it wouldn't drip wax onto the paper.

An endless sea of tax law and income estimates spread out before her. Comprised of page after page of calculations, the labyrinth of imperial accounting far exceeded the finances she'd managed at the abbey. How could she hope to understand this?

Fryni and the other acolytes leaned in around Sophie, lifting their candles to shed more light. Sophie closed her eyes and took a deep breath. She didn't need a detailed understanding of Meyatha's entire economy, just an awareness of what resources she had to work with. She stopped focusing on every line of numbers, looking specifically for revenue and expense figures instead.

Everywhere she looked, expense numbers loomed far higher than the imperial revenue. Sophie's eyes widened. She must have missed something. She scattered more pages across the desk, but they only confirmed her findings. The Laskaris family's own holdings brought in some income, but it disappeared into the vast depths of upkeeping Heratia's infrastructure. The senatorial families barely contributed, and if Sophie understood what she was reading, what they did pay was largely voluntary.

Demetra's own House Kalgari paid by far the greatest tithe to the empero; the other houses gave next to nothing. Instead the Meyathan state borrowed money from them to pay expenses at whatever rates and terms the senators felt like setting. It was practically extortion. Sophie's hands trembled, and she nearly dropped the candle. She took a deep breath to calm herself. "Sol, blessed daughter, may I see with your clarity."

The candle had burned down to its base. She switched to a new one and turned to another page. Then another. So far as she could tell, the empire's finances were collapsing. No wonder Heratia was deteriorating. In this state, it wouldn't be long before citizens died in crumbled buildings or the sewers backed up and turned the capital into a cesspit of disease. Heratia had the labor to halt this deterioration, but those with the coin refused to spend it. Instead citizens starved from inadequate wages, if they had work at all.

The acolytes drifted away to other tasks. The candles burned down as Sophie kept looking, scouring each page for some fragment of unspent income. She found a handful of entries in the positive, family holdings that had produced more than expected the previous year. It wasn't much, but the money could buy enough grain to grant hungry citizens some reprieve.

There were still so many pages left just for Heratia. The numbers blurred into incoherent lines. Sophie's eyelids drooped; she would rest them, just for a minute. Her head slumped forward, and her grip slackened on the candle.

Fryni's hand took hers, steadying the flame. "This paper won't make a good pillow," she said, putting her other arm around Sophie's shoulders. "It's good I came to check on you. Even the blessed daughters need to rest eventually."

Sophie blinked, staring for a moment at the priceless records she had nearly set alight. She let the younger woman lead her away from the desk. How long had she sat there? Long enough that her back ached from hunching over. The walk back was a blur of palace halls and passages.

Finally they reached the rooms cleared out for sleeping, a wing of guest quarters near the west wall. Most of the fine bedding had been taken or ruined, but they'd salvaged enough to make mats at least as soft as what they'd slept on at the abbey, and heavy shutters meant the rooms were warm.

Sophie lay down on one of the mats and let the ache drain from her muscles. Her eyelids slid shut. The last thing she felt was someone putting a blanket over her.

***

A hand shook Sophie's shoulder, rocking her out of a dreamless sleep. Sophie groaned. She was being woken already? Something must have gone wrong. She cracked an eye open. Sunlight streamed in through the open window. She'd slept through the night and missed the sun's rising. That wasn't like her; at the abbey they rose at dawn, unless it was winter, when they rose earlier.

"The speaker's back, Sister Sophie," Fryni said, giving Sophie's shoulder another shake. "She's brought a train of soldiers and servants, and she wants to talk to you." Fryni grinned. "I told her you were meditating on the Mother's works so you could have a few extra minutes. Very spiritual, couldn't be disturbed."

Sophie groaned and sat up. "The Mother and I both appreciate your quick thinking, dearest one." Her back twinged from leaning over tax papers all night, and not even the morning sunlight could convince her mind that it was time to abandon sleep. "I'll be up presently. At any moment."

Fryni took hold of Sophie's arm and hoisted her up. "Sorry, Sister Sophie," she said with a sheepish grin. "I think I already pushed the speaker's patience as far as it'll go. Probably best not to keep her longer."

Sophie rolled her eyes. "Yes, thank you, I'm up." She stretched until some of the stiffness retreated, then slipped on a fresh tunic and trousers. They were as plain as what she'd worn since arriving at the abbey twenty-three years ago, but at least they were clean. She took a moment to wash her face in a chipped porcelain basin—even with the chip it was worth more than half the abbey—and draped her black shawl over her shoulders. Time to meet with the speaker.

Demetra waited in the entrance hall, still giving directions to the small army of servants and house guards that accompanied her. She was dressed in resplendent green robes with emeralds embroidered in the collar, all signs of hard traveling erased. Guards split off to begin patrols of the palace's outer wall while the servants brought out straw brooms and tubs of acrid-smelling soap. Some carried out the few remaining chunks of debris the acolytes had missed, and others set to work scrubbing scorch marks off the wall.

Out in the courtyard, workers in clothing even plainer than Sophie's own loaded the debris into wide carts. Sophie frowned. Much of the debris was stone, heavy enough that lifting it alone could be dangerous. How much was Demetra paying these laborers? She shook her head. Time enough to think of that once the larger problems were dealt with.

Demetra turned as Sophie approached and gave a short bow. "I hope your meditation was enlightening." Sophie glanced at Fryni as the acolyte did a poor job hiding her grin, but the speaker went on, "Savvas has indeed been busy, but he has failed to bring a select number of influential senators to his side. With swift action, we may turn the tide against him."

Sophie nodded. "Thank you, but there is something you must see." Demetra was more familiar with imperial law than Sophie; perhaps she could see something in the tax records to make the situation less dire.

Expression curious, Demetra agreed to follow and handed off authority to one of her stewards. Sophie led her to the accounting chamber, where some of the acolytes had done a serviceable job repairing two more desks before pushing them together so there was room to lay out more of the record.

Rays of sunlight filtered down from the high windows, but even during the day, the room was dark enough that the acolytes still needed to light candles. Demetra read line after line, her expression losing its curiosity and turning graver with each page. Finally she stopped and looked away, blinking her eyes back into focus. "Enough, I don't need to see any more."

"My fears are true, then," Sophie said. "The empire is destitute."

Demetra massaged her temples. "It seems so. Mihail never showed me these records. I knew things were dire, but not how near we've crept to the edge."

"I didn't realize my father would keep secrets from his speaker."

Demetra sighed, and her voice turned wistful. "Neither did I. Mihail did try, you know. He was up before dawn most days, entertaining important guests, working on them to support this or that project he was sure would strengthen Meyatha. This"—she gestured at the papers—"is the result of all his compromises."

"If this is the result," Sophie said, "perhaps he should have slept in more often."

When Demetra spoke again, her voice had none of the anger Sophie expected. "This decline has been building steam for a long time, and losses against Skaldre invasions only made it worse for Mihail. Your grandmother reversed it for a time, and we had such hopes for Taisa, but now the empire's hopes are in you."

Demetra stood up, the emeralds at her throat catching the light in flashes of green fire. "Enough bathing in our sorrows, there is work to do. Have you found any coin at all in that mess?"

"Some," Sophie said. What would Demetra, a woman who wore silks and emeralds, need with what little silver she could squeeze from the imperial accounts?

Demetra clasped her hands together. "Good. I've met with the most influential senators not already in Savvas's pocket, and after many favors exchanged, they've agreed to postpone any further support from him until they've had a chance to meet you. To that end, we shall host them here at the palace, where they will find themselves dazzled by your wit and charm."

Sophie's eyebrows rose. The Mother knew she had never dazzled anyone, let alone senatorial aristocrats, even before she had spent twenty-three years working her hands to calluses at the abbey. But that seemed the lesser problem with Demetra's plan. "You think we shall entertain senators here?" She spread her hands to encompass the scorched walls and the floor still covered with soiled paper. Her choice to stay in the palace had been an important symbol, but hosting the empire's elite was another matter.

"It won't be easy," Demetra said. "But it must be done. If we entertained them at my home, it would cement in their minds forever that you are only my puppet and not a true Laskaris."

Demetra extended the fingers of one hand, counting them off. "We'll need more cleaners for the interior, craftsfolk to repair the gates, and more besides to make the outer walls presentable. Inside we'll keep guests to a small area, the rest of the palace can wait." The speaker took a breath. "My agents have located a handful of palace servants, but senior imperial officials and most of the guard seem to have fled the city, justifiably fearing retribution from Savvas and his new regime. My estate can provide something, but we'll still need to hire new servers, cooks, and the like. Plus food, decorations, clothes—you can see why we need all available coin."

Sophie took a step back under the avalanche of costs. "There are people starving in the street. What coin I have should go to them, not be wasted on feasting those who already have more than they can ever spend."

Demetra let out an exasperated breath. "And who do you think will help those wretches after Savvas throws your body into the Marshrun? My family's resources are already stretched to breaking, and this is the only way you will ever sit on the Falcon Throne. Once you are empero and your power is secure, then you can think of lesser matters."

The words "lesser matters" rankled Sophie, but she kept her expression stoic. Demetra was right. She could not feed a few today and call it justice if she let all of Meyatha starve tomorrow. "I understand," she said, not trusting herself to say more.

"Good," Demetra said. "This will take some time to arrange, and in that time we shall practice what you will say to them. You must emphasize stability above all. House Laskaris has ruled Meyatha for generations, you are a continuation of that tradition. If they press you, falling back on religion is acceptable, but only the most conservative interpretations. You are loyal to your empire, kind to your neighbors, that sort of thing."

Sophie blinked. The thought of a senatorial dinner in the palace had been absurd enough, but this? "You want me to position myself as the moderate alternative to Savvas's radical ideas? And you think they will believe that?"

"They will if you sell it to them," Demetra said. "Most senators want things to continue as they are. They stand to gain both money and power if Savvas destroys the rights of citizenship, but that would still be change, and change is dangerous. Our only hope of preserving what good remains in Meyatha is convincing them that you are safe."

Sophie laughed, a short and bitter sound. "Safe. I was safe at the abbey. Here I seem increasingly useless."

Demetra's brows furrowed. "Don't speak as if I've ruined your childhood dreams. This is politics, this is what it means to be an empero." She leaned close to Sophie. "Once the throne is yours, then we shall see."

Yes, Sophie didn't doubt they would. And how many such obstacles would spring from the shadows if she did claim her birthright? The throne wasn't even hers, and she was already compromising. Was this what her forebearers had faced? How many of *their* dreams had turned to smoke in light of imperial reality? She shook her head. That didn't matter now; she needed to be empero, or everything was for naught.

"Very well," she said. "I shall dance to the tune they play for me, and let us hope I do not trip."

Chapter 10

Demetra left the palace shortly after Sophie agreed to her plans. There was much to do: invitations to be sent, craftsfolk to be hired, clothing to be tailored. Sophie put herself back to work alongside her acolytes and Demetra's servants. The entire scheme depended on at least a small part of the palace projecting imperial grandeur, and that was something that only hard work could achieve.

Some of the servants gave uncomfortable looks to the imperial heir working among them, but Sophie ignored them. There were tasks to be done, and she wouldn't leave them unfinished when her only other option was to wait quietly for Demetra's plans to bear fruit. So she scrubbed the soiled walls until her hands were sore and carried debris to the waiting carts until she ached from knees to neck.

They had just finished sweeping splinters and broken crockery from one of the palace's many dining rooms when Alkestis approached Sophie and ushered her off to a side chamber. Once they were beyond the hearing of Demetra's servants, the acolyte spoke.

"Scholar Makis is here to see you," she said. "He's waiting out beyond the palace walls, I didn't think it wise to bring him inside with the speaker's people about."

With the thought of Makis waiting to speak to her, Sophie's aches didn't seem so pressing. "That was well reasoned," she said. "Bring him to the western annex. Demetra didn't send enough guards to patrol that far." If any of the servants asked why she was going out to the annex, Sophie would explain that she needed to see if any useful supplies had survived the looting, but such questions seemed unlikely. The servants would likely be happy to have her out of the way.

Alkestis turned to go, but burning curiosity got the better of Sophie. "Is there anyone else with him?" she asked. It was too much to hope that she'd see any others today—Makis could likely go about with far more freedom than they could—but she had to know.

"Yes," Alkestis said. "A woman, late in her fifth decade by my estimate, broad in the shoulder and northern by her complexion, with a hard stare and more scars than I could count."

Sophie's heart leapt. That had to be Faidra. She had been the uprising's general, interested more in how to win street fights than give speeches. But she had a keen mind as well. Many nights they had stayed up into the dawn hours debating what the new Meyatha would look like, whether there were any need for the country to exist at all, and always they woke the next day more exhilarated for it. Their parting had been less harmonious. Faidra wanted to fight on even as all hope was lost, but at least she had lived thanks to Sophie's surrender. That had to count for something after all this time.

Sophie let Alkestis go on her way and whispered a quiet prayer of thanks. The details of her banishment had been kept secret, so none of her old comrades could reach out to her. Now, after twenty-three years, she could finally look upon two of her dear friends again. She took a circuitous route out of the palace proper, Fryni falling into step beside her as she went out through the western gate.

The annex was a squat building made of plain gray stone and brick rather than the palace's elegant marble. Before Sophie's exile, it had been the palace's storage depot, holding the incalculable reserves of cutlery, candles, tableware, tools, and the other myriad supplies needed to keep the imperial household running. The doors had been broken open and most of the contents carried away, but the building itself had escaped the worst of the damage.

Alkestis met them at the entrance. She and Fryni exchanged a few quiet words before Alkestis took up sentry just inside the doors and Fryni preceded Sophie inside. Nerves thrumming with anticipation, Sophie followed her militia captain into a small room lit by late-afternoon sunlight that seeped in through windows just high enough that no one outside would see the occupants.

Two people stood waiting for her. The first was a slightly stooped man with pale skin and thinning gray hair on his head that became a full beard on his chin. The second was as Alkestis had said: a powerfully built woman, her ruddy skin flecked with many scars over corded muscle. They were older, but Sophie would have recognized Makis and Faidra anywhere.

Makis's face lit with a wide grin. He wrapped his long arms around Sophie in a warm embrace. "Sophie! Mother and Her blessed daughters, it really is you. I thought that acolyte was putting me on at first, but here you are!"

"Yes, here I am," Sophie said, pulling her old friend closer. "And by the Mother's blessing, you've both come back to me."

Faidra's voice was level. "The acolyte's garb suits you, Sophie." She gestured in the direction of the palace. "A palace surrounded by senatorial house guards, not so much."

Sophie released Makis from her embrace. "An unfortunate necessity," she said. She took a step toward embracing Faidra next, but the tension in the other woman's stance stopped her. Sophie smothered the pang of hurt. She'd been safe at the abbey all this time; she had no idea what Faidra had gone through. "Tell me of the others," she said instead. "Alexandra, Petros, Styliani? What mischief have you all been up to?"

Makis laughed and shook his head. "You ride in out of legend and expect to hear our stories? No, you have that responsibility first. Half the city thinks you're dead and this is all a hoax, while the other half is saying you defeated the entire Skaldre army just to get here."

"Hardly an army," Sophie said. She sat on one of the rough-hewn wooden chairs that adorned the room. "Only an ambush, but it was danger enough." She gestured to Fryni standing guard. "Fryni and the others fought like lions to get us through, I was practically a sightseer."

In her position by the door, Fryni preened under the praise.

Iris's memory loomed over Sophie, but she kept her voice light. This was a happy occasion. "Surely you don't want to hear about all the time I spent away?"

Makis insisted that he did, so Sophie told him of arriving at the abbey, of organizing the younger acolytes into a militia to do the work that should have fallen on an imperial garrison. She spoke of failed harvests and the hard years that followed, of mediating local blood feuds, and of the day the others chose her to be abbess. She left out most details and focused on the broad strokes, but even then the sun was lower on the horizon when she finished. Makis paid rapt attention, asking questions and demanding more context. Faidra stayed quiet.

"But that is too much about me," Sophie said as she finally caught up with the present. "I've only just arrived, and I've already seen the black sunburst. That's your doing, I assume?"

"All Faidra," Makis said. "The university takes up all my time now. Scribes and those gifted with figures are always in demand. But I keep up my research when I can, and—"

"Enough," Faidra said. She fixed a hard stare at Sophie. "Is it true? Have you returned to become empero?"

A cold knot formed in Sophie's gut. She'd dreaded this, but she owed her old comrades an answer. "Yes," she said. "If I do not, Savvas Carenthus will take the throne and turn Meyatha into a feudal state. I must be empero if I am to protect what little our citizens still have."

Faidra snorted. "And how will you accomplish this? With the Senate's consent? They are the ones who produce monsters like Savvas in the first place." She stood and paced the short length of the room. "Will you turn them to the cause of liberation, convince them to give up all the wealth and power they've hoarded? Or will you continue the surrender you started on the Solstice, making greater and greater concessions like every empero before you?"

Sophie's cheeks went hot at the words. "It isn't that simple," she said. "I need the Senate's support for now. Once I'm established, things can change."

"We're supposed to believe that?" Faidra asked. "When you have chained your star to Demetra Kalgari? There is no one more devoted to keeping things as they are in all Meyatha." She pointed an accusing finger at Sophie. "If you wanted change, you'd be in the streets with us, not hiding here in the ashes of your family's glory."

Fryni slammed her staff against the floor, her light-brown cheeks turning darker with anger. "You don't know what you're talking about. Sister Sophie is doing the Mother's work, bringing justice for all Meyathans!"

Sophie stood and placed both hands on Fryni's shoulders before the acolyte could say more. "Fryni, please, give me a few moments alone with my old friends." This kind of talk would only make Faidra angrier, and it wasn't a defense Sophie rightly deserved anyway.

The anger on Fryni's face turned to surprise and hurt, but she obeyed, stalking from the room with her head held high. Faidra watched the younger woman go with a raised eyebrow. "So, you're a savior now as well as empero. Was that part of the deal Kalgari offered you?"

Makis cleared his throat. "Faidra, is that necessary?"

"She's the one who wants absolute power over us," Faidra said. "I just want her to explain herself."

"Please," Sophie said, her heart beating faster. "There's no time for another uprising, or I'd join you this moment. The rights of citizenship are in danger, and the Skaldre are massing on the border. Meyatha must be united if it is to survive."

"The Skaldre, oh, that's clever." Faidra took a step closer, staring Sophie down. "Always when we demand change, there are the

Skaldre or the Free Provinces or someone else threatening to invade." She turned for the door. "This is pointless. I came to see if the rebel heir had recovered the spirit that made her stand with us at the barricades, but nothing about you has changed since the day you surrendered our cause."

"Wait," Sophie said, desperation rising. "At least help me find the others. No matter what you think of me, don't I deserve to see them again?"

Faidra turned back, her eyes boring into Sophie. "The others?"

"Faidra," Makis said, a warning in his tone.

"She asked," Faidra said. "The others are dead."

Sophie reeled. No, it couldn't be true. She looked to Makis, desperate for him to deny it, but he said nothing. "All of them?"

"Everyone with a connection to the Solstice Council," Faidra said. "We three are the only ones left."

"H-how?"

"How do you think?" Faidra snapped. "Alexandra went a year after the uprising. She broke into Senica Cathedral and preached about the blood on the empero's hands. They cut off her head before the falcon mosaic at this palace."

Bile rose in Sophie's throat. She had walked through those gates on her way to power, over the long-spilled blood of a priestess whose fiery sermons had agitated Heratia's faithful to rise up.

"Petros took his ship and sailed south to become a pirate in the Marmian Sea," Faidra continued. "He sent us a portion of his haul every year until they caught him and hung his body out for the crows."

Sophie sat down hard on the rough-hewn chair. No, they were supposed to live. They were supposed to live! Had her surrender to Irena been for nothing?

Faidra wasn't finished. "Styliani was the worst. After Irena Ironheart dissolved the People's Chamber, Styliani's husband left her and went back to his family estates. He wouldn't even let Styliani see her son! She wasted away for years, writing pamphlets we couldn't distribute. She died at her desk—it was her heart, we think. She never lost faith in you. To her last breath, she was sure you'd come back and lead us."

A sob wracked Sophie's body. Tribune Styliani Dellis of the People's Chamber, the woman who had taught Sophie how unjust the imperial system was, dead. Without her family, without even the satisfaction of teaching others. Passing on knowledge had been Styliani's joy. Sophie would never forget the way her tutor's severe gray eyes crinkled in a smile when Sophie solved a difficult problem.

Summoning all her resolve, Sophie met Faidra's gaze with eyes blurry from tears. "I'm here now."

"Styliani wouldn't recognize you," Faidra snarled. "The Sophie she believed in vanished when you sold our uprising to the empero. You betrayed us then, you're still betraying us now."

Faidra strode out of the annex, leaving only the sting of her words behind.

Sophie and Makis sat in silence for a few moments. Sophie wiped at her tears with the rough wool of her sleeve until Makis handed her a silk kerchief.

"Thank you," Sophie said, clearing the water from her eyes. "Doesn't she understand? I have no army, barely any money to speak of. I need the Senate's backing if I'm to accomplish anything. Can't she see this is only temporary?"

"I'm sorry," Makis said. "But I'm afraid we heard talk like that from your father for years, when he deigned to address the people at all. Whenever he reduced food aid to the poor or seized silver vessels from a church, it was a temporary measure. Faidra doesn't trust anyone who talks like that."

"Is she right not to?"

Makis shrugged. "I've led a privileged life since the uprising, free to research what I want so long as I do it quietly. It's not my place to say what someone in Faidra's position should believe."

"I've been so childish," Sophie said. "I imagined you all here waiting for me as if nothing had changed."

Makis squeezed her hand. "The others never stopped fighting, especially Faidra. In daylight she organizes workers to bargain for what rights they can claw from their employers, and by night she leads bands to vandalize the property of wealthy citizens who mistreat the unfortunate. It will get her killed one day. Don't judge her too harshly."

Sophie nodded. She had no wish to judge Faidra, even while the stabbing pain of her accusations remained. Sophie only feared that Faidra was right.

"I'm afraid I can't stay much longer myself," Makis said. "Is there anything I can do for you?"

A thought broke through Sophie's despair. "Actually, there is. If I gave you a copy of the imperial tax records, could you unsnarl it for me? I can see that the senatorial families are evading the collectors somehow, but everything is such smoke and mirrors that I cannot see who properly owes what."

Makis agreed, though perhaps he was simply humoring her. Her father had employed the best accountants in Meyatha. If they had not been able to right the empire's finances, what hope was there? Nevertheless, she directed Makis to speak with Alkestis and arrange for a copy of the records to be sent away with him. Mihail had kept duplicates of nearly all his records at least.

Finally Sophie sat alone, the weight of her reunion pinning her to the chair. But she couldn't stay here; she had to speak with Fryni. The young acolyte deserved more than the rough dismissal Sophie had given her.

She found Fryni whirling through a martial-training form just outside the annex, staff darting around an imaginary opponent's guard so quickly that Sophie could barely keep track of it. Sweat flew from Fryni's brow as she threw herself into each motion, face flushed with the exertion.

Fryni's head shifted slightly as she caught sight of Sophie. "That woman shouldn't have spoken to you that way."

"Fryni, please listen to me," Sophie said.

Fryni finished the form and came to a halt, leaning on her staff for support. "You deserve better. Next time that bitter old relic insults you, I'll teach her a lesson."

Sophie put her hands on Fryni's shoulders and looked the younger woman in the eyes. "That bitter old relic was once my best friend, and while I was safe with you protecting me at the abbey, she was risking her life for the people here who have nothing. The Mother asks for kindness, so we can forgive her a few harsh words, can't we?"

Fryni looked down and mumbled something.

Sophie gave her shoulders a squeeze. "What was that?"

"I suppose," Fryni said louder. "For the Mother and Her blessed daughters."

Sophie smiled, then winced as the rush from her encounter with Faidra ended, leaving her exhausted and heavy eyed despite the sun still shining high in the sky. "We should return to the others," she said. "There's much to do if Demetra's plan is to go forward." Her fatigue could wait; others had worked harder and with less rest.

They walked back toward the palace, its cracked walls and burned-out towers silhouetted before the setting sun. With the details lost in shadow, Sophie's childhood home looked once again like a residence for the empire's most powerful family. There was no telling whether that power could be restored one day, and Sophie was less sure than ever if that was what she wanted.

Chapter 11

They only had three more days to prepare the palace for Demetra's planned dinner. If they pushed the date out any further, it would look like they were stalling. The first day was more scrubbing and shifting debris. Sophie, her acolytes, and Demetra's servants all joined in the effort. Cleaning the entire palace complex would take weeks, if not longer, so they focused their efforts on a path from the entrance to a dining hall Demetra had chosen. It was large enough to suggest imperial power, she claimed, but small enough so the guests would feel they had spent personal time with the empero-in-waiting.

Demetra's promised craftsfolk arrived on the second day and set to work on the palace's exterior, repairing the gates and setting new glass into the public-facing windows. Sophie spent much of the day with Demetra, assessing what most needed work and what could be left until later. The speaker had thrown together a workforce of hundreds, but, even so, their task was daunting. From the main gate, the repairs would be passable. Anyone approaching from other directions would see how much damage remained, but that couldn't be helped. Wrapped up in preparations, Sophie heard nothing from Makis, and she had no time to see more of the city.

The day of the dinner, they saw to interior decorations. New portraits and wall hangings had been bought or commissioned and new statues brought in to replace the smashed wreckage. With the assistance of Fryni and the other acolytes, Sophie papered over damage that had so far resisted their efforts. Then they hung a tapestry across scored wall paneling and shifted a statue atop cracked floor tiles.

Demetra wanted Sophie to pose so a sculptor might carve something in her image, but there was no time, something Sophie thanked the Mother for. There were too many statues of her family in Heratia already. Instead Demetra somehow acquired a marble soldier who bore a passing resemblance so long as one did not look overly close. Sophie contemplated how much she could sell the thing for once this was over.

Food was another matter still. Only the rarest delights could be served to the influential senators who might be swayed to Sophie's side. Servants brought in the tenderest meats and finest vegetables, many of them imported from beyond the empire's borders. With them came cooks to sear and spice the feast just so. As the speaker had predicted, preparing for it strained the Kalgari family's finances, and they had needed every coin Sophie was able to pry from the imperial ledgers.

Far too soon, evening arrived. The rich scent and the sizzle of cooking permeated from the kitchen, and Sophie's stomach growled. As unjust as this extravagant feast was, Sophie couldn't help looking forward to it. After twenty-three years of being concerned with all the acolytes having enough to eat, the olive oil and spices of Heratia made every meal a treasure, and she couldn't resist fantasizing about what each dish would taste like. Sophie bit her lip. The food wasn't the point; she had a job to do.

Demetra had agonized over Sophie's outfit all through the preparations, particularly the color. Purple was reserved for the imperial family, and wearing a gown of it would certainly send a message. But Demetra had wondered if it would be too strong a message. It could make the senators feel like Sophie was putting herself above them, as though she was assuming their support when it was not yet given.

Eventually they settled on a purple sash.

"It will remind them who you are," Demetra said, "but not so much that they feel threatened."

The rest of Sophie's outfit was a gown of deepest-blue silk, high necked and long sleeved, the finest garment she had worn in a long time. It felt like a cool wind over her skin after years of rough wool.

Thinking of how much the silk had cost made Sophie's heart beat faster, and she nearly flinched away as Demetra placed a net of sparkling diamonds over her hair.

Seeing Sophie's distress, Demetra assured her that this was subdued by the standards of senatorial fashion. When that did not seem to help, she added, "Without the proper appearances, we have no hope." She held up a mirror. "See? This is an empero to dazzle them."

In the mirror, Sophie's reflection gawked back at her. The blue gown complemented her dark-brown skin, and the diamonds sparkled like stars against her black hair. At the abbey, the acolytes had shared half a dozen pieces of costume jewelry between them on occasions when they wanted to dress up—nothing that could hold a candle to this.

A twinge of regret nagged at Sophie. Her black shawl, a symbol of the Mother's grace, lay folded neatly on a side table. This would be the first time in years she hadn't worn it. *Greater and greater concessions,* Faidra had said.

Sophie took a deep breath. "Let us face our guests, then." She was committed; it was too late for reservations.

While the Meyathan Senate numbered just over two hundred in total, Demetra had only invited a few dozen that night: those who she judged most amenable to their cause. Ariadne arrived first, dressed in the sky blue of House Ducas to match her light complexion, with a necklace of sparkling green emeralds announcing her alignment with Demetra.

The slender senator eyed Sophie's apparel and turned to the speaker. "I'd have included more finery. A brooch and a few rings, at least. The empero should make an unforgettable impression."

A muscle in Sophie's cheek twitched. So she was to be considered a political prop by Demetra's allies: useful, but not an equal partner to be addressed.

Ariadne glanced at Sophie again. "The sash is a nice touch though."

"Thank you, Senator," Sophie said with a carefully constructed smile. "Demetra and I are pleased to receive you in the palace of my ancestors."

"Yes," Demetra said, clapping her hands together through the tension. "Now, let us all be on our most charming behavior. We have many guests to win over before we catch up to Savvas."

The next of those guests arrived even as she spoke, riding in carriages of the finest black-stained wood, escorted by house guards in shining mail adorned with the crests of their houses. The senators emerged from within and surrounded Sophie like finely dressed wolves. They circled her, offering polite greetings while their eyes scrutinized her for weaknesses. A few wore House Kalgari's green, but most of the invitations had gone to neutral senators as they were the ones whose votes could make the difference. Sophie took refuge within the armor of her attire. She fit here as well as they did, and the Mother knew she had paid enough for the privilege.

"Welcome, senators of Meyatha," she said. Most of the faces she saw were her own age or older, as Demetra had limited invitations to those of greatest influence. But she also saw that the majority of them were light skinned, suggesting a provincial background. That made them less likely to have strong memories of the Solstice Uprising if they had been minding their personal estates during the fighting. Demetra had chosen her guest list well.

"Join me inside," Sophie continued. "We shall have entertainment as we wait for the other guests." She led them into the palace through the restored entrance hall and into the dining room where a collection of Heratia's finest musicians played a soothing melody. Demetra's servants flitted in among the guests, offering glasses of crisp white wine. Others carried trays of fruit pastries dusted in white sugar, honey-fried dates, and olives stuffed with savory cheeses. Fryni and the other acolytes stood sentry on the room's edges, eyes watchful and staves held straight at their sides.

After their initial salvo of polite greetings, the attending senators bombarded Sophie with questions. What steps would she take to honor her deceased father and sister? What would she do about labor shortages on the docks? What measures would she take to protect Meyathan merchants threatened by competition from the Free Provinces?

How would she deal with the Skaldre threat?

Demetra had drilled Sophie on all these questions and more. She demurred whenever possible, explaining that of course she would seek the Senate's guidance before taking any critical actions. Naturally her fallen family would be given full state honors, and she would see that the empire's own traders had preferential tax rates over foreigners. The question of labor shortages rankled—likely the employers weren't paying enough to attract workers to a hard life—but she gritted her teeth and explained that as empero she would do what was necessary. She would say whatever it took to get through this evening and bite her tongue to keep the rest inside.

A senator with a northern accent caught Sophie's attention. "Enough of inconsequential matters," he said. "You must agree to reinforce Heliopolis's garrison and begin construction of a new curtain wall immediately. My city will be the first target when Thane Eidsson crosses the border."

The request was sensible enough, given the increased Skaldre threat and Heliopolis's proximity to the frontier, but another senator spoke up before Sophie could respond. "The north already has most of our legions," this second one said, bearing the sun-weathered look of someone who worked outdoors. "What we need is a campaign to take a port on the Marmian Sea. That way our navy can finally put Gallia in its place and secure our southern trade routes."

Even after twenty-three years in exile, Sophie remembered how the empire's northern and southern frontiers competed for resources from Heratia. With Demetra's coaching, she was prepared for the specifics as well. "The Skaldre requires our most immediate attention," she said. "But we have not forgotten the Free Provinces." She gestured toward Demetra. "My speaker is already making inquiries among Gallia's rivals."

"Indeed," Demetra said, picking up the practiced reply. "There is no need to waste Meyathan lives when for a little silver, we can have the Free Provinces fight each." That brought murmurs of appreciation from the senators, though Sophie didn't know where they would find the coin in question. No matter—this was a night for reassurances.

A third senator, an older woman with a regal bearing, spoke up. "It is good to hear that you take the Free Provinces' threat seriously, but what of your choice to grant a Gallian duchess access to the Falcon Piers, in the face of all imperial custom and tradition? A bit presumptuous, don't you think?"

The other senators watched with interest as Sophie turned to face her questioner. Demetra had prepared an answer for this too, about how greater trade would bring prosperity to all of Meyatha, but Sophie had shown her neck enough this evening.

"Not at all," Sophie said. "The Falcon Piers are property of the Laskaris family, and I know how important it is that citizens have control of their own property, Senator."

Several of the guests chuckled as the questioning senator bowed her head in acknowledgment of Sophie's point. Even Demetra smiled. Sophie relaxed her stance. If she could mediate between farmers desperate to feed their families, she could handle these senators.

"Wisely spoken," Ariadne said. "The speaker has brought us an empero who understands the pillars of Meyatha." She raised a wine glass. "May she bring us a reign of peace and prosperity."

The guests raised their glasses in response, but some with less enthusiasm than others. Sophie winced. Ally or no, the senator might have overplayed her hand by speaking of reigns so early in the evening.

A servant approached Demetra and leaned to whisper in the speaker's ear. Demetra's mouth set in a hard line. She turned to Sophie, voice cold and low. "Savvas Carenthus is at the gates."

Sophie kept her breathing even. "Then we had best admit him."

They'd known he might attend, though Demetra had sent him no invitation. Denying him entrance would only announce that she was afraid of him, assuming he didn't take it as an excuse to force the palace with his soldiers. Neither option was acceptable.

The other guests stopped to listen as their own servants brought news of the latest arrival. The dining-hall doors swung open, admitting a tall man to stride through them. Sophie only looked from the corner of her eye, facing Demetra like nothing of significance was occurring. The man was perhaps in his mid-forties, with light-brown skin that sported several dashing scars. His dark beard was neatly trimmed, and his mouth was set in a relaxed smile. In place of a robe he wore ceremonial armor, each plate polished to a mirror shine, the breast adorned with rubies in the shape of his house crest: a rearing stallion. Savvas Carenthus.

Senators, acolytes, and servants alike fell silent. All eyes shifted between Sophie and the newcomer, between empero and pretender, though only the Mother knew who deserved which title. Sophie turned carefully, letting the movement ripple up her gown like it was a ship's sail. She raised her eyebrows as if she'd only just noticed a new guest.

"Welcome, Senator Carenthus," she said, spreading her hands. "It is always a pleasure to host one of Meyatha's great public servants." She was to flatter him but remind the others that he was below her.

Savvas took a step toward her, and along the wall, Fryni's posture went even more rigid than before.

"You honor me," Savvas said, "Abbess."

That caused a ripple: some guests tsked with dismay at the disrespect, while others chuckled at the subtle jab.

Demetra took her own step forward. "Petty disrespect is beneath someone of your record," she said. "Unless you don't believe the imperial heir deserves her proper title within the palace itself."

"You mistake me," Savvas said. "It is simply that I do not know what other title to use." He counted off on his fingers. "She is not confirmed by the Senate, so 'Your Majesty' is inappropriate. I might call her 'Lady Laskaris,' but that venerable family disowned her, so it doesn't fit. Surely you do not wish me to call her by her given name?"

The words hurt more than Sophie expected. Was no one willing to leave her family to their rest? She put on the mask of a smile. There was nothing Demetra could say to rescue her from this. "Abbess is acceptable. I am not ashamed of my time serving the Mother and Her blessed daughters."

"It clearly suits you," Savvas said. "You should consider going back there, away from the dangers of this city."

The other senators made startled murmurs. Fryni tensed, ready to strike, knuckles white around her staff.

Demetra's voice forestalled her. "Honored guests." The speaker's tone was as calm as a frozen lake. "The first course is served, shall we sit?"

Angry heat built under Sophie's collar even as she followed Demetra's timely intervention. This man would enslave her people, and now he saw fit to dredge up her family's ghosts to threaten her?

In her grandmother's time, a pretender like Savvas would have his head on a pike before he knew what had happened.

They all took seats at a long table, the polished wood piled high with dishes of finest silver and porcelain, their contents fresh and steaming from the kitchen. The heavenly scents barely registered as Sophie stared down to the table's far end, where Savvas took the seat opposite hers. Demetra's hand on Sophie's arm pushed back the fog of anger. She needed calm. He wanted her upset so she would make a mistake.

"If you will join me in thanking the Mother's generosity," Sophie said. "We may begin."

She chose a long blessing, invoking Sol's gift of sunlight to bless the fields and Luna's watchful eye to keep pests away. She needed the familiar mantra to center herself, and no one could object to properly invoking the divine. To her annoyance, Savvas didn't show any sign of impatience or irritation. He spoke the entire blessing without faltering, even as most of the other guests mumbled their way through.

As she spoke the final words, some of her calm returned. She could weather any barbs this enslaver hurled at her; she had to. The senators attacked their plates with gusto, many offering compliments to the palace's cooking. Sophie accepted each bit of praise with grace, but she ate very little herself. Tastes that had tantalized her mere hours before now seemed as ash.

One of the older senators offered a toast to Empero Mihail. "It is a shame we cannot drink the empero's health, but may he find peace among Luna's starry children."

They all drank, the wine in their cups worth a common citizen's yearly income.

"Peace was always Mihail's first love," another senator said. "He would treat anyone willing to listen."

Someone muttered, "Including Thane Eidsson and the entire Skaldre army."

Sophie looked over her guests, but the speaker had been too quiet to tell who it was. However, from the mix of chuckles and disapproving frowns, their voice had been loud enough to carry the table's length.

A younger senator, bold with wine, took up the barb. "Savvas here'll rescind the invitation, like he did the last one!"

Those close to Savvas gripped his shoulder or clapped him on the back in adoration.

Demetra kept silent, but Ariadne made an irritated noise and spoke. "The empero, Mother embrace him, served Meyatha in countless ways. The negotiating table is as important as the battlefield."

Savvas nodded, his face solemn. "Indeed, we all help the empire as we are able," he said. His mouth quirked up in a half grin. "I'm only sorry that being the son of Irena Ironheart wasn't quite enough to give our departed empero mastery of the cavalry charge."

This time chuckles turned into full laughter. Sophie's cheeks burned with embarrassment as much as anger. Demetra hadn't covered whatever was being joked about during her preparation. She looked to the older woman, surprised to find that Demetra's calm expression had cracked into a snarl.

Demetra leaned in so only Sophie could hear. "Mihail tried to make peace with the Skaldre when they last attacked," she said between clenched teeth. "Eidsson betrayed him, and when the empero took the field, it went badly. Only Savvas's arrival stopped the Skaldre advance."

Sophie took a long drink of wine. Was there no end to her family's failures? She put the glass down to find the table quiet, the guests staring at her in expectation and Savvas with a satisfied smirk.

He must have asked her something that Sophie had been too lost in thought to register. She cleared her throat and tried to look apologetic. "Your pardon, Senator, I was thinking of Meyatha's many glorious victories."

Savvas waved the apology away. "No bother," he said. "It had just occurred to me that I'm not the only one here with military experience. What were they called, the Solstice Riots? Untrained rabble against the imperial elite. It was impressive, even if it was treasonous." The other guests held their breath, waiting for Sophie's reply.

She forced a laugh. "I was barely past my majority," she said. "Surely we are all allowed a youthful indiscretion or two?" She was ashamed of the words even as she said them. Thousands had died in the uprising, and they deserved infinitely more than a vapid dismissal, but she needed to think of the living now.

The gathered senators laughed and slapped the table in uproarious applause; several shared anecdotes of their own wild youth. Ariadne's eyebrows raised, but then she nodded in approval. Sophie sat rigid, keeping her smile in place through force of will. It was all a game to them. The lives lost, the freedoms endangered... none of it mattered.

Demetra squeezed her hand and spoke under her breath. "Well done, they're warming up to you."

Politics, that was why Sophie was here. That was all that mattered.

The applause calmed enough for Savvas to speak. "I would not hold anyone's youth against them, but it seems some troublemakers haven't forgotten." His smirk returned. "They deface our property and interfere with critical functions of the capital. Your father never managed to round them all up, I trust you will do better?"

Demetra smiled. "Her Majesty will deal with many problems once she is properly confirmed as empero."

That brought appreciative sounds from the dinner guests, and for a moment, Savvas hesitated, likely realizing he had suggested a future in which Sophie was empero rather than he. Still, Sophie's hackles rose. Faidra and her people being discussed in such company couldn't lead to anything good.

Savvas nodded and raised his glass to acknowledge the point. "Fairly said, Speaker." He paused, one hand on his chin. "In that case, maybe we can find some common ground? To assure the empire its leaders will not let vandals run wild in the capital, even in this difficult time."

"It would be more appropriate," Demetra said, "to speak of the Skaldre threat on our northern border, and what can be done about it."

Sophie held back a sigh of relief. Anything to keep Faidra out of the conversation.

"Wait," Ariadne said. "It can't do any harm to hear him out."

Before Sophie or Demetra could object, Savvas pressed on. "The abbess and myself should address the citizens together, make it clear we will not tolerate any sabotage while the empire is under threat, that the watch and garrison are fully empowered to deal with any internal disruption."

A chill ran through Sophie. Fully empowered. With the empire's very existence in question, Savvas proposed to unleash imperial troops against their fellow citizens. And in this room, his proposal did not seem at all unpopular.

"We're too gentle with them, that's the problem," one guest said. "Give the watch a free hand and the city will be back in order before the troublemakers know what's happened. That's the only way to protect our property, the only way we'll have justice." More agreement.

Demetra stood. "A moment, please. Her Majesty and I must confer." She put a hand on Sophie's shoulder, guiding her as far away from the table as the dining hall would allow. "I didn't expect this," Demetra said in a whisper, "but it is an opportunity."

"An opportunity?" Sophie asked. "He asks me to join him in declaring war against our own people because they broke into a few shops. Meyathan citizens will die."

Demetra's dark-brown face creased in a frown. "We can mitigate the damage, and this would quiet any who wish to use the uprising against you."

Ariadne stepped up to the speaker's side, her emerald necklace sparkling green in the light. "What is there to discuss?" she asked. "This would build our support among the merchants, assure those senators who doubt us, and give us greater influence over the garrison. Our answer is obvious."

Sophie's nails bit into her palms. Faidra and her people struck out in desperation, and these senators could only see it in terms of coins lost and influence gained. They spoke of summary sentencing and the Mother's justice in the same breath. No matter what mitigations Demetra concocted, citizens would die if she accepted Savvas's proposal, and he no doubt knew it.

"It isn't a complicated offer," Savvas called from his seat at the table. The other guests were whispering among themselves. "Unless you haven't actually left your radical beliefs behind."

Demetra's voice was in her ear. "For the Mother's grace, Sophie, tell him yes. We'll deal with the consequences later, just tell them what they want to hear."

Yes, say what she needed to say for the Falcon Throne. Appease the coddled elite, laughing over the desperation of the people they abused. Tell them she would murder her people so they wouldn't have to deal with the inconvenience of treating their workers with dignity.

Sophie pushed past Demetra and Ariadne. "No," she said, eyes locked with Savvas's. "I will not join you in spreading terror through

Heratia." She lifted her gaze to the other guests. "These citizens you condemn are desperate. They destroy your property because it is the only way they know to make you listen." She spread her hands. "It doesn't have to be this way. If we keep the Mother's loyalty to each other, we can build a stronger Meyatha together."

Absolute silence greeted Sophie's speech, many of the guests staring at her with open mouths. Then came a frenzy of whispered conversation as Demetra pressed her hands to her face.

Only Savvas's voice rose above the muttering clamor. "Well," he said. "It seems the rebel heir is still with us."

Ariadne shook her head, staring at Demetra. "She will never hold the Falcon Throne." The light-skinned senator unfastened her emerald necklace and let it clatter to the floor. "This abbess will be your destruction, Demetra. Cast her off before it is too late." Ariadne turned and strode out of the hall, leaving a speechless Demetra in her wake.

Other guests stood to follow the senator of House Ducas, one at a time at first, then in larger groups until the table was nearly empty. Sophie watched them go. This was her fault for not playing along as Demetra had begged her to, but she couldn't regret it. Some costs were too high, even for a throne.

When Savvas himself stood, he did not turn for the exit but instead strode up the table's length toward Sophie. This time Fryni did not restrain herself. In half a breath she and two other acolytes were between Sophie and Savvas, their staves held at the ready.

Savvas raised his hands, palms open. "Peace, sisters. I have only words for your abbess."

"Let him through," Sophie said. This night was a disaster already; she would not have it said that she was a coward in the face of her enemy.

Fryni glared at Savvas for a moment longer, then stood aside and motioned her fellow acolytes to do the same. Savvas approached

Sophie, hands still open. "I served your father loyally, whatever his flaws," he said. "And I would have served your sister too, Mother embrace her."

"You have a strange sense of loyalty then, Senator," Sophie said.

"I am loyal to Meyatha first," Savvas said. "And I will not let you destroy it with your treasonous ideas. But I would rather not spill Laskaris blood. Go back to your abbey before the Senate votes, and I will let you live. If you are still here on that day, I will storm this palace and kill everyone inside."

He spun on his heel and strode briskly out the room. Sophie shook in his absence. He would kill Fryni, Alkestis, all of the others, without mercy. Sophie's gaze settled on the marble statue that Demetra had acquired to grace the dining hall, the one that was meant to resemble Sophie herself. Whom the statue actually depicted was long forgotten, and its weathered features had seen many years of hardship, but it still stood with sword and shield ready.

Sophie stilled her shaking and straightened her spine. If Savvas wanted a fight, she would give him one.

Chapter 12

Several days passed after the disastrous dinner, and the situation only grew worse. Demetra spent every waking moment going from the house of one influential senator to another, but her reports to Sophie each evening were grim. Word of Sophie's speech had spread among Heratia's elite, and even the rumor that she favored Faidra's rebels was enough to turn the entire senatorial class against her.

Reports reached the capital that Thane Eidsson had officially claimed responsibility for the deaths of Taisa and her family. Worse news followed, of Skaldre armies on the move to besiege the border cities of Heliopolis and Karotia. With losses mounting at the frontier, much of Heratia's garrison marched north to reinforce what remained of the field armies. This only made Demetra's task more difficult. With war against the Skaldre a glaring reality, senators and citizens both wanted a proven general leading them.

If Savvas won another victory against Eidsson, his hold on power would be unbreakable. If he lost, then northern Meyatha would burn. There was too much bad blood between Meyathans and the Skaldre for Sophie to hope for any other result.

If Sophie fled in the night, at least her acolytes would be safe. But what about the rest of Meyatha? She couldn't leave her people to the mercy of those who saw them as little more than an exploitable resource. Sophie wouldn't run, not while there was even the slightest chance she could save her people from that fate. And if she couldn't, then this time she would die fighting.

Her only solace was that despite the incident with the guards when she arrived at the palace, few people knew what she looked like. She could still go into the city without being noticed. Demetra disapproved, but she did not argue so long as Sophie took her acolytes along as escorts and gave her word not to attract attention.

Sophie took the chance to visit Heratia's western side, where the dense housing for the city's poor crowded up against foundries and tanneries. As she expected, poverty was worse here among the working crowds, with far more citizens sleeping on the streets and asking alms from passersby.

But she also saw signs of Faidra's handywork. Cloaked Heratians handed out food and coin, then vanished when watch officers approached. Stones and offal were hurled at warehouses. The black sunburst was everywhere, and alongside it graffiti stating in no uncertain terms what the artist thought of those who sought the Falcon Throne. While there was some disagreement, the consensus portrayed Savvas as a tyrant and Sophie as ineffective, something she could hardly dispute.

On the fourth morning after Sophie's dinner speech, she was dressing herself for another outing when Demetra bustled into the sleeping chamber, wearing robes of fiery orange with a gold circlet around her head.

"I address the full Senate today," Demetra said. "If everything goes right, they may agree to delay Savvas's confirmation vote."

"You certainly look the part of speaker," Sophie said.

Demetra paused for a moment, as if she had not expected the compliment. "Thank you," she said. "I ask that you remain in the palace today. If things go badly, it is important that you have suitable protection."

"If that is your wish," Sophie said. She had no strength left to argue nor explain to Demetra that if Savvas and the Senate came for her, being in the palace would only make her easier to find. She'd done enough damage already by speaking her mind.

"I will return as soon as I can," Demetra said. She turned to go, then paused. "I will find a way to salvage this. I swear."

Sophie took Demetra's hand in hers. "The Mother appreciates your kindness, Speaker, but she does not need your guilt. I chose to come here. If I suffer for that, it is from my choice."

Demetra blinked and opened her mouth but said nothing. After a few moments, she nodded and hurried out. Sophie watched her go. Both their heads were on the chopping block now. If only there were some way she could convince Fryni and the others to return to Gray Falls before the blade fell.

As if summoned by her thoughts, an acolyte appeared at the doorway, a lacquered scroll case in her hands.

"A courier brought this for you, Sister Sophie," the acolyte said, holding out the case. Calliope was her name. She'd been wounded in the Skaldre ambush, but the gash down her side had healed nicely.

"Thank you," Sophie said, taking the cool wood in her hands. "Please tell Fryni and the others that we shall stay in today. And tell her that you're all to relax for the morning, you've been working far too hard."

Calliope bowed. "I don't think Fryni knows how to relax, but the rest of us have found some intact books in the library. We'll convince her to read with us and call it practicing our letters."

Sophie nodded with a warm smile, and Calliope padded out, silent on the stone floor. She was a little older than Fryni, but still so young. All of them, even Alkestis, the eldest, were so young.

Sophie opened the case and broke the seal. The letter was short, written in a flowing hand.

Most esteemed Sophie,

The Falcon Piers are indeed excellent docks, just as you promised. I would love to tell you I am most pleased with them. However, the city watch will still not let me access them. Something about the property's status being uncertain due to inheritance laws. I know you must be busy, but I confess that waiting for anything makes me irritable.

The letter ended with the signature of Duchess Constantia de Beltane.

She had written "Sophie," not "Your Majesty." So Constantia knew that Sophie was not empero in truth then. With everything else happening, it was hardly a surprise that someone in a position of power had decided that she didn't actually have authority over her family's property after all. Sophie folded the letter and stowed it in her tunic. Now she could add a powerful Gallian duchess to her list of enemies. If Savvas didn't finish her, Constantia would be pleased to do it for him.

Sophie left her sleeping chamber and walked to the palace chapel. She lit a single candle, letting the flickering light paint shapes across the walls in the warm darkness. She sank down to kneel. The chamber's carpet provided some cushioning, but her knees still protested as always.

Constantia's letter weighed heavy in her pocket, and the knowledge of how easily Savvas could storm the palace pressed even heavier upon her. Was this how she would die? Trapped in her family home with enemies on all sides? When she had taken up arms against her family twenty-three years ago, she had failed. Now she had tried to claim her heritage as a Laskaris, and again she had failed. Failure appeared all she was good at.

She wound her black shawl around her hands. "Mother, I walk in cold and darkness. If I am not to feel the warmth of Your love, I hope You will grant me some measure of clarity to see through the Void as You do." She breathed in. "I walk in the Void, the Void surrounds me."

Some of the weight on her shoulders lifted as she repeated the meditation mantras. She'd lost count of the repetitions when a gentle cough brought her out of it. She opened her eyes to bright sunlight streaming in through the chapel's open doors. Calliope stood there, her expression pensive.

"What is it?" Sophie asked. "Is Fryni making you practice forms again?" That young woman needed to find something she could take pleasure in beyond her responsibilities. Of course, whose fault was that but Sophie's?

"No, no," Calliope said. "She has her nose in a book of poetry, if you can believe it."

A snort escaped Sophie's lips. "Poetry? That I might have to come down and see." She straightened, shielding her eyes from the high sun's light. "But I assume it's not the reason you're here?"

"There's a man with a cart in the courtyard," Calliope said. "Some of the speaker's guards brought him in, and now he's arguing with them."

Sophie frowned. What new trouble was this? Had she made another enemy without noticing? There seemed no shortage of them. "Thank you," she said. "I'll see what the difficulty is. Fetch Fryni and the others, if you would. Just in case."

Calliope bowed and sprinted off toward the library, favoring her weak side only a little. Sophie walked briskly and reached the courtyard's threshold just in time to hear an irritated guard snap, "We've no record of your services, and you expect us to believe you were sent for?"

"Perhaps the empero does not confide everything in you, young man," came the reply. It was Makis's voice, stern and unbending as if he addressed unruly students.

Why was he here? What had happened? Sophie stepped into the sunlight and beheld a dozen Kalgari house guards surrounding Makis and his cart, which was piled high with boxes. Of course, she'd asked him to look into the imperial records. It hadn't seemed important after she'd destroyed her only real chance at the throne.

"I called for him," she said. The guards turned to her, and she took a step forward. "Leave him be."

The guard captain glanced between them for a few moments before bowing to Sophie. "As you say, Lady Laskaris." He directed the other guards back to their patrols, clearing the space around Makis's cart.

Sophie stood silent for a moment. So she was "Lady Laskaris" and not "Your Majesty" to Demetra's retainers as well. She couldn't blame them for hedging their bets, not if they knew the half of how poorly Sophie's position stood.

She roused herself from those dark thoughts and stepped closer to Makis. "I'm sorry for that," she said. "I didn't realize you'd be here today."

Color rose in Makis's cheeks, and his voice turned from stern to embarrassed. "I'd meant to signal your acolyte Alkestis and meet you unannounced, but one of those guards noticed me on a side street, and all I could think to do was act like I was called for."

Sophie nodded. She would have preferred to keep her meetings with Makis from Demetra, but there was no helping it now. With luck, the speaker still did not know that the venerable Scholar Makis Logos had once sat on the Solstice Council.

"No matter," Sophie said. "But you shouldn't stay. My star isn't high at the moment, and it might go badly for you to be seen with me."

Makis patted one of the boxes. "I think these will be worth making the time for. Besides, the life of a scholar offers few opportunities for danger." He winked at her. "Hitching myself to a falling star is just the opportunity I've been waiting for."

Before Sophie could voice her exasperation, soft footfalls alerted her to the arrival of Fryni and the others. They fanned out across the courtyard, eyes alert and staves in hand.

"It's alright," Sophie said. "There's no danger, I'm sorry for calling you out here." She eyed the pile of boxes in Makis's cart. If the scholar wanted her to see their contents, then so be it. "Though, if you're willing, we could use some assistance bringing these inside."

Working together, they all brought the boxes to the inauspicious dining room. It was the only cleaned-out chamber with enough space. Sophie took the opportunity to brew Makis and herself cups of strong tea, one of the many imports Heratia boasted that would sell dearly out in the empire's provinces.

Sophie took a long sip of the bitter liquid. "So, what have you brought me?"

Makis ignored his own tea and spread documents on the table. "Much of this is what you gave me," he said. "But these"—he indicated a line of documents printed on crisp, clean paper—"these are the senatorial houses' own records. They hire out the finest university scribes, and a few owed me favors." He shrugged. "It is what little I could do."

Sophie smiled and smacked her hand against his shoulder. "What little you could do indeed." Twenty-three years hadn't dulled Makis's talent for producing the most amazing documents. She sighed. "Oh, what I could do with these if I were ever to actually become empero."

She had always planned a full audit of the state, but with detailed understandings of where the wealthiest citizens invested their coin, she could have done so much more. Still, what was the harm in knowing? She picked up one of the documents, squinting at the tiny script.

"Ah," Makis said, leaning over Sophie's shoulder. "That one is from the house of your good friend Savvas Carenthus. You'll see how his family uses a loophole in imperial law to register their southern vineyards as abbeys. A neat trick."

Sophie let out a long breath. Sacrilege alongside subterfuge. "Show me more," she said.

Makis did. His style of lecturing did not have the flair she remembered from lessons with Styliani, but it sufficed. He walked her through the intricate steps each senatorial house used to obscure their fortunes. They weren't the only ones, of course—nearly all wealthy Meyathans hid something from the tax collectors—but it seemed the wealthier one was, the more one could hide.

The documents spread out before them, filling more and more of the table. Sophie read of schemes to manipulate the Meyathan census and thus reduce the amount owed to the capital. The pages told of complex inheritance webs that kept vast fortunes just out of the tax collector's reach, and more straightforward methods like placing silver reserves on board foreign ships where imperial agents had no jurisdiction.

She went through two cups of tea, and there was still more. Perhaps it had no end. Meyatha was as wealthy as it had ever been, and yet it was crumbling because that wealth lay locked away behind a fortress of bent laws.

Sophie put down her empty cup. And it would always be that way, even if Demetra produced a miracle and put Sophie on the Falcon Throne. This creeping death was older than Sophie. It was older than her father. He had tried to halt it, but his efforts were thwarted at every turn. Even Sophie's grandmother hadn't stopped it, not with all her fearsome steel. With the many compromises Sophie would need just to gain the throne, she had no chance.

Makis paused in the middle of explaining some new scheme of misrepresenting livestock as wild herds. "Sophie, is something wrong?"

"They're just going to keep doing it, Makis," she said. "Until the empire collapses around their ears, and then they'll wonder why."

"I suspect so," Makis said.

It wasn't just Sophie's own death staring at her from these documents. Even if she somehow convinced Fryni and the others to flee, how long would the abbey last as Meyatha crumbled and its enemies rushed in from all sides? And if Savvas or Demetra kept the wolves from the door for now, how long could it possibly go on? All the teeming life of Heratia had perhaps a generation or two left. The rest of the empire wouldn't last much longer.

"Someone needs to stop it," Sophie said, her hands clenched at her sides. She had danced to the Senate's tune even as it devoured the marrow of her empire. "*I* have to stop it." There was no one else. If she died now or returned to exile, it would be the ultimate betrayal of her people.

Makis nodded, tugging a strand of his beard. "No argument from me. It's the how that's the sticking point."

"Tell Faidra I need to meet with her," Sophie said. "Tell her it's urgent." She had no plan yet, only a certainty that she could not save Meyatha by begging for the Senate's confirmation as Demetra advocated. She would need to force their hand. With so many soldiers sent to hold off the Skaldre, it might be possible.

"It'll take time, assuming she agrees," Makis said. "Faidra's even deeper underground than normal with all the senators clamoring for her head."

Sophie smiled a tired smile. "I know the feeling. Do what you can, and hurry."

***

When Makis was safely away, Sophie gathered her acolytes together in the chapel, their faces lit only by the dancing flames of her candelabra. The familiar darkness and the shifting wall murals soothed Sophie's nerves. She walked in the Mother's shadow.

"A bit early for evening prayers, isn't it?" one of the acolytes asked.

"Maybe we're in trouble because Fryni lazed about reading poetry," another said. Several others giggled.

"It was only a few verses," Fryni said, but her smile showed even in the candlelight. She turned to Sophie. "We're here for you, whatever you need."

Sophie smiled in return. "I'm glad, because I need you to take two others with you back to the abbey with and—"

"Back to the abbey?" Fryni interrupted. "No, I won't run away when you're in danger!"

Several others murmured agreement.

Sophie held up her hands. "If I might finish, I need you to assemble as much of the militia as you can and return here with all speed." The abbey's acolytes formed the core of Gray Falls' militia, but in times of need, every family in the province had pledged at least one youth. It was a fighting force some two hundred strong, each of them trained and armed for war. Sophie would need every loyal spear to have any hope.

Some of the indignance faded from Fryni's shadowed expression. "Still," she said. "If that bastard Savvas tries something, I should be here to protect you."

"Alkestis will see to my safety," Sophie said. "I need you to get past whatever patrols Savvas has put in place outside the city." It was the logical move for any general preparing to seize power, preventing enemies from sending messages past the walls. She had called her acolytes to the chapel because it was the least likely place for them to be overheard. Better not to risk the loyalty of Demetra's soldiers and servants.

Fryni stood straighter. "I understand, Sister Sophie. We'll run circles around Carenthus's goons." She glanced at the other acolytes. "Anna, Evi, you feel up to a run back home?"

Both acolytes nodded their affirmation. Anna, her arm still in a sling from Tallirod, grinned. "Don't worry, Sister Sophie, we'll make better time than on the way out here without a caravan or a senator's carriage to slow us down."

Evi let out an exaggerated groan and held her sides. "And here I was getting lazy and indolent in a beautiful palace." The other acolytes laughed, surrounding their sisters and wishing them good fortune.

Fryni wrapped her arms around Sophie and squeezed. "Luna keep you in her shadow and Sol light your way. Stay safe until I get back."

Sophie returned the embrace. She wished she could promise that she'd be fine while Fryni was gone, but even at a fast march, it was a long journey to the abbey and then back. Anything could happen in that time.

***

Demetra returned to the palace just as the sun dipped down to the western horizon, long after Fryni, Anna, and Evi had gathered their supplies and departed. The speaker's pace was slow and deliberate as she entered Sophie's chamber, sweat stains showing on her robe. She sank down into the room's only chair and let out a long groan. "Day long sessions aren't meant for a senator of my age," she said.

Sophie doubted the Senate ever met for long when they weren't deciding who would sit on the Falcon Throne. So much time spent in governance would mean less time for enriching themselves. "And the results?"

"They were ready to confirm Savvas today," Demetra said. "Ariadne pushed hard for it, all dressed up with her red band as if Sol couldn't see her traitor's heart." She took a deep breath. "I convinced them to wait until next Sol's Day. That's the traditional time for confirming a new empero."

"A week isn't much time," Sophie said. Fryni would need eight days at the very least to reach the abbey and return. Longer, likely. But they couldn't afford to wait. Sophie paused. The next part required delicate handling; she still needed Demetra on her side. "What do you think we can do to change their votes in that time?"

Demetra looked at Sophie, opened her mouth, closed it, then sighed. "I'm not sure, but I will think of something."

"You said you wanted me on the throne," Sophie said. "That it was vital for the empire's survival. Do you still want me there?"

Demetra's eyebrows rose. "Of course I do. Why else did I defend you for hours to a Senate that sees you as chaos incarnate?"

"Then we must change tactics. It doesn't matter how much we placate them, the senators will never believe that I am the empero they want. If you wish me on the Falcon Throne, we shall have to take it from them."

A scowl settled on Demetra's face. "What are you talking about? The garrison and the watch have gone over to Savvas completely. My house guard is well trained, but they would be hopelessly outnumbered, even if my few remaining allies were to reinforce them."

Demetra had objected on the grounds of practicality, not morality. That was more than Sophie had hoped for. "I don't intend a conventional battle, I mean to ally with my old comrades and stage a mass uprising. We can paralyze the city and threaten what the senatorial houses value most: their property." All of that would require Faidra's help if it were possible at all, but she'd deal with that later.

The scowl vanished from Demetra's face, replaced by a wide-eyed expression. "How can you suggest that? Did the Solstice Uprising teach you nothing?"

The words cut like a razor, but Sophie stood her ground. "I learned that the best time for an uprising is when there's no reigning empero to crush it." Let Savvas try. She had faced Irena Ironheart; she could handle him.

Demetra shook her head. "The Senate will send in all the soldiers at its disposal. Even if you somehow win, blood will run in the streets, and Heratia will burn."

"I think not," Sophie said. "Half the garrison is already out of the city to reinforce the north. If we create a threat to the Senate's southern holdings, they will send out the rest to protect their coin, and then we strike."

"Mother and Her blessed daughters," Demetra said. "How long have you planned this? No, more importantly, how do we create a threat in the south? Do you have some army I don't know about?"

Sophie kept her voice neutral, though Demetra even considering the idea made her want to shout with triumph. The most difficult parts were still ahead. "For that, we must speak with Constantia de Beltane."

Chapter 13

Once it was clear that Demetra would not quit the cause over Constantia's inclusion, Sophie dispatched a message to the Gallian's home requesting an urgent meeting. At Demetra's insistence, the message also contained a stipulation that they meet on neutral ground.

"Everything I said about her before is still true," Demetra said. "Now that she knows your true standing, if you go into her home, you might not come out again except to be sold to Savvas."

Sophie agreed, though it rankled her to make a demand of Constantia when the merchant already hadn't received the Falcon Piers berths that Sophie had promised. The response came quickly, written in Constantia's flowing hand.

You have no shortage of surprises, most esteemed Sophie. Very well, I shall be at Senica Cathedral two hours past sunset for Luna's hymns. Be on time if you wish a meeting; I shall not wait for you.

Below the message, a different hand had scribbled the number of a private box at the cathedral.

"Typical," Demetra said after Sophie read the letter aloud. "Never misses a chance to show off her wealth, that one."

Sophie glanced at the speaker's fine robes but did not comment. Outside, the last of the sun's orb passed below the horizon. "We must move quickly."

Sophie's plain tunic and trousers would see them thrown out of Senica's private boxes, so she shrugged on the deep-blue gown that had seen her through one harrowing meeting already. It was not in the style for an evening out, but it would suffice. She skipped the net of jewels and the purple sash, taking her black shawl instead. If she couldn't wear her sacred black in Senica, where could she?

They traveled from the palace in Demetra's carriage. Sophie would have preferred to walk, but, once again, appearances took priority. Fortunately traffic was light so late in the evening, and they reached the great dome of Senica Cathedral before Constantia's deadline expired. Inside, a priest wearing luxurious robes led them away from the main entrance and up a winding set of marble stairs.

The interior of Senica was cavernous, with room for thousands of common worshippers on the floor below the private boxes. The dome rose above them all, inset with star-cut pieces of glass that twinkled in the low candlelight. In a city where smoke from the foundries often obscured the sky, it was the best chance many had to look upon the starry Void.

As Sophie and Demetra reached the upper level, the soft tones of Luna's choir drifted in through unoccupied boxes. The words were of loss and responsibility, of Luna's separation from her sister so she and her starry children could guide lost souls at night. The fine harmony could only mean trained professionals. In Gray Falls, every acolyte sang in the choir, and enthusiasm was the best they ever hoped for.

Finally they reached Constantia's box, where two guards gestured them inside. Constantia was alone, head tilted to one side as the choir reached a crescendo. She wore a gown of golds and reds, with a cluster of black diamonds around her neck on a woven chain and her dark hair in elaborate braids. She had the perfect lines of a statue carved by masters. Sophie tried not to stare.

The hymn faded past its crescendo, and the citizens gathered below lifted their faces to the starry ceiling.

Constantia turned to face Sophie and Demetra. "This cathedral is a triumph of Meyatha, isn't it?" she said. "Nothing like it anywhere else on the continent. Of course"—she swept a hand over the lip of her box toward gilded statues of the Mother and Her blessed daughters on the cathedral floor—"some of this grandeur came from Gallia, back when the empire could command us." She grinned. "No more, I'm afraid."

Demetra glowered. "Is posturing the style in Gallia this season?"

Constantia continued as if she had not heard the speaker. "I must admit," she said, "I did not expect to see either of you again except as a spectator at your execution." She wagged a finger at Sophie. "Impolite of you to promise me something that wasn't yours to give."

Sophie bowed. "I will honor our contract as soon as I am able." She had no time or patience for any sparring. "But to grant you berths on the Falcon Piers, I must be confirmed as empero of Meyatha, and to do that I need your help once again."

"Mother and Her blessed daughters," Constantia said with a chuckle. "The audacity of you. You've come here just to ask that I throw more good money away?"

Sophie lifted her head and met Constantia's gaze, unblinking. "I ask you to invest. You will have profits aplenty, and if my head rolls down the palace steps, do you really think someone with Savvas's antiforeigner stance will be friendly to your business dealings in Meyatha?"

Constantia sighed. "Always straight to the point with you." She leaned forward. "Very well, what is this help you need from me?"

This was the moment then. "You will send word to Gallia for mercenary companies to sail upriver and threaten senatorial holdings in the southern interior."

Demetra made a strangled gasp, but Sophie kept on. "With Taisa's death and the Skaldre in the north, the southern provinces are lightly garrisoned. The Senate will panic and send more troops out of the city to protect their interests. When Heratia is empty, my forces will seize control."

A wide grin revealed Constantia's teeth. "I have not yet seen the beginnings of your audacity. What an empero you will make, assuming we do not all die just for speaking of this."

Demetra's expression was back to blank neutrality. Her voice was calm. "If Gallia is not strong enough to meet the empero's request, say so."

Sophie nodded in acknowledgment of the words, the gesture inadequate to express her gratitude. Asking Constantia for help had to gall Demetra, yet the speaker did her part to goad the Gallian into acceptance.

Constantia's eyes narrowed. "It will not be cheap. You ask that I mobilize a substantial force on short notice, and it sounds as though you do not actually wish them pillaging through southern Meyatha. All of that requires gold."

"You shall be paid double whatever it costs you," Sophie said. It was not the sort of expenditure she wished to start her reign with, especially since Constantia would almost certainly pad the ledger, but time was short. Demetra's grip tightened on the armrests of her chair, but she stayed silent.

The Gallian nodded. "A start, but not enough. To seal this bargain, I will have a voice in your new Meyatha, a way to make sure both my interests and Gallia's interests are protected."

Sophie frowned, not understanding. "Do you mean to be my adviser? I would welcome the counsel, but I don't see how you benefit."

"No, dear Sophie," Constantia said. She bared her teeth. "I mean to have the Beltane family's old Senate seat, granted to me with all privileges due the office."

The demand broke Demetra's silence. "Is there no end to your ambition, your greed?"

Constantia touched the cluster of diamonds around her neck. "If there is, I haven't found it yet." She gestured to Sophie. "What shall it be, Your Majesty?"

Sophie thought back to her history classes. The Senate seats of Gallia's elite families had been empty ever since the city broke away from Meyatha over a century previous. It was the same with all of the Free Provinces. But those seats had never been formally dissolved so far as she knew, all part of the polite fiction that the empire had let the Free Provinces go rather than fail to hold them.

"If you do this," Demetra said, "there will be a Gallian merchant lord in the heart of Meyatha. She will know our every move as soon as we do."

It was true; Constantia would not only have a wealth of information about the empire's internal workings but a vote on Meyathan law. And with most of Constantia's holdings out of reach in the Free Provinces, Sophie would have little leverage to compel her, even as empero. It was an unthinkable demand. Constantia was already wealthy, and access to the halls of imperial government would give her a formidable edge over any potential rivals. It would also infuriate the other senators, but they would have far more to rouse their anger shortly.

Constantia tapped one manicured nail on the arm of her chair. "Well, Sophie? Would you be empero or not?"

Sophie marshaled her nerve to meet the duchess's predatory gaze. "I accept your terms, on one condition." She gestured to the space around her. "You will invest a third of any profits you make in the empire in rebuilding Meyathan infrastructure. A senator should have a stake in the land over which they preside." And it would give Sophie something of Constantia's that she could reach if necessary.

Constantia smiled. "A fifth of any Meyathan profits."

"A quarter."

"Done."

Some tension left Sophie's shoulders, only to settle in the back of her mind. It was something, but Constantia would know better than anyone how to take the greatest advantage of their deal and give the least in return. She could be as bad as Savvas—or worse. But that was a mountain to climb tomorrow.

***

Demetra was silent as they left Senica Cathedral, heading back down the marble stairs and out to her waiting carriage. Crowds of darkly dressed faithful streamed out of the church and parted around the carriage like water. Their chatter nearly drowned out the speaker's voice. "This is treason. Treason in conspiracy with a foreign power."

Sophie put a hand on Demetra's shoulder and squeezed. "We do what we must for Meyatha."

"I am a traitor to everything I've worked for," Demetra went on. Her voice shook. "If I had caught anyone in such a plot during your father's reign, I'd have had them executed without a thought."

"There is still time," Sophie said. She needed Demetra; she couldn't afford to have the speaker unsure about her choices. "Tell Savvas and the Senate what I've done, and I will be dead before tomorrow's sunset."

Demetra stared at Sophie, tears glistening at the corners of her eyes. The silence hung heavy as the crowds outside cleared and the driver snapped the reins, sending the carriage into a gentle roll forward.

Finally Demetra shook her head. "No. I fought for a Meyatha where a strong Laskaris empero worked side by side with the Senate to keep the peace and protect the empire's grateful citizens. But that Meyatha doesn't exist anymore. Savvas would enslave the citizens to strengthen the Senate, and you would weaken the Senate to protect the citizens. I can only choose between you." She met Sophie's eyes. "You are all I have left, Sophie Laskaris, may the Void Mother be kind to me."

It was not a devoted oath of loyalty, but Sophie hadn't expected such a thing. "Then we must return to the palace and begin plans for the uprising." An uprising that wouldn't be possible without Faidra's help, and Faidra saw Sophie as a traitor.

Chapter 14

Sophie spent the next several days in constant awareness of how little time she could afford to lose. Constantia had sent coded letters south with the fastest couriers silver could buy, and news of the mercenary raiders might arrive at any hour. When it did, Sophie would had a narrow window to act. When the rest of Heratia's garrison marched south, it would only be a matter of time before they realized the Gallian attack was a feint. Once the garrison returned to the city, it would be too late, and Sophie didn't even know if Makis had managed to get Faidra a message.

Demetra quietly prepared her house guard for battle and laid hands on whatever supplies she could for the rest of their force that did not exist yet. After some discussion, they decided it would not be safe to bring the supplies to either the palace or Demetra's home. When fighting broke out, the Senatorial District would be firmly in enemy hands.

Instead they used several Kalgari family holdings as caches: a bakery near the Marshrun river, a tailor shop at the base of the western wall, places out of sight from prying eyes. Unfortunately even Demetra's resources could produce only a modest bounty of extra weapons and armor. With war brewing, most available arms went straight to the garrisons or field armies.

"We will have enough spears and swords to outfit a few hundred fighters," Demetra said over the supply ledger. "Anyone beyond that number will have to arm themself or make do with clubs and slings." She frowned. "And we have no heavy armor at all."

"Can your house guards spare any further equipment?" Sophie asked. She doubted Faidra's underground could afford an arsenal of their own, else their resistance would likely have been more violent these long years.

Demetra shook her head. "Not if we wish to preserve them as a fighting force. Most of their spares have already been requisitioned to replace weapons and armor lost in the field." She snorted. "It was a burden all houses were meant to share equally in defense of Meyatha, but I suspect other senators held back more than I."

They would have to depend on numbers then. Seize the city and force the Senate to surrender without a fight or be starved out inside their manors. Of course, the Senate would be led by a general who was famous for his victories in the face of a larger force. Sophie frowned. It was the last course left to them; she would see it through.

After only four days, word reached Heratia of heavily armed Free Province raiders sailing up the Silvervein into the heart of Meyatha's vineyard country. Constantia had kept her part of the bargain, and in so little time. Had she merely diverted forces intended for a real raid?

One thing went right at least: the Senate reacted as expected, dispatching most of the city's remaining garrison south. Demetra's spies reported that Savvas had disapproved of the measure, but to keep the support of his fickle allies, he'd agreed to leave Heratia protected only by an overstretched city watch and the senatorial-house guards. Hearing this gave Sophie a thrill of vindictive pleasure.

But still no word came from Faidra. Nor from Fryni, though Sophie knew she could not expect anything from her acolyte so soon. Hearing nothing of the acolytes was good; it meant Fryni had slipped through Savvas's patrols undetected. It could also mean that she'd been caught, and they hadn't bothered to bring her body back to the city.

The image of Fryni's body lying unmourned on some remote stretch of the road gripped Sophie, making her drop the map she'd been studying. She knelt and took deep, regular breaths. She wouldn't think that way. Fryni walked with the Void Mother and Her blessed daughters. Fryni would make it through; she had to.

Finally Makis returned to the palace, alone and with dark bags under his eyes. "She'll meet with you," he said. "But not here. You're to come to her this time, in a warehouse her people control by the docks."

Sophie embraced her old friend. "Thank you, Makis. Tell her I will be there tonight."

"I don't like it," Demetra said. "Bad enough to dance when a Gallian duchess plays, but now this street tough wants to order you around?"

Makis glared at the speaker. "That street tough has done more to help Meyatha than you did in fifteen years leading the Senate."

Sophie raised her hands between them. "Peace, please." She turned to Demetra. "I don't ask you to like Faidra, but recognize that without her, our plan is already over. That gives her the right to dictate a few terms."

Demetra didn't look pleased, but she raised no further objection. After Makis had left, Sophie determined she would take her nine remaining acolytes, but with staves only. No need to make Faidra feel under threat.

***

As evening came, they donned plain tunics and strode out on a circuitous route that Sophie hoped would take them to Faidra without being seen. They had timed their journey to mix in with the late-evening crowds, when it was dark enough to make proper identification difficult but before the streets emptied in the night.

The docks stayed active long after the rest of the city had retired, with strings of lanterns hung up to shed light on the workers as they moved cargo to and from the endless line of ships docking from both north and south.

A few laborers paused to glance at Sophie and her acolytes before taskmasters swooped in to drive them back to work with sharp words or the whistle of a heavy crop. Sophie winced, and Alkestis gestured some of the more hot-blooded acolytes back. Starting a confrontation here would help no one.

Sophie stayed to watch just a moment longer. In the lantern light, many of the workers bore scars of old wounds, hands and limbs gnarled after broken bones hadn't been given time to heal properly. Others were startlingly thin, a sign they didn't get enough to eat for such physically demanding work, worse than anything Sophie had seen in the capital before her exile. She had struggled for years to eliminate that look in Gray Falls, and here it was in the city at the center of the world.

"We should move on, Sister Sophie," Alkestis said.

Sophie nodded. There was nothing they could do here, not yet. Faidra's warehouse was tucked away on the dock's western side beside the Dusk Gate, far from the water and away from the teeming lines of night workers. Heavy cloth and wooden shutters covered the windows, but tiny slivers of light shone out from the edges. Muffled conversation sounded from inside.

As they approached, over a dozen figures emerged from the alleys on either side. In the moonlight, they wore loose cloaks with hoods to obscure their faces. Some carried staves or clubs; others kept their hands hidden. Alkestis and the other acolytes drew in tighter around Sophie but left their staves at their sides.

One of the strangers stepped forward. "Sophie Laskaris?"

"Yes," Sophie said. "I've come to speak with Faidra Remi."

The stranger lifted the hood off a lantern and held it up to illuminate Sophie's face. She blinked in the bright light but resisted the impulse to look away or shield her face. The stranger's own face was that of an elderly man with dark Heratian skin baked by decades in the sun, a man who'd have clear memories of the Solstice Uprising.

"It's her," the stranger said. "Let them through." He stood aside and gave a quick bow. "Mother's kindness on you, Sister Sophie. You'll need it."

The way clear, Sophie let Alkestis precede her, pushing through the warehouse doors into a haze of smoky light cast by braziers and tallow candles. The buzz of conversation ceased as the milling crowd within turned their eyes on the newcomers. There were too many to count, at least a hundred. Most were young, with skin tones ranging from the Skaldre's northern pale to Heratia's deepest brown. Nearly all had the thick build and calloused hands of those who did hard labor for a living.

At the center of the crowded room was a raised platform with two chairs. Faidra leaned back in one of them, a satisfied grin on her scarred face. The simple arrangement sparked Sophie's memory. In the uprising, when two comrades disagreed on a course of action, they would meet before as great an assembly as could be gathered and debate the point.

This wasn't the same thing, of course. In the uprising, the assembly listened to every view and weighed the options. This room was full of Faidra's people; they would likely do as she said. Faidra was the one Sophie had to convince. The rest was pageantry to remind Sophie who had stayed closer to their shared roots.

Sophie motioned to Alkestis. "Wait here while I speak with Faidra."

Alkestis eyed the crowd. "Fryni won't be pleased if something happens to you while I'm standing by the door."

"They won't hurt me," Sophie said. Not until they'd heard her out, anyway. If tension gave way to violence, her acolytes would have the best chance to escape near the main exit. Alkestis frowned, but she and the others held their positions as Sophie stepped into the crowd.

The expressions on those around her ranged from curiosity to suspicion to plain hostility. One woman spat at Sophie's feet as she passed and spoke an exaggerated "Your Majesty," which raised chuckles from several others.

Sophie clambered up onto the platform, doing her best to look dignified. Every eye in the warehouse fell on her, and she paused for a moment to center herself. "Faidra," she said with a nod. "My thanks for the chance to address you and your comrades tonight." She sat down in the chair opposite her old friend.

"We didn't expect to see you here," Faidra said. "Fine dining with the Senate didn't turn out like you hoped?" This brought more chuckles from Faidra's supporters, and a few stamped their feet.

"I hoped we could have justice without the need for another uprising," Sophie said. There was no point in telling Faidra why the senatorial dinner had gone so poorly; it would just be making excuses. She went on, "I also hoped you'd understand, even if it was a naive wish. We lost so many the first time."

Faidra's severe expression cracked for a moment. "I haven't forgotten." She shook her head. "Now you're back with us. Why?"

"Diplomacy failed," Sophie said. "Force will have its way. You've noticed there are almost no soldiers in the capital. If we seize control, bring the Senate's precious commerce to a standstill, they will have no choice but to confirm me."

A stir of mutters went through the gathered crowd. Faidra raised an eyebrow. "We, is it? And why should my people risk their lives for you?" She turned to address the crowd. "We don't want a nice empero, we want no empero at all!"

The crowd roared in agreement, clapping hands and stamping feet. Near the door, Alkestis and the other acolytes glanced around, assessing threats, but Sophie felt a surge of the old thrill. If Faidra wanted a debate, Sophie could give her one.

"If you could have overthrown the Senate on your own," Sophie said, "it would already be done. Even now that I've emptied the garrison for you, the best you can hope for is a short civil war before the Skaldre sweep out of the north and burn Meyatha to the ground."

Faidra's confident smile set in a grim line, but Sophie wasn't finished. She faced the crowd. "And that assumes you can hold the capital. If Savvas takes the Falcon Throne for himself, he will destroy the rights of citizenship and turn Heratia into his personal estate. All your problems will increase tenfold. Together, we can stop things from getting worse, and once the crisis is past, make them better."

A young woman shouted from the crowd. "Some of us are starving now, what if we can't wait that long?"

"Quite right," Sophie said. "It does no good to speak of a better world to those who will not survive to see it." She turned back to Faidra. "If you help me, we will seize and open the imperial grain stores to any who need it, no questions asked or limits imposed." Demetra would object, would point out that the grain there was to supply Heratia in case of a siege, but Sophie's city was already under siege. She would feed her people.

Some in the crowd nodded at Sophie's words. Others murmured to each other in unsure tones.

Faidra's expression softened just a touch. "And what of those with no place to sleep?"

"I will find beds for them," Sophie said.

"Even in the palace? Or will you put that burden only on others?"

Sophie gave an exaggerated shrug. "My home is in no fit state to entertain guests, but if they wish to stay, I will not bar the door." That brought a few laughs from the crowd, and fewer of the stares that fell on Sophie were overtly hostile.

The elderly man who had met Sophie outside stepped forward. "And what of the fighting itself? In the Solstice, we had weapons from the People's Chamber. Now we have clubs and a few rusty swords. Even with just the Senate's house guards, Savvas can cut us to pieces."

Sophie acknowledged him with a nod. "He speaks the truth. I will provide what weapons and armor I can, but, even so, it will be a hard fight. Our best hope is to bottle the Senate up and frighten them to the negotiating table. If that fails, I will stand beside you, and we will all face their soldiers together."

Some younger members of the crowd cheered, fists raised in the air. Perhaps Sophie had misread them. They did not simply hang on Faidra's every word; they were eager for someone, anyone, to give them a tangible course of action.

Faidra waited until the cheers faded. "The abbey hasn't dulled your oratory skills. Styliani would be pleased by that, at least." She paused for a moment. "Mother embrace her and all those we've lost."

Sophie's breath caught, and tears pricked at the corners of her eyes. "Thank you," she said, not trusting herself to say more.

"However," Faidra said. "You haven't addressed the main issue. A rule of one over many is unjust."

Sophie couldn't resist a small smile. Her old friend hadn't lost that keen sense of the matter's heart. "I do not want to rule as a tyrant, benevolent or otherwise," Sophie said. "When the throne is mine, I will restrict the Senate's power and see elections held in Meyatha once again. The People's Chamber shall be restored, and its voice will decide our future, not mine."

"And how long will that take?" someone shouted from the crowd. "Once you're gone, what's to stop another Ironheart from plunging us all back into tyranny?"

Faidra nodded. "That's the truth, Sophie. Even if you keep every promise, you cannot make the same guarantee for whoever follows you on the Falcon Throne."

No cheers this time, only quiet murmurs of agreement. Faidra was right, of course. Emperos had risen with popular support before, making radical promises on the redistribution of land or the democratizing of imperial power. Their progressive visions had rarely outlived them, as the next empero turned back to the tradition of consolidating power for themself. The Laskaris bloodline was as guilty as those that had preceded it. Sophie took a long breath. There was only one choice in the Mother's eyes.

"If you support me," she said, "I will be the last empero of Meyatha. I will bear no children, I will adopt no heirs. The Laskaris line will end with me." Sophie's heart sank even as she said it. There would be no redemption for her family. They had been murdered by their enemies, and now future generations would only know them as tyrants. Once she was gone, Sophie had little doubt that every glass statue commemorating their lives would be shattered. But they were already dead, down to the last. She just had to let them go. She locked eyes with Faidra. "That is the most I can offer. Is it satisfactory?"

Faidra was quiet for a moment, and when she spoke, her voice had a slight hitch to it. "That is the rebel heir that I remember." She swept a hand over the crowd. "But my voice is not important. What say you, friends and comrades? Do we rise with the last empero?"

The crowd roared in response, stamping their feet hard enough to shake the warehouse. A chant started somewhere and spread until it was on every lip: "Rise, rise, rise!"

Faidra clasped Sophie's arm and held it tight. In Sophie's ear, she said, "A second uprising is yours, Sophie. Mother's kindness on us all."

Chapter 15

The plan was to gather their forces just before sunrise, but Sophie's restless thoughts woke her early. It left her nothing to do but watch the stars and contemplate what she had set in motion: a second uprising, one that could end in even greater disaster than the first. Speed would be essential. They had to force Savvas and the Senate's capitulation within days at most, or Heratia's garrison would return and crush any uprising.

Three targets were essential to take in the opening hours. First the docks, Heratia's economic heart. Without the docks in their hands, the rebels would have little leverage over senatorial finances, and Savvas could easily call in reinforcements from across Godstep Lake. At least taking the docks would be relatively easy, as they were the center of Faidra's strength in the city. Next the Dawn Gate, to prevent the Senate from fleeing the city. Faidra would lead that operation herself. If the Dawn Gate fell, the Senate would escape, and the rebellion would become a civil war.

Finally they needed the imperial grain stores. That was Sophie's task, and she did not relish it. The city watch's headquarters was just down the street, and with the garrison depleted, it represented the largest concentration of troops in Heratia. The watch had stations across the city, but they always kept their largest force near grain stores.

Sophie was only glad that the stores themselves were too large to fit inside the watch's walled compound. She looked at the acolytes sleeping around her. More than anything she wanted to keep them safe, but soon she would lead them into battle against Meyathan legionnaires. There was no other way. Without the grain, the rebellion could never hope to attract Heratia's hungry poor to its banner or even feed itself.

Demetra's task would be to buy the uprising time. While they seized critical areas of Heratia, the speaker would keep Savvas and his allies bottled up in the Senatorial District. To accomplish the task she had her own house guards plus those of a select few senators she trusted enough to recruit. They would be outnumbered, but with surprise, they might keep the rest of the Senate from combining their forces.

At last the hour before dawn arrived. Sophie and her acolytes donned their chain mail, picked up their spears, and quietly took their leave of the palace. Sophie paused for just a moment in the barely repaired entrance hall. The palace was part of a life she had never wanted to return to. Leaving it now, perhaps for the last time, felt like losing that final part of herself that still called it home. She squared her shoulders and kept walking.

Demetra joined them at the palace gates, dressed in steel scales and escorted by a handful of her most trusted retainers while her house guards assembled further away from prying eyes. They left the Senatorial District behind and took back streets to a bakery that was one of their makeshift supply depots. Faidra and some of her people were already there, opening the bakery's rear doors and distributing their limited supply of arms and armor.

Faidra hefted a blacksmith's hammer and a wooden shield. "Weapons are nearly all handed out," she said. "It would be helpful if there were more, but then it wouldn't feel like old times."

Sophie put on a mock serious expression. "We could always go unarmed. To give Savvas a sporting chance."

They both laughed, and, for just a moment, the twenty-three-year chasm between them vanished.

Demetra cleared her throat, voice impatient. "Whenever you're both ready."

Faidra's eyes locked on Demetra. "Why, Speaker Demetra Kalgari. I honestly didn't think you'd have the nerve to join us."

Demetra checked her heavy shortsword, then slid the weapon back into its sheath. "I fight for House Laskaris," she said. "Not for you or your rabble."

Faidra's smile bared her teeth. "So long as we know where we both stand."

Sophie stepped forward before the argument could go any further. "Any difficulties with the watch?"

"Not yet," Faidra said. "They're clustered in their stations like we expected, with the biggest group around the grain." She spat. "They never much cared for night patrol. If you're fast, you can capture the stores before troops in the outlying stations respond." More of her people emerged from alleys and stepped out of deep shadows. "My best fighters are ready to hold the Dawn Gate. We'll have Savvas surrounded before he knows what's happening, and I've sent reserves to seize the docks."

Demetra tsked. "Savvas is Meyatha's greatest general, he's almost certainly planned for this."

"Then we shall put his plans to the test," Sophie said. It was too late for second-guessing now. She clasped Faidra by the shoulders. "Sol's grace on you."

Faidra returned the gesture. "And on you."

The rebel leader left to join her troops, motioning them to head east toward the Dawn Gate.

Demetra turned to leave and hesitated, gazing off toward the center of the city and the waiting grain stores. Her mouth set in a frown. "Heratia's surplus took years to build," the speaker said. "If you're successful, we shall give it away in days, if that."

Sophie patted the speaker's armored shoulder. "A city works better when it is well-fed. We shall find a way to replenish the stores."

"We shall have to," Demetra said. She turned to go, but Sophie kept her hand on the speaker's shoulder.

"Sol watch over you as well," Sophie said. "I wouldn't care to take the throne without you as my speaker."

Demetra's expression shifted to surprise. "I... I assumed you would have little use for me. Not among your old comrades and their revolutionary spirit."

Sophie shook her head. "Nothing we're about to do would be possible without you, Demetra." Sophie meant it. The speaker's politics had many shortcomings, but she cared for Meyatha with undeniable fervor.

"Then I will see you crowned this day," Demetra said, her voice thick. "Your Majesty." With a deep bow, she left to rendezvous with her force of house guards in the Senatorial District.

Sophie focused on her own task. With dawn cresting the horizon, she led her acolytes and their contingent toward the grain stores at the city's center. She and the other leaders had arranged signal-horn patterns for basic commands: advance, retreat, ambush, surrender, and a handful of other contingencies. It wasn't fine control, but it was a system that had served Meyatha well for all its history. Their strategy had been crafted with the lessons learned twenty-three years ago. It would work this time; it had to.

Alkestis looked back over the hundreds of citizens that marched with them, formed into ordered ranks like a military column. "Fryni will be disappointed she missed this. Sol's mercy, I didn't expect so many people would answer your call on such little notice."

"Faidra's call more than mine," Sophie said. "But this is something that's been bubbling under the surface for years, maybe as far back as the Solstice Uprising." More citizens emerged from side streets to join them, clubs and staves in hand. "I only hope Savvas and his allies can be made to see reason. If they fight to the last, the city will drown in blood."

***

The sun was an hour higher in the sky as they advanced. The imperial grain stores were a cluster of brick warehouses in Heratia's central district, the spur of land between the Marshrun and Silvervein rivers. Beside the grain stores, the thick walls of the watch's headquarters rose, a small fortress in the heart of Heratia. Sophie thanked the Mother that they didn't have to lay siege to it. The watch would have to come out if they wished to protect the grain stores, and that battle would be difficult enough.

It being still early in the morning, the streets were mostly clear as Sophie's force approached the intersection before the watch's fortress. She positioned herself and her remaining acolytes at the rebel formation's vanguard, with the most heavily armed of Faidra's rebels alongside them. Those with slings or a rare bow she sent up to the roofs of nearby buildings. The rest she ordered down side streets. They were lightly armed, but, even so, they might attack from the flanks and cause chaos. She gave them all instructions not to attack without her signal. She would not give up the chance to prevail through diplomacy.

The rest of Sophie's force emerged from side streets, assembling on the main avenue before the fortress. Sentries in the fortress blew signal horns as they spotted the rebels drawing near. Moments later the watch's gates swung open, and a column of armored soldiers emerged, all bearing the bronze shield-crest. They formed up in the wide intersection that bordered both their fortress and the grain stores, shields locked together and spears at the ready. Sophie made a rough count of the enemy by Sol's rising light. She had greater numbers, but the watch was better armed and better trained. This would be a hard fight, and it was only the first of many.

A few curious citizens looked out of doors and windows, their eyes flicking between the watch and the rebels closing in. Sophie signaled a halt. The two sides stared at each other, separated by only a few dozen yards. Sophie's breath caught, and she forced herself to let it out, breathing slowly and evenly. The Solstice Uprising had started this way, except they had confronted the watch outside the Senate's Grand Forum rather than the grain stores. This time she knew what was really important.

An officer stepped forward from the watch's ranks, tall and broad shouldered, with gold filigree decorating her breastplate and the rearing stallion of House Carenthus emblazoned on her shield. "Clear this street at once!" she shouted. "This is imperial property, your disrespect will not be tolerated."

Sophie inhaled so she could match the officer's volume. "I am Sophie Laskaris, daughter of Mihail, sister of Taisa, empero of Meyatha." She extended a hand to the forces gathered around her. "These are loyal citizens of my empire." She pointed one finger toward the officer. "These stores are mine, this city is mine." If the watch believed her, perhaps they could yet avoid bloodshed. "Stand aside."

A few of the guards muttered to each other. The officer silenced them by snapping her spear against her shield. "Don't listen to her. She hasn't been confirmed, she's just a rebel looking to take what isn't hers." She aimed her spear at Sophie. "Clear these streets or you will die on them."

Sophie stared the officer down. So much for avoiding bloodshed. More faces appeared at windows and doorways, gaping out at the two sides preparing for battle.

Sophie turned to address the crowd instead of the watch. "She's right," Sophie called out as loudly as she could. "I have not been confirmed by the Senate. I come here with a higher authority: the Mother's justice.

"Some of you are old enough to remember the Solstice Uprising," Sophie went on. "We promised you an end to the system that ground you down until you had nothing left to give. We failed."

Murmurs passed through the gathering onlookers. Alkestis gave Sophie a questioning look.

Sophie raised her voice once more. "I am here before you not to make more promises, but to ask for your help. Savvas Carenthus wishes to destroy your rights of citizenship, and Thane Eidsson marches from the north to see Meyatha burn. Even as empero, I cannot stop them alone."

The watch soldiers tensed, but the crowd listened, the many faces of Heratia's citizenry looking on with hard expressions.

Sophie drew in a final breath. "If you will join me, lend me your strength, then we shall face these dangers. We shall triumph over them in the name of all Meyatha." She raised her spear toward the grain stores. "And our first act shall be to open these stores to any who need them."

That brought a cheer from the crowd and a snarl from the watch officer.

"Spears ready!" the officer shouted. The soldiers extended their spears. The rebels braced to meet the charge. The watch officer raised her hand to signal the attack.

Sophie set her own spear. There was nothing else for it. "Loose!" she shouted. Her slingers and archers let fly a volley just as the watch rushed forward. Nearly all the arrows and stones deflected off the watch's armor, lacking the power or precise aim to break through.

The watch's charge crashed into Sophie's line. Shield smashed against shield, and spearpoints thrust through the gaps, probing for vulnerable flesh. Sophie dug her feet in and leaned forward into her shield. The watch had an entire column of professional soldiers; she had only a thin line of rebels and acolytes with the weapons to hold the enemy back.

More rebels flooded in from side streets to attack the watch's flanks, but these rebels were armed only with clubs and homemade spears. The outnumbered watch rebuffed the charge with bloody spear thrusts, sending the first wave of rebels sprawling back in panic.

Sophie thrust overhand with her spear, aiming for a seam in her enemy's armor, but her strike only glanced to one side. She put all her strength into keeping her shield in place. They had to hold the line long enough for her flanking troops to regroup and attack again. It was their only chance.

A signal horn blew from the east in a pattern Sophie didn't recognize. It wasn't one of the signals she had arranged with Faidra and Demetra.

The watch commander raised her voice. "Back," she shouted. "Fall back!"

As a single unit, the watch soldiers retreated, ending the shoving match and opening space between the shield walls. Many of the rebels cheered and shouted insults after the retreating watch, convinced they had sent the enemy running. But unease slithered up Sophie's spine. The watch had been in a strong position. Why had a signal called them to retreat?

The watch soldiers kept moving, heading past their fortress and north toward one of the bridges over the Silvervein.

Alkestis stared after the soldiers in disbelief. "Their position was still secure, what are they doing?"

Sophie traced the watch's course in her mind. The bridge would take the watch soldiers east, toward the Senatorial District. "Savvas is consolidating his soldiers," she said. "Though I don't know for what."

"To outflank Demetra's forces?" Alkestis asked. "If she is doing well against Savvas, he might need the extra help."

"Possibly," Sophie said. She shook her head. "But I don't believe so. If Demetra is already winning that battle, the watch won't arrive in time to be of any use."

"Do we pursue?" Alkestis asked.

Sophie considered it. Chasing down the watch soldiers might disrupt Savvas's plan, but it would also mean leaving the grain stores behind, and as long as the enemy was retreating, there was still a chance Sophie could negotiate a peaceful end to this.

"No," Sophie said. "Secure the stores." She called to the still-gathering crowd. "Let it be known, all who need grain may have it, by the order of Empero Sophie."

That brought a full-throated cheer from the crowd. Many came forward, baskets and sacks in hand, while others ran to spread the word. Alkestis took charge of distribution, and before long people were thronging in from every direction, chasing the rumor of free grain.

The stores were extensive, enough to feed all of Gray Falls for a half a decade, but even that did not seem like so much in the face of Heratia's lean masses. At first she feared the hungry citizens would stampede, but each waited their turn. Watching the orderly Heratians take their measure of grain, Sophie smiled. Even if all else failed, more of her people would eat this night than the one before. That was something.

Signal horns sounded from the north and east, prearranged patterns to indicate Faidra's people had control of the docks and the Dawn Gate. A runner arrived from the east to deliver more detailed news: the docks had fallen with relative ease, and while the watch had made a few probing attacks at the Dawn Gates, nothing substantial had come from the Senatorial District where Demetra's forces waited.

"And we've brought piles of rubble to block the gate," the runner said. "Even if they take it, they'll be hours getting it open."

Sophie didn't like it. Savvas must have known what was happening by now; where was his response?

Sophie paced beside Alkestis as the hours wore on. More and more citizens arrived at the grain stores, the crowd swelling until it seemed the entire city had converged on them. Some were impatient, sure that if they didn't get to the grain now, it would all be gone. But a group of Faidra's people calmed them, and the orderly distribution continued without incident.

"It's been too long," Sophie finally said. "I need to meet with Faidra, find out what Savvas is—"

A flurry of frantic signal horns interrupted her from the east. They overlapped, so Sophie couldn't tell if they were from her people or not. She thought she heard the signal for an enemy attack, but she couldn't be sure.

"To arms, my sisters," Sophie called. "We must go, something is very wrong."

Alkestis and the other acolytes let waiting volunteers take their places distributing grain and fell into step beside Sophie. More signal horns sounded from the east, and this time Sophie clearly heard the pattern for retreat. Somewhere in the city, her soldiers were being overwhelmed.

On the bridge over the Silvervein, a young man raced toward them, blood streaming from a gash in his temple. "Empero," he gasped. "Empero Sophie, they need you!"

"Peace," Sophie said, steadying the young man as Alkestis wrapped a bandage around his forehead. He couldn't be any older than Fryni. Was it Sophie's destiny to put children in danger? "Tell me what has happened."

The youth gulped more air. "We assembled with Speaker Kalgari to block the Senatorial District, but General Carenthus found a way to outflank us. We tried to retreat, but his soldiers were everywhere. The speaker led a breakout." He shuddered. "But most of us didn't make it."

Sophie put her hand over the young soldier's. "You're safe now, and your service to the empire is noted. Where are Savvas and the speaker now?"

The youth held Sophie's hand in a vice grip. "After they broke us, Savvas and his soldiers left the Senatorial District through its north gate. They have wagons with them, dozens, full of the senators' families and their gold. Last I saw the speaker, she was shadowing the enemy, but they've gotten reinforcements from the watch, so I don't know what she can do."

Sophie glanced at Alkestis. The district's north gate meant Savvas wasn't taking the shortest route out of the city toward the Dawn Gate, where Faidra's best-equipped rebels were fortified and waiting to contain him.

"The docks," Alkestis said.

Sophie nodded as the pieces clicked into place. Savvas was leading the Senate on a break toward Heratia's docks with all the wealth they could carry. It was further away, but it was also the most lightly protected of the rebellion's objectives, and the ships there would allow the senators to carry away far more of their wealth than if they'd escaped by land.

A less-experienced commander would have stayed to fight, but Sophie had studied Savvas's tactics. He was no doubt thinking that if the senatorial families were out of the city, he could launch a counterattack without even the barest restraint that Irena Ironheart had shown during the Solstice Uprising. Heratia would be a charred ruin before he finished with it. Demetra was right; he had planned for this.

Sophie turned back to the messenger. "Where is Faidra Remi?"

"She says to meet her on Luna's Hill," the youth said. "If you don't get there soon, she'll join up with the speaker and they'll try to stop General Carenthus together."

Sophie nodded. "Your task is finished. Go to the grain stores, they will tend your wound there."

The youth bowed. "Mother's kindness on Your Majesty."

Alkestis grimaced. "If the reports are accurate, then Savvas has already defeated our best soldiers." She looked at the acolytes and the Heratian citizens gathered behind them. "I do not see how we can stop him."

"We'll find a way," Sophie said. "We have to. I will not let everything we've done today be in vain." How she was going to do that, only the Void Mother knew.

Chapter 16

There was only one place nearby where Sophie could get a good view of the docks: Luna's Hill. It was the highest point in Heratia's central district. It was also where she had surrendered the uprising to Irena Ironheart twenty-three years ago, where Sophie had earned Taisa's scornful hatred and given up any chance of helping the people of Meyatha.

The hilltop was mostly as Sophie remembered it, open ground with a handful of trees for shade and a freestanding mosaic of the goddess Luna scattering her starry children into the night sky. The weeds around the mosaic's base were overgrown, but the largest change was a bronze statue of a falcon closing its talons around a black sunburst. A monument to Empero Irena crushing the Solstice Uprising.

Sophie glared at the statue, which was nearly as tall as she was. An urge bubbled up to cast the hunk of metal off the hill, but Sophie resisted. The statue was bronze and stone; moving it would take hours, and she had more immediate problems.

She stepped around the statue and mosaic and led her acolytes to the hill's crest. It offered a clear overlook of the city's streets, from the docks in the north to the Senatorial District in the southeast. Faidra and Demetra were already there, along with a motley collection of surviving house guards and Heratian revolutionaries. The speaker herself was uninjured, though her armor bore the scratches and dents of heavy fighting.

"Your Majesty," Demetra said, her eyes downcast. "My house guards fought like lions, but I did not see Savvas's trap until it was too late. We pushed him back into the Senatorial District, but he hid a flanking detachment inside a temple that we didn't check thoroughly enough. Mother abandoned me, I should have expected it."

"We cannot predict war," Sophie said. She needed the speaker at her best, not agonizing over a defeat. "We can only accept what fortune hands us and fight on."

Demetra nodded. "Then look there." She pointed down to the city below them, where a long line of wagons still snaked out of the district's northern gate, protected by a column of at least two thousand heavily armored house guards. "Savvas is still on the move, but he'll be at the docks soon."

Faidra turned to Sophie, her face grim. "This is the real test," she said. "My people are trying to slow them down, but they can't hold out for long."

The convoy had already broken through one barricade, and Sophie's eyes widened in horror as the frontline of elite house guards reached a second, swarming over the makeshift defense and falling on the rebels. The untrained defenders had no chance against their enemy's practiced attacks. Some broke and ran at the first contact; others held their ground and were cut down.

Bands of rebels regrouped behind the column, and though there were many, they were uncoordinated, only able to harass the senatorial rear guard. Even then, the lightly armored rebels paid a dear price in blood every time they attacked. Sophie's throat constricted. How many had already died?

Faidra's voice cut into Sophie's grief. "They're on Triumph Causeway now," the rebel leader said. "The buildings there are all stone, we should send people up to the roofs to drop burning pitch on their wagons."

"I agree," Demetra said. The speaker and Faidra exchanged surprised looks before Demetra went on, "It's our best chance to stop them."

Sophie recoiled at the idea. Those wagons held children and elderly. Desperate as they were, it couldn't come to that. "There must be another way," she said.

Demetra looked at Sophie with a hard expression. "If Savvas escapes, he can gather the imperial army and set a noose around Heratia's neck. We must stop him or what Irena Ironheart did on the Solstice will seem like a mercy."

"I know that," Sophie said. She knew it better than most. "But if their wagons burn, they may realize it's best to leave them behind. We only have the time we do because they're trying to take their wealth with them."

"Then what do you suggest?" Faidra asked. "We can't let them reach the docks."

Sophie squinted against the nearly overhead sun, measuring the distance Savvas's column had yet to travel on the long Triumph Causeway. Maybe if she had Fryni and all of the Gray Falls militia they could set up a shield wall that would halt the column's advance, but for all the bravery of Faidra's rebels, they would never stand up to Savvas's disciplined soldiers in open battle.

"We'll circle around and hold them at the Coin Gate," she said. "It's the closest entry to the docks that can accommodate those wagons." The Coin Gate was designed to stop attacks from Godstep Lake to the north, not to bottle up an enemy inside the city, but it was their best chance. It had battlements and strong walls; even Savvas's elite guards would struggle to scale it.

Sophie went on, "Send harriers to the roofs with weighted lines to tangle in the wagon wheels. That will slow them down at least. Have all of our people in the northern districts converge at the harbor. Everyone else, assemble behind Savvas on Triumph Causeway. If we can hold him at the gate, he'll be surrounded."

It was the most questionable 'if' Sophie could remember uttering, but there was no other hope.

Faidra passed the orders along, but Sophie was already moving. Her acolytes were few in number, and they could do the most good at a choke point like the Coin Gate. They had to reach it before Savvas if there were to be any hope of preventing a breakthrough.

***

They ran a circuitous route toward the docks, avoiding Triumph Causeway by crossing over the Marshrun river into western Heratia. Heratians rallied to them on the way, some with the makeshift weapons and armor of Faidra's rebels, others dressed for long hours of labor as if they had planned for this to be any other day. A few even wore the finer linens of artisans and intellectuals, classes of Heratia's population far outside Faidra's normal support base.

Combined with the forces already at the docks, Sophie estimated they would outnumber Savvas two to one. Even that would never be enough, not with the house guards' great advantages in training and equipment. But with the harbor district's interior walls to stand upon, they at least had a chance. Finally they crossed into the docks at one of the smaller western gates. A rebel lookout reported that despite their longer route, they had arrived ahead of Savvas's column, slowed as it was by treasure-laden wagons.

Sophie led her force toward the Coin Gate, approaching from the harbor side. The wall on either side of the gate sectioned the docks off from the rest of the city, crossing the Marshrun and Silvervein rivers where they flowed south out of Godstep Lake. Both rivers were wide enough to carry the empire's vital trade ships. The Marshrun flowed away to the southwest, far away from Savvas's force, but the Silvervein ran southeast, its near bank just a few dozen strides from the gate itself.

Sophie breathed a sigh of relief when she saw the heavy iron grates had been lowered into the rivers to block anyone from entering by water. That path, at least, was secure. Nearby, the black marble statue of Empero Hera the Great stood over them, looking down on the berth where Sophie had first stepped into the city.

A cluster of rebels stood before the Coin Gate, but instead of reinforcing the gate, they argued in raised voices. "—suicide to defend here," one was saying as Sophie approached. "The gate won't hold!"

Sophie turned to the gate itself and saw what they meant. The heavy timbers were stained with mold and cracked through in a dozen places, held up only by rusted iron bolts. The wind shifted, bringing rot and mildew with it. How long since anyone had tested it? How long since anyone had simply tried to close it? Even here Heratia's slow starvation showed. As if that weren't enough, the Coin Gate was built to defend against attacks from the harbor. The narrow stairs to the battlements were on the landward side, where Savvas would make his attack. They would need to be blocked.

"We must make our stand here," she said. The argument ceased as the rebels turned to her. "There is nowhere else. If the gate will not serve us, then we make our own barricade." Sophie swept her arm over the gathered rebels, then pointed at Hera's statue. "All of you, pull that down across the gate. Once that's done, bring up wagons, crates, anything we can pile up."

The rebels stared at her. One of them spoke up. "The founder's statue? We can't just knock it down."

Sophie breathed out in exasperation. She put on the voice she used for leading sermons at the abbey. "I am the last Laskaris alive, I absolve you. Now bring it down!"

The rebels jumped to obey, looping rope around the statue's base and forming teams to pull it into position. Thankfully the gates opened into the docks, so Savvas wouldn't be able to pull them open, and the wall on either side was in better condition than the gate itself.

Sophie turned to Faidra and Demetra. "We need a force on the battlements," Sophie said. "To stop them climbing over that way."

Faidra nodded. "Already done." She waved behind her to where dozens of rebels rushed toward the gate with ladders carried between them. They placed them against the wall to one side and scrambled up. Their fellows on the ground brought them ropes to haul up wooden planks and bags of rubble so the landward-facing stairs might be blocked. More rebels ran down the walls in either direction, spreading out so they could at least raise an alarm if Savvas tried to cross somewhere else.

Sophie pointed to her acolytes. "Calliope, Alkestis, up the battlements with them to watch for the enemy." Calliope had the sharpest eyes, and Alkestis knew Heratia's streets better than anyone else from Gray Falls. The acolytes snapped to obey.

The other rebels finished tying ropes to Hera the Great's statue. They pulled, and the marble base ground over the cobblestones, the statue turning as it moved until its face pointed in Sophie's direction. In the glaring sunlight, Hera's stone expression looked like a smile.

"Enemy in sight," Calliope shouted from the battlements. "They're carrying a stone column like a ram between them."

"How long until they arrive?" Sophie called back.

Alkestis shielded her eyes from the sun. "A few minutes at most. They have ladders as well."

Sophie sprinted to the statue's base and took up a slack place in the rope, heaving with all her might as someone shouted a time. The statue stood firm; they needed more people.

Demetra took a place beside Sophie. The speaker's expression was solemn. "Mother forgive me," she whispered, "for this sacrilege I commit against your champion of old." She took hold of the rope and leaned against the stone Hera's vast weight. Then Faidra was on Sophie's other side, and the three of them pulled together.

The statue shifted, tilted onto a corner of its base, then toppled to the ground with a crash that rattled Sophie's bones and threw clouds of dust into the air. Hera the Great's stone body shattered into dozens of fragments, most of them still heavier than a grown adult.

Sophie coughed as the coarse dust attacked her throat. Half the statue's head rolled to a stop at her feet; Hera the Great's triumphant face was split down the middle. With only half an expression, the statue looked almost questioning, as if Hera was asking, "You've pulled me down, now what?"

"Now, Ancestor," Sophie whispered just to herself, "we liberate the city that meant so much to you." Tension eased out of Sophie's shoulders. Whatever her politics had been, Hera the Great wanted Heratia to prosper. On that much, at least, she and Sophie could agree.

Faidra raised her voice as the dust finally settled. "Alright, it was just a statue, and now it's rubble we need. Let's get it into place!"

The rebels shifted back into motion, pushing the stone fragments that had once been an empero against the Coin Gate to block the rotted timbers from opening and allowing the enemy through.

Sophie retrieved her spear, raising the weapon over her head so the steel point glittered in the sun. "To the battlements!"

A hand on Sophie's arm stopped her. She turned to see Demetra, her shortsword in hand. "I will lead them," the speaker said. "Those battlements will be a killing ground even if fortune goes our way."

"Then I should be there," Sophie said, pulling away.

Demetra held her ground. "Maybe you were all equal in the Solstice Uprising, but here today, if we lose you, we lose everything."

Faidra spoke up. "She's right. I hate it, but she is. And we don't have time to argue."

Sophie grimaced. "Go, then. Brave Sol guide your blade and shine in your enemies' eyes."

Demetra drew her sword and aimed it at the top of the wall. "For Heratia!"

The gathered rebels echoed her cry, and together they surged up the ladders to the Coin Gate's battlements.

Calliope shouted down from the wall as Demetra and her people neared the top. "Sister Sophie, Savvas's vanguard nearly has their ladders in place and—"

A crossbow bolt sheared through Calliope's chain mail and buried itself in her side. She slumped forward, toppling over the battlements even as Alkestis made a desperate grab for her. Sophie and two other acolytes lunged forward. Together they caught Calliope before she struck the cobblestone, blood from the bolt running across her chain mail.

"Get her back," Sophie shouted as the clack of ladders striking stone sounded from atop the wall. Something heavy thudded against the rotting gate from the other side, cracking the wood and shaking the piled rubble.

Calliope reached for her fallen spear. "I can still—" She winced as the movement jostled her wound. "I can still fight. We promised Fryni we'd keep you safe."

"You'll fulfill that promise when you're healed, Sister," Sophie said. She stepped back so a stocky Heratian could take some of Calliope's armored weight. "Move her."

Battle cries and screams of pain sounded from the walls above, along with the ring of clashing steel and the hard impacts of bodies falling from the ramparts. Sophie couldn't see what was happening over the parapet's edge; she could only pray for the people fighting up there.

Metal groaned from further down the wall, and Sophie's gaze snapped toward the sound. A small boat bumped against the Silvervein's iron grating from the landward side, a score of house-guard soldiers crammed aboard. They hacked away at a section of the grate with saws and hammers, tearing away metal that was nearly rusted through. More boats lined up behind them, pushing forward one at a time.

"Mother abandon me," Sophie swore. She should have guessed that the river grates would be in poor repair as well. Other rebels realized what was happening and shouted an alarm. Sophie shook her head. No time for dwelling on her failures; the enemy was nearly through.

Sophie brought up her spear. "On me! We must not let them flank us." She led the rebels and acolytes around her in a charge just as soldiers from the first boat broke through the grate and scrambled up the Silvervein's banks, their shining coats of mail streaked with lines of river mud.

She angled her spear to catch a soldier climbing up onto the bank. The soldier tried to raise her shield. *Too slow.* Sophie's spear slammed into the soldier's chest, crunching through steel scales and into flesh beneath. The impact jarred the breath from Sophie's body. The soldier crumpled and fell back into the Silvervein as Sophie pulled the spear free. *Mother embrace her.*

"Push them back into the river!" Sophie shouted. Another soldier was already climbing up. Sophie brought up her spear again, but without the momentum of a charge, she wasn't fast enough. The soldier deflected the thrust with his shield and struck out with a shortsword, landing a heavy blow on Sophie's shoulder. The chain mail held, but her vision sparked and swam.

Sophie gave ground, opening a gap where she could aim her spear, and then her few remaining acolytes were there, locking their shields together in a wall between Sophie and the enemy. Sophie glanced left and right. All around her, rebels surrounded the outnumbered house guard, but it wasn't enough. With their armor and training, Savvas's soldiers cut down any within reach. Those behind them widened the gap in the grating, allowing more of their number to pass through.

Behind Sophie, the Coin Gate shuddered again from a hard blow. Faidra's voice sounded from somewhere outside her vision. "Sophie, get back, we have to withdraw!"

"No!" Sophie bellowed. "This is our only chance!" If they fell back, Demetra and her defenders on the battlements would be slaughtered. She looked behind her. Calliope and many other wounded were laid out not far away; they couldn't be moved without aggravating their injuries. Mother's loyalty, she couldn't abandon them.

More soldiers climbed up the Silvervein's banks. One sprinted round Sophie's remaining acolytes and charged for her, heavy chopping blade raised high. Sophie ducked low and stabbed her spear into the man's lightly armored thigh. The soldier grunted as his leg gave out, but his sword still came down. Sophie raised her shield and the sword glanced off it, the flat of the blade arcing up to strike her helmet with an earsplitting ring.

Sophie's vision exploded into stars, and she fell to the hard stone street. Air escaped her lips, but she couldn't hear the sound. The roaring in her ears was too loud, the sky and earth spinning too fast. She blinked. The soldier was still moving, on his knees now, his sword raised high above her for a killing strike.

Faidra leapt over Sophie's prone form, hair flying out behind her. Her hammer caught the stunned soldier across the jaw, and he crumpled with a wet crunch. More soldiers broke through the rebel line. Faidra screamed her challenge and charged to meet them. The Coin Gate shuddered under another impact; the gate itself cracked open, and the statue remnants slid outward. One of Hera's arms stretched toward Sophie as though reaching for her help while soldiers squeezed through the gap to climb over the broken remains.

Sophie pressed her hand to the ground. Where was her spear? She couldn't reach it. *Up*—she had to get up. Mother's loyalty, her people were dying around her. Sophie tried to rise, but the motion sent another ripple through the world, and she collapsed back to the paving stones. Her limbs wouldn't obey. Maybe that was fitting. She'd failed so many others, and now her body had failed her. Had the same thing happened to Taisa? Tears pricked Sophie's eyes. When she met her sister in the Void, would they share a memory of being too weak to stand as enemies closed in all around them?

Feet pounded the stone around her. Rebels? Soldiers? She wasn't sure. This was her end; she couldn't fight. At least she hadn't surrendered. That would make Faidra happy. Sophie even heard the sacred hymns welcoming her to the Mother's embrace. Hymns sung without skill or training, but with all the enthusiasm of acolytes gathered together for warmth on a cold Gray Falls night.

She tilted her head up, blinking until the spots cleared. The hymns were real, coming from a ship just bumping up against the docks. Her acolytes stood at the rail, and behind them the fighters of Gray Falls, their spears a sharp forest of glittering steel.

A wide ramp thudded down onto the docks, and the sounds of battle quieted as both sides paused to gape at the sight of twenty sacred sisters forming a vanguard for two hundred militia soldiers.

Fryni stood tall at their head with her spear raised high, Anna and Evi by her side. "The Mother's justice!" she shouted.

The rest of the militia responded with a roaring cry: "JUSTICE!"

As a wave they charged down the ramp, their heavy boots hitting the stone dock in a pounding rhythm. Rebels threw themselves out of the way as Fryni's line met the advancing senatorial troops.

Spears and shields ground together as both sides shoved for position, but the house guards who'd made it into the docks were outnumbered. They'd pushed through the poorly trained rebels, but against a larger, equally disciplined force they had no choice but to give way, scrambling back the way they'd come. The acolytes let them go, offering a path of retreat instead of forcing them to stand and fight. Pride warmed Sophie's heart.

Hands clutched at Sophie's shoulders. "Sister Sophie?" Fryni's voice, desperate and raw. "Mother forgive me, I'm too late!"

"No, no, dearest one," Sophie mumbled. "I live, help me stand." How could Fryni and the others be here so soon? They should have been several more days out at least.

"Oh, Sophie," Fryni said with palpable relief. "Steady now, you'll be up in a moment." The young woman's hands shifted, and with a gentle strength they lifted Sophie up to her feet.

Sophie forced down the bile that came with every motion. The world was not spinning; it was just the blow to her head. "I walk in the Void, the Void surrounds me," Sophie whispered, focusing on the words until some of the nausea faded. She looked at the battlefield, where the entirety of the Gray Falls militia helped wounded rebels back to shelter or climbed up to reinforce Demetra's position on the battlements.

"How can you be here?" Sophie asked. "No one could have traveled that quickly." She wobbled on her feet, but Fryni's shoulder was there, supporting her.

Fryni looked up at Sophie with a wide smile. "We met them on the road, Anna, Evi, and me. The abbey heard about what happened in Tallirod, didn't know what had become of us, so they called up the militia to look for us. They'd tracked the Skaldre who attacked us, and they were about to turn north when we found them and got them going in the right direction. We'd have been here sooner, but it took some time to convince the people crewing the harbor chain that we were on your side."

Sophie marveled. Of all the Mother's blessed luck.

The Coin Gate shuddered a final time, the wood splintering to pieces and the piled rubble sliding away to either side. Moments later a soldier in shining plate-mail armor strode through, breastplate emblazoned with the crest of a rearing stallion. Savvas Carenthus, his polished armor bearing the dents and bloodstains of battle. More house guards flanked him on either side, their weapons gleaming in the sun.

"Form up!" Fryni shouted.

As one, the militia rushed in around Sophie and Fryni, locking their shields together in a tight phalanx.

Fryni drew in a breath. "Spears out!"

The militia extended their spears with a challenging shout.

Savvas paused in his tracks, heavy mace hanging at his side, staring at the formation of acolytes and Gray Falls youths. Sophie couldn't see his face under the helmet's visor, but she could guess the calculations going through his head. With two hundred well-armed and disciplined soldiers blocking the Coin Gate, his main escape was cut off, and the bulk of Faidra's people still assembled behind him. He couldn't retreat to one of the city's land gates. His soldiers might break out on their own, but not if they wanted to protect the senators' wealth and families.

But the fighting would not be painless for Sophie's side either. Even with the uprising's greater numbers, grinding down Savvas and his elite guard would cost time and lives that Meyatha could not afford.

"Savvas," she called out. "I seek parley with you." This might be her best chance.

Savvas's deep baritone boomed back a reply. "Agreed."

After a meaningful look from Sophie, Fryni ordered that the acolyte's formation open so that she could meet Savvas halfway between the lines. Most of the spinning was gone now, but Sophie couldn't trust her legs to obey, so she kept Fryni close.

All sounds of battle faded now, replaced only by the moans of the wounded and the cawing of crows.

Savvas glanced back at the rubble before the Coin Gate. "You used the founder's sacred likeness as a barricade. Is any depth too low for you?"

Sophie shrugged. "I value living citizens more than dead emperos." She blinked to clear more spots from her vision. "Your escape is over. It's time to end this bloodshed."

Savvas lifted his visor to reveal a hard expression. "Pulling these sisters from Mother knows where is a good trick, I'll grant that. But with Demetra's force smashed, my real soldiers still outnumber yours ten to one. Get out of the way, and we won't have to cut our way through you."

Fryni tensed at Sophie's side. Sophie squeezed the younger woman's shoulder through her chain mail.

"You do have those numbers," Sophie said. "But we can hold you at this gate for hours. In that time, more of my people will be up behind you. Then your force will be the one outnumbered ten to one, if not more so. And while your soldiers fight for their lives, who will protect the senators and their families? You'll be surrounded. There's no way out of this for you." It was true, but the cost in blood would make the stars weep.

Savvas stared at her, his eyes searching her face. "Then what alternative do you offer?"

"Only one," Sophie said. "The Senate will confirm me as empero, unanimously. Each family who raised arms against me will surrender two-thirds of their wealth to the state. In return—"

"Two-thirds?" Savvas interrupted. "You can't be serious."

"I am," Sophie said. "So much of that wealth is hidden in various schemes that they'll hardly notice it's gone. Unanimous confirmation, two-thirds of the Senate's wealth, and my guarantee of their safety."

Savvas shook his head. "You ask too much. Leave the senators' property intact, and I will see to it that they confirm you."

"I am not negotiating." Sophie leaned closer to him. "If you fight, it is only a matter of time until the senatorial families under your protection die a bloody death. You know my intervention is the only way they will keep their lives. Accept, and when you stand trial for your crimes against our people, I will ensure that execution is withheld. Or you can go to the Mother's embrace now, on the streets of Heratia."

Savvas's eyes narrowed. "I am a general of the imperial army, I will not be sent to molder away in a cell when the empire is under threat of a Skaldre invasion."

Faidra shouldered her way beside Sophie. Blood from a cut on her forehead had dried in rivulets down one cheek. "Did I hear that right? Does he think we'd let him stay anywhere near power after what he tried to do?"

At Sophie's side, Fryni spoke up. "He seems to think he's the only general in Meyatha."

"I *know*," Savvas said, a muscle twitching in his jaw, "that you need me. Unless you have a plan to deal with the Skaldre."

"Enough arguing," Sophie said. "Savvas, the sooner you surrender, the sooner I can organize relief forces to lift the sieges at Heliopolis and Karotia. You are only prolonging their suffering."

Savvas looked at her for a moment, then barked out a short laugh. "You don't know, then? The northern sieges are a diversion to draw our attention. The main Skaldre army marches directly south, to assault Heratia itself."

"I knew you were a monster," Faidra said. "But I'd never dreamed you were such a poor liar."

Sophie stared at her enemy, a tremor running down both hands. Why make up such a farfetched lie at this late hour?

"No lies," Savvas said. "Only a truth you don't want to hear. My northern agents captured Thane Eidsson's battle plans weeks ago, and I have been scraping together a force to stop him ever since. It assembles north of Godstep Lake even now, and its commanders will serve you only if I wish it."

"Do you have proof of anything you say?" Sophie asked.

Savvas motioned behind him, and one of his soldiers brought forth a thin sheaf of papers and offered them with an extended hand. Fryni kept Sophie back; she moved forward to take the papers herself and then retreated back from Savvas's side, eyes watchful.

Sophie took the pages from her acolyte and stared at them, desperate to find evidence of Savvas's dishonesty. Instead she found maps of the roads through northern Meyatha and orders in the Skaldre script to converge on Heratia.

"So he knows how to draw a map and a few words of Skaldre," Faidra said, glancing over Sophie's shoulder. "It changes nothing."

Savvas shrugged. "Find your friend Demetra if she's still alive. She'll recognize Thane Eidsson's handwriting."

"Even if she does," Faidra said, hand clenching around her hammer, "the rest could still be lies."

"March without me then," Savvas said. "See what happens. Do you really think I'd have let the capital's forces get so depleted if I didn't need every soldier assembled elsewhere?"

"*If* this is the thane's handwriting," Sophie said, "it doesn't change our demands." She met her enemy's cool gaze, keeping her voice level. "I will have the Senate's hoarded wealth, both because I need it to rebuild Meyatha, and to break their power so they do not depose me from the throne."

Savvas tensed, hand drifting toward his mace.

"However," Sophie said. Her guts roiled as she choked out the next words. "I will allow you to retain your command, to march north with me and defeat the Skaldre."

Faidra's eyes turned from Savvas to Sophie, and she whispered, "Sophie, no, please don't do this."

"I have no choice," Sophie said. "If he's telling the truth, we need him."

"Even if every word is true," Faidra said, "it's not worth the cost. Not after what he's done."

"Faidra," Sophie said, reaching a hand out to her friend. "Think of this city, of its people. I must protect them from invasion just as I protect them from the Senate. If keeping Savvas is the only way to do both, then so be it."

Faidra raised her arm and Fryni tensed with her spear, but Faidra only knocked Sophie's hand away. "You promised us justice," Faidra said, voice rough. "Your acolytes screamed it when they charged. This is a strange way to go about it."

Faidra took a step back. She wouldn't meet Sophie's eyes.

After a moment, Sophie turned away from her old comrade to face Savvas. Her tone was icy. "You have my offer, General Carenthus. What is your answer?"

Savvas stood silently for a moment. Then he took a slow breath, bent one knee, and knelt down, his eyes never leaving Sophie's. "I accept," he said, "Your Majesty."

Sophie's heart skipped a beat. She had done it. The city was hers, or, at least, it was hers until the Skaldre took it from her. Technically the other senators still needed to agree, but she couldn't believe any of them would defy their great protector.

"Return to your people and order them to surrender their weapons," she managed at last. "Once I have confirmed your proof with Demetra, we shall escort you to the palace."

Savvas rose and turned to march back the way he had come, signaling his soldiers to fall in behind him.

Sophie watched him go, expecting him to signal a fresh attack at any moment, but he didn't. They really had done it. She turned to find Faidra, but the other woman had retreated back through their own lines. Looking for her friend, Sophie beheld how many bodies the fighting had left behind. Even more wounded were being cared for under makeshift tents. Calliope was there, the bolt drawn from her side, her normally ruddy face having taken on a deathly pallor. How many others hadn't been so lucky?

Demetra descended the battlement stairs. Her scale mail was rent through, a blood-soaked bandage was tied over her leg, and she walked with a limp, leaning on a borrowed spear. "Show me these supposed Skaldre orders," she said, extending a hand.

Sophie handed over the thin sheaf. If the speaker identified them as false, this cursed deal could still be undone. But Sophie didn't believe Demetra would find any such thing.

"This..." Demetra said, furrowing her brow, "is Starkad Eidsson's hand, without a doubt. I recognize it from his correspondence with Empero Mihail."

Sophie let out her breath. "It's true, then. I must accept Savvas's aid or see my nation crushed." She swayed on her feet, a sliver of dizziness from the blow to her head returning. Fryni and Demetra both put out their hands to steady her.

"This is still a victory," Demetra said.

Fryni made a fist with the hand that wasn't supporting Sophie. "The speaker's right. Whatever deal he's wriggled into, we stopped him cold."

Demetra squeezed Sophie's shoulder. "Now, let us see you crowned, Your Majesty."

Sophie's balance returned, and warmth blossomed within her. "Thank you both. Without you, I could not have won today." She took a step forward, making sure she could stand on her own. "Now, let us make good our victory, so that we can face our next enemy."

Chapter 17

It took Sophie all of the next day to begin the process of putting Heratia back together from the battle. First her militia had to take custody of the surrendered senators, their families, and their wagons of hoarded wealth. Then Sophie ordered the city's physicians be brought together to treat those wounded who could be saved and ease the suffering of those who could not. Savvas's disarmed soldiers were tasked to look after their fallen, while volunteer citizens, Faidra's rebels, and the Gray Falls militia saw to the rest. Clergy arrived from Senica Cathedral to say prayers and blessings over the bodies, and from there it was a matter for the gravediggers. Putting the dead to rest would take several more days at least, but Sophie did not have the time to oversee it herself.

Two days after the battle, at first light, Sophie's forces assembled at their temporary camp in the docks for a somber coronation march back to the palace. Demetra met Sophie in her tent, a cane to support her injured leg in one hand, a robe of deepest-purple silk in the other.

"Whatever arrangement you made with Faidra," Demetra said, in response to Sophie's questioning look, "we are still crowning you to the Falcon Throne. For that, you must wear your family's color."

Sophie consented without further argument, donning the robe and wrapping her black shawl around it. The robe's featherlight fabric floated against her skin, weighed down only by the needs of a teetering empire.

Outside the tent, Sophie's supporters stood in ranks, ready to march. After the anger of their last parting, Sophie worried that Faidra would refuse to attend, but the stone-faced rebel took her place of honor at the vanguard even as she refused to meet Sophie's gaze.

The citizens of Heratia watched them pass down Triumph Causeway. The people were wary: glad that the violence was over, but unsure what would happen next. Sophie didn't blame them. Still, a new empero wasn't crowned often, and the procession gathered more and more people as it went.

The senators of Meyatha met Sophie's procession at the entrance to their district. Each senator wore their finest house colors, but most had the dejected looks of those attending a funeral. Only Demetra's handful of loyalists looked at all pleased.

In the senators' midst was Savvas Carenthus, clad in the same armor he had worn in battle, though the grime had been cleaned away and the dents repaired. The rubies of his house crest caught the morning light, reflecting a crimson hue on any who stood near.

Traditionally emperos were confirmed at the Grand Forum where the Senate met, but Sophie and Demetra had both agreed a more potent symbol of their victory was required, so they made for the imperial palace instead. Senators and common citizens alike crowded through the palace gates. Their path was clear of debris and ash but still bereft of the lavish decorations that normally adorned it. Sophie didn't mind. If she were to be the last empero of Meyatha, it was well to begin her reign without the conventional trappings of imperium.

Finally Sophie's procession reached the audience chamber, where the black onyx of the Falcon Throne waited. All bowed low to Sophie as she approached the imperial dais—all but one. Faidra still stood tall, which suited Sophie fine. She would be perfectly content if no one ever bowed to her again.

Sophie concentrated on the throne itself, which was still missing one of its armrests. The falcon crest shone in the evening sunlight, a beacon of her responsibilities. She stood before the throne and turned to face her people, hands out with palms open. Previous emperos would scatter coins at their coronation, but Sophie had no gold to spare. She could only offer herself.

Demetra addressed the senators, her voice strong and clear. "Honored senators, this daughter of House Laskaris seeks Meyatha's imperial throne. Who among you consents to her rule?"

"We so consent," came the unanimous response, every senator crossing an arm over their chest in salute, even a glaring Ariadne Ducas. Savvas's expression was grim, but he crossed his arm with the others. A handful of senators had been wounded in the fighting, and a few more were out of the city, but that still left nearly the full two hundred. Only a dozen of Demetra's loyalists gave their vote with any genuine enthusiasm, likely because most of their property had been spared. Sophie marked their faces. She would need partners in the Senate.

Demetra approached Sophie and placed a sapphire-studded diadem over her head. It wasn't the imperial diadem her father and grandmother had worn—no one had yet been able to locate that—but it would suffice. "Sophie Laskaris," Demetra said. "As speaker of the Senate and representative of the people, I proclaim you Empero of all Meyatha."

Sophie lowered herself down onto the Falcon Throne. Its stone was cold and unyielding. It didn't seem like something she could sit in for long without aching all over. Should she have cushions added, or would that undercut her authority?

Fryni and the other acolytes broke into cheers that quickly spread to the crowd of citizens and even to a few of the senators, though most only stared.

Sophie acknowledged the crowd with a dip of her head, careful not to dislodge the jeweled diadem. When the cheering faded, she spoke. "I am only here on this throne because you shed blood to win it for me. With the Mother's blessing, I shall repay that loyalty as I work for a Meyatha that no longer has any need of me."

A normal coronation would have included far more pomp and ceremony, but Sophie dispensed with it. There was much to do and little time to do it. She spent the rest of the day enacting her promised edicts. All citizens were granted full amnesty for the uprising, and the state would pay for all funeral expenses. She opened the imperial grain stores and the city's hospitals and proclaimed that any unoccupied building might be used for shelter without fear of arrest.

These measures were a bandage on the capital's wounds. To staunch the flow of Heratian blood, she turned to monetary pronouncements. House Carenthus and those that had joined it would turn over two-thirds of their wealth as promised, and in return there would be no retaliation against them or their remaining property. To enforce this, she unleashed Scholar Makis and an army of clerks from the Imperial University. Makis bowed to her, touching his balding head to the floor, and swore not a single piece of silver would escape his sight.

With finances handled for the time being and an immediate influx of gold and silver that the senators had helpfully piled into wagons, Sophie made it known that from that day forward, the Meyathan state alone would be responsible for all army pay. She dispatched messengers to field commanders so they would know the situation and recognize who now controlled their coin.

In the midst of implementing new policies, Sophie made time to restore an old one. She rescinded Empero Irena's decree of dissolution against the People's Chamber, reinstating that ancient institution to the full powers of government. It would take time to organize elections just in Heratia, let alone the rest of the empire, but the people would have their arm of government restored.

For now she was content knowing that Styliani Dellis's legacy was ensured. Her old teacher had labored for years writing treatises she couldn't show to anyone, and now they would see the light of day at last. She hoped Styliani was proud of her in the Mother's embrace.

When the Skaldre threat was past—*if* it passed—Sophie would find Styliani's son and ensure he knew of his mother's legacy.

The final order of business was to honor promises. Sophie called for Constantia de Beltane to appear before her, and, with full imperial honors, invested her with the Beltane family's old Senate seat. A few senators scowled, but none openly protested. Constantia smiled wide and swept into a low, elegant bow, her many jewels flashing a cascade of colors in the candlelight. "A worthy gift, Your Majesty," she said. "I look forward to future favors."

"No doubt," Sophie said. Constantia would have her voice in Meyathan affairs. How long would it be until Sophie had to contain the Gallian's influence? It did no good to overthrow one class of tyrants only to invite another in, but she had more immediate concerns. "If you would join me, I am calling a council of war."

***

In the next hour, Sophie dismissed the gathered Senate, sending them back to their homes under guard. The last thing she needed now was her political enemies demanding a say in the empire's defense. Her handpicked council gathered in the palace war room. Its heavy oak table had survived the looting, but the detailed imperial maps that had once adorned the walls were gone, either taken or torn to useless shreds.

Fryni and half a dozen acolytes went in first, standing guard around the chamber. Sophie took her place at the head of the table. Two more acolytes helped Demetra in, offering their arms so the speaker could keep weight off her leg. Following her came Constantia and Makis. Demetra sank into the seat on Sophie's left. Her gaze met Constantia's in a glare, but neither woman said anything.

Faidra came in next, striding forward with casual confidence to stand over the seat on Sophie's right. She'd replaced her blacksmith's hammer with a heavy-bladed broadsword and was technically committing high treason by going armed before the empero.

"Does the *empero* object?" Faidra asked in a cool voice, tapping the sword on her belt. It was the most she had said to Sophie since the battle's end.

Sophie shook her head. "If you'd wanted me dead, you could have just let that soldier kill me on the docks." She waved to encompass the room around them. "Of course, then you'd be the one having to put up with all the pomp and ceremony."

Faidra gave a short chuckle as she sat down. "And wouldn't that be a fate worse than death?"

The two of them exchanged the slightest of grins before Demetra cleared her throat, which announced the arrival of Savvas Carenthus. The handsome general had doffed his armor, now wearing plain robes embellished only with the rearing stallion of his house. He carried a tied bundle of long scrolls under one arm. Sophie's jaw muscles tightened when she saw him. This man had planned to turn her people into serfs, and only force had stayed his hand. She would prefer never to see him again, but she had given her word, and Meyatha still needed its best general.

"There he is," Faidra said, leaning back and rolling her shoulders. "Our great savior, other than the minor incident where he tried to enslave us, of course."

Savvas shrugged. "The empero called me to her council of war, but I suppose we can also talk of all the ways you might smash Skaldre shops or scrawl puerile graffiti on their homes. I'm sure it will be just as helpful."

Makis started to speak, but Demetra preempted him. "Her people took the capital out from under you," she said. "Will Thane Eidsson send you running just as easily?" She stopped, looking surprised that she had come to Faidra's defense, though not half so surprised as Faidra herself.

Sophie rapped one hand on the table. "If we could focus on the matter at hand?" She harbored the same anger that Faidra did, but this wasn't the time.

"But, Your Majesty," Constantia said with a wicked grin, "it's just getting good."

Sophie closed her eyes for a moment, then focused on Savvas. "Proceed, General."

Savvas untied one of his long scrolls and unrolled it across the table to reveal a map of Meyatha, with its hourglass shape beginning in the north, narrowing to a point at Heratia, then widening again south of the Serate Mountains.

"Last reports paint a grim picture," Savvas said. He tapped several points in northern Meyatha. "Eidsson's ruse at Heliopolis and Karotia worked exactly as he intended, luring the majority of our northern-frontier armies to 'relieve' those cities. The Skaldre forces there have fought skillful delaying actions, leaving central Meyatha and Heratia open to the main attack."

That drew the room's attention, even Faidra's. Sophie stared at the map. No matter how destructive the empire's wars had been in the past, Heratia itself had always been safe. No longer, it seemed.

Constantia studied the map. "Curious. That's a very long way to travel for a raid. Wouldn't it make more sense for him to claim territory he can actually hold on to?"

Demetra snorted. "Heratia is a far more tempting target than any of your Free Province cities. Our walls have never been breached by a foreign power, the wealth of this city could sustain the northern barbarians for a hundred years."

Constantia examined one of her sparkling rings. "Why, of course." She smiled at Demetra. "And since these walls were indeed breached by their own empero, Thane Eidsson must believe it is not an overly challenging task."

Sophie raised her voice. "Enough, we are at war with the Skaldre, not each other." The animosity between Demetra and Constantia would be a problem if it continued to fester, but Sophie couldn't afford to dismiss either of them.

Makis cleared his throat. "Perhaps this isn't a mere raid. Eidsson assassinated Heir Taisa, Mother embrace her. Perhaps he expects us to still be squabbling over the succession, easy pickings for conquest. He would not be the first conqueror to exploit such divisions."

Sophie raised her brows. She wouldn't have believed it but for seeing how effectively the Skaldre tactics had subverted Meyatha's defenses. Perhaps Eidsson was right to think he could hold Heratia. And though he wouldn't know it, her own edicts meant Heratia's reserves of food were too low to withstand a long siege. This could be the Skaldre's chance to knock out their sworn enemy once and for all. The eternal Meyathan Empire, conquered by Thane Eidsson's hand.

Savvas leaned forward. "I trust you understand the danger, Your Majesty. Our armies are scattered, and Heratia's granaries are dangerously low." His eyes found Sophie's in a pointed look.

Sophie met the general's gaze. "Indeed. Please, continue." She needed him, but she would not apologize for feeding her own people.

"Fortunately," Savvas said, "by pulling forces from garrisons in the east and west, I have assembled a force just beyond Godstep Lake. I will take that force and secure the Golden Fields to restock the city's grain supply." Savvas traced a new path north from the capital. His hand stopped at a green valley bordered by thick forests on one side and sheer cliffs on the other. "Eidsson will want the fields to feed his own soldiers, so that is where we shall meet him in battle. Two days to assemble, another two marching north at a brisk march, and we should just beat him there."

Sophie examined the map. The Golden Fields were the breadbasket of Meyatha's northern provinces. This far into autumn, the crops would all have been harvested, waiting in silos for collections by imperial agents. Or by an invading army looking to resupply.

"Then we must waste no time," Sophie said. "We shall depart as soon as arms and provisions are accounted for."

Constantia looked up from the map. "You plan to go yourself? Isn't that unwise after all the work to put you on the throne?"

"I must," Sophie said. "I cannot ask my people to face this battle while I sit safe in the palace." Her two hundred-strong militia wouldn't have much impact as part of a force that was set to number over ten thousand, assuming they could locate the scattered Meyathan forces, but her presence would be critical for morale. And she was not about to trust Savvas with sole command of the army.

Constantia switched her gaze to Demetra. "And you approve of this?"

"I do not like it," Demetra said, her eyes narrowed. "But Meyatha's survival is at stake, our soldiers must see that the empero stands with them."

Faidra stood. "I'm going too." She pointed at Savvas. "I don't trust you alone with Sophie, and none of my people will ever follow your orders."

Savvas raised an eyebrow. "This will be a real battle, not street brawling."

Faidra took a step toward him. "I served my tour with the legions before you were old enough to enlist." She looked back at Sophie. "Many of my people did the same. Give them proper arms and they'll fight as well as any soldier."

"Agreed," Sophie said. She would not turn down any offer of more reinforcements, and fighting side by side seemed to be all that was left of her old friendship with Faidra. "I name you General Faidra Remi, commander of our infantry as General Carenthus commands our cavalry."

Faidra only shrugged, but Savvas spoke up. "Her, a general? My officers will not stand for it. Most of my cavalry riders hail from the very senatorial families she tried to annihilate!"

Sophie turned her gaze on him. "You will convince them. Faidra has proven her worth." It wasn't as if Savvas had anyone better. Most of Meyatha's best commanders were in border fortresses like those the Skaldre had already overrun.

After a moment, Savvas nodded. "Yes, Your Majesty."

Sophie addressed the rest of the table. "Demetra, I leave you as my representative in Heratia. Makis will advise you on spending priorities, he speaks with my voice."

Speaker and scholar both bowed.

"And what of me?" Constantia asked.

Sophie turned to her. "From you, I need assurances that the Free Provinces will not take advantage of our war against the Skaldre. That seems only fair, since your profits are tied to ours now, and you hold a seat in our Senate."

Constantia smiled. "I'll do what I can. I may have a few friends back home who value my counsel."

After that it was simply a matter of discussing logistics, most of which would be handed off to the re-forming imperial bureaucracy in the morning. Sophie dismissed the meeting a short time later. It was past midnight, and they all needed sleep.

Demetra stayed behind as the others filed out, waving off the acolytes who offered to help her. "A moment, Your Majesty," she said.

Sophie sighed. "My name will do fine, don't you think?" When Demetra only frowned, she went on, "Never mind, what mistake have I made this time?"

"None," Demetra said. "I agree that we need Savvas Carenthus for this campaign, but I do not trust him no matter how many oaths he swears. Even if he serves you loyally in battle, a victory might be all he needs to turn traitor." She took a breath. "At your word, I can send people who will make sure he does not survive contact with the enemy."

Sophie took a step back. Kill Savvas in cold blood? "No."

"No one will ever know," Demetra said. "If by some chance my people are discovered, I will take full responsibility. Savvas will never think you capable of such an act."

"No," Sophie repeated. "I do not refuse out of practicality. I will not harm a man who has sworn to serve me."

"Not even after all he's done? What he would have done to your people?"

"I have granted him a second chance," Sophie said. "The Mother's kindness demands it of me, and that is all I will say on the matter. Good night, Speaker."

Chapter 18

The Meyathan imperial army, or what little of it could be scraped together, marched to the docks two days later. It was hardly the mighty sea of soldiers Sophie remembered her grandmother leading off to battle. They were a rough mix of senatorial house guards, the returning detachment of Heratia's garrison, reserve soldiers drafted from surrounding towns, Faidra's rebels, and the Gray Falls militia.

All told, they had mustered some six thousand soldiers from Heratia. It was a greater force than anything Sophie had seen since before her exile, but it seemed small indeed to make war with the Skaldre. Demetra had begun recruiting from the citizenry to form new legions, but they were unlikely to be ready in time to do any good. At least the force Sophie had was well equipped with arms and armor taken from the Senate's holdings. It would be some time before everything was properly cataloged, but already the seizures were proving their worth.

Sophie herself rode at the column's center as it flowed down Triumph Causeway toward the Coin Gate, where so many had died in her name. The blood had been cleared away, but a foot from Hera the Great's statue was still there, propping up the sagging gate. Sophie focused on her balance as the roan horse shifted beneath her. It had been twenty-three years since she'd ridden anything, and they gave her the tallest charger in the city.

Her new armor, a shining suit of plated mail with the deep-purple falcon etched across the breastplate, wasn't helping. The weight wasn't any worse than the chain mail she was used to, but the armor pinched if she moved wrong. It had been commissioned for her sister, Taisa, and it wasn't quite Sophie's size.

She would take the blasted thing off as soon as they reached the ships, but Demetra had insisted that the citizenry needed to see their empero riding a warhorse in full armor, off to smite their enemies.

"If I cannot go with you to battle," the speaker said, "I can at least see that your departure is properly celebrated."

Sophie had conceded, but she doubted even the speaker's carefully engineered pomp could rouse the spirit of tired Heratia.

Citizens lined the causeway on either side, staring at the soldiers as they marched past. A few cheered, but most only cast wary gazes upon them. They had no reason to believe Sophie would return, that she could protect them against the Skaldre juggernaut. And yet there was no panic, no flight from the city. Sophie crossed an arm over her chest in silent thanks for that. Many of the elder citizens returned her silent salute, those old enough to remember the last time Sophie had defended them. This time she would do better.

A fleet of warships, barges, and fishing boats sailed the army north across the Godstep, leaving Heratia and the towering Serate Mountains behind them. Just north of the lake, they met the army Savvas had promised as it prepared to break camp, more than doubling their numbers. The two columns joined together, falling easily into formation. The force swelled further as it marched, scattered field-army contingents flowing into its ranks.

Unlike the decay Sophie had witnessed everywhere else she visited in the empire, these soldiers were well-fed and equipped. The infantry carried long spears alongside heavy round shields, and their chain mail showed not a speck of rust. The cavalry all sported powerful bows of horn and sinew, with lances for the charge and heavy maces for close-in work. Their scale mail rippled in the late-afternoon sun. It wasn't a surprise that the legions received an outsized portion of the state's resources, just another reminder of how much work Sophie had ahead of her.

The first day of marching came to an end, and the army began the task of setting up their fortified camp. This was something every Meyathan soldier learned, practiced with the same regularity as their martial skills. In Gray Falls, Sophie had trained her militia in the same manner, and they pitched in with the regular army as if they were all of the same barracks.

First a trench was dug around the perimeter, then the dirt piled up to form a rampart. Once the defenses were in place, officers marked squares where the tents were to be set up, always in the same formation so that soldiers could find their way in the dark.

Savvas swung down from the saddle and approached Sophie while she held up a tent pole so two of her acolytes could fix it in the ground. Savvas's eyes glanced around, his mouth in a thin line. "Your Majesty," he said. "We have a tent set up for you near the western parapet, if you would care to inspect it."

Sophie let Fryni take her place and turned to face her former enemy. "Thank you, General Carenthus, but this tent will suit my needs." Savvas would have her camp among the cavalry, and it was a tempting offer, despite how she felt about the general. As the scions of aristocratic families, cavalry riders had warmer tents and softer blankets, which would tell in the autumn chill. But the infantry were her people too, and if Sophie asked them to fight and die for her, the least she could do was share their quarters.

Savvas only shook his head and made no further attempt to convince her.

Fryni snorted when the general was gone. "Did he really think you would sleep where any of his riders could put a knife in your back?"

Sophie gave a rueful smile. She'd completely failed to consider the security implications of Savvas's offer. She really was tired.

As the army broke camp the next morning, Sophie found what little anonymity she had previously enjoyed was gone. Soldiers turned to look at her whenever she passed, some in curiosity, others with open contempt until Fryni took a pointed step toward them and they hurried about their business. One young cavalry officer stared at her so long that Sophie began to wonder if she'd seen him somewhere before. Something about the set of his face and his gray eyes tickled her memory.

But her thoughts were interrupted by a scouting report, which required all of the army's leaders to gather and hear how the Skaldre had still not been spotted. Sophie pinched herself to keep from nodding off. These reports were vital, she told herself. It was important to know where the enemy was not, even if it felt like the long wait before the blow fell. At least at the abbey, even in the most mundane drudgery, she was doing something. Now there was only watching the sun go by.

Faidra and the army's other leaders dispersed back to their regiments once the report was finished, but Sophie steered her horse toward Savvas after they'd both remounted. Perhaps there was something she could do after all: it would serve Meyatha better if she had a relationship with her best general beyond strained mercy.

"The army has assembled in greater numbers than I dared hope," she said. "And the soldiers know their business. A credit to your organization."

Savvas bowed his head, keeping his eyes off Sophie's. "It is nothing compared to what we could have mustered in your grandmother's day. I only hope it is enough."

Sophie hid a grimace behind her hand. Was the reference to her grandmother a deliberate slight, or was she only seeing the worst in a vanquished enemy? She needed to keep the Mother's kindness. "Once the Skaldre are pushed back," she said, "restoring the northern defenses will be a top priority."

Savvas looked toward the sinking sun. "If that's true, then you should begin by revoking citizens' right of travel and relocating as many as you can from the south."

An angry heat flared in Sophie's cheeks. "I shall do no such thing!" But she regretted the outburst as soon as it left her lips. Of course Savvas knew she would never issue such a decree; they had already fought this argument with spear and blood. She took a breath to calm herself. "My mandate as empero is to expand the citizens' rights, not constrain them further."

This time Savvas did look at her. "It is those rights that weakened us in the first place. Citizens fled south to avoid the hardships of war, and so we had fewer soldiers when we desperately needed them." His eyes locked on Sophie's. "Your sister knew what needed to be done, and she would have already made it so in your place."

Sophie shook her head. "General, citizens flee south because the state does not protect them. They avoid military service because there is no guarantee their farms and homes will still be there when they return." She could make him understand, the way Styliani had made her understand so many years ago.

Savvas's expression went rigid. "If the empero decrees it, then it must be the truth."

Sophie sighed. Such reformations did not occur in a day. "See to the ordering of my army, General."

The march continued until the great limestone cliffs of the Empero's Teeth rose up in the distance, the Golden Fields' eastern boundary. The fields themselves were still hidden behind the horizon, but if Savvas's prediction of the Skaldre's movements held true, Sophie's army would meet the enemy soon.

With the sun low in the west, Savvas called a halt. "The infantry needs a rest," he said to Sophie and the assembled officers. He pointed off the road to where a range of low hills formed a nearly closed curve, the opening narrow and easy to defend. "You should make camp there. Legions have used the Horseshoe since Hera the Great's time." He bowed to Sophie. "With your blessing, I will take the cavalry and ensure that the next crossroad is free of enemy presence. If the Skaldre reach it before we do, they could block us from reaching the Golden Fields entirely. We shall reunite our forces in the morning."

Sophie raised an eyebrow. "What if you encounter Thane Eidsson in the dark?"

Savvas showed his teeth. "Our scouts know this terrain even at midnight. If the Skaldre dare face us when they cannot see, so much the better."

Sophie agreed, and in short order Savvas had separated off most of the cavalry regiments at a stiff canter.

Faidra watched him ride off, her eyes narrowed. "A silver coin says he never returns."

Sophie laughed. "You think he would ride off with only a night's worth of supplies? Doesn't sound like a Meyathan general at all."

The Horseshoe's interior was easily large enough to accommodate the Meyathan infantry, though it would have been a tight squeeze if Savvas and the cavalry had remained. As Sophie rode through the narrow opening, it was clear why the legions preferred to camp here. The ridgeline kept out the wind's chill and offered a commanding view of the surrounding countryside. Outside the Horseshoe, the ground was carefully cleared for long stretches in every direction and maintained by imperial patrols. Any enemy would be spotted long before they could attack, even in the dark.

For a second time, the soldiers set up their camp with practiced ease. This time at least they did not have to dig fortifications, except at the Horseshoe's mouth. Sophie was glad for that. A few hours of extra sleep would be invaluable if they met the Skaldre tomorrow.

Once the last tents were up and a light drizzle caressed the camp, Sophie lay her head down and tried to still her thoughts for sleep. Tomorrow they would face the enemy, but at least they would do so on ground of their choosing. "Mother embrace those who die under my banner," Sophie whispered.

"And may the skies weep for them," Fryni answered from her place at the tent's mouth. "And the earth turn their bones to mighty trees that reach up toward the Void."

Sophie raised an eyebrow. That wasn't from any prayer she knew. "And what sacred text did you find that in?"

Color bloomed in Fryni's cheeks. "It's from the poetry book I found in the palace library. It sounded right."

"It did indeed." Sophie smiled. "When we get back, I'll make sure you have time to read more poetry. You clearly have a knack for it."

Fryni beamed, and Sophie lay down on her mat. They were as prepared as they could possibly be.

Chapter 19

The tone of a signal horn jolted Sophie out of sleep. Its note was cut abruptly short. Had that been the signal for an enemy attack? Did she hear shouting? Yes, shouting outside, and the frenzied ring of steel against steel, coming from the Horseshoe's mouth. But how? The sentries along its low ridge should have signaled long before the enemy was close enough to strike.

Something tore through the tent's ceiling and thudded into the earth beside Sophie's face. She turned her head and stared. An arrow, half-buried in the dirt, its goose-feather fletching still quivering. Sophie jumped to her feet. *An arrow*—they were under attack. She scanned the tent for her round shield. Where there was one archer, there would be others.

More arrows showered down through the tent, raining down around Sophie. *There*—her shield was leaning against the far wall. Sophie stepped forward to retrieve it, and an arrow grazed her arm, drawing a line of red across the skin. She flinched back.

A breath later Fryni was there, holding her round shield over them both. A fresh volley thudded into the oak disc, but it held firm.

Sophie let out a shuddering breath. "Thank you. I'm not quite ready to join the Mother's embrace just yet."

Fryni's hand grasped Sophie's. "We have to move," the young captain said. "Outside where we can see what's happening."

Sophie nodded, picking up her own shield and spear from the ground. No time to don her armor, not if the enemy were already upon them. Outside, as predawn light shone through a golden mist, the camp was in chaos. Meyathan soldiers ran in every direction, some diving for what little cover presented itself, others only running as if that would save them from the arrows plummeting down in all directions. A few soldiers had their shields up as Fryni and Sophie did and gathered together in small knots. Bodies littered the earth, blood mixing with the early-morning dew.

Sophie swept her eyes across the camp. Where were the arrows coming from—where was the enemy? Her eyes caught movement atop the Horseshoe's walls. A long line of archers were drawing back bows as tall as they were, silhouetted against the western sky. The Skaldre had climbed up the ridge in force, giving them a deadly vantage over the camp below, but where were the Meyathan sentries that had been posted there? Why hadn't they raised an alarm in time? She couldn't worry about that now; she needed to focus on preserving her army.

Heavy footfalls sounded on the packed earth, and Faidra appeared out of the gloom, her armor half on, a line of blood down one cheek. "Sophie," she said, "we're surrounded. They have archers all around the Horseshoe's ridge, and heavy infantry assaulting our barricades at the mouth. The guard regiment is holding there, but I doubt for much longer."

Sophie took in the news. That must be the sounds of fighting she could still hear over the general din, some part of her army struggling to hold the camp's fortified entrance. If the Skaldre broke through, they could slaughter her soldiers as they tried to don armor and form battle lines. Even if the Skaldre didn't break through, their archers would simply kill her soldiers instead. The infantry had trusted Sophie, and she'd led them right into an ambush with no escape.

Fryni spoke up. "We need to get Sophie out of here. Gather anyone we can and break out."

Faidra nodded, looking at Sophie. "The acolyte's right. We break through, retreat, and regroup."

Sophie shook her head. "We can't escape through the valley mouth," she said. "Not with Thane Eidsson's army camped there."

"It's our best chance," Faidra said. "Stay here, and we all die. Try to break out, at least a few of us will make it through."

Sophie's arm ached from holding her shield above her head. More arrows fell around them, one biting into her shield so deep that the point broke through and drew a bead of blood from her arm. "A breakout is exactly what they expect us to try," Sophie said. "They'll be ready for it. Our only hope is to hold here, exhaust their arrows."

Before Faidra or Fryni could argue, Sophie raised her voice above the din. "All Meyathans to me, to your empero! Raise your shields high, protect your fellows!"

The soldiers around them obeyed. First came the other acolytes and the Gray Falls militia, accustomed to heeding Sophie's call. They stood together, their shields overlapping in a tight phalanx.

Then the regular soldiers began to form up around them, mimicking the militia's formation. Those who had shields raised them; others grabbed barrel lids or lifted up leather saddles. Chaos subsided as Meyathan discipline took over, even with the unceasing torrent of arrows.

Beneath their shields, Faidra gave Sophie a long look. Then she bellowed new commands. "Bring wagons up to cover the wounded! Anyone with armor, reinforce the guard regiment."

The soldiers followed her commands, even breaking the cover of their phalanxes to drag supply wagons to protect their injured comrades. When they faltered under a fresh barrage, Fryni and the other acolytes darted out to pick up the slack, forming the wagons into a rough semicircle so that the wounded could get some shelter from the inner wall as well as from lying beneath. Sophie let out a relieved breath when Fryni returned to the phalanx bearing a triumphant grin.

Elsewhere in the camp, Sophie heard officers shouting orders for their own soldiers to form similar defensive formations, bringing back some level of discipline.

More arrows weighed their shields down, and Faidra grimaced. "The guard regiment won't hold much longer, and we can't drop our shields long enough to don armor. It'll be a slaughter when the Skaldre break through."

"They won't," Sophie said. "Not while their archers are still loosing. They won't charge into their own arrows." But Faidra was right; they couldn't stay here forever. Eventually her soldiers would tire and drop their shields, or the Skaldre would break through and cut them down.

"This is Savvas's doing," Faidra muttered beside Sophie. "He left us to die."

"Maybe," Sophie said. She didn't think Savvas would ally with the Skaldre, but there was no way to know. She needed to find a way out of this trap. Through tiny gaps in the Meyathan shields, she could pick out more of the Skaldre archers. There were so many of them, all with the perfect angle to shoot down into the Horseshoe. But the slope up to their position wasn't steep, not compared to the Serate Mountains she had climbed at Gray Falls.

"We have one chance," she said. "Charge up the ridge and attack the archers, then get away from here and regroup." It was desperate, perhaps desperate enough that the Skaldre would not expect it.

Faidra stared at Sophie, eyes wide.

Fryni nodded. "The other acolytes and I will lead, Sister Sophie."

"Not yet," Sophie said. "If we break ranks now we'll be dead of arrows before we reach the slope. We must wait until they run low, they can only have brought so many."

Sophie raised her voice so it carried across the makeshift phalanx. "Meyathans, we hold. We hold until this rain slackens." She couldn't be sure how far her voice carried beyond her formation, and she had no horn to signal with. She could only hope that the other phalanxes hunkered down and waited for orders.

Another volley of arrows thudded into their shields. Moments after the impact, acrid smoke tickled Sophie's note. She risked lowering her shield enough to see one of the many arrows stuck in it had a burning rag tied around its shaft.

More fire arrows smoldered in the other shields of her phalanx. A soldier shouted in pain as ashes leaked in through a crack between shields and burned his shoulder.

"They'll burn us alive," someone else cried. "The Mother will never find our ashes!"

Panicked mutters spread through the formation as more ash and smoke drifted over them.

Faidra's voice boomed over it. "No!" she shouted. "There's too much dew in the air, the wood won't catch." She glanced at Sophie. "Stand with your empero as she stands with you."

A few ragged cheers answered, and the panic subsided. Sophie smiled a brief thanks at Faidra, but loyalty to their empero couldn't keep these soldiers on their feet forever. Even as Sophie watched, some of them buckled from standing in place with shields high for so long, the arrows adding more fatigue with each volley.

One soldier's arm gave out, opening a gap in the wooden roof. Barbed arrows streamed through, shearing into flesh and bone. Meyathans screamed and fought to get away from the opening, which only brought down more shields and widened the gap.

Fryni gave a wordless cry and pushed her way from the formation's outer edge to the breach, a dozen other acolytes in her wake. They raised their shields just as the next volley came down. Sophie forced herself to breathe. Fryni wouldn't be able to save them a second time, not when she was already anchoring the phalanx's center. If even one soldier lost their nerve, it would mean death for them all. Sophie needed to do something; these people were here in her name.

She drew in a breath and belted out the first line of a sacred hymn. "Brave Sol stepped into the Void that day, she held the darkness all at bay!"

For a moment, only silence greeted her. Then Faidra raised her voice in the next verse. "Brave Sol did veil the world in light, so those below could trust their sight."

Soldiers and acolytes took up the hymn, singing the story of the first blessed daughter's quest to shine light upon the Void Mother's faithful. When the verses ran out, Sophie began another hymn, and then another. Arrows poured down onto their raised shields, but each Meyathan stood, singing their faith in defiance.

At last the tide of barbed shafts ebbed. Sophie held her spear tighter. Either the Skaldre were low on arrows, or they had decided to let the axe folk close in for their turn. No matter which, this was the only chance she and her Meyathans would get.

"Follow me!" Sophie shouted, her voice clear despite singing a month's worth of sacred hymns. Her stiff legs protested, but she propelled herself forward nonetheless, the tightly packed Meyathan formation opening to let her through. Soldiers all around her dropped their arrow-riddled shields and picked up whatever weapons they had at hand before following after her with wordless shouts.

Soldiers of the other phalanxes stared as Sophie charged past them. She didn't look back, but the growing thunder of running feet told her at least some were following.

They hit the valley's slope just as the sun broke through the morning clouds, blinding the Skaldre archers with a barrage of golden light. The Skaldre flinched, buying the Meyathans precious seconds, but before Sophie was halfway up the slope, the enemy recovered, once again putting shaft to string.

A volley tore into the Meyathan ranks, one arrow just flitting past Sophie's ear. She pressed on, leaning on her spear as the ascent steepened. All that mattered was the charge. If they stopped, they were all dead.

The Skaldre archers held their ground, loosing arrows until the Meyathans were mere paces from them. Then they drew shortswords and lunged forward to crash into the Meyathan battle line, raising a frenzy of battle cries.

Sophie's spear took a blond-haired soldier in the chest, biting through his light chain armor and sending him toppling back over the ridge's far side. Sophie's spear went with him, ripped from her hands. She fumbled for her own shortsword as two Skaldre ran at her from either side. She got the sword free just in time to deflect the first strike, then she dodged low. The attack from her other side went over her head.

Sophie stayed crouched, keeping her center of balance close to the ground on the uneven ridge. This wasn't her first time fighting on a slope, not after twenty-three years leading acolytes in the Serate Mountains, but her opponents were not so experienced. They stood tall, aiming down at her.

With one foot, Sophie swept the legs out from under her first opponent, sending the Skaldre woman tumbling down into the rising Meyathan ranks. Her second opponent adjusted his footing, and in that moment of hesitation, Sophie thrust her sword up under the Skaldre's shirt of chain mail.

This time Sophie kept hold of her weapon as her enemy fell, but there were more behind him and even more to her other side. With only a shortsword, she had no chance against a charge from both directions.

Then a Meyathan soldier, one of the few who had managed to don any armor during the ambush, clambered onto the ridge behind her. He raised his spear and shouted, "To me, protect your empero!"

More soldiers followed, and then Fryni was at Sophie's side, casting her a scolding look. "A leader should not outrun their soldiers," she said. "At least that's what an abbess I once knew taught me."

A tired laugh escaped Sophie's lips. "Forgive me, it slipped my mind."

Together soldiers and acolytes shielded Sophie from further attack. They spread out in both directions along the ridge as more Meyathans ascended the slope behind them. The remaining Skaldre archers tried to rally, but they were no match for Meyathan discipline in hand-to-hand. The enemy line bent, then shattered, with the Skaldre either dead or tumbling down the ridge's far side to escape.

Down at the Horseshoe's mouth, the Meyathan guard regiments had fallen back to the second barricade. The frantic notes of their signal horns reached Sophie's ears: soon they would retreat in earnest or be overrun. Sophie nodded to herself. Now that they'd secured a place on the ridge to withdraw over, that was fine. The guard regiments could make a fighting retreat and then slip away once they were all out of the valley.

From the north came the notes of other Meyathan signal horns and a rising dust cloud: Savvas's cavalry galloping back toward the Horseshoe. They must have realized something was wrong. That or Faidra was right and Savvas was on his way to finish what Thane Eidsson had started. Sophie could only trust that wasn't the case, or they were all done for.

On the cleared ground below them, ranks of armored Skaldre soldiers retreated from the Horseshoe, thousands of them at least. The sun shone on their many banners, the leaping wolf of Thane Eidsson most prominent among them. Sophie stared down at the enemy. Was the thane among them even now, or had he sent a lieutenant to oversee the ambush?

Fryni growled from deep in her throat. "Cowards. Their ambush failed, so now they're running away."

To Sophie, the retreat had more prudence to it than cowardice. The Skaldre forces, nearly all on foot, were marching toward forested ground, where the Meyathan cavalry wouldn't be able to follow them. The Skaldre hoped to slip away before Savvas arrived, preserving their army to fight another day.

Sophie's hand tightened around her sword. Whether he was here or not, Thane Eidsson had tried to wipe her soldiers out while they slept. His army wasn't getting away. She measured the Horseshoe's outer slope. It was steep, but not too steep for a charge. The Skaldre were fully equipped for battle, while almost none of Sophie's soldiers wore armor, and some lacked even proper weapons, making do with whatever they could find. The Meyathan infantry could never win a conventional battle in this state, but they didn't have to. They only needed to tie the Skaldre down until the cavalry arrived.

Sophie pointed her sword at the retreating enemy and raised her voice in a shout. "Soldiers of Meyatha, we attack!"

A roar of approval greeted her words, and the Meyathan infantry surged down the Horseshoe's slopes. Sophie ran at their head, Fryni beside her.

The rear line of Skaldre shouted confused warnings to their comrades and turned to meet the charge. Fryni darted ahead of Sophie, raising her shield to absorb the deadly arc of a Skaldre soldier's axe. Sophie lunged past her militia captain and buried her sword in the Skaldre's throat.

Beside them, Faidra struck out with her sword, and it bit into an enemy's shield. With her other hand, she shoved Sophie back.

"Will you keep away from their axes, for the Mother's sake?" Faidra said between clenched teeth. "You're no good to any of us with your head split open."

The old rebel was right, and Sophie let a line of imperial soldiers fill the gap between her and the enemy. More of the Skaldre host turned around to face the charge. Their weapons took a bloody toll from the unarmored Meyathans.

Then the first rank of riders appeared around a curve in the road, their officer waving the purple falcon of Meyatha and, below it, the rearing-stallion crest of Savvas Carenthus. They unleashed a volley of arrows into the Skaldre ranks before wheeling to one side, turning in the saddle to loose another flight while making way for the ranks behind them.

Most of the Skaldre archers had died on the ridge, so they had few bows to answer. The forward ranks of Skaldre tried to form a line against this new threat, but with Savvas's cavalry still pouring arrows into them, the line was awkward and disorganized. The second line rank of riders aimed their lances and charged. The two sides clashed, and the Skaldre gave way. Tight wedges of Meyathan cavalry punched through the Skaldre line, their lances red with blood.

It was too much for the surrounded Skaldre. Some broke and ran; others threw down their weapons and shouted their surrender in Meyathan. Sophie took charge of the second group and sent Fryni and Alkestis to ensure that no prisoners were harmed.

She could do nothing for the Skaldre who ran, and most of them were cut down by the Meyathan cavalry. A few reached the woods, where it was too dense for horses to pursue. Signal horns told Sophie that the Horseshoe was clear of the enemy, with a handful of surviving Skaldre archers fleeing toward the woods. Savvas's riders gave chase, picking off the stragglers until only a few escaped.

A helmeted Meyathan rider galloped toward Sophie, visor down to protect against dust and arrows. He reined up his horse and bowed from the saddle, a colonel's emblem on one shoulder. "Your Majesty," he said, "what's left of this Skaldre force is fleeing toward the Golden Fields, where scouts indicate the rest of Thane Eidsson's army is regrouping."

Sophie raised an eyebrow. "Regrouping? Not retreating?" After a defeat like this, most commanders would withdraw as quickly as possible.

The rider shook his head. "No, Your Majesty. With survivors from the Horseshoe and soldiers held in reserve, General Carenthus estimates roughly half of the Skaldre army is still able to fight."

Sophie's brow furrowed. It was still a considerable force, but not enough to defeat her own army except by the most unlikely of luck. Did Thane Eidsson have another army hidden somewhere? Was this a trap within a trap?

"Tell the general I must speak with him immediately," Sophie said.

The rider nodded and flipped his visor up. "I will, Your Majesty. Mother preserve the empero!"

In the moment that Sophie saw the rider's face before he wheeled around, she glimpsed something familiar about his eyes. Was this the same officer who had stared at her earlier in the march? He was already galloping away before Sophie could call out to him.

Sophie shook her head and leaned on a spear someone had given her. She would solve that mystery later, after the Skaldre were finished. Her army had dealt the enemy an injury, but not a knockout blow. Their fight wasn't over yet.

Chapter 20

Savvas brought his charger to a halt just in front of Sophie, his stallion banner flapping in the breeze and specks of blood adorning his plate-mail armor. He dismounted with practiced grace and bowed.

"Your Majesty," he said. "I apologize for our late arrival. If we'd known you were under attack, we'd have been here sooner."

Beside Sophie, Faidra snorted.

Sophie pinched the bridge of her nose. She had no love for Savvas, but he had just dealt a hard blow to their common enemy. "You were just on time," she said. "For that, you have our gratitude. Now, report."

Savvas nodded. "We scouted the main Skaldre army on the Golden Fields last evening, but when it was smaller than expected, I thought they might have sent a force ahead to harass our supply lines." He gestured at the battlefield, where the dead of both sides still littered the field. "I had no idea they would attempt something like this."

"And what of Thane Eidsson himself?" Sophie asked. "Did he lead this ambush personally?"

"I don't know," Savvas said. His expression turned to a frown. "We have not found his body, and he is not among the prisoners. But perhaps four in ten of the ambushers reached the woods, he could have been with them." The general bowed again. "I will see to it they do not escape again."

His hard expression gave Sophie the urge to step back. She did not think Savvas's idea of preventing escape included taking prisoners. She pushed the thought aside. There was no time for it now, not when the enemy was still within striking range.

"Very well," Sophie said. "Let us see to the wounded, then determine how the Skaldre managed to attack us unnoticed."

With the Skaldre gone, the Meyathans quickly reclaimed their camp, setting up sick tents for the wounded and stockades for the prisoners. Soldiers organized into their regiments so their officers could take account of the losses.

Savvas brought Sophie, Fryni, and Faidra to a place outside the valley walls where a pit had been dug into the slope, large enough for a score of armed soldiers to hide in. Inside were the bodies of several Meyathan sentries, their throats slit.

"We've found half a dozen pits like this one dug around the Horseshoe's exterior," Savvas said. "An advanced force hid in them, and once night fell, they emerged to take your sentries by surprise. Then the rest of their force took up positions from a camp deeper into the forest."

Sophie remembered the lone signal horn that woke her just before the first arrows struck. "One of our sentries survived long enough to sound the alarm. They bought us a few seconds before the killing started." Sophie would likely never know that soldier's name; she could only offer a whispered prayer on their behalf.

Faidra sucked air through her teeth, staring at the deep pit. "This couldn't have been done quickly," said. "Thane Eidsson knew we were coming and where we'd camp when we got there."

Sophie grimaced. "Then someone *has* betrayed us." It was the only explanation, and the list of suspects was short. None of the soldiers had known the army's marching route, only those who had been in the room when it was planned: herself, Demetra, Constantia, Makis, Faidra, and Savvas. Fryni and a guard of other acolytes had also been there, but it couldn't have been one of them, could it? Sophie would sooner suspect her family's angry ghosts.

She came out of her thoughts to find Fryni guarding her closely and Faidra staring hard at Savvas.

The general shifted, glaring back at Faidra. "You can't believe it was me," he said. "I returned, I saved you all."

"Yes," Faidra said. "And earned much glory in the process. Very clever. If Sophie had died, you could be empero, and if she lived, then she would owe you a great debt." Her hand came to rest on her sword. "I'd love to see Thane Eidsson's face when he discovers you double-crossed him."

"And what would I have done if the Skaldre succeeded in their ambush? Fight their entire army with just my cavalry?" Savvas turned to Sophie. "Perhaps Speaker Kalgari arranged it, now that it's clear she can't control her pet empero anymore." He pointed at Faidra. "Or maybe you accuse me to cover your own guilt."

Faidra snorted. "I must have iron nerves to catch myself in an ambush."

"You seem to prize plunging the empire into chaos."

Sophie held up a hand. "Enough." She did not believe Savvas would work with his hated enemy, no matter how he felt about Sophie, and surely Demetra would not betray her after all the work they'd done together. "We will not discover the traitor here, shouting at each other. We must focus our efforts on defeating Thane Eidsson before we turn on each other."

Savvas bowed his head. "I obey the empero's command."

Faidra shrugged. "Keep this viper in your closet if you like, Sophie. It's your hand he'll bite first."

Sophie sighed in relief. It was the best response she could have hoped for.

Alkestis jogged into view from the camp, a scroll in hand. The tall acolyte came to a stop, nodded to Fryni, and offered the scroll to Sophie. "The count of losses, Sister Sophie. Ours and what we could guess of the Skaldre."

Sophie took the scroll and unrolled it. It told a grim story. Nearly three in ten of the Meyathan infantry had died or been injured too badly to fight. And yet the Skaldre had suffered worse, losing over two-thirds of the force they had sent, and their fine equipment marked them as Thane Eidsson's elite.

"Well?" Faidra asked, turning her gaze away from Savvas.

"Bad," Sophie said. "But not catastrophic. I believe we should march north immediately and either chase Thane Eidsson from our territory or force his surrender." She offered the scroll first to Faidra, then Savvas. "Are we in agreement?"

"Yes," Savvas said. "If our scouting yesterday was true, Eidsson still has a considerable army at his command. We cannot let them roam free within the empire."

After a moment, Faidra nodded. "There's no telling how much damage he'll do if we let him retreat in his own time. We have to go after him."

The army assembled and marched out in short order, demonstrating the famed efficiency that had once seen the Meyathan Empire stretch from the continent's southern coast to deep in the far north. This time the infantry were ready for battle, armor shining and weapons in hand. They consolidated their ranks to fill the holes left by casualties until there was no outward sign of their losses.

Sophie rode in her dead sister's plate-mail armor, Fryni and the other acolytes on foot around her. Before the noon hour passed, scouts brought back reports that the remnants of Thane Eidsson's force remained camped upon the Golden Fields, not even arrayed for battle.

Sophie blinked at the news. "A trap, do you think?" she asked.

"I do not see how," Savvas said. "My scouts have scoured the edges of the Golden Fields, their attendant villages, and the forests beyond. There is nowhere for Eidsson to hide more soldiers."

Faidra bared her teeth. "He has already evaded your scouts once."

Savvas's mouth set in a thin line. "True. If you would care to scout yourself, then by all means."

Sophie shook her head. "For the last time, peace." She looked at the reports again. "We cannot let ourselves be frightened by shadows. If Eidsson has another scheme, we will never be more ready to face it."

The army marched on, and soon the imperial road opened up onto the Golden Fields: miles of flat plain, bearing the crushed remnants of autumn's harvest that would blossom into golden wheat again come spring. To the west lay dense forest broken up by the many villages that worked the fields. To the east, the high, jagged cliffs of the Empero's Teeth.

Just as the scouts had said, the Skaldre army had pitched their tents upon the field. A trench marked the camp's perimeter, but otherwise it showed no defenses. From the Meyathan army's position at the fields' southern border, it looked to Sophie like nearly half the camp was empty. That still left Eidsson with a sizeable force, but no match for her soldiers.

As the Meyathans assembled into battle ranks, a patrol of Skaldre soldiers left their camp and marched toward the imperial army, a white flag of parley in their leader's hands.

Sophie raised an eyebrow. "I hoped for a surrender, I did not expect it to come so soon."

A squadron of Meyathan cavalry met the Skaldre delegation halfway between the two sides. After a few minutes, one of the riders wheeled his horse around and galloped back to the Meyathan lines. It was the young man that Sophie had seen twice now: first staring at her just after they crossed the Godstep, and then again outside the Horseshoe. Clean-shaven, light-brown skin—something about the set of his severe expression itched at Sophie's memories.

The young colonel nodded to Savvas, then bowed to Sophie. "Thane Eidsson wishes to parley with you, Your Majesty. To discuss his surrender to the empero, he claims."

Faidra cracked her knuckles. "Is that his game?" She looked at Sophie. "Lure you out and ambush you? I suppose he's not the mastermind we all feared."

Savvas nodded. "I agree." He gave Faidra a long look. "This could easily be a trap."

"And yet," Sophie said, "we have no choice but to hear him out. I will not sacrifice any further Meyathan lives if it can be avoided." She turned to the young cavalry colonel. "Arrange a parley with Thane Eidsson. Inform him that my soldiers will be armed and his will not. There is no negotiation on that point."

The colonel nodded, turned his horse, and galloped back out to deliver the message. Shortly afterward, the details were set, and Sophie rode out with Faidra on her right, Savvas on her left, surrounded by acolytes and Meyathan riders.

The meeting place was a small hill about halfway between the Meyathan army and the Skaldre camp. Even this raised ground was covered in the trampled remnants of wheat left after harvesttime. Savvas had insisted on this spot, where they would have the best chance of spotting any potential ambush.

The Skaldre delegation approached on foot from the other side, a dozen in all, most with their people's distinctive blond hair and pale skin. They wore no weapons, so far as Sophie could see, and moved together in a tight knot, gazes darting over the Meyathans. Sophie couldn't blame them, walking unarmed into a meeting with their bitter enemies.

The lead Skaldre was a tall, broad-shouldered man with his golden hair and beard tied in thin braids. He wore a tunic of fine green silk, with the wolf crest sewn in gold. Thane Eidsson, Sophie guessed, though she had never seen him in person. Most of the other Skaldre bore a familial resemblance to him, in the shape of their face or the set of their eyes. Had he brought hostages to offer?

Sophie and the other Meyathans dismounted and strode forward. Silence stretched by as Meyathan and Skaldre stared at each other, before Sophie remembered that as the empero, custom demanded she speak first. "Thane Eidsson," she said. "We accept your request for parley."

Eidsson spread his hands and replied in perfect Meyathan, "Indeed, I bring a great gift for my southern neighbors. I can offer you—"

"You can offer us your unconditional surrender," Sophie said. Angry heat spread up from the base of her neck. "You have invaded Meyathan lands and slain Meyathan citizens. Lay down your arms or stand to fight. We are interested in nothing else."

Savvas nodded, a grim smile on his face. Faidra crossed her arms and yawned.

Eidsson grinned. "You dismiss me, and yet I have brought you Meyatha's true empero." He snapped his fingers, and the knot of Skaldre behind him separated to reveal a young Meyathan woman, with curly black hair and skin as dark brown as Sophie's own.

Taisa. Sophie stared. Her sister hadn't changed at all, from the elegant bones of her face and her piercing eyes to her very stance, proud and challenging. A bruise marred her cheek, but otherwise she was the very image of how she'd looked the day Sophie was banished. No, that had been twenty-three years ago. This young woman couldn't be much over sixteen.

"I present to you," Eidsson said, "Dafni Laskaris, rightful heir to the Falcon Throne." He and the other Skaldre knelt, bowing their heads to the silent young woman.

No one spoke among the Meyathans. Savvas's eyes were wide. Faidra's posture went rigid. Sophie's voice stuck in her throat. *Dafni.* Her niece was alive. Alive and standing before her. How was it possible? Demetra had been certain she was dead with the rest of her family. But Demetra had rushed to Gray Falls the moment news had reached her. How reliable had her first reports been?

Savvas recovered first, hand on the hilt of his mace. "What is the meaning of this?"

"My soldiers rescued her from a raid on your northern border," Eidsson said, standing to his full height. "We were coming south to install her as empero in Heratia."

He would have gone on, but Dafni herself stepped forward, cutting him off. "This man"—she indicated Thane Eidsson—"murdered my imperial mother and my father. He would have killed me as well if my brother had survived the ambush. He meant to use me as a puppet to control Meyatha."

She spoke the words with a calm certainty, like a general describing the facts of a battlefield. If Dafni had any anger over her family's death, Sophie couldn't detect it. Was that the imperial training, or was Sophie's niece simply numb from her loss?

Savvas snarled and drew his mace. "Say the word and you will have vengeance here and now."

Eidsson took a step back, but Dafni waved Savvas down. "It is not necessary. His army is broken and his plans are in ruins. To save his own life, he has sworn loyalty to me before his own soldiers and offered his family as hostages. I have his obedience, if not his loyalty." Her eyes swept over the Meyathan delegation, settling first on Savvas, then on Sophie. "The only question now is if you will serve your rightful empero."

Savvas dropped to his knees and bowed his head so low it nearly touched the crushed wheat beneath his feet. "My life, my loyalty, my soldiers are Your Majesty's."

Faidra sucked in a hissing breath. Fryni motioned, and the other acolytes closed in around Sophie, their eyes now on Savvas, the Skaldre, and the Meyathan riders.

Dafni stepped toward Sophie, and her imperious expression melted into a warm smile. She reached out a hand, fingers already carrying the calluses of sword practice, and touched Sophie's cheek.

"You must be my Aunt Sophie," Dafni said. "I've always wanted to meet you."

"You—you have?" Sophie asked, her voice choked.

Daphni nodded. "My mother—" The young woman's voice caught for a moment. "She called you a traitor, but I know she missed you, and I always wanted to meet the woman who gave old Ironheart such a run of trouble."

Sophie could barely breathe. Taisa had missed her? Dafni wanted to know her? "I didn't know you were alive," Sophie gasped out. "If I had..."

"I know," Dafni said, her voice calm and understanding as if she were twenty-seven years Sophie's elder and not the other way around. Dafni shot a baleful look at the Skaldre delegation. "The thane planned to use me as a puppet empero, but now that you have defeated him, he will be *my* puppet in exchange for imperial support in keeping his place as leader of the Skaldre confederation."

"You negotiated that, as his prisoner?" Sophie asked, her voice incredulous.

"I convinced him it was either that or your army would chase him down like a dog," Dafni said. She stood to her full height, nearly eye to eye with Sophie. "All that's left is for you to escort me back to Heratia and my throne."

"Sophie," Faidra said, more than a note of warning in the single word.

Sophie heard the tension in her old friend's voice. "Much has occurred," Sophie said to Dafni. "I have reinstated the People's Chamber, opened Heratia's granaries, and confiscated the wealth of rebellious senators."

Dafni's nostrils flared. "You should not have overstepped so." Then her voice softened again. "No matter, we can talk about it later, once we're home." The mask of regal magnanimity was back in place.

But Sophie had seen. For a moment, Dafni had shown less of her mother Taisa and more of Irena Ironheart. "There is still so much to do," Sophie said. "I cannot simply give up the throne."

"Of course you can, Aunt Sophie," Dafni said. Her warm gaze turned piercing. "Step down from a throne that is no longer yours, and save the empire yet more bloodshed."

Sophie swallowed the lump in her throat. Bloodshed? Would she have to fight Dafni? Could she? Sophie was officially empero, but in imperial law, Dafni had by far the stronger claim. She was next in line after Taisa and Mihail, while Sophie had forced the Senate to ignore her own removal from the Laskaris family inheritance and confirm her. Sophie had to say something, but no words came.

Dafni went on. "You have done well securing the empire in my absence, as my imperial mother would have wanted. Show your loyalty and you will be welcome in my palace, adviser to my throne, and tutor to my children when I have them."

That brought a quiet curse from Faidra, and Sophie couldn't blame her. Sophie had sworn to be the last empero, the last Laskaris. But she was not the last after all. Sophie could never mend her rift with Taisa, but here was Taisa's daughter, alive and asking Sophie to join her. The palace could be home again, not just a means to power. Dafni had been through so much, and yet here she stood, sounding like an empero already. Could Sophie turn her down?

Dafni cleared her throat. "I require an answer, Aunt Sophie."

"I request a recess," Sophie said at last. Time, she needed time. "I must discuss this with my advisers." She gestured at the scene. "Surely that is not too much to ask under the circumstances."

Dafni's eyes narrowed, and her voice took on a hint of anger. "Fine. I will await your answer in one hour, not a moment longer."

She turned to Savvas. "General Carenthus, you will escort me and my hostages. I desire to be among Meyathans again."

Savvas nodded and climbed up onto his horse. One of his riders dismounted and offered Dafni their horse's reins. She swung up into the saddle with a fluid motion.

"Riders, on me," Savvas said. "We hear our empero's command and obey." A gloating smile touched his lips as he met Sophie's gaze. Then his cavalry formed up around him and Dafni, the horse's hooves churning up the earth as they turned back to Meyathan lines.

Sophie watched them go, the last true Laskaris riding to her people.

Chapter 21

Sophie returned to the Meyathan lines in a daze, but preoccupied as she was, even she couldn't miss the way Savvas's cavalry regiments had separated from the rest of the army, moving a good distance away and circling up into a temporary camp. Perhaps Savvas feared Sophie would send someone to kill Dafni, a reasonable fear considering Demetra's plan to kill *him*.

She followed Faidra to a tent that had been set up for them. Only Fryni followed them inside, while Alkestis took command of the other acolytes outside. Once the flap closed, its thick canvas muffling sounds from outside, Faidra lit a candle and turned to Sophie.

"That was smart, playing for time. Now we need a plan while she thinks we're still considering her offer." She paused, and her eyes narrowed at Sophie. "We *are* only pretending to consider it, yes?"

Sophie looked away. "I'm not certain. Perhaps." She couldn't meet Faidra's eyes.

"I can't believe you," Faidra said. She set the candle down and stalked toward Sophie. "You'd betray everything we've fought for, betray me, for the word of some child?"

Dull anger replaced some of Sophie's shame. How much abuse did Faidra expect her to put up with? "Maybe Dafni *should* be empero," Sophie said, finally meeting Faidra's gaze. "She already looks and sounds the part. She wouldn't have to fight the Senate tooth and nail to get anything done."

"She won't have to fight because she'll do exactly what the Senate wants," Faidra said. She leaned in close to Sophie's face. "Just like her grandfather and her great-grandmother. She'll let the senators take more and more until there's nothing left. We have to stop her."

Sophie held her ground. "Stop her? Do you know what that would mean? We'd have to fight Dafni, Savvas, and the Skaldre for that matter. And even if we somehow win, there's no guarantee we can stop her here. If Dafni's cause spreads, it could become a full civil war."

That took Faidra back a step. Both women were quiet for a moment. Sophie shivered. Bloody as it had been, their uprising in Heratia was nothing compared to the conflicts that had ravaged Meyatha in the past between rival claimants to the throne. Faidra knew the same history; even she wouldn't eagerly court that again.

Sophie raised both hands, palms open. "Perhaps we can negotiate with Dafni, convince her to guarantee the gains we've already made." Even as she said the words, Sophie recalled the easy confidence with which Dafni had demanded imperial power and how the young woman had balked when Sophie didn't immediately acquiesce. Negotiations would not be easy.

Faidra shook her head, but her voice was quiet. "It wouldn't last, not once she's back in Heratia, surrounded by Savvas and his ilk." Now it was Faidra who wouldn't meet Sophie's gaze.

Sophie put a hand on her old friend's shoulder. "I'd be there too. I can help her understand." For all her imperial bearing, Dafni was still only sixteen. Sophie might be able to influence the young empero. It wasn't what Faidra wanted, it wasn't what they had fought for, but what choice did she have? She had promised to be the last of her line when she thought her entire family was dead. She couldn't fight her flesh and blood, not again.

"We promised the people justice." Fryni's voice rang out, startling Sophie and Faidra both. The young captain looked at Sophie. "You promised it to them at the imperial grain stores, and we acolytes promised it when we charged off the ships. We swore to create a Meyatha where no one starved, where their freedoms wouldn't be sold to the highest bidder. People gave their lives for it. Is it the Mother's justice to let your niece take the Falcon Throne, Sister Sophie?"

The gentle rebuke hit Sophie like a slingstone. She sank down onto a low stool, the strength to stand completely gone.

Faidra whistled. "Damn. Fryni, wasn't it? If we'd had you in the first uprising, convincing people to sign up wouldn't have been a problem."

Fryni shrugged. "Sister Sophie will know what to do."

Sophie pressed a hand to her temple. How could Fryni still trust her so? Sophie had just nearly given up everything that others had fought and died to gain. Meyatha was so close to a better future, and she was ready to throw it away for the sake of family. This couldn't be about family; it had to be about justice.

"Dearest one," Sophie said, "your estimation of me is too high, but I will try." She took a deep breath. "You're both right. We've come too far to give up." She looked to Faidra. "My niece will not give up her claim through talk, she made that much clear. The question now is if we have any chance of stopping her. Will the army even follow me?"

"Not the cavalry," Faidra said. "Savvas trained half of them himself, and they're mostly from senatorial families anyway. But the infantry, they stood with you under Skaldre arrows, and you led them out of it. They'll follow, I think." She paused. "But all the same, it might be better not to tell them who we're marching against. Just say Savvas betrayed us."

Sophie shook her head. "No. If they follow me, they deserve to know why." She doubted she could keep this kind of news from the soldiers anyway, and not acknowledging it would only damage morale further. "I'll address them myself."

She stood and, with Fryni preceding her, emerged from the tent. Outside the Meyathan infantry stood in loose ranks, many of them glancing to where Savvas's cavalry had moved closer to the Skaldre camp. They no longer flew the rearing stallion of House Carenthus but the imperial falcon, an honor reserved for an army led personally by the empero.

Fryni and Faidra dispatched messengers to spread the word that the remaining soldiers should gather to hear Sophie speak. It did not take long for the infantry to assemble, as most of them had already been arrayed for battle. One of Sophie's acolytes found a crate from the supply wagons for her to stand on, which raised her up just enough so the soldiers in the very back lines could see her.

Sophie took a breath. If these soldiers would not follow her, then all the conviction in the world did not matter. She projected her voice out over the armored ranks. "Thane Eidsson has just revealed that he kept my niece, Dafni Laskaris, alive to be made a puppet empero."

Several soldiers booed; others looked at each other in confusion. Sophie held up a hand for quiet. "That was his plan, but he has no hope of achieving it now. Instead he has sworn loyalty to Dafni to save his own life. General Savvas Carenthus and those loyal to him have gone over as well, and they plan to put her on the Falcon Throne in my place."

To this the soldiers responded with total silence. Even the ever-present clink of armored links rubbing together was muffled as they stood still as statues, eyes fixed on Sophie.

She went on, "Carenthus follows Dafni because her blood is closer to the line of succession than my own, and because she will undo the reforms we won in Heratia." She paused for a moment, letting her words sink in. "But for my part, I believe that Meyatha's people are more important than the vagaries of imperial inheritance." Most of the faces watching her were rank-and-file soldiers, not Faidra's rebels. Sophie couldn't know how they'd react to such a plea, but she had to try. "Your fellow citizens chose me, and we are here as an instrument of their will."

She spread her arms, encompassing every soldier. "I stood with you under Skaldre arrows, and together we escaped that killing ground. When this campaign is finished, I will see that no citizen ever goes hungry again. I will make your voices heard in the halls of power. *I* will ensure that you never need fear senatorial encroachment again. If that makes me worthy to lead you, then together we have the strength to keep Meyatha out of traitors' hands. If not, then you have the power to end this right here." She tilted her head slightly to the side, exposing her neck.

Faidra and Fryni shot her alarmed looks, but this was the path they had all chosen. Either the army would follow her, or it would not.

A few soldiers shifted from their rigid poses, hands drifting near weapons. Then one man stepped forward out of the front rank. He was old by a soldier's standard, nearing forty at least. He turned his back toward Sophie and faced the other soldiers, then banged his spear against his shield. "Sophie!" he shouted. He knocked spear and shield together a second time. "Sophie!"

A second soldier took up the chant, banging his spear and shield in time with the first. Then a third, and then a fourth. One by one, the ranks of soldiers raised their voices. "Sophie! Sophie! Sophie!" The chant spread until thousands of Meyathan legionnaires shouted Sophie's name together, echoing until anyone within half a dozen miles would know who they served.

A weight lifted off Sophie's shoulders. Her cause wasn't doomed; she still had an army to protect what fragile gains had been made in Heratia. She turned to Faidra. "Send a messenger to inform my niece that I will not abdicate. If she acknowledges that I am empero, rightly confirmed by the Senate, this can still end peacefully." Dafni would do no such thing, not the young woman with all the world's fire in her eyes, but Sophie had to give her the chance.

Faidra raised an eyebrow. "You don't wish to speak with her yourself?"

Sophie shook her head. "The empero does not negotiate with pretenders."

Chapter 22

As the Meyathan infantry re-formed into battle ranks, shouts echoed from Savvas's cavalry formation across the Golden Fields. Sophie squinted. Neither Savvas nor the Skaldre were yet arrayed for battle. What was happening?

Savvas's rightmost regiment broke away from his lines, nearly a thousand riders and their mounts moving toward Sophie's infantry at a full gallop. Sophie found her horse and climbed up into the saddle. Was this some kind of attack? It seemed poorly planned and sloppy, even for a general less skilled than Savvas Carenthus. No, the remaining riders had drawn bows and loosed arrows after their galloping comrades. Several fell. It wasn't an attack; some of Savvas's cavalry were fleeing his lines.

Arrows flew after the fleeing riders for a few moments as they drew closer to Sophie's side. Though Savvas's remaining force greatly outnumbered the deserters, they could not pursue without leaving their Skaldre allies behind. Soon the fleeing riders were out of range. The escape had been well planned.

The deserters crossed the Golden Fields at a lightning pace, a full regiment of Meyathan cavalry armed and armored for battle. They reined up just outside the range of an easy bow shot, and one rider continued on alone with a parley flag raised.

Several of Sophie's soldiers and acolytes tensed, but Sophie waved them down. "Let him through," she commanded.

As the rider drew closer, she recognized him: the young colonel who'd delivered them news of the Skaldre camp, who had stared at her on the march north. He bowed from the saddle. "Your Majesty," he said. "I am Omiros Leonid, of the Thirteenth Cavalry. My riders and I pledge ourselves to your service against the pretender."

"Welcome," Sophie said. "If you would fight with us, then you are the Mother's own blessing." Some cavalry of her own could easily make the difference against an enemy like Savvas.

Faidra made a disapproving noise. "A blessing straight from Savvas, eh? Did he gift wrap you himself?"

The young colonel set his jaw as color sprang to his light-brown cheeks. Sophie tilted her head. There was something so familiar about the way he did that. He spoke. "Twoscore of my riders fell when they loosed arrows after us." He turned to look back across the field. "I would not sacrifice them like that just to betray you."

Faidra shrugged. "I might, to get a regiment of my elite cavalry into the enemy's ranks." She leaned forward in her saddle. "And I know Savvas would."

"A moment," Sophie said. This arguing could go in circles until Savvas overran them, and she had to know. "Who are you, young Omiros Leonid? I have never heard your name but with Sol's eyes I swear I have seen your face before."

Omiros bowed again. "Leonid is my father's house, and I honor it," he said. "It has allowed me to rise quickly in the ranks. But at my birth, my mother named me Omiros Dellis."

Sophie's heart skipped a beat. *Dellis.* This was the son of Styliani Dellis, her teacher who had passed away writing truths no one could read. Mother and Her blessed daughters, of course she recognized him. The tone of his skin and severe gray eyes were exactly the same as his mother's, especially when he was arguing. A glance at Faidra showed an expression of shock and recognition.

"Forgive me," Faidra said. "I should have—" Her voice caught. "I should have recognized you. I thought you'd been assigned to a southern garrison, to get you away from Heratia and its politics."

Omiros nodded. "That was my father's wish. Even before the first uprising, he begged my mother to keep me out of her radical movement, so he tells me." He looked up and met Sophie's eyes. "But she always spoke well of you, Your Majesty, when I was allowed to see her. Even as her health faded. Even at the end."

Sophie swallowed around the lump in her throat. "It is good to finally meet you, son of my teacher." She cleared her throat. "Bring your riders across the line, *General* Leonid, so they might fight beside us."

Omiros's eyes widened. "Your Majesty, I am only a colonel. It will be years before I am ready for promotion."

Sophie waved the objection away. "You command the empero's cavalry, and none of my other officers have experience leading from horseback. Fetch your riders, General, so we may have my second council of war in less than a week."

***

Sophie gathered her war council on the highest piece of ground they could find. Atop this modest hillock, they at least had a full view of the enemy force, as well as their own. The fields stretched north for miles, bordered on its eastern side by the jagged cliffs of the Empero's Teeth and on the western side by thick timber forests.

Sophie's war council consisted of herself, Fryni, Faidra, the newly promoted Omiros, and half a dozen of the senior infantry officers. Except for Faidra and Sophie herself, they were all so young. Sophie couldn't be sure how many of them had ever seen a real battle. Her own experience was limited to the street fights of the uprisings and repelling raiders in Gray Falls, nothing like the massive clash that was before them.

They gathered around their best maps of the Golden Fields, which they had spread on a rickety table. Omiros spoke. "Savvas must get past us before he takes Dafni to the capital." He pointed at the map. "He will deploy his cavalry here, on the fields' west side, where the ground is flat and firm. It's too uneven near the Empero's

Teeth for good charges." He gestured at the eastern side of the plain, where flat wheat fields broke up into foothills of the jagged cliffs.

Omiros went on, "He'll split the Skaldre infantry between his center and eastern side. Their only job is to hold until his cavalry break through and sweep us aside from the west."

The other officers voiced their agreement with the assessment, adding minor opinions about where the remaining Skaldre archers would be placed and other details, but it seemed to Sophie that the greater part of Savvas's battle plan would be brutally simple.

Meyathan military doctrine called for infantry to stand their ground while cavalry broke through on one or both flanks and either annihilated the enemy or forced them to retreat depending on the goals of a campaign. The cavalry's speed and the range of their bows meant that as long as they had room to maneuver, they could only be engaged with arrows or other cavalry. Their charge was a force to be reckoned with as well, as every rider was trained with the lance.

In contrast, the Skaldre traditionally depended on charging infantry to break an enemy weakened by withering arrow volleys. With Thane Eidsson's forces badly reduced from their loss at the Horseshoe, Savvas would likely not rely on them for his primary attack.

Sophie had barely a quarter of the riders that her enemies possessed. Her infantry wielded spear and shield; they were trained to hold their own line, not break through the enemy's. They could outlast the weakened Skaldre formations, but they would never route the enemy infantry before Savvas's cavalry broke through Sophie's western flank and enveloped them.

Faidra sighed. "Do we have any defense against this brilliant plan by Savvas, or do we march into a doomed battle hoping the Mother delivers a miracle?"

Uncomfortable silence settled after Faidra's question.

Finally Fryni spoke up. "Can we return the favor? Send our cavalry to the eastern side and break through the Skaldre infantry there?"

Omiros shook his head. "My regiment alone isn't enough, and the ground close to the Empero's Teeth is too uneven for good maneuvering on horseback." He straightened up. "I believe our best chance is for my regiment to engage Savvas's riders with our bows. It is possible we may hold him long enough for our infantry to overwhelm the Skaldre foot soldiers."

"You'll die," Faidra said. "Savvas's arrows will cut you to pieces long before the infantry can make any headway."

Omiros protested, and they argued back and forth about his plan's viability and whether they had any alternative. Sophie was inclined to agree with Faidra. They had very few archers among their infantry, which would leave Omiros and his riders without any support. If her infantry tried to close in on Savvas's cavalry for spear work, Savvas had miles of plain to retreat through while showering them with arrows the whole time. Something about Fryni's suggestion tugged at her though.

"Savvas will deploy all his cavalry in the west," Sophie said, interrupting the argument, "and not leave any to reinforce the center or the eastern flank?"

Omiros nodded. "It's what I would do. The more concentrated his cavalry, the better they can punch through our line."

"And the Skaldre morale will be low," Sophie continued, the shape of a plan forming in her mind. "They came here as conquerors, now they are vassals to the young woman who should have been their puppet."

Faidra made a frustrated sound in her throat. "Yes, but what's the point? Even if their morale is low, they won't break in time to do any good."

"Not in an honest fight," Sophie said. She tapped the eastern side of the map. "But if I lead my acolytes and the Gray Falls militia up the Empero's Teeth, we can get around the far end of their line and climb down to attack them from behind. The Skaldre's eastern flank will break, and their center will follow after it."

She pressed her index finger down in the middle of the battle map. "That will open a gap in the center, which Omiros will bring his riders through to engage Savvas's cavalry with lances from the side. That will tie them down long enough for our infantry to surround them," she finished with a flourish.

A barrage of objections greeted her plan. Sophie raised her hands for silence. "One at a time, please." She nodded to Omiros.

"It's too difficult a climb," the newly minted general said. "For long stretches there's nothing but sheer limestone. You'll have to carry armor and weapons, you won't make it."

Sophie resisted the urge to pat the young man's arm. "In Gray Falls, my militia and I conquered far more dangerous ascents. It was the only way to reach the most isolated villages."

One of the infantry officers spoke up. "But your militia is less than two hundred soldiers, that's barely enough to dent the Skaldre's numbers."

"We do not need great numbers," Sophie said. "The shock of being surrounded is what will break the Skaldre." She hoped she was right, but there was only one way to find out.

"But what about the Skaldre archers?" another officer asked. "If they see you coming, they'll have an easy time picking you off the cliffs with their longbows."

"That's true," Sophie said. She did not relish the prospect of scaling the cliffs under a hail of arrows. "But if we leave immediately, we can be at least part of the way there before they're in position. The alternative is a battle we are sure to lose, and I would rather take my chances with the cliff."

Finally Faidra spoke. "It's a decent plan." She pointed a finger at Sophie. "But you can't lead it."

Heat spread over Sophie's face. Would Faidra ever do anything but contradict her? "We all know how dangerous that climb is," Sophie said. "I can't ask my acolytes to face it alone."

"Yes," Faidra said, "you can. You're the empero. We've bet everything on you." She leaned forward, a hand on her chest. "*My* people bet everything on you. If you die, winning this battle doesn't matter."

Before Sophie could reply, Fryni joined the argument. "She's right, Sister Sophie, even if she's rude," she said with a frown in Faidra's direction. "I'll lead the climb."

Sophie's heart raced. She took Fryni's hand. "Dearest one, no, I can't ask that." This brilliant young woman wouldn't even be here, fighting and killing far from home, if not for Sophie.

Fryni squeezed Sophie's hand. "You're not asking, Sister Sophie. I'm captain of the Gray Falls militia, leading them is my charge." She grinned and poked Sophie in the ribs. "Besides, you told me climbing mountains was a young woman's game."

A pit widened in Sophie's chest. They were right, Void take them all, they were right. She pulled Fryni in close and held her in a tight embrace. "Brave Sol keep you in her sight," she said.

Fryni returned the hug. "She'll be busy watching you while I'm gone."

Omiros cleared his throat. "Even if the plan goes perfectly, that will leave Savvas plenty of time to attack us on the western flank."

Sophie released Fryni. "Then we shall have to hold the line until Fryni is in position." It was a plan at least. A plan with too many points of failure, but it gave them better odds than being ground under Savvas's cavalry.

"I have one more question," Faidra said. "A third of the enemy out there is wearing Meyathan uniform. How do we tell each other apart?" She looked at Omiros. "When I knock a rider down, I'd like to know it's not one of yours."

"Ah, yes," Omiros said. He bowed again to Sophie. "I'm sorry, Your Majesty, that point slipped my mind." He straightened. "Before my regiment and I broke out, Savvas had given orders to cut several old banners into purple armbands, I believe at the pretender's direction."

Sophie chuckled. "My niece has a flair for the dramatic. The imperial color on her soldiers to show she is the rightful empero."

"It's clever," Fryni said. "It makes her side look legitimate, like we're the pretenders. And we can't exactly copy her."

Sophie clapped her hands together. "Then we shall have to appeal to the only power higher than the empero."

Chapter 23

Sophie's army arrayed itself for battle in the afternoon's warm sun. Eight regiments of Meyathans split into their battle units, spreading out across the Golden Fields from the Empero's Teeth in the east to the timber forests in the west. With spear and shield they marched in disciplined lines, their few archers concentrated in the western flank where they could provide some cover against Savvas's cavalry. Every soldier, from the highest officer to the newest recruit, wore a swatch of black fabric on one arm: the mark that both identified their allegiance to Sophie and their faith in the Void Mother.

Dafni's army deployed itself precisely as Omiros had predicted, close enough for Sophie to see the crests on their banners. Thane Eidsson's six remaining regiments held the center and eastern flank, their infantry carrying round shields and a mix of axes and swords. The Skaldre's surviving archers spread out among them, depleted but still dangerous. Meanwhile, the entirety of Savvas's cavalry concentrated itself on the western flank across from Sophie, bows and lances at the ready. Row upon row stood waiting for the order to attack, both horses and riders covered in shining steel scales. Above them fluttered the imperial falcon banner, a sign that the woman they would make empero rode with them.

To Sophie's left, a warm afternoon breeze rustled the dense trees that formed the battlefield's western edge. She glanced east, toward the Empero's Teeth. Though Sophie couldn't see them from so far off, Fryni and the other acolytes were up there now. Fryni would stick to shadowed crevices, leading her sisters and militia up until they could climb back down behind the Skaldre line.

"Merciful Luna, do not take them from me," Sophie whispered. "Great Mother, keep them cloaked in your Void." Fryni's best chance was for the battle to begin as soon as possible so the remaining Skaldre archers would have something else to occupy their attention.

Omiros and his riders were stationed in the center behind the infantry. He had insisted on detaching twoscore riders to act as Sophie's escort and emergency reserve. She had agreed, provided he swore not to move the rest of his force until the Skaldre began to break. Her army would have only one chance to pin down Savvas's cavalry, if the chance came at all, and Sophie did not intend to lose it. If the enemy riders were not enveloped, they had all of the Golden Fields to retreat down. Dafni would escape to raise her banner elsewhere in the empire, a fire Sophie would never be able to quench.

All of that was assuming Savvas didn't break Sophie's western flank first and annihilate the rest of her army on the spot. She looked at her new squadron of bodyguards, then to Faidra. Her old friend sat mounted among a group of former rebels, those with the skill to ride. Faidra looked at ease, just as she always had during the uprising, whether it was the triumphant early days or the last few hours before their final defeat.

There was nothing else for it. "Signal the advance," Sophie said.

Faidra raised a signal horn to her lips and blew out three short tones followed by a single longer tone. The pattern spread across Sophie's army as each unit's standard-bearer took it. A different set of tones sounded from across the field, Dafni's own call to battle.

Sophie's Meyathan infantry in the center and east stepped forward in unified ranks, shields high and spears level. The Skaldre infantry opposite them held their ground, standing as their longbow archers loosed volley after volley of goose-feathered shafts. While there were too few archers for them to be a serious threat, they aimed their arrows well. Most buried themselves in Meyathan shields or glanced off steel helmets, but some found gaps, and a handful of Sophie's soldiers fell to the firm earth. Soldiers from the reserves pulled their fallen comrades back to the physicians' tents, but some were already dead.

Sophie made herself breathe. They were not the first to die for her, and they would not be the last. As the distance between Skaldre and Meyathan lines shrank, the enemy archers loosed their last volley. Both sides' war cries merged into a wordless roar, the two lines crashing together in a cacophony of soldiers and steel that thundered across the plain. Now the eastern and center fronts were a shoving match between two shield walls, and the first to break would pay a heavy toll indeed.

Only on the western flank, far enough across the Golden Plain that Sophie's eastern soldiers were tiny blurs to her eye, did the Meyathan line hold rather than charge. Chasing Savvas's cavalry was pointless. The first move was his. Sophie did not have long to wait. The enemy's standard-bearers blew a sharp sequence of notes, and the first rank of riders cantered forward, arrows drawn to bowstrings.

A storm of barbed shafts lanced out from the first rank of riders. Sophie's infantry locked their shields in a tight phalanx, but they couldn't cover every gap, and these riders were much closer than their Skaldre allies had been. Arrows found their way into gaps and cracks. Soldiers fell. Others rushed forward to take their place, but it was a grueling stand, with the enemy dispensing death from just out of reach.

For two units in the front lines, it was too much. They broke ranks and charged, spears held high. Sophie's guts tightened into a hard knot. This was exactly what Savvas wanted. If her infantry left their protected phalanx, his riders could cut them down with ease, then turn and envelop the rest of the army.

Sophie urged her horse forward into the gap between two of her infantry phalanxes. Her startled escort pushed hard to keep up.

"Hold!" Sophie shouted to the soldiers who still kept their positions. "Soldiers of Meyatha, hold your line!"

An arrow glanced off the metal plate protecting her shoulder, the impact jerking her in the saddle.

The captain of Sophie's escort, a fresh-faced woman with alarmed eyes, shouted for Sophie to turn back. Sophie kept on. If her line broke here, everything else would fall to pieces. Her plate-mail armor gave Sophie better protection than any of her soldiers; she could risk a few arrows.

With the imperial falcon shining on her breastplate, Sophie steered her horse out in front of the line and rode parallel to her soldiers. "You stood with me under the shields," she called out at the top of her lungs. "Stand with me now!"

At their captain's direction, Sophie's escort shifted around her, steering their mounts to form a wall between Sophie and the enemy. They caught most of the arrows on their shields or armor, but one rider fell from the saddle, a shaft jutting from between bent steel scales. Sophie kept her eyes forward. She couldn't think about every soldier who fell in her name, not when the whole battle relied on her formations holding.

The rest of her soldiers kept their position as Sophie rode up and down the line. Reserve troops came up to fill the space left by the two units that had chased after Savvas's riders. The barrage of arrows slackened as the enemy's quivers ran low. Finally, they turned their mounts pulled back toward their own line where fresh arrows awaited them, no doubt.

Sophie watched them pull back, and her eyes fell on what remained of the two units that had broken formation. Arrows bristled from their bodies; all of them were dead upon the field. It must have happened as she had enjoined their comrades to stand firm. Outside the phalanx of shields, the wayward soldiers had possessed no defense against attacks from the side. There was nothing she could do for them now, not until the battle was won and there was time for Luna and her starry children to guide the fallen into the Void.

The captain of Sophie's escort cleared her throat. "Your Majesty, if we might get you behind the front line?" She jerked her hand toward the enemy side. "They'll be back, and one arrow is all it takes."

Sophie nodded. "Proceed, Captain." This part of the line was steady for now at least. The captain and her riders guided Sophie between the forward ranks and toward the reserve. Soldiers on either side knocked shield and spear together in salute as Sophie passed. She acknowledged them with an arm crossed over her chest.

Faidra and her riders approached at a fast trot as Sophie reached the rearmost ranks. "Good of you to survive," Faidra said. "The eastern flank is holding steady, and the Skaldre have given some ground in the center, but not enough to do us any good."

Her next words were cut off by a long tone from the enemy signal horns, which was followed by a complex series of shorter tones. Across the field, the bulk of Savvas's cavalry squadrons shifted into arrowhead formations, each creating a deadly point meant to punch through a weakened enemy. As Sophie watched, the front rank of riders stowed their bows and took up their lances.

Faidra's voice was incredulous. "They can't be planning a charge. Savvas might as well hand us the battle fried in olive oil."

"General Carenthus wouldn't throw his riders' lives away like that," the captain of Sophie's cavalry guard said.

Sophie could only agree. Meyathan cavalry charges were devastating when there was an opening to exploit, but her infantry's formation was unbroken. Crashing his riders into them would give Savvas nothing but bodies; surely he knew that. For that matter, surely Dafni knew it too, with an imperial heir's education.

And yet the enemy riders lowered their spears and urged their horses to a full gallop, thundering across the plain. Sophie's infantry braced, a forest of spears growing from a wall of shields. Then, seconds before contact, the leading edge of Savvas's charge wheeled their horses around and swept back the way they had come. The next rank repeated this graceful pirouette, and the next. Sophie's breath caught. It was a dance in the center of a battlefield.

Then she saw one of her forward infantry platoons break ranks and charge after the retreating cavalry. She couldn't blame them; the enemy was so close, and they were retreating just slowly enough that a frustrated foot soldier might believe they could catch up. And yet if more than a handful of platoons took the bait, her entire army was doomed.

"Damn you, Savvas," Sophie muttered.

She took up her reins, but Faidra's voice stopped her. "No. This is why Omiros gave you a cavalry reserve." She waved a hand at the young captain and her riders. "We're not giving Savvas and his imperial brat another free shot at your head."

The captain nodded. "We fight at the empero's command."

Sophie quashed her urge to protest. Faidra was right. She couldn't risk her own life when there were others to risk their lives for her. Perhaps one day that fact would stop making her nauseous.

"Sol light your way," she said to the captain. "May your spears strike true in her sight."

The captain gestured to her riders. "Lances, on me. We ride for the Falcon Throne."

The squadron wheeled as one and thundered toward the front line at a full gallop. The reserve ranks of infantry parted to let the riders through even as more of their frontline comrades fell for Savvas's trap, charging after the enemy despite their officers' frantic orders.

The young captain and her squadron struck with deadly precision, cutting down half a dozen of Savvas's cavalry in the first few moments. Their charge spent, Sophie's riders dropped their spears, drawing swords and maces for close-in work.

In the next second, another squadron of Savvas's cavalry arrived, and this time the momentum was theirs as they cut into Sophie's riders like a scythe. The captain took a blow in the leg and tumbled from the saddle, disappearing from sight in the melee.

Sophie clutched her reins and focused on keeping her breath steady. Another mark on the tally of people Sophie had sent to their deaths, and Sophie had not even known the woman's name. Faidra put a hand on Sophie's shoulder, a comforting weight even through steel armor.

By now Sophie's infantry were in motion, fanning out to envelop the hated enemy cavalry that the mounted reserve had bogged down. A few of Savvas's riders managed to cut their way free, but most were pulled from the saddle or impaled on long spears as they tried to escape. The next wave of charging cavalry wheeled early and began a true retreat back to their line. They knew better than to get entangled in melee with Sophie's infantry when Savvas had the luxury of time to break them with arrows.

The infantry that had taken Savvas's bait turned back for the relative safety of their line, but most were cut down by riders going the other way or by arrows loosed from Savvas's reserve squadrons. More soldiers advanced to fill their places in the line. Wounded were carried back by auxiliaries, then taken off the battlefield and toward the physicians' tents.

Sophie's line held, but after two near disasters it was a ragged thing, the reserves thinning, soldiers in the front exhausted from standing their ground while the enemy danced just out of reach.

Finally the call of a horn sounded down Sophie's line from the far eastern side of the battlefield. The Gray Falls militia had begun their attack. If it went well, and if Sophie's guess about Skaldre morale had been right, then the enemy infantry would soon begin to break, leaving Omiros and his riders a path to pin Savvas down from the side.

A different horn blared: not one of Sophie's, and it came from much closer. Sophie and Faidra both turned their heads to the west, following the sound toward the woods on their left.

A flight of arrows loosed from between the trees and tore into the Meyathan infantry's flank with the driving power of Skaldre longbows.

"Ambush!" Faidra shouted to her people, shifting her horse so she was between Sophie and the new threat. "Close ranks!"

More arrows flew from the woods, but all were aimed at the reeling Meyathan soldiers. Sophie and Faidra were far enough away that even a longbow would struggle to reach them, and Sophie doubted these new attackers would waste their arrows so.

The second volley ceased, and a line of armored Skaldre soldiers roared from the woods, led by a tall man with golden hair streaming from under his helmet and a wolf crest on his armor. It could only be Thane Eidsson and his personal guards that fell upon the Meyathan flank, hacking with sword and axe as Sophie's soldiers struggled to respond.

"We have to help them," Sophie said, blood pounding in her ears. "They can't fight the Skaldre *and* hold the line against Savvas's cavalry."

Faidra's hand gripped her sword hilt. "I know." She swept her eyes left and right. "But I'm not putting you in the thick of a melee, and there's no one else left to protect you if I go."

Sophie caught her old friend's gaze and held it. "If our line breaks, not even you can stop Savvas from killing me. Trust that I can take care of myself and save us while there is still time."

Faidra was silent for a moment, hints of moisture glinting in her eyes. "Don't die," she said. "You still have a lot to do."

"I won't," Sophie said. They exchanged grim smiles, and, for just a moment, Sophie was back on the Solstice barricades with her old friends, before time and choices had driven them apart.

Faidra looked away and addressed her people gathered around them. "You all heard our comrade. We fight today to keep what we won in Heratia. With me!"

Faidra urged her horse forward, sword in hand, and her people fell in behind her. Some rode with the casual ease of former soldiers, while others concentrated only on staying in the saddle, but they kept their formation nonetheless.

They galloped toward the Skaldre ambush, and if their formation did not have the precision of imperial cavalry, the thunder of hooves caught the enemy's attention all the same. The Skaldre shifted, Eidsson leading half his force to form a new line against Faidra's charge.

The Skaldre drew back on bows as tall as they were. Sophie's hands clenched. The Skaldre loosed. Arrows punched through Meyathan armor as Faidra's people drew closer. The man to Faidra's left tumbled from the saddle, a feathered shaft buried in his chest.

The Skaldre drew again, Eidsson himself aiming directly for Faidra. Sophie's breath froze in her throat. The Skaldre loosed. Faidra sprang from the saddle and rolled, the arrow scything past just over her head. She came up within a dozen paces of Eidsson, too close for the Skaldre thane to draw another arrow.

Faidra lunged, swinging her sword up in a long arc as the rest of her people met the Skaldre around her. Eidsson dropped the longbow and drew his own sword just in time to deflect Faidra's attack. Sophie lost sight of them in the swirling melee, but then they were in the open once again, this time with Eidsson on the attack. Despite Faidra's ferocity, he had reach and height, driving her back with powerful swings.

Faidra stumbled, and Sophie suppressed the urge to call out. It would only distract her friend. Eidsson saw his opening and struck, driving his sword forward. The swordpoint scoured a deep gash through the weaker armor at Faidra's waist, but then Faidra brought her own sword up and drove it through the light mail protecting Eidsson's neck even as his momentum still carried him forward.

The Skaldre thane shuddered once and dropped to the ground, where he lay unmoving. Faidra stood over him, raising her bloody sword high even as her own wound wept red. Around Faidra, Meyathans rallied, soldiers and former rebels both pushing their enemy back into the trees.

Faidra turned to face Sophie across the many paces that separated them. Even from this distance, Faidra's expression was visible, a rigid mask against the pain of her injury. Slowly, she crossed an arm over her chest in salute. Then she swayed on her feet and collapsed.

Sophie cried out, reaching a hand toward her fallen friend despite the space between them. In moments Faidra's people were with her, hoisting her onto a makeshift stretcher of saddle belts tied between two spears. Faidra disappeared into the mass of wounded being carried toward the physicians' tents, and Sophie forced herself to look back toward the front line. There was nothing she could do for Faidra now, and a battle still required her attention.

Infantry in the western flank before her still held firm, their phalanx intact despite Eidsson's ambush. In the center, Skaldre and Meyathan still fought shield to shield, but something had changed in the tenor of the battle further east. More shouting, fewer clashes of steel against steel. Sophie turned to look. On the eastern flank, Skaldre banners wavered. One banner fell, then another. Others shifted back as their bearers took flight. Signal horns sounded, but Sophie didn't need them; the Skaldre were breaking.

The infantry of Sophie's eastern flank pivoted in perfect order to pressure the Skaldre units holding the center, and, like an ebbing tide, the center units fled as well, many throwing down their weapons in desperation to escape a doomed battle.

Then Omiros's cavalry charged through the gap the Skaldre left behind, thundering forward until they came parallel with Savvas's regiments, then flowing west toward the enemy. Savvas's riders turned to meet the charge, and the two cavalry forces came together with a thunderous crash.

Sophie drew a breath. It was working. Omiros had Savvas tied down; they could end the battle here and now. She drew her signal horn and sounded the tone to charge. As one, her infantry surged forward, all fatigue forgotten. They swarmed around the enemy cavalry, and their spears ran red as they stabbed at both rider and horse.

Sophie followed her soldiers at a trot. She couldn't help them, but she could at least bear witness to the carnage. Realizing they were surrounded, Savvas's riders formed up in tight knots, their spears taking a heavy toll out of any who came close. And yet Sophie's infantry did not relent. They answered with spears of their own, and when those broke, they pulled the riders down to hack at them with shortswords.

The largest group of riders flew the banner of House Carenthus beneath Dafni's imperial falcon. In among them, Sophie glimpsed a tall rider in plate mail emblazoned with a rearing stallion and, beside him, a smaller figure in plain armor. Savvas and Dafni, the young heir wearing no crests both for her own protection and because her side had not possessed any imperial armor.

As the Meyathan infantry closed in around them, Savvas shouted an order Sophie couldn't hear. Dafni vanished behind a curtain of armored riders as the group split in two, half of them dashing north in a full gallop while the other half plunged into Sophie's oncoming soldiers. Savvas led the charge himself, buying time for Dafni's escape. If Omiros's riders didn't catch her, she would have a second chance to light Meyatha aflame.

Sophie shook her head. There was nothing she could do about Dafni now; Omiros would bring her back or he wouldn't. Savvas's countercharge caught Sophie's soldiers by surprise. Dozens died in the initial contact, impaled on lances or crushed under steel-shod hooves. The line wavered until a dark-skinned sergeant picked up the unit's standard and raised it high.

"The empero is watching!" she bellowed. "Stand your ground!"

The infantry's resolve hardened, and they pushed back against Savvas's riders, several shouting Sophie's name. The two formations ground together, Meyathans dying on both sides. Revulsion churned inside Sophie. How many would lose their lives with her name on their lips? How many would die fighting to win Dafni a throne? It wasn't fair. Thousands of citizens had already bled their lives away for the sake of this Laskaris feud, and thousands more were sure to follow. Savvas's riders were cornered now; they would fight to their last breath.

She should withdraw. The enemy was too close, and she had no guards. She needed to find if there was anything left of her escort or at least move further from the melee. But that would leave even more of her citizens to die.

Savvas was on the outside of his formation now, fighting to turn the infantry's flank. A thrill rippled through Sophie. In his zeal, Savvas had moved beyond the protection of his riders. He was vulnerable, for however brief a time. If he fell, the rest of his riders might lose the will to fight. She could end this now.

Sophie lowered her visor and leveled her spear for a charge. With a shield on her other arm, she urged her horse into a gallop with just her legs, a technique remembered from long training under her grandmother's eye.

Savvas saw her and peeled off from the rest of his riders, bringing his own mount to a gallop toward Sophie. His spear and shield were gone, leaving him with only his heavy mace. The force of Sophie's charge would punch her spear through Savvas's armor before his own weapon was in range. As long as she didn't miss, victory was hers.

The distance vanished between them. Sophie adjusted her spear. He would pass on her right side, and then she had him.

Savvas made the slightest motion with his body and his warhorse shifted to pass on Sophie's left. He transferred his mace from one hand to the other in the same moment. Sophie's spear couldn't reach him on that side; her mount's neck blocked the way. In a surge of fear, she urged her horse to turn aside, but it was too late.

Savvas's mace smashed into Sophie's shield as they passed. Splinters sprayed in the air. The impact nearly wrenched Sophie from the saddle. She only held on by tangling the fingers of her spear hand in the reins, which her well-trained mount took as a signal to stop. Something was wrong with her left arm. It hung limp, bent at a sharp angle where the mace had dented the plate-mail armor in. Drops of blood seeped through cracks in the metal.

Then the pain hit, waves of white coals traveling up her shattered arm and scorching through the rest of her body. Sophie groaned. She wanted to curl up around the injury, cradle it until someone came to take her away from this.

Sophie shook her head. She'd been injured before; she couldn't let this pain stop her, not with Savvas out to finish the job. "I walk in the Void," she muttered, "the Void surrounds me."

She repeated the mantra and turned to find Savvas bearing down on her, his mace raised high. Her spear was still the longer weapon, and she thrust out at him, striking once, twice. Both times the spearhead skittered off Savvas's plate-mail armor. Without the momentum of a charge, she didn't have the strength to break through it, while Savvas's mace was purpose-built to take armor apart piece by piece. She was doomed if she gave him room to swing it.

Savvas closed in to within arm's reach. He swung the mace down. Sophie dropped her spear and lunged out of the saddle, smashing into Savvas with her good shoulder and robbing his swing of momentum. He grunted in surprise as the impact carried them both over his horse's side. He flailed for purchase, but it was too late. Sophie gripped him with her good arm, keeping him beneath her so when they hit the ground her full weight came down on top of his chest.

The impact drove the air from both of them, and something cracked beneath Savvas's armor. He hissed in pain. A rib, Sophie hoped. Her ruined arm throbbed so badly that stars clouded her vision. Then Savvas's left hand was grasping at her; it held her still while his right hand reached for something. She twisted her head to see, the helmet limiting her vision. Savvas had lost his mace in the fall, but from his belt he drew a wicked dirk, perfect for killing at close quarters.

Savvas plunged his dagger toward the broken gap in Sophie's armor beneath her left shoulder. She would bleed out in minutes if his blade found her there. With all her strength, Sophie twisted away. A red line of pain ran under her injured arm as the dirk pricked her, but the cut was shallow. She wasn't dead yet.

She rolled onto her left arm, and her vision blacked out completely. Daylight returned a moment later, and she turned over to see Savvas struggling to rise, wheezing as if breathing pained him. She kicked out, and her boot struck his abdomen with all the fury she could muster for a man who had betrayed her so he could slaughter his own people.

Even with his armor, the blow sent Savvas back to the firm earth, his labored breaths turned to choking wheezes. Sophie pushed against the ground with her good arm. She'd lost her shortsword in the fall. She had to stand, had to find a weapon. If Savvas regained his footing, she was dead, and she couldn't outwrestle him either. *There*—her spear lay on the trampled wheat stalks just a few paces away. She only needed to reach it.

Her left arm throbbed with fire at every move. "I walk in the Void," she repeated, "the Void surrounds me." She got one knee under her. "I walk in the Void, the Void surrounds me." She was halfway up. "I walk in the Void, the Void surrounds me!"

With a shouted verse of her prayer, Sophie made it to her feet. She scooped up her fallen spear and turned back to Savvas, who had recovered just enough to sit up. She pressed the spearpoint to the seam where his breastplate met the armor around his neck, forcing him back down.

"It's over, Savvas," she said. "Surrender." She leaned over the spear haft, ready to put all her weight behind it to thrust the point through the armor's seam.

Savvas coughed out a laugh. "Why? So you may spare my life a second time, O merciful Abbess-Empero?"

"No," Sophie said. "You will die for this, and I won't insult you by pretending otherwise. But if you order your soldiers to stand down, I will protect your family from all retribution." She leaned just a little of her weight on the spear. "You know Demetra will be eager to destroy them."

And the speaker would be wise to do it; even Sophie knew that. Leaving Savvas's family intact to plot revenge was courting disaster, and yet they had nothing to do with his treachery. Even threatening them with retribution violated the Mother's justice.

Savvas's expression was unreadable beneath the steel of his helmet. "I am loyal to the empire," he said at last, as the battle still raged around them. "If my family must pay for that, then so be it."

Sophie's voice rose. "The empire is bleeding to death across this plain!" Tilting her head down, she managed to raise her visor without letting go of her spear. "You've lost, but Meyatha's best soldiers still slaughter each other while we are surrounded by enemies on every side. Is that what you want? Is that what your loyalty means?"

Savvas lifted his own visor, his expression drawn with pain. "Do you have the strength and the will to defend Meyatha?"

Sophie bared her teeth. "I've beaten you, haven't I?"

A weak chuckle escaped Savvas's lips. "Yes, Your Majesty, you have." With one hand, he unhooked the signal horn from his belt and brought it to his lips. He sounded five long tones, three short, and a final tone that went on until he ran out of breath.

For a few moments, nothing happened. The battle raged unabated. Then what remained of Savvas's standard-bearers repeated the signal, and the sounds of battle began to dissipate. Around Sophie, the remaining knots of Savvas's cavalry put down their weapons and raised their hands in surrender. The rush of battle slowly drained from Sophie's muscles. It was over. They had won.

She let Savvas stand and gave his custody over to a platoon of her infantry. His fate was sealed, but she would not send him to his death before giving him the chance to bathe and eat a hot meal. It was all the Mother's kindness she had left for him.

To Sophie's surprise, a much-battered squadron of cavalry approached her as the infantry rounded up prisoners. Sophie tensed for a moment, but then she saw the black cloth bands they wore. Her eyes widened. It was the escort Omiros had assigned to her. They were reduced by nearly half, but the sight still eased some of the weight from Sophie's shoulders. She'd thought her orders had sent every rider among them to their deaths.

The young captain's armor was gouged in places, and a thick bandage bound one leg. Her light-skinned face went even paler than usual when she saw Sophie's arm.

"Your Majesty," the captain said, shifting to swing down from the saddle, but she stopped with a grimace as her injured leg refused to move. "I plead your forgiveness, I should have found you sooner."

Sophie resisted the urge to laugh. That would have been cruel, and it would probably evoke a fresh wave of pain from her arm. "You were where the empire needed," she said instead. "And we won the battle because of it. Well done, Captain..?"

"Antonina, Your Majesty," the captain said. She straightened in the saddle. "Antonina Ducas."

That made Sophie blink. This woman was related to Ariadne Ducas, Demetra's former ally, one of many senators who had lost prestige and wealth when Sophie took the throne. Perhaps it had been better that she hadn't known the captain's name during the battle, or else Sophie would have been constantly tempted to look over her shoulder.

Antonina's expression turned from pride to alarm. "I'm only distantly related to Senator Ducas, Your Majesty," she said, doing her best to bow from the saddle without jostling her leg. "It's a big family."

Sophie waved it away. Who was she to start judging people for their relatives? "Your general will hear only good things about you and your riders from me." She paused, as even the act of speaking drew sparks of pain. "Mother embrace those you have lost."

Antonina recovered her composure and gave a solemn salute. "Thank you, Your Majesty." Her eyes landed on Sophie's arm again. "But we must take you to the physicians' tents."

"Yes," Sophie said. "That would be best." She needed to check on Faidra, and Fryni could find her there. Sophie smiled despite the fresh assault of pain. Fryni wouldn't leave her side for months once she saw Sophie's injuries. Perhaps she would take some comfort from knowing that her flanking force had turned the battle and saved them all.

Two of her escorts came to help Sophie up into the saddle, but they stopped as another troop of riders approached, all of them bearing the black cloth of Sophie's side. As they drew closer, Sophie recognized Omiros leading them, his face grim. Two of his riders restrained a smaller figure in the saddle between them, the prisoner's hands bound tight together. Dafni Laskaris.

Sophie's niece had lost her helmet, and blood spattered her armor, but otherwise she appeared unharmed. Indeed, with her curly black hair flying in the wind, she looked regal even as a prisoner. Her expression was unconcerned, as if she rode among loyal supporters and not a victorious enemy.

Omiros slowed his riders to a stop before Sophie. He gestured at the ground; Dafni swung down from the saddle and managed a graceful landing even with her hands tied. Omiros dismounted behind her, a hand on the pommel of his shortsword.

"The traitor, Your Majesty," he said, bowing his head to Sophie. "She killed two of my riders *after* General Carenthus ordered a surrender."

Dafni looked at Sophie with a face so like Taisa's. "I do not recognize a surrender ordered by disloyal followers."

Omiros drew his sword. "Say the word and she dies here."

Sophie blinked. Kill Dafni, her niece, here? Now? It made brutal sense. The longer Dafni was alive, the more time her support had to grow. And Sophie had already committed to Savvas's execution. What other choice did she have?

"I..." she began, but no other words came.

Dafni shook a strand of hair out of her eyes. "If you are going to kill me, Aunt Sophie, do be quick about it."

Sophie could only stare. Her sister's child stood there, daring Sophie to kill her. Mother and Her blessed daughters, what was she to do? Even with the threat of death over her head, Dafni showed no sign that she would ever accept Sophie's reign. But what else could she expect from a child who had been told the throne was her destiny all her life? Would Dafni have hesitated if the battle had gone the other way? Her mother certainly wouldn't have. Taisa had made it quite clear what she believed Sophie's fate should be.

Omiros took a step closer to Dafni, bringing his sword to her throat. "Your Majesty," he said, "every moment she's alive is a threat to your rule. Faidra would say the same if she were here."

That brought a grim smile to Sophie's lips. Omiros was only wrong in that Faidra would likely have killed Dafni herself to save all the arguing. Dafni's eyes fixed on the general's sword, and she leaned back just a touch, the first sign of fear Sophie had ever seen from her.

That did it. Sophie was not Faidra, and she was not her sister.

"No," Sophie said. "She swore no vows to me, I will not have her killed for trying to take the throne she was promised."

"If the rest of Meyatha discovers she is alive," Omiros said, "this could all have been for nothing." He held his arm out to encompass the Golden Fields and the thousands of fallen strewn upon it.

"She is sixteen years old," Sophie said. "Barely more than a child." She waved away Omiros's next objection. "Assign your most loyal soldiers to guard her. When we return to Heratia I will find somewhere to keep her away from would-be rebels." The pain in her arm flared up again. "For now, I am going to the physicians' tent."

To Sophie's surprise, it was Dafni who spoke next. "The empire will never be yours!" A flush turned her dark-brown cheeks even darker. "Sleep lightly, Aunt Sophie."

Sophie turned away from the young Laskaris and, with her escort's help, clambered into the saddle. Her arm only made her fight back a scream twice. She clicked the reins with her good hand and sent the horse into a gentle walk. She didn't look back at her niece. It was true that the empire wasn't Sophie's, but she had never imagined it was. She only hoped she could leave Meyatha better than she found it.

Chapter 24

The physicians' tents were filled to capacity with wounded, Meyathan soldiers from both sides crowding every available space. There were even a few of Thane Eidsson's Skaldre, though Eidsson himself had died at Faidra's hand. The army's healers worked alongside locals from the surrounding towns, and they kept an ordered operation despite the crowding, with patients organized into neat rows for better access.

At first the healers tried to have a special tent erected for Sophie, but she refused. She would not take physicians away from the other wounded just so she could have a private space. Instead of arguing, the healers gave her a bitter tea that dulled some of the pain, then cut the armor off her wounded arm and told her to bite down on a strip of leather. She did, and she screamed through her clenched teeth as they set the bone. The pain receded as a healer bound Sophie's injured arm in place, leaving nausea and dizziness in equal measure.

Hurried footsteps turned Sophie's head, but it was an effort to focus her eyes. Alkestis raced down the aisle toward her, skidding to a stop and breathing hard. "Sister Sophie," the tall acolyte said between breaths, "I've been looking, I couldn't find you..."

Further words failed Alkestis as the exhausted acolyte struggled to regain her breath.

Sophie's chest tightened, and her good hand shook. Her voice was barely a whisper. "Fryni?" *Mother in all Her wisdom, not that.*

"She lives," Alkestis said. "But she's badly hurt. This way."

Sophie followed Alkestis in a blur, losing track of where among the healers' tents they were. Fryni, hurt? Fryni was never hurt; she was fearless, and she never slowed down for anyone. Sophie nearly ran into Alkestis when the tall acolyte halted near the back of the tent. Sophie looked down.

Fryni lay on the cot at Sophie's feet. A bloody gash ran from the young woman's hairline to her jaw, the wound barely covered with a linen cloth. Her short black hair was crusted with dirt and blood. Her eyes stared at the ceiling in a glassy daze. Leather cords bit into the flesh of her right arm just below the shoulder, tied tightly enough to cut off all blood flow. The rest of the arm was gone, heavy bandages hiding the place where Fryni's flesh suddenly ended.

Alkestis was saying something. Sophie tried to listen. The arm had been too badly injured; the physicians saved Fryni's life by removing it. They thought she would make it, but it had been a near thing. Sophie swallowed. While she had spared her niece's life among the fallen, Fryni had been under a physician's blade.

Sophie knelt down by Fryni's side. "Fryni," she whispered. "Dearest one. I'm here."

Fryni blinked, and a smile curled her mouth. "Sister Sophie. We did it. I didn't fail you."

"You never could have," Sophie said, her relief at hearing Fryni's voice warring with the guilt over such a grievous injury.

In the silence, Fryni's eyes focused on Sophie's own wounded arm. "We almost match," the young acolyte said, her voice ragged. "Except yours is on the wrong side." One corner of her mouth twitched up. "And still there."

A laugh escaped Sophie's lips. "I'll try to coordinate which side I'm struck on next time." She took Fryni's left hand, Fryni's remaining hand, in her own. "We couldn't have won today without you. Your climb turned the tide."

Fryni drew a weak breath. "It was nearly a disaster. The Skaldre flank guards spotted us when it was just me and a few sisters on the ground, with the rest of the militia still climbing down the rock face."

She was quiet for a moment, sweat soaking her brow. Sophie took a cloth from the basin of cool water beside the cot and wiped

Fryni's forehead. Then Sophie waited, letting Fryni decide if she wanted to continue.

When Fryni spoke again, her voice was stronger. "I had to stop the flank guards from rallying help, or our militia would be slaughtered." Her expression turned triumphant. "The sisters and I charged before they could signal. Bought time for everyone else to get down." She turned her head toward her wounded shoulder. "One of the Skaldre was faster than I expected. Got past my guard with an axe. I was in the Void for a while after that."

"You protected your soldiers and led them to victory," Sophie said, her voice unsteady with pride for this fierce young woman who kept Sophie safe when no one else could. "And now you'll have time to rest."

Fryni's labored breathing turned rapid, her eyes widening. "You're sending me back to the abbey? I won't go. I don't care how many arms I've lost!"

"Mother's loyalty, no!" Sophie said, gripping Fryni's hand tighter. "To Heratia. I need you now more than ever, to train and lead a new Laskaris guard so that your sisters who do wish for a return to Gray Falls are free to go. But first"—she took on her sternest abbess voice—"you will rest."

"That, that makes sense," Fryni said, her burst of energy gone. Her eyes drooped, and her breaths came more evenly. "I'll be here. Just don't go anywhere without me." In moments, the young acolyte fell asleep.

Sophie wiped Fryni's brow once more, then stood. She stopped a passing physician and confirmed that to the best of their skill and knowledge, Fryni was out of immediate danger. Tears beaded in Sophie's eyes as she thanked the healers. The young woman she had raised like a daughter would not go to the Mother that day.

Moments later, Sophie dried the tears from her eyes. There was someone else she had to see, an old comrade to whom Sophie owed more than could ever be repaid.

Faidra's cot wasn't far away, in a quiet corner of the tent reserved for those who could no longer be helped. Half a dozen of her people stood and sat around her, many bearing bandages and splints that marked serious injuries of their own. A few nodded to Sophie; others ignored her.

Faidra herself looked almost relaxed, as if she lounged on a feather couch in Heratia rather than on rough canvas with dirt caked in her hair and bloody bandages tied round a lethal wound in her gut. Sophie's gorge rose. With an effort, she held herself back from rushing forward and saying how sorry she was. If Faidra wanted to talk, she would say.

The old rebel's eyes focused on Sophie after a moment, and her voice was clear. "Hey, everyone. Give me a minute, yeah?" She paused for breath. "I'd like to catch up with my old friend."

As the others retreated to give them privacy, Sophie knelt down and offered her hand.

Faidra watched, eyes narrowing. "You're not here to apologize for Eidsson sticking a sword through me, are you?"

"No," Sophie said. A sob built inside her, but she took a shaky breath and pushed it down. These moments weren't hers; they were for Faidra. "I wouldn't insult you like that."

"Good," Faidra said. She took Sophie's offered hand and weakly pulled her closer. Gently Sophie put her uninjured arm around Faidra's shoulders, careful not to jostle the dying woman.

A shudder ran through Faidra. "Mother and Her blessed daughters," she said. "I'm not afraid to die, but there's so much work left to do."

Sophie held her close. "I know. I hope you can trust me to do it."

Faidra gasped against a fresh wave of pain. "Savvas?" she asked after a moment.

"A prisoner," Sophie said. "Bound for execution before we return to Heratia."

Faidra grunted. "Wasn't sure you had it in you. Your niece?"

"I have spared her life," Sophie said. "Gray Falls kept one Laskaris secret from the world. It can keep another."

"Not what I would have done," Faidra said, her voice slipping until Sophie could barely hear her. "But she's young, no one can see the future." Another tremor ran through her, and she spoke through clenched teeth. "Promise me, Sophie. That you won't let them take it all back, that this is just the start."

"I swear it," Sophie said. "Everything we fought for on the Solstice and more." She blinked away the tears burning behind her eyes.

"I believe you," Faidra said. She relaxed in Sophie's arms, letting out a long breath. "Sophie," she said after a moment.

"Yes, Faidra?" Sophie said, her voice finally breaking.

"I'd like you to sing my rites," Faidra said. Her breath rattled. "I've never done much praying, will the Void Mother mind?"

"Of course I'll sing them," Sophie said. "And the Void Mother cares what you do, not how much devotion you show Her."

"Ah," Faidra said, but Sophie couldn't tell if it was a word or just an exhalation.

Sophie released her arm from around Faidra's shoulders and leaned back so she would have room to sing the first verse in a soft croon.

"The sun will light your way, dear friend, you have no need to fear this end."

She saw the day when Faidra had first invited her to debate before the gathered dissidents who would one day launch the Solstice Uprising.

"The moon will guide you at night, dear one, if ever you should miss the sun."

A daring radical raced through Sophie's memories, breaking open senatorial coffers and dispersing the treasure to those most in need.

"For you will sail on the starry sea, they know the course that's set for thee."

And then that radical became the uprising's general, leading them in righteous rebellion and desperate street battles both, a soldier who never gave up the fight.

"And then you'll rest in the Void, my friend. Eternal rest in the Void."

Faidra sighed and closed her eyes. She didn't open them again, even though her breaths still came for a little while longer. Sophie sang more hymns while Alkestis and the other acolytes joined Faidra's followers in cleaning the fallen rebel of battlefield grime.

When Faidra took her final breath, the acolytes gathered around Sophie and wrapped her in their arms. Fryni's cot had been moved close enough that she could reach out with her remaining hand and grasp Sophie's.

A sob wracked Sophie's body. "I shouldn't," she muttered. What right did she have to comfort? "I shouldn't be like this, others have lost so much in my name."

Fryni held her tighter. "This is who *you* lost," she said. "Even an empero is allowed to grieve."

Sophie relaxed into the acolytes' embrace and wept.

***

A week after the battle at the Golden Fields, the afternoon sun shone gently down on a crisp autumn day in Heratia, caressing Sophie's dark skin as she prepared to finish the task of putting her old friend to rest.

A long-neglected cemetery in northwestern Heratia would be the last resting place not just for Faidra but for most of those who had fallen on Sophie's side in the capital and on the field, excepting only those of Omiros's riders who were bound for family estates. In just a few days, imperial craftsfolk had patched the low perimeter wall, cleaned the central statue of the Void Mother, cleared away the overgrown brambles, and planted trees that would one day offer shade to any who visited the graves.

Once home to only a few dozen markers, now the cemetery grounds were filled to the brim with circles of black stone, each etched with the name of one who had died to put Sophie on the Falcon Throne. Between those rows and around the low wall stood the witnesses: Meyathans from all walks of life gathered in their hundreds to see the final departure of friends, comrades, loved ones. They watched so the fallen would know they were not forgotten in the Void.

Sophie wore a serviceable gray tunic and pants, her black shawl around her shoulders. Stripes of purple adorned the ends of her sleeves, and an amethyst falcon rested against her brow in a light circlet of silver. It marked her as Sophie Laskaris II, empero of Meyatha, but it was far from full imperial regalia. Today she walked among her people.

Meyathan citizens stood shoulder to shoulder between the neat rows of stone markers. More ringed the cemetery's perimeter. Scholars in their gray robes stood next to spark-scarred smiths from the capital's foundries. Chariot racers in their team colors clustered beside plain-robed Heratian acolytes. Hundreds, possibly thousands, gathered to see off their honored dead.

Among the crowd were those who now wore the black sunburst openly as a mark of allegiance. The Solstice Radicals they called themselves, for all that Sophie had thought of them as Faidra's people. They'd given Sophie a wide berth since the battle, and she didn't blame them. Their leader had made an ally of Sophie, and now that leader was dead, leaving an empty place in their command and in Sophie's heart.

Around Sophie, before the last grave whose marker had not been placed, stood her inner circle: those without whom she would not be empero. Demetra wore her finest green silks, and Makis had styled his long beard in elegant curls. Omiros's ceremonial armor gleamed with a mirror shine, while Constantia had shrouded herself in an unusually somber gray cloak. And at Sophie's right hand stood Fryni, heading the Gray Falls acolytes in their new suits of custom-fitted steel plate, armor worthy of imperial bodyguards. Clean linen bandages still covered the gash down one side of Fryni's face and the not yet fully healed remnant of her right arm.

They all formed a loose circle around Faidra's grave, the last to still be marked with its own black stone. Makis was just finishing his farewell to Faidra, pitched in a lecturer's voice so it filled the crowded cemetery. "For twenty-three years," he said, "she kept the uprising alive. She sheltered the flame until today, when it burns in the black sunburst once more."

The Solstice Radicals raised their fists at his words but remained silent as all eyes turned to Sophie. As empero, it fell on her to honor both Faidra and all those who had gone before. Fryni gave her an encouraging smile, and Sophie took a deep breath.

"Faidra always told the truth," she said, raising her voice to carry as far as it could. "I never had to worry that she would only tell me what I wanted to hear."

That brought a chuckle from Makis that caught in his throat. Sophie squeezed his hand in hers.

She continued, "And while Faidra and I did not always agree, she was more committed to justice than anyone I knew." Moisture pricked at her eyes, and she did not brush it away. "Now she's left us to join Luna's starry children," Sophie said. She made her voice louder to keep it from breaking. "Her sacrifice was not for any throne, but so that no Meyathan would go hungry when there was food to give or freeze when there was room for them by the fire."

Sophie extended her arms to encompass the entire cemetery. "Each citizen who rests here can say the same. With their spears and their lives, they saved us, first here in Heratia, and then on the Golden Plain. Their fight is now in our hands, to protect what they died for and to see that it is only the start."

She turned to Makis and Fryni. "Will you help me place her marker?"

Together they lifted the polished black marble circle from the small cart on which it rested, Makis with two hands on one side, Sophie and Fryni with a single hand each on the other. The disk drank in sunlight, and the etched letters of Faidra's name were only visible from just the right angle. The marker had been carved from a fragment of Hera the Great's statue, which Sophie hoped she and Faidra would laugh about when they met one day in the Void Mother's embrace.

Makis, Fryni, and Sophie carefully lowered the stone circle to the soft earth over Faidra's grave. A murmur swept through the crowd as each Meyathan present said a quiet prayer for those they'd lost. Sophie herself stayed silent. She had already made her promise to Faidra; the proof would be in her actions.

Some of the adherents drifted away while others knelt by marker stones to say a more private farewell. From the crowd, a young man approached Sophie, the black sunburst prominent on his collar. His skin was dark, darkened even further by the same long solar caress that had lightened his hair. Both Omiros and Fryni glanced at Sophie, but she gave them an affirming nod. If one of the radicals wanted to speak with her, she was happy to listen.

"Sophie Laskaris," the young man said, briefly inclining his head. "I'm Gaius Lepidus. I was in charge of organizing down in Ravian, but with Faidra gone, it seemed I'd be of more use here."

Sophie studied the man. His smooth face seemed very young to lead the radicals of Ravian, Meyatha's largest city in the south. But Sophie supposed she herself had once been very young to lead an uprising. "I'm afraid Faidra didn't mention you to me," she said after a moment.

Gaius shrugged. "Not surprising, Faidra and I didn't agree on much. You know how it could be."

Sophie couldn't resist a wistful smile. She did indeed.

"For example," Gaius went on, "if I'd been in charge here, we'd never have supported a Laskaris in anything."

Demetra looked up from where she conferred with a retainer, a scowl on her face, while Fryni's brow twitched and Constantia gave a slight roll of her eyes, but none of them said anything. Sophie was grateful for that.

"I can understand that," Sophie said. "But I hope you see that we don't need to be enemies. One of my promises to Faidra was changing the government so there's no need for an empero, from House Laskaris or any other."

"I heard," Gaius said. He glanced at the freshly placed marker stone. "Faidra believed in that promise enough to die for it, which buys you a bit of grace." He leaned closer to Sophie, his expression grim. "But we're watching you. We won't be bought off with empty gestures."

Sophie met his gaze, unblinking. "I am in the process of re-forming the People's Chamber," she said. "You should stand for election. The citizens will need voices like yours to represent their interests."

Gaius paused, one eyebrow raised. "Maybe I'll do that," he said at last. "Enjoy the afternoon, Sophie Laskaris." He turned and strode back to his fellow radicals as the crowd continued to thin.

Constantia covered an exaggerated yawn. "Mother be praised, I thought he'd never leave. Shall we depart? We should still be able to enjoy some of the celebrations if we hurry."

"Yes," Demetra said. "The empero should be seen by her people as they are flush with victory." She noticed Sophie's slight frown. "And don't look so dour. Whatever your plans for the future, you are the empero *today*."

"Too right," Constantia said. She unfastened her cloak and handed it to a valet, revealing a figure-hugging blue gown with swirls of white and a teardrop-shaped jade pendant at her throat. "And the empero has promised to show me around the capital, as a courtesy to a visiting ambassador." She gave a bright smile and entwined her arm with Sophie's.

Sophie's cheeks grew hot as Fryni smirked on her other side. "Shall we, Your Majesty?" the acolyte captain asked, her voice only slightly mocking.

Sophie cleared her throat. "Yes, let us proceed."

The six of them—Sophie, Constantia, Fryni, Demetra, Makis, and Omiros—left the cemetery together, escorted by a loose ring of Omiros's soldiers and Fryni's acolytes. Alkestis had left days ago with the militia to escort Dafni on her way to Peaceful Rest Abbey, but Anna, Evi, Calliope, and the others were all there.

Outside the cemetery, Heratia's forges and glassworks were quiet, but signs of the city's rebuilding program were already visible. Freshly cut paving stones had replaced cracked ones, and scaffolds cocooned dilapidated tenements that were otherwise on the verge of collapse. The stink of sewage was much reduced thanks to temporary patches, if not completely gone.

Sophie had much greater plans. The Senate's confiscated treasure and new taxes would fund reconstruction across Meyatha, repairing vital infrastructure and cutting away at least some of the rot that had beset her nation over the centuries. No doubt it would be far from easy, but it was working for now.

The sounds of celebration grew as they approached the wider streets. Excited voices blended into raucous music as the people of Heratia celebrated a victory over both foreign invasion and domestic oppression. Bright streamers crisscrossed between the buildings, people dancing beneath them in shifting lines and circles, pausing only to help themselves at one of the dozen food carts and stands that lined the street.

The scents rolled over Sophie a moment later: freshly baked bread and the heavenly aroma of cheese and meats frying in olive oil that made her mouth water. Citizens paused in their celebrations, turning their heads as Sophie and her escort approached. While imperial processions were a common part of Heratian life, they were always carried out from horseback. An empero had never *walked* among them before.

Some bowed low or even knelt on the ground while others crossed an arm over their chest in salute, and still others only gave wary looks. All moved out of the way as Sophie's escort of acolytes and soldiers approached. With her good arm entangled in Constantia's and her other arm still in a sling, Sophie couldn't return the people's salutes, but she met the eyes of as many as possible, just for a moment.

Fresh graffiti adorned many of the buildings that lined the streets, much of the art depicting either the uprising's black sunburst or the Laskaris family's falcon, though the latter was mostly done in dark blue rather than expensive purple. On one workshop's wall, the falcon and sunburst had been painted over each other until they were a nearly incomprehensible mess.

"That is troubling," Omiros said as they passed the competing graffiti. "If the citizens are dividing into camps over who deserves credit for our victory, it will not be well for us."

Makis put a hand to his beard. "Perhaps it is a sign of unity instead." He pointed to the overlapping symbols. "We cannot say where one begins and the other ends."

"The optimism of a scholar," Demetra said, her tone skeptical. She leaned on a sturdy cane, letting it take most of the weight from her still-recovering leg. "It stinks of factions and division to me."

To Sophie's eye, it looked as though the artists had simply run out of wall space, but she was happy to let her advisers speculate. If Meyathans saw her as opposed to the uprising, it was a problem to deal with, but not today.

"Let's wait here a moment," Constantia said as they drew near one of the food stands. "That smells simply divine." Sophie nodded her agreement as the stand's proprietor melted cheese and peppered cuts of meat across long pieces of flatbread.

Constantia fished a coin pouch out of a pocket with her free hand. "Your pardon, sir," she said to the proprietor. "One of those for any who desire it, from my purse, of course."

The proprietor blinked, looking up from his work and seeing who stood before him. "It's, uh, it's all free for the celebration, my lady," he said. "Compliments of, well" —he gestured at Sophie—"Her Majesty."

Constantia gave Sophie a look. "Dear Sophie, you do make it difficult sometimes." She set the coin pouch on the stand with a flourish. "Keep it anyway, good sir, as Gallia's contribution to the festivities."

The proprietor didn't argue, vanishing the coins away into a pocket of his tunic. Makis took a piece of flatbread for himself as Omiros and Fryni gave clearance for any of the soldiers and acolytes under their command who were hungry.

Constantia picked the largest piece of flatbread, then grinned at Sophie. "Why, my dear empero, it seems you do not have a hand free."

Sophie's cheeks turned even hotter. The duchess was right, but she failed to mention that her own arm was firmly entwined around Sophie's uninjured one.

"Allow me to assist," Constantia said. Her long eyelashes fluttered. "Your Majesty." She held up the flatbread, steam rising from its surface.

Before she could think further, Sophie leaned forward and took a bite. The bread was soft and chewy beneath its toasted crust, the melted cheese providing a tangy kick on top of the meat's smoky flavor. Garlic and basil ignited on her tongue. Sophie closed her eyes, savoring the morsel.

Omiros cleared his throat. "Your Grace," he said to Constantia. "If you seek the empero's favor, there are protocols to follow."

Fryni stifled a giggle.

Constantia let out a dramatic sigh. "It's the tragic truth," the Gallian woman said. "You Meyathans have a protocol for everything."

"We do," Demetra said. She glanced at where Sophie and Constantia's arms were still entwined. "But I think we can relax them, if just for today." She placed her cane out in front of her. "Come, we must make our appearances elsewhere."

With Constantia's help, Sophie finished the flatbread as they walked, enjoying the warm contact of the other woman's arm in hers. Romantic affection wasn't uncommon at the abbey, but Sophie had never made the time for it, and now it had been so long that she found herself unsure of the Gallian duchess's intentions. Was this only a bit of fun for the day, or did Constantia want something more? If she did want more, what were the political implications?

Sophie put the thoughts out of her mind when she glanced to her left and saw Fryni wearing a frustrated frown as she tugged at the buckles that held her armor's right shoulder in place. With a quiet murmur, Sophie disentangled herself from Constantia and approached the young acolyte captain.

"Having trouble with the new plate?" Sophie asked.

"The weight's all wrong," Fryni said. She bit her lip in concentration. "With a metal sleeve on just one side, it throws off my balance."

Sophie put her hand over Fryni's. "The smiths say that the shield frame will be ready soon. Once your shoulder is healed, we can attach it and see if it helps with balance."

"What if it's not right?" Fryni asked. Her voice was light but had a note of tension in it. "What if it just throws me off on the other side and they can't fix it?"

"Then you'll learn to fight without a shield," Sophie tapped her left arm, still held immobile in a tight sling. "We can learn together."

Fryni considered for a moment. "That'll be easier with armor like this instead of the old chain." She tapped the steel plate, then her eyes flicked up ahead and widened. "Oh, Sister Sophie, look! We have to stop and watch." She pointed to a small park at one corner of the upcoming intersection, where a large crowd was gathered around a raised stage.

On the stage stood a dozen or so actors dressed in stiff cloth painted to look like amor. They swung wooden swords at each other, always careful to pull their swings at the last moment, relying on their fellows to reel back as if struck. Half wore black armbands to mark them as Sophie's while the other half wore purple.

Demetra grinned. "Fryni's right. This we must witness."

Sophie frowned. "It seems to me that such plays are for those who did not see what they depict firsthand." If she wished to see the battle again, she only had to close her eyes. The pain and blood would come unbidden.

Demetra let out a breath. "Sophie, the point is not to study the events as history, but to see how your people imagine them."

"And besides," Fryni said, her eyes wide and excited, "I missed most of the battle when I was climbing the Empero's Teeth."

Sophie sighed. "Alright, we'll watch for a brief time." If Fryni wanted to see more of a battle she'd lost so much for, Sophie wouldn't deny her.

As Sophie's party approached, the battling actors separated to reveal two figures, one bearing the Laskaris falcon, the other with House Carenthus's stallion sewn into his costume armor. Representations of herself and Savvas, it seemed.

The two new actors paused, staring at Sophie and her escort. Sweat broke out on their faces that had nothing to do with the late-afternoon sun.

Demetra waved a hand. "Continue, good citizens. The empero wishes to see your performance."

The actors bowed and turned back to face each other. The woman portraying Sophie drew a two-handed prop sword and raised it over her head. "Brave Sol sees the treachery in your heart," she shouted. "Her sacred light will burn it out!"

The words sounded faraway to Sophie. It wasn't a bad line, but it was so far from anything she'd had the presence of mind to say. The actor leapt forward, swinging her huge sword in great two-handed arcs. She did *not* fall to the ground and struggle just to stand, her left arm broken and useless.

Sophie turned to Makis. "You'll write the history like it really happened, won't you? Future Meyathans deserve to know I couldn't even stay on my horse."

"Of course," Makis said. "I already have a team of scholars compiling accounts of the battle."

Demetra's eyes sparkled as she watched the staged combat. "He'll write what happened," the speaker said. "But *this* is how the people will remember it."

On the stage, Sophie's actor drove her sword forward in a dramatic thrust. Savvas's actor fell back, tearing open the front of his costume armor and tossing out red ribbons in place of blood. The watching crowd exploded into applause. Demetra and Constantia enthusiastically joined in, while Fryni stamped a foot in appreciation.

The ribbons drew Sophie's gaze and held it in a vice grip. She hadn't killed Savvas herself, hadn't even shed his blood in battle, but she'd looked him in the eye as the executioner's blade fell. The general's courage had held to the last.

"It's time we moved on," Sophie said, her voice almost lost in the crowd.

Fryni heard her anyway. The acolyte captain let out a sharp whistle. "Sister Sophie says it's time to go. Everyone, form up!"

The mixed escort of soldiers and acolytes snapped to obey, forming a wedge that gently but firmly urged passing citizens out of the way as Sophie and her fellows departed.

With the sun sinking lower in the sky, the empero's party turned east so Sophie could make her appearances across the Marshrun and Silvervein before retiring to the palace.

At the first bridge, the smooth paving stones stirred the depths of Sophie's memory. Her muscles echoed the old ache of pushing barricades into place in a vain attempt to hold off Irena Ironheart's onslaught. The bridge where she and Faidra had fought side by side all those years ago. The bridge where their friendship had shattered under the weight of defeat.

Sophie placed her hand on the bridge's stone rail, dark waters of the Marshrun drifting past below her. "No more surrender," Sophie said in a soft voice. "Not here, not ever."

Fryni glanced back. "Something wrong, Sister Sophie?"

Sophie shook her head. "Nothing, just a promise." She took her hand off the rail and quickened her step. Behind her, the bridge and what she'd lost there remained, a stone fixture of both the city and Sophie's mind.

Heratia's wealthier eastern side celebrated Sophie's victory as well but with a distinctly different tenor. Along Triumph Causeway, the black sunburst was nearly absent. Instead citizens paraded captured and broken Skaldre standards down the wide street. Craftsfolk tossed out garlands of dried wheat to celebrate victory at the Golden Fields while artisans displayed paintings of the battle that showed stalwart legionnaires battling northern invaders.

The capital's great chariot-racing stadium rose up across the causeway, and on its nearest wall, workers were busy placing the first tiles of a towering mosaic. Sophie squinted, trying to make sense of the colored glass and painted ceramic. Two figures faced each other, of that she was sure, one tall and with a long beard, the other broad in the shoulder and with ruddy-colored skin.

Beside her, Makis sucked in a breath. "It's Faidra," he said, pointing to the mosaic. "Faidra facing off against Eidsson."

Sophie's eyes widened. Makis was right. The artist had captured Faidra's profile perfectly, and though the face was far from finished, several of Faidra's many scars were already visible.

"It's..." Sophie paused, taken aback by yet another reminder of her fallen friend. "It appears to be a good likeness."

"It's a mockery," Makis said, a thread of raw fury in his voice. The gray-haired scholar's fists clenched. "These people wanted Faidra dead for resisting their dominion, and now they celebrate her as a hero?"

Demetra glanced at Makis but said nothing, perhaps knowing that anything from her would only raise further anger.

Sophie took Makis's hand in hers and squeezed until some of its tension slackened. "It is Faidra's victory. The people she fought for decades now pay her tribute." Her eyes found Makis's. "At least, that's how I choose to view it. But if you feel differently, say the word and I'll have it stopped."

Makis took a deep breath and shook his head. When he spoke, his voice was calm again. "No, it's only a mosaic. Let Heratia's fortunate celebrate how they like." He turned away from the stadium and quickened his step until he was just behind the forward edge of Sophie's escort.

From behind Sophie, Demetra muttered, "What does he expect? Savvas was a hero to many, they can't celebrate his defeat here. So they've found a courageous Meyathan vanquishing our traditional enemy."

Constantia made a noncommittal noise in reply. Sophie let out a long breath. Yet another way that some citizens would remember her victory differently than others. And this was just in the capital. Reports from the more remote provinces wouldn't be complete for months. She sighed to herself. Another order of business for the empero.

"Your Majesty," Omiros said, his voice cutting through her thoughts. He pointed ahead. "Trouble."

Sophie followed the direction of his arm. Just in front of her escort, the crowd had cleared except for one young woman, perhaps in her early twenties, with light-brown skin and black hair in a short braid. She wore no visible weapons, but she held herself with a fighter's confidence. A rearing red stallion was embroidered on the shoulder of her otherwise-plain tunic.

Demetra spoke the woman's name, but Sophie already knew it: Justinia Carenthus, Savvas's eldest daughter.

At a motion from Fryni, acolytes and soldiers formed rank shoulder to shoulder, a wall of steel between Sophie and the new leader of House Carenthus. For a moment, Justinia stared them down. Then she knelt, eyes to the ground and hands across her knee.

"I seek an audience with Her Majesty, Empero Sophie," Justinia said, "so that I might swear allegiance and take up my family's seat in the venerable Senate of Meyatha."

Stepping close to Sophie, Constantia rolled her eyes. "How dramatic. Send this stripling on her way. She can apply for an audience like everyone else."

The idea of simply pushing Justinia to one side was tantalizing, like not having to lift something heavy and awkward until another day. But Sophie already knew she couldn't.

"She's faced down my entire retinue alone and unarmed," Sophie said with a sad shake of her head. "If I send her away, it will look like I'm afraid of her."

"The empero is right," Demetra said. "Unfortunately."

"She may approach," Sophie said, trying to give her voice some of the imperious tone her grandmother had displayed so casually.

With coordinated precision, the empero's escort separated in the center, leaving an opening just wide enough for a single person to pass through. Justinia stood and walked toward Sophie, her step light, as if she were on an afternoon stroll. Fryni stepped just next to the newcomer's path at a dozen paces from where Sophie stood. While the acolyte captain said nothing, the message was clear: no closer.

Justinia stopped. She bowed to Sophie and nodded to Demetra. "Your Majesty. Honored Speaker," said the scion of House Carenthus. "I stand here to speak my oath as a servant of the empire, before the Mother and Her blessed daughters."

"Speak it, then," Demetra said, her voice cool. "With these citizens as your witness."

Justinia stood straighter, some of her casual confidence gone. "I swear to uphold Meyathan law, to further the empire's interests in word and deed, and..." She paused, her eyes focusing on Sophie. "Accord all glory to the empero."

Sophie realized she didn't know the proper response. It had been decades since she'd last heard a senator's oath, and embarrassed heat crept up her neck as the silence stretched out.

Then Demetra leaned over and whispered in Sophie's ear. Sophie repeated the words. "I hear your oath and accept it. In sight of the Mother and Meyathans all, you are welcome in the Senate's venerable halls."

"Thank you, Your Majesty." Justinia said. She paused, expression set as if gathering her nerve. Finally she blurted out, "The soldiers say you gave my father a clean death. Is it true?"

For a moment, the woman standing before Sophie wasn't a political enemy but a child mourning their parent. "Yes," Sophie said. "It was quick. He did not suffer or beg."

Justinia's eyes flashed in the evening sun. "I will remember that," she said. "And everything else." She bowed to Sophie a final time, turned on her heel, and strode away. At a motion from Omiros, Sophie's escort once again opened to let the senator of House Carenthus through.

Demetra watched the younger woman go. "You should have let me deal with the whole family," the speaker said. "Justinia is young, but she already has a reputation for winning battles against Free Province raids. She'll be trouble."

"Alternatively," Makis said with a sly smile, "you could make her irrelevant by abolishing the Senate completely."

Demetra pressed a hand to her temple. "Yes, and why not stop paying the army while we're at it? To really maximize the number of revolts Sophie would face."

Sophie let them argue. Demetra pointed out the Senate's political value as a way to legitimize Sophie's reforms, especially since the senators most opposed to the reform were currently eating out of the speaker's hand in the hope of having some of their fortune restored. Makis countered that such compliance was temporary, and, at the very least, limits needed to be placed on the Senate's power to keep it from overshadowing the people's will.

They were both right, of course. Just another balance Sophie would have to strike, further complicated by the need to build a just system that could endure without an empero holding it together.

From Triumph Causeway, it wasn't much further to the imperial palace, Sophie's eventual destination that evening. Unlike the rest of Heratia, the Senatorial District was quiet as they passed through it, most of its residents still smarting from defeat.

At the palace, Sophie brought her companions to a newly refurbished meeting room, smaller and less ostentatious than the war room they had used to plan the campaign against Eidsson's invasion. Fryni, Demetra, Constantia, Makis, and Omiros all joined Sophie around a circular table as newly hired palace clerks brought them the latest reports on everything from tax revenue and troop movements to food distribution and infrastructure repair.

Demetra glared at one report. "The governor of Palzena is dithering on recognizing your ascension," she said. "He's playing for time while he sees if anyone will support him."

Sophie looked at the paper. Palzena was a coastal province northwest of Heratia, most valuable as the anchorage for Meyatha's western naval fleet. "Omiros," Sophie said. "Your opinion?"

"Palzena's garrison is small," Omiros said. "And morale among our loyal troops is high." He frowned. "But the terrain is rugged, good for a prolonged defense."

"If he's stalling," Fryni said, her hand tapping the sword at her belt, "he probably doesn't want to fight. If we show up right away, I bet he suddenly remembers that he meant to recognize Sister Sophie all along."

Sophie considered. The thought of more fighting in Meyatha made her stomach churn, but her control of the outer province was still tenuous. She couldn't afford to let a governor flaunt her authority.

"Send an envoy to the western admirals," she said to Demetra. "See if we can learn how many of them support the governor. If few do, he won't be able to supply by sea, and there won't be any need for fighting." She turned to Constantia. "Do you know a way the envoy could get through without the governor realizing?"

Constantia put a finger to her lips. "I might be able to find something." She winked at Sophie. "If Your Majesty promises not to tell."

Heat built in Sophie's cheeks once again, which she tried to ignore. "Omiros, you will assemble a force to show the governor we are unwilling to wait, and force the issue if it comes to that."

"Yes, Your Majesty," Omiros said, crossing an arm over his chest in salute.

"If I may," Makis said, looking carefully at a different report. "The most recent electoral divisions are hopelessly outdated. We have two decades of shifting populations to reckon with if we wish to elect a new cohort to the People's Chamber before the end of next year."

"I trust you to do the job," Sophie said. "Use whatever resources you need. Restoring the citizens' voice is our most critical task."

Makis nodded. "I'll reach out to any surviving tribunes. Their contacts will be invaluable."

"You should check in Ravian first," Demetra said. "Many from the chamber settled there after Irena's dissolution."

Omiros suggested a few of his mother Styliani's friends who still lived, which Makis carefully copied down. Fryni asked about strengthening the northern border defenses to ensure another Skaldre leader didn't follow in Eidsson's footsteps. Constantia countered with a plan to play one Skaldre ruler off against another.

Sophie listened to the discussion and felt the day's fatigue lift from her shoulders. This was the point, what it had all been for: putting Meyatha's resources to work for the benefit of its people. From blood and sacrifice, that chance was finally hers.

There was only one point that still pricked at her like a barb in her foot: someone had betrayed her army's route to the Skaldre, enabling their ambush at the Horseshoe. Savvas had sworn that Eidsson hadn't told either Dafni or himself who the traitor was, and if his words were true, then the only remaining possibilities were the people helping her shape Meyatha's destiny. Omiros hadn't known the route they would take in advance, and she couldn't believe it of Fryni, leaving just Demetra, Makis, and Constantia.

Sophie didn't want to believe any of them guilty, but she couldn't let that be the end of it. The ambush had cost her army precious soldiers. If not for that ambush, she might have had enough soldiers to win the day without sending Faidra to her death at Thane Eidsson's hands. Sophie gritted her teeth. She would find out whoever it was, and they would learn what the Mother's justice really meant.

Acknowledgements

More than anyone else, I owe a deep debt to my partner and colleague, Chris Winkle. This book would not exist without her, as she worked tirelessly with me from the outline stage all the way to the final draft. Once that stage was finished, my copy editor Avery provided invaluable assistance in polishing the story's prose. Thanks to them, you don't have to see "rain of arrows" nine times across three chapters.

Artist Caio Eduardo is the force behind the amazing cover, while Tiffany Munro turned my extremely basic sketch into a beautiful map. Thank you both!

Next, it's time for the beta readers. There are a lot of them, as this book took several rounds to get right. But each of them deserves my thanks, so there they are:

Alex Van Putten, Anne-Marie Beaudoin-Bégin, Danita Rambo, Elly Bangs, Jessyca Yoppolo, Kathy Ferguson, Michelle Christine Julseth, Mike Foxman, Olivia Bernard, Paul Chiusano, Peter Schaefer, Pm Weizenbaum, Sam Stryker, SG, Svea Phillips, Thyanna Voisine, and Valerie Paquin. I couldn't have gotten this book to where it is without all of your help!

Finally, I need to acknowledge the Byzantine Empire for inspiring this story in the first place. I got through writer's block more than a few times by reading about the adventures of Justinian and Alexios. Rest easy, Romans of the east.

About the Author

Oren Ashkenazi grew up in Hawaii, where he annoyed his parents by constantly thinking up ways that the latest Star Trek episode could have happened differently. It wasn't until embarrassingly late in his teens that he discovered science fiction's magical cousin, fantasy, but it was love at first sight once he did. Novels, video games, tabletop roleplaying games, there was no limit to the stories of swords and dragons that he would consume.

After college, Oren was approached to be part of Mythcreants. Since he had media opinions aplenty, it was an easy fit! Soon, he wasn't just writing articles, he was also working with clients as a content editor. At least, all those hours spent revising Star Trek episodes would come in handy! As an editor, Oren focuses on helping authors figure out what kind of story they want to tell, and then focusing on how best to do this. The common refrain is "your story can be about anything, but it can't be about *everything*."

When Oren isn't writing for Mythcreants or working on a client manuscript, he likes to run roleplaying campaigns, design roleplaying systems, and work on his own stories.

You can learn storytelling from Oren at https://mythcreants.com.

Read more at https://mythcreants.com/.